"It's a girl."

Molly watched as the doctor placed her blue-eyed, black-haired daughter into her sister's arms, and she suffered a jolt of loss so wrenching, she almost cried out.

"Have you chosen a name?" the nurse asked.

Lena was smiling down at the baby girl as if the entire world had just been handed to her on a silver platter. "Grace," she said as she lifted her gaze to Molly. "Grace Margaret Longworth."

Molly was moved by her sister using her name as the baby's middle name. As for Grace, she realized Lena had chosen well. This infant was, indeed, a very special gift from God.

Thy will be done, Molly prayed silently. And struggled not to weep.

NO REGRETS

Also available from MIRA Books and
JoANN ROSS

LEGACY OF LIES
CONFESSIONS
SOUTHERN COMFORTS

JoANN ROSS

NO REGRETS

MIRA BOOKS

ISBN 1-55166-282-5

NO REGRETS

Copyright © 1997 by JoAnn Ross.

To Marisa Ann Ross, who reminds me
that miracles do exist.

And, as always, to Jay, for all the years.

Once again, with heartfelt appreciation
to my editor and friend,
Malle Vallik.

Prologue

1972

It was Christmas in Los Angeles. Although the temperature was in the mid-eighties the residents of the City of Angels were determined to rev up that old holiday spirit.

The venerable *Queen Mary* was decked out in its winter wonderland finery, Dickens's *A Christmas Carol* was playing to standing-room-only crowds at the Hollywood Bowl, and at the Shrine Auditorium the *Nutcracker* ballet continued to entrance.

Richard Burton was narrating *A Child's Christmas in Wales* at the Shubert Theatre, the Mickey Mouse Very Merry Christmas Parade had returned to Disneyland's Main Street, and even the hookers strolling Hollywood Boulevard had gotten into the act, dressing for the season in skimpy red-and-white outfits.

But inside a small pink stucco house, located in the

shadow of Dodger Stadium, the mood was anything
but festive.

"Molly," Lena McBride whispered desperately,
"I'm going to pee in my pants."

Ten-year-old Molly McBride drew her sister a little
tighter against her. "No, you're not, Lena," she whispered back without taking her eyes from their daddy.
"You can hold on."

"No, I can't. Please, Molly," she hissed, as she
recrossed her legs and pressed her small hand between them. "You have to *do* something."

It was a common refrain, one Molly had grown up
hearing. Although there was only two years' difference between them, sometimes she felt more like
Lena's mother than her sister.

"Would you two brats shut the fuck up?" Rory
McBride roared, aiming his gun away from his wife
and at Molly and Lena.

Amazingly, his shout failed to wake three-year-old
Tessa, who continued to sleep on the rug in the center
of the room. Her baby sister had been cranky that
morning with a cold. Afraid at what might happen if
Tessa woke and began fussing, Molly was relieved
that the cough medicine seemed to have knocked her
out.

"How's a man supposed to think around here with
you brats babbling all the time?"

Having learned to keep quiet when her parents
were drinking, which her daddy had been doing until
he'd run out of liquor around sundown, Molly didn't
point out that it was the first thing either one of them
had said since this all started six hours earlier. When

her mama had come home from her afternoon shift at Denny's smelling—as Rory had put it—of sex and sin, instead of cigarette smoke and fried eggs.

"Lena needs to go to the bathroom," she announced.

"She'll have to hold it, because she's not goin' anywhere."

Molly lifted her chin and met his bleary, red-rimmed eyes with a level look of her own. "She needs to go to the bathroom." Her voice was quiet. But insistent.

He drew in a long drag on a cigarette—his last—exhaled the smoke through his nose like a fire-breathing dragon and glared at her through the blue cloud. "You always have been a real mouthy little bitch, Molly McBride." He shook his head with mock regret. "I think it's high time your daddy shut you up."

He pointed the revolver straight at her, winked and pulled the trigger.

A phalanx of police cars was parked out in front of the house. Klieg lights lit up the area, making it as bright as day. Behind the police barricade, despite the fact that it was nearly midnight on Christmas Eve, spectators stood in groups, talking about the action as if they were watching a taping of "The Rookies" while video crews from every television station in the city were jockeying over the best vantage positions.

"What we've got inside that house is potential multiple homicides," Lieutenant Alex Kovaleski reminded his men. "The guy's been threatening to kill himself and his wife and daughters for hours." As chief negotiator of the Los Angeles Police hostage team, it was Alex's responsibility to see that didn't happen.

"Why don't we just rush the house?" a young, impatient rookie asked.

"This isn't some Hollywood movie. We do that and there'll be lots of gunfire that'll look real dandy on the nightly news, but we could end up taking three little girls out of there in body bags."

Alex knew all too well that when a guy took his kids hostage, his real agenda was to get back at his wife for some grievance, either real or imagined. Killing the kids was a surefire way to hurt a spouse, but Alex wasn't going to allow any children to die tonight.

"Time's on our side," he reminded everyone. "If we get tired, we go home and they send in another fifty cops to take our place. And fifty more. Then fifty more after that. Hell, we can keep rotating cops until doomsday. We can outlast the son of a bitch."

They'd already cut off the power and water to the McBride house. Intimidation tactics, certainly. The entire idea of hostage negotiation was to control the hostage-taker's environment.

"I'm going to kill the fuckin' bitch," Rory McBride insisted yet again. It was the fourth time Alex had spoken with him on the phone since the standoff had begun. The previous three times the conversation had ended with McBride hanging up.

"That's what you keep saying," Alex agreed mildly. "But you know, Rory, I don't think you want to do that. Not really."

"What I want is a goddamn drink. And some cig-arettes."

"Can't give you any alcohol, Rory. It's against the rules, remember?" They'd been through this earlier, when he'd threatened to blow out his wife's brains if the cops didn't get him a bottle of Jim Beam. "But I suppose I could send a pack of cigarettes in."

There was a long silence. Then a curse. "Okay. Make 'em Camels. Filterless."

"Sorry, but that's not quite the way it works." The way it worked was that the cops took everything away. Then negotiated things back, one item at a time. "Tell you what I'll do, Rory. Since I'm feeling generous tonight, and I'd like to get this over with so we can all get some sleep, I'll trade you two packs of Camels for those little girls."

Rory McBride's answer was a ripe curse. When the sound of a receiver being slammed down reverberated in his ear, Alex muttered his own curse.

Deciding to give McBride a few minutes to calm down, Alex studied the sketch of the interior of the house that had been drawn by a woman down the street who was friends with Mrs. McBride. The front door opened right onto the living room, which in turn opened to the kitchen, which meant that sitting on the couch, McBride would have a view of both the front and side doors.

It wasn't the kind of house you could easily slip a gunman into. Which meant that they'd just have to wait. For as long as it took.

In that fleeting flash of time after she watched her daddy pull the trigger of the ugly black gun, Molly

waited for the roar, stiffened in preparation for the
expected pain. And even as she wondered how badly
it would hurt to die, she worried how her little sisters
would survive without her.

She heard the click of the trigger being pulled, her
mama's shriek, Lena's scream. Then she heard her
daddy's harsh, cigarette-roughened laugh.

"You flinched," he said, his grin showing that he'd
enjoyed his cruel trick immensely. "Guess you're not
so tough after all, little girl."

Leftover fear mingled with fury as her heart continued to pound in her ears. She heard Lena sob something about an accident, felt the moisture running
down her own bare legs and realized her sister was
not the only one who'd wet herself.

"You had no right to do that, Rory McBride, you
sadistic son of a bitch," Karla yelled. "Molly's never
done anything to you."

"If you hadn't gotten knocked up with that snotty
little brat in the first place, I could've played pro ball.
I was state high school All-Star first baseman for three
straight years," he reminded her. And himself. Sometimes those glory days seemed very far away.

"I didn't get pregnant all by myself, hotshot," Karla flared. "You were the one who was always tryin'
to get beneath my skirt."

"A guy didn't have to try all that hard," he countered on a snort. "Hell, you were pulling your panties
down three minutes after I met you."

It was an old argument. Molly had heard it so many
times, she could recite the lines from memory. She
leaned her head against the back of the couch and
closed her eyes.

Everyone in the neighborhood knew you were a slut. She mentally said the words along with her daddy. *If I hadn't been so drunk that day you told me you were pregnant, I would've figured out that it probably wasn't even my kid.*

Molly was already thinking ahead to her mother's line that if *she* hadn't been so stoned, she never would have married such a miserable loser, and, just to set the record straight, there weren't any goddamn base-ball teams in the country that would have signed a player with two bad knees, when a sound like a gun-shot rang out.

Molly's eyes flew open. She saw her mama's hand still resting on her daddy's cheek and watched as a muscle jerked violently beneath Karla's scarlet-tipped fingers.

Rory slapped her back, a hard, backhanded blow that sent her peroxide-blond head reeling. Then he smiled evilly at his two older daughters.

"I'm going to kill your mama now." He put the gun to Karla's temple and pulled the trigger. This time there was a roar, followed by a blinding spray of blood.

As Molly and Lena watched in horror, their daddy stuck the barrel of the revolver against the roof of his mouth.

The thunderous bang reverberated through Molly's head, followed by the crashing sound of wood splin-tering as the front door was kicked in.

Alex took in the murder scene—the woman sprawled on the floor, the man draped over her, the blood and pieces of brain tissue darkening the wall behind them.

On a raggedy brown couch facing the door, two little girls sat side by side, their arms wrapped tightly around each other, their eyes wide, their complexions as pale as wraiths'. Nearby, a pink-cheeked toddler sat in the center of a stained rug and screeched.

"Aw, hell."

Alex dragged his palms down his face, and as the rest of the city celebrated the season of peace and joy, he found himself wishing that he'd listened to his mother and gone to law school.

Part One

Chapter One

December 24, 1986

Later, Molly McBride would look back on this night and wonder if the disappearance of the baby Jesus hadn't been a sign. A portent that her life was about to dramatically and inexorably change.

At the moment, however, attempting to get to work on time, she had no time to ponder the existence of signs or omens. During the half-block walk between her bus stop and the hospital, she'd been approached by three panhandlers.

"'Give to him who begs from you. He who has two coats, let him share with him who has none, and he who has food must do likewise.'"

A cloud of foul breath strong enough to down a mastodon wafted between Molly and an emaciated man, but she did not back away. The quiz, administered by the former Jesuit seminarian, was a daily event. And as much as she worried about the man she only knew as Thomas—Doubting Thomas, he'd informed her one day—Molly had come to enjoy them.

"Those are easy, Thomas. The first is from Matthew, the second Luke."

She cheerfully handed over the cheese sandwich she'd made that morning. "Now I have one for you."

He bowed and gave her a go-ahead sign as, with yellowed teeth, he began tearing the wrapping off the sandwich.

"God created us without us but he did not will to *save* us without us." She waited, not willing to admit that she'd spent hours looking up that obscure quote.

Thomas wolfed down nearly a quarter of the sandwich, rewrapped the remainder and stuck it in his pocket. Then he rocked back on the run-down heels of his cowboy boots and clucked his tongue.

"Me dear, darling, Saint Molly." His brogue could have fooled any of Molly's ancestors back in County Cork. "A keenly educated Catholic girl such as yourself should know that Saint Augustine is required reading in any seminary."

"Actually, I was thinking more of Saint Augustine's message telling us that we must take responsibility for our salvation, and our lives, than winning today's contest. If you're not careful, you're going to end up in the hospital."

Beneath his filthy Raiders jacket he shrugged shoulders that reminded her of a wire hanger. "It won't be the first time."

"No. But it could be the last." She put her hand on his sleeve. "I worry about you, Thomas."

His smile was sad. "You worry about everyone. When are you going to realize, Saint Molly, that no matter what Saint Augustine told us, you can't save the world?"

"I'll pray for you, Thomas." It was what she always said.

"Save your prayers." It was what he always said. "I'm beyond redemption."

Molly sighed as he walked away. Then continued on.

Mercy Samaritan Hospital sprawled over a no-man's land in the shadow of the Harbor Freeway and Santa Monica Freeway interchange like a huge gray stone Goliath. The neighborhood where Molly spent her nights was home to some of the roughest bars, seediest transients and oldest whores in the City of Angels.

Thanks to gang members' propensity for shooting out streetlights, once the sun went down, the streets and alleys were as dark as tombs. To the residents of these mean streets, the gilt excess of Beverly Hills and the sparkling sun-drenched beaches of Malibu might as well have belonged to another planet.

Mercy Sam, a teaching hospital established by the Sisters of Mercy nearly a century ago, had been more than a place of healing; it had been a living symbol of hope and compassion. Hope had long since fled, along with most of the population of the inner city. Fortunately, although Molly was the only Sister of Mercy still on staff, compassion had remained.

A visual affront to Frank Lloyd Wright's famed concept of organic architecture, the building featured a hulking main building with two wings. Various outbuildings had cropped up over the years like weeds.

The pneumatic doors opened with a hiss as Molly

entered the emergency department beneath the bright red neon sign. The triage area was nearly deserted, as were the fast-track cubicles, where patients with level-one complaints—bloody noses, scrapes and bruises, migraines, intestinal upsets, minor burns and strep throats—were treated.

She went into the staff lounge, changed into the cranberry red scrubs that had recently replaced the hated pink ones and joined the other nurses in The Pit, as the ER was routinely called.

"Merry Christmas," Yolanda Brown greeted her.

"Happy Holidays to you, too." Nothing in Molly's voice revealed her painful memories of Christmas Eve. "I'm sorry I'm late."

"It's getting tougher and tougher to run that gauntlet," Yolanda said with a frown. "Nobody rides the bus in L.A. Especially not at night and in this neighborhood. You really ought to get yourself a car."

Molly smiled, feeling the shadows drift away as her equilibrium returned. "Why don't you write a letter to the Pope and suggest he cosign a loan?"

Yolanda's shrug suggested she'd expected that answer to the ongoing argument, but intended to keep on trying, anyway. "You didn't miss anything," she said. "It's turning out to be a blessedly silent night. According to Banning's report, it was pretty quiet on the day shift, too. Which is pretty amazing, given that not only is it a holiday, it's a full moon.

"They had only half a dozen patients during their last three hours," Yolanda continued. "The last one was some guy who sliced his finger to the bone trying to put together a bicycle for his eight-year-old son. He was stitched up, given a tetanus shot, advised to pay the ten bucks to have the store do it next time and was leaving just as I was coming on duty.

"By the way," she tacked on as an afterthought, "the baby Jesus is gone."

"I noticed as I walked by the crèche." Molly sighed. "I suppose it isn't surprising. Putting a baby doll outside in this neighborhood is just asking to have it stolen, especially this time of year."

Molly was of two minds about the theft. She found the act wrong, but she couldn't help envisioning the joy on the face of whatever child received the doll on Christmas morning.

"Santa's gonna be paying a surprise visit to some kid's house," Yolanda said. "Apparently from now on, the swaddled babe is going to be a bunch of rolled-up towels. The visual impact won't be the same, but administration has decided it might last through the night."

Molly wasn't so certain about that, since clean towels were even more precious than baby dolls around there.

It was almost eerily quiet. There were no metal-bound triage charts in the racks, crisp white sheets covered the high-wheeled gurneys lined up in the hallway outside trauma area A and all the booths were empty, curtains pulled back in anticipation of patients. Molly was Irish enough to be vaguely superstitious of such calm.

"Where's Reece?" Molly asked.

"Your handsome young brother-in-law is hiding away in waiting room A. Seems he's got a hundred bucks' bet with Dr. Bernstein on the Houston Rockets over the Bulls—it's the third quarter, Jordan's on a roll and he's starting to get nervous that his bride is going to murder him when she finds out.''

"Lena would never murder Reece. She adores him.''

And rightfully so, Molly thought. Dr. Reece Longworth, Mercy Sam's ER resident, was the nicest man she'd ever met. He was also her best friend.

"And he's nuts about her. The guy lights up from the inside like a Christmas tree whenever she's around.'' Yolanda sighed. "If I could ever find me a man who looked at me the way Reece looks at your little sister, I'd marry him in a heartbeat.''

"Lena's lucky,'' Molly agreed. Lena had met Reece one night two years ago when she'd shown up unexpectedly to eat dinner with Molly in the cafeteria. Instantly smitten, Reece had proposed within the week. It had taken him six months to convince Lena to marry him.

Until Reece, Lena's choices in men had been disastrous, eerily similar to their own mother's. All of her lovers—and there had been many—had been carbon copies of their abusive, alcoholic father. Molly often thought that Lena hadn't believed she was deserving of love, even though she'd been ravenous for it all her life. During those bad years, Lena had reminded Molly of a bottomless, fragile porcelain bowl—impossible to fill and capable of shattering at a touch.

Molly sat staring at the lights of the small artificial tree atop a filing cabinet at the nurses' station thinking that Lena's first Christmas Eve with Reece had probably been the only truly happy one she'd ever had. The lights blinked red, green and white, flashing gaily on yellowed and cracked plaster walls in the unnaturally quiet room.

Normally, Molly would never have questioned the rare peace. Emergencies came in spurts. But she could never remember it being as quiet as this.

"You know, this really is starting to get a little spooky," she said thirty minutes later as she bit into a bell-shaped cookie covered with red sugar sprinkles. "So where are all the customers?"

She'd no sooner spoken than the dam broke—a drive-by shooting; an attempted suicide who'd washed a bottle of nitroglycerin tablets down with a fifth of Beefeaters gin, then burned the inside of his mouth trying to blow himself up with a Bic lighter; and a cop carrying a newspaper-wrapped bundle.

"One of the bums found her in a Dumpster," he said, shoving the bundle into Molly's arms.

Sensing what she was about to see, Molly gently placed the newspapers onto a gurney and carefully opened them up. The baby's eyelids were sealed shut, its pale blue skin gelatinous. She was wet and so tiny, she reminded Molly of a newly hatched hummingbird.

Reece, who'd just finished the unenviable task of telling the shell-shocked parents of the thirteen-year-old honor student that he'd been unable to save their son, paused on his way to check out a lacerated scalp.

"Aw, hell," he responded in his characteristically even tone that was faintly softened with the accent of the deep South. "Get a neonatologist on the line, stat," he told the clerk. "Tell him we've got an extramural preemie delivery. And start arranging for a transfer upstairs to NICU, just in case."

Unlike so many other physicians Molly worked with, Reece Longworth never raised his voice except when it was necessary in order to be heard over the din. Few had ever seen him get angry. Such a relaxed, informal demeanor helped calm the staff, as well as thousands of anxious patients. The fluorescent red plastic button he wore on his green scrub shirt reading *Don't Panic* probably didn't hurt, either.

"She's so small," Yolanda murmured as Reece managed, just barely, to put the blade of the infant laryngoscope into the baby girl's rosebud mouth. "She could fit in the palm of my hand."

"Probably another crack kid," the cop muttered as he stood on the sidelines and watched.

While Reece slid the tube between the tiny vocal chords, Molly said a quick, silent prayer and checked for a pulse.

"Sixty," she announced grimly. She did not have to add that it was much too slow for a preemie.

"Dr. Winston's the neonatologist on call," the clerk announced as Reece put in an umbilical line to start pushing drugs. "He wants to know how much the baby weighs. Because if it's less than five hundred grams, the kid's not viable."

As soon as the line was in, Reece bagged the baby girl, forcing air directly into immature lungs through the tube. Molly wrapped a towel around the frail infant in an attempt to warm it.

"See if you can find a nursery scale," Reece instructed Yolanda. "And round up an Isolette, too."

When the baby suddenly kicked, Molly felt her own pulse leap in response.

"It doesn't mean anything," Reece warned as they

exchanged a look. "It's only reflex. No matter what she weighs, we're not even talking long shot here, Molly."

"I know."

Yet, even as she prepared for the worst, even as she saw the infant crumping before her eyes, Molly took the weak little kick as a sign of encouragement. Death was a frequent companion in her line of work, but Molly had also witnessed enough miracles to allow her to hang on to hope now.

Yolanda came back with the scale and a hush suddenly came over the room as Molly placed the baby girl on it.

"Four hundred and twenty grams." Molly closed her eyes and heard the onlookers sigh in unison.

"Too light to fake it," Reece said what everyone already knew.

The clerk passed the information on to the neonatologist still waiting on the phone. "Winston says to pull the plug. The kid's FTD."

Fixing to Die. Accustomed as she was to the term, Molly was irritated by it now.

As was Reece. "Easy for Winston to say," he muttered. With an icy, controlled fury that was almost palpable, he marched the few feet to the phone and snatched the receiver from the clerk's hand.

"As much as I appreciate your consult, Dr. Winston, we don't throw terms around like that in my emergency department. She may be small, but she deserves the same respect we'd show your child, or wife, or mother, if they showed up down here."

He hung up.

"All we can do now is make her as comfortable

as possible,'' he said. Every eye in the room was riveted on him as he turned off the line, pulled the plug from the baby's lungs, wrapped the painfully tiny girl up again and placed her in the Isolette.

"She's still breathing,'' Yolanda pointed out unnecessarily.

"She'll stop.''

An aide popped her head into the room. "You've got a stab wound in treatment room B, Dr. Longworth.''

He turned to Molly. "I'll need you to assist.'' Without waiting for an answer, he cast one more quick, regretful look at the baby and left the room.

After asking the clerk to page Father Dennis Murphy, who she'd seen going upstairs to bring Christmas communion to Catholics on the medical wards, Molly followed Reece.

After stitching up the wound that had resulted from an argument over whether "Away in a Manger'' or "Silent Night'' was the Christmas carol most appropriate to the season, Reece stopped by to check the baby again and found her still breathing. They also found the cop still standing beside the Isolette.

"I'm off duty,'' he said, as if worried they'd think he was shirking his work. "My daughter's pregnant with her first. This could be her kid.''

Despite the tragedy of their situation, Molly managed a smile at the thought of a new life on the way. "I'll add your daughter to my prayers.''

"Thank you, Sister.'' Patrolman Tom Walsh, a frequent visitor to the ER due to his work patrolling the seediest parts of the city, managed a smile. "Someone needs to baptize her.''

"Father Murphy didn't answer his page," the clerk, who overheard his statement informed Molly. "The guard said he left about thirty minutes ago."

"Looks like it's up to you, Sister," Walsh said. "How about naming her Mary?" he suggested. "That's my mother's name. And it *is* Christmas, so it fits."

It took all Molly's inner strength to grace him with a smile when she wanted to weep. "Mary's perfect."

The patrolman put his hat over his heart. Molly sprinkled water over the tiny bald head, wishing for the usual cries, but the infant didn't so much as flinch. Even so, the hopelessly immature lungs valiantly continued to draw in rasping breaths of air like tiny bellows.

"Mary, I baptize you in the name of the Father, the Son and the Holy Spirit."

Walsh exhaled a long breath. "Thank you, Sister. I feel a lot better."

Molly was grateful that she'd managed to bring one of them comfort. With a no-nonsense attitude that had always served her well, she reminded herself that such emotionally painful situations came with the territory. She'd chosen to live out her vocation in the real world, where a sacred moment was when someone shared with you—like Thomas earlier, and Officer Walsh now. If she'd wanted her life to be one of quiet dedication contemplating holy mysteries, she would have joined an order of cloistered nuns.

Baby Mary fought on. Two hours later, when the flood of patients had slowed to a trickle, Molly slipped back into the room and took the swaddled infant who was no heavier than a handful of feathers out of the Isolette. She held her in her arms and felt the tiny, birdlike heart flutter in a last futile attempt to keep beating. Then it finally went still.

As a grim-faced Reece called the death for the record, and Patrolman Tom Walsh made a sign of the cross, Molly, who was suddenly having trouble breathing herself, escaped from the room.

Reece found her on the rooftop, looking out over the lights of the city.

"Repeat Longworth's rules of critical care," he said.

The rules—known as Longworthisms—were a joke around the ER. They were also right on the money.

"Number one—air goes in, air goes out," Molly answered remotely. She didn't feel like joking at the moment. "Number two—blood goes round and round. Number three—bleeding always stops." She drew in a weary breath. "Number four—oxygen is good."

"Very good." He nodded his satisfaction. "But you forgot the most important."

"What's that?"

"Dr. Reece Longworth's Rule Number Five. Patients always leave." In an affectionate gesture more suited to a friend and brother-in-law than a physician, he skimmed his finger down the slope of her nose. "It's a good one to keep in mind. Getting too involved can end up in a flame-out."

"But it's not fair. That was an innocent child, Reece, a little girl who'd never done anything but do her best to beat impossible odds. She was so tiny. And so brave." Believing all life was a gift from God, Molly hated seeing such a gift not being honored.

"I know." Reece sighed and put his arm around her. "Some days are harder than others," he allowed. "But you're still too softhearted for your own good. You've got to save a little of that caring for yourself."

Molly knew he was right. Emergency room nurses—and doctors—burned out all the time. But she couldn't just turn off her emotions like a water tap.

When she didn't answer, Reece ran the back of his hand down her cheek in a soothing fraternal gesture that carried absolutely no sexual overtones.

"You know, I suppose the truth is, deep down, I don't want you to change, either." Both his expression and his tone were serious. "The patients are lucky to have you. *I'm* lucky to have you. But you've got to learn to let go."

"I know." She sighed. "But sometimes it's difficult not to worry. When you care so deeply."

It was Reece's turn to sigh. A faint shadow moved across his eyes. "On that we're in full agreement."

Venice Beach was deserted save for a few couples walking their dogs along the strand. The full moon hanging in the sky created a glittering silver path on the jet water, but as she sat in the sidewalk café, Lena Longworth's interest was not in the view, but on the woman across the table from her.

"You've been having problems at home," the young woman, who looked a bit like a blond Gypsy, with her wild long spiral perm, floating gauze skirt and heavy sweater, announced.

"Not really," Lena lied. The truth was, that although Reece was a man of uncommon tolerance, she

knew her obsession with having a child had been
straining his patience lately.

Although the woman smiled benignly back at her,
Lena knew she wasn't fooling her for a moment. She
took a sip of her cola and wished it were something
stronger. But she'd promised Reece that she'd never
drink and drive. Having been forced to treat too many
casualties of such reckless behavior in the ER, he was
adamant on the subject.

A silence settled over them. A pregnant silence,
Lena thought wryly.

"I have a friend who told me that your cards had
predicted she'd have children. Even when the doctors
said it was impossible," she said finally. "Three
months later, she got pregnant."

"The cards are not some magical fortune-telling
computer," the woman who'd introduced herself as
Ophelia, said. "I can't make them give you the answer you're seeking. I can only interpret them."

"That's a start."

"Fine." Ophelia smiled again. "Have you ever had
a reading before?"

"No." Lena refrained from mentioning that she'd
always found such superstitious behavior foolish. She
was a sensible woman. She had a degree in education.
She taught kindergarten and was married to a physician. She didn't need New Age mumbo jumbo to
make her happy. But still...

Ophelia held out the deck of colorful cards. "Some
readers prefer to shuffle the cards themselves. Personally, I believe it's better if you instill them with your
own energy first."

Although she knew it was only her imagination,

Lena could have sworn her fingertips tingled as she shuffled the cards.

"You can deal out your first card whenever you're ready," Ophelia instructed. "This will tell us your present position."

Lena drew the first card from the shuffled deck. The image was of a young man, sitting in front of a tree. In front of him were three goblets; a hand coming out of the clouds was offering him a fourth, but his arms were folded in a gesture that suggested his unwillingness to accept.

"The Four of Cups." Ophelia nodded. "You can see this is a very lucky man. Unfortunately, he's so caught up in his own despair he can't see life offering him a great deal."

Lena twisted her wedding ring and stared down at the cards. This was already hitting a bit too close to home.

Her marriage had been strained lately. But as soon as she got pregnant, that would change. All she wanted was a child. Someone all her own to love. Someone who'd love her back.

"Why don't you deal the next card," Ophelia suggested, her gentle voice breaking into Lena's unhappy thoughts.

Lena nearly groaned as she looked down at the card depicting a woman sitting in bed, obviously in deep despair, her head in her hands as a row of swords hung ominously overhead.

"The Nine of Swords suggests the seeker senses impending doom and disaster," Ophelia divulged, once again hitting unnervingly close to reality.

Lena wanted to jump up and run away, but she

found herself spellbound by the sight of that anguished, sleepless woman. It could have been a self-portrait.

"As you'll see, although she's obviously caught up in her fears, the swords do not touch the woman." The psychic's dark eyes swept over Lena's face. "Often the fear of disaster is worse than the reality."

"The only thing we have to fear is fear itself?" Lena muttered.

Ophelia remained unscathed by Lena's sarcasm. "That's often the case."

Irritated and unnerved, Lena dealt another card. This time the woman was standing alone in a vineyard, a falcon on her arm, a manor house in the background.

"As you can see, the woman is at peace with herself. And her surroundings, which are quite lush and suggest material success. This is a woman who does not need to cling to past or even present relationships. A woman who does not need constant companionship to feel content."

"So, the cards are saying I'm going to be alone?" Panic surged through Lena's veins like ice water. One of the reasons she'd agreed to marry Reece was because he'd offered security and protection. If he were to leave...

"The cards don't imply the woman is without relationships," Ophelia stressed calmly. "Only that she's at peace with herself. And her situation."

Lena's fear ebbed slightly, even as she glumly wondered if this meant that she and Reece were destined never to have children.

She dealt another card. The Wheel of Fortune.

"The Wheel teaches us that although our circumstances are predetermined, we remain responsible for our own destiny. When joy or sorrow come into our lives, what's important is that we turn to face it. We're all constantly being presented with decisions and choices to make. Learning to take responsibility for our own destiny is the most difficult of life's lessons. But it's well worth the struggle," Ophelia said encouragingly. "And now the last one. Which will foresee your long-term future."

Feeling again as if her fingertips were tingling, Lena dealt a fifth card and drew in a harsh breath as she viewed the evil half-goat, half-human figure holding a flaming torch toward a couple who stood naked and vulnerable, chains around their necks. "A devil?" she whispered feeling goose bumps rise on her flesh.

"Like everything in life, this card cannot be taken at face value," Ophelia assured her. "The devil represents all energy, positive and negative. He teaches us that if we don't accept both sides of our nature—the light and the dark—we can develop inhibitions. And phobias. In many cases, he represents the shadowy side of our psyches we prefer to ignore."

Having taken an intro psych course in college, Lena recognized the Jungian shadow term. Although she'd received an A in the course, she'd never thought of the concept in relation to her own personality.

She stared down at the unappealing card for a long time, allowing another silence to stretch between them.

"Although it's not wise to take the cards too literally," Ophelia said quietly, "the devil often symbolizes the removal of fears and inhibitions that hinder personal growth.''

"Like not being able to love openly?"

"That could be an example. In the fifth position, this is a very good card. You're facing a time of great growth. A time when much good could come from apparent evil."

Lena knew a lot about evil. The trick was to somehow learn to accept the good.

"Thank you." She reached into her purse and added more bills to the ones she'd already paid when she'd first sat down. "You've given me a great deal to think about."

"It was your own willingness to open your heart and your mind to the message of the cards," Ophelia reminded her.

Open your heart. The words reverberated over and over again in her mind as Lena drove away from funky Venice to the privileged enclaves of Pacific Palisades. That was something she'd never been able to do. Not since that long-ago Christmas Eve.

She'd tried to tell Reece that she didn't have it in her to love him the way a wife should love her husband. Oh, she admired him, of course. And respected him without question, which wasn't difficult since he was the most noble, honorable, caring man she'd ever met. And she was truly fond of him.

Her mind drifted back to that day, six months after they'd first met, when he'd taken her hand and led her to a secluded bench in Griffith Park.

"I love you, Lena." His handsome face had been so earnest, so sincere, it almost made her weep.

She'd dragged her gaze from his to the children

pouring out of the yellow school bus that had pulled into the planetarium parking lot. Dressed in a parochial school uniform similar to the one she'd once worn, they were laughing and obviously enjoying their field trip. Lena had been unable to remember a time while growing up when she'd felt even half as carefree as those children looked.

She'd been about to tell Reece yet again that she couldn't marry him. But as she watched the children lining up in double lines, something inside her moved. The response to the children was as unbidden as it was unfamiliar. Perhaps, she'd thought, if she married Reece and had a child, she wouldn't feel so empty.

She'd drawn in a deep breath and hoped she was making the right decision. "If you're really serious..."

"Of course I am," he'd answered in that calm, rational way she assumed he must have learned growing up in that mansion in North Carolina.

Feeling as if she were perched on the edge of a steep and dangerous precipice, she'd taken another deep breath and leapt daringly over the edge. "Then my answer's yes. I'll marry you."

His joyous whoop had drawn the attention of the children, who'd laughed at the sight of the man picking the pretty woman up and twirling her around in his arms. What neither they, nor Reece had seen, was the shimmer of tears in Lena's eyes.

The memory of that day, along with the knowledge of how unfair she'd been to the only man who'd ever loved her, made Lena's eyes fill with tears all over again.

Open your heart. Dear Lord, how she wanted to do that! For Reece, and for herself.

As she turned onto the winding road leading up the cliff to their ocean-view house, Lena realized that unfortunately she had no idea where—or how—to begin.

Then the answer came to her, so bright and vivid, she wondered why it hadn't occurred to her before.

Molly could help her sort this out. As she had every other problem in Lena's life. Even before that horrifying night their daddy had gotten drunk and made them orphans.

She'd talk to her big sister first thing tomorrow, Lena decided. After Christmas dinner.

Although it had been a very long time since she could remember having anything to feel hopeful about, Lena was smiling as she pulled her Jaguar into the half-moon driveway.

Chapter Two

"**E**mergency Department." Impatience crackled in Molly's usually calm and reassuring voice. She sighed and prayed, as she was so often forced to do, for patience.

"Hello?" There was a slight pause. "Is this Mercy Samaritan Hospital?" Molly thought the hesitant female voice sounded slightly slurred.

"Yes. You've reached the emergency department. How can I help you?"

"It's my husband."

Molly groaned inwardly, realizing this was going to be one of those calls in which she had to drag the information out one word at a time. Frustrated, she pushed a long jet curl that had come loose from the knot at the back of her neck.

"Has he been injured?"

"Not yet." There was a sound somewhere between a sob and a laugh. "Although I'm thinking about cutting his prick off with the electric carving knife." The words were definitely slurred.

"I'd advise against that, ma'am. The police frown on such things. Meanwhile, if your husband isn't hurt right now, I'm afraid we're very busy and—"

"He's got the clap. And he didn't get it from me."

Molly rubbed unconsciously at her temples where a headache hammered. "I see."

"And now I have this goddamn rash, which is the only reason the son of a bitch confessed to screwing around in the first place. So, I guess I'd better come in for a test."

"That would be my suggestion. You need to be seen by a doctor and get started on antibiotic treatment," she told the caller. "You should also have an AIDS test."

"You think I have AIDS?"

Molly heard the sudden panic in the woman's voice. "I'm only suggesting the test as a precaution," she said as soothingly as possible. "Since your sexual relationship with your husband was not the monogamous one you believed it to be—"

"I'm not taking any AIDS test."

"It can be done confidentially, if you're worried about—"

"If you have AIDS, you die. And if I'm gonna die, I damn well don't want to know it. I'm also going to kill the bastard if he gave it to me." That said, the woman slammed down the receiver.

Her ears ringing, Molly took a deep breath, said a quick prayer for both the philandering husband and his angry wife, then returned to the fray.

Her next patient was a two-year-old child who'd been nipped by the family's new German shepherd puppy.

"It's okay, sweetheart," Molly soothed as she cleaned the puncture wound, gave the little girl a tetanus shot and advised the mother to keep the child away from the puppy until things quieted down after the holidays.

"I need a prescription for a seven-day course of penicillin," she told Reece, when he paused at the desk to pick up the next chart. "It's for a dog bite."

He pulled a prescription pad from a pocket bulging with tongue depressors, a pen light and ampoules of medications.

"I wish people would listen when the Humane Society tells them this is the worst time of year to try to introduce a new animal into the home." He scribbled the order onto the pad. "Was that a VD call I heard you taking?"

"You've got good ears." Molly wondered how he could have heard anything over the din.

"Nah. I'm just nosy." He ripped the script off and handed it to her. "So, have you heard the county health department's new venereal disease slogan?"

"I don't think so. What is it?"

"VD is nothing to clap about."

Although it was a terrible pun, an involuntary giggle escaped her lips. "You're making that up."

"That's the trouble with working with you, Sister Molly," he said on an exaggerated sigh. "You make it impossible to lie. But it's still pretty good, don't you think?"

"I think I should have Dr. Bernstein come down for a consult." Alan Bernstein was the psych resident. "No one should remain this upbeat at the twenty-fourth hour of a thirty-six-hour shift." Before he could answer, she was off to meet another paramedic who was wheeling in a woman on a gurney.

The patient was dressed for a party in a thigh-high, formfitting red sequined dress and skyscraper heels, one of which had cracked in two. Her hair, the color of a new penny, had been fashioned in an elaborate upsweep and Christmas trees had been airbrushed onto each of her long, scarlet fingernails. Her dress had been torn up one side, and one sleeve had been cut open to allow for an IV drip.

"She was crossing Sunset and got hit by a car," the paramedic began. The man, whose badge read Sam Browning, had earned the nickname Big E his first night on the job when he'd excitedly radioed that he and his partner were bringing in a twenty-year-old male who'd been "ejaculated" from his Corvette.

"It was my fault," the patient interrupted, struggling to sit up. "I wasn't watching where I was going."

"Fault's for the cops to decide," Big E said. "Why don't you just lie down, ma'am, and let me tell the nurse what she needs to know to treat you, okay?"

"I'm sorry." The woman gave Molly an apologetic look through lashes coated with navy blue mascara. Molly was momentarily distracted by the thin row of rhinestones bordering her eyelids.

"That's all right," she soothed. "I can understand you've suffered a great deal of stress."

"I just don't want that poor driver to get in trouble. Especially on Christmas Eve."

"The driver's pretty shook up," Big E told Molly. "He insisted on coming along. He's out in the waiting room. You might want to talk to him after you're finished.''

"I'll do that."

"You won't be sorry. He's very handsome," the patient informed Molly, earning a glare from the paramedic who was obviously frustrated at having been interrupted again. "A girl could certainly do worse."

"Anyway," Big E doggedly continued, "according to witnesses, the patient suffered a brief period of unconsciousness—"

"I suppose that's why I can't remember what happened."

"It's possible you've suffered a slight concussion," Molly said.

"She had some labored breathing in the vehicle coming over here, which suggests a cracked rib," Big E said, grimly determined to finish his report. "We started her on glucose, thiamine and naloxone. As you can see, there's no loss of verbal skills and her only other symptoms are retrograde amnesia and a few scrapes and bruises."

"I skinned my leg when I landed," the patient revealed as Molly took her blood pressure.

Molly observed the red-and-purple scrape along one firm thigh. The skin around it was darkly bruised. "Don't worry, we'll have the gravel cleaned out in no time."

"But it won't scar?"

"No." Molly smiled reassuringly. "It shouldn't."

"I'm so relieved. I'm a dancer. My legs are my livelihood."

"When I was a little girl, I wanted to be a ballerina."

"Why didn't you?"

"My family couldn't afford the lessons."

"Oh." The woman pursed her vermilion lips and thought about that for a moment. "That's too bad."

"Not really." Molly began swabbing the wound while she waited for Reece to arrive. "Because I know now I was meant to be a nurse." She didn't mention being a nun, since that always seemed to lead to questions, and this patient was already talkative enough.

"I've always admired caretaker personalities," the woman said. "Unfortunately, there aren't enough of them in the world. Especially these days."

"I don't know about the world, but we could use a few more in here tonight."

"Amen," Reece agreed as he joined them in the curtained cubicle. "I'm Dr. Longworth. Looks as if someone had a close encounter with Santa's sleigh."

The woman laughed, as Reece had intended. When the laugh deteriorated into a wheezing cough, he and Molly exchanged a look.

"I'm afraid we're going to have to remove your dress, Ms...."

"Fuller. Dana Fuller," the woman responded in a breathy voice that Molly suspected had little to do with a possible cracked rib.

Molly had seen this happen innumerable times. Reece Longworth was a devastatingly attractive man; whenever he appeared in the emergency room, women invariably took one look at his laughing emerald eyes, perpetually tousled chestnut hair, boyish smile and lean muscular body, and experienced an immediate increase in their heart rates.

"And I'll be more than happy to take off anything you'd like, Doctor."

The sexual invitation was unmistakable. Molly was amused by the flush rising from the collar of Reece's white jacket.

As Molly helped Reece remove the sequined dress, he stared in momentary puzzlement at the flat brown nipples. As comprehension crashed down on him he lifted the sheet he and Molly were pulling up over the patient's chest and viewed the penis nestled in the curly dark hair.

He'd learned in medical school never to make assumptions, and he assured himself that the only reason he hadn't realized he was treating a man was because he'd already been working for twenty-four hours. Now, as he managed to keep a straight face and examine the patient's breathing, Reece reminded himself again why he was hooked on the ER.

He enjoyed the action, the constant surprises. There was nothing worse, he reminded himself as he referred the patient to neurology for a CAT scan, than being bored. Fortunately, that damn sure wasn't going to happen tonight.

The driver of the car that had struck the cross-dressing dancer was still pacing the waiting room when Molly came to assure him that the patient was going to survive with a minimum of injuries.

"Thank God." He took both her hands in his. "I've been so worried."

"I can certainly understand that." Molly smiled her professional caretaker's smile. "But you can go home now and sleep easy."

"Sleep." He thrust his hands through his hair. He

was a good-looking man in his mid-thirties. "Lord, I doubt if I'll sleep for a week, after this."

"If you'd like, I can ask the physician on duty to prescribe a sleeping pill for you. Just for tonight."

"No." He shook his head. "I'll be all right." He took another deep breath. "I want to thank you, Nurse…" He glanced down at her name tag, which, due to security measures lobbied for by the female employees of the hospital, had only her first name along with the alphabet soup of initials representing her numerous professional credentials.

He tilted his head and studied her. "I hope you don't take this the wrong way, but you don't look much like a Margaret."

"My friends call me Molly."

"Molly." He considered that a moment. "That's much better. Do you have a last name?"

"McBride."

"Ah." He nodded. "I can see the emerald isle in your face, Molly McBride. My mother, Mary Keegan, was black Irish. I should have recognized those lovely blue eyes and dark hair right away."

"You had other things on your mind."

"True. But the day I fail to notice a beautiful woman is the day I need to reassess my priorities. My name is Patrick Nelson."

The conversation was getting more than a little sticky. Molly pulled her hand out of his grasp. "Well, it's a very busy night, Mr. Nelson, and I'd better get back to work—"

"Would you have a drink with me when you get off shift, Molly?"

"I'm sorry, but—"

"A cup of coffee, then. Or a glass of eggnog. It's Christmas," he reminded her. "I transferred down here from San Francisco last month and don't know many people. I'll also admit to being so desperate for company that I'm throwing myself on your mercy."

Patrick Nelson seemed sincere. And nice. Which left Molly feeling a bit like the Grinch about to steal his Christmas. "I'm sorry, but I don't think that's such a good idea."

"If you're involved with someone, that's all right. I'm not going to lie and say that I don't find you very attractive, Nurse Molly, but if you just want to share some friendly, platonic conversation, that'd be great, too."

From the flirtatious, masculine gleam in his eyes, she suspected he was looking for more than mere conversation. "Mr. Nelson—"

"Patrick," he reminded her.

"Patrick." She decided the best way to handle this was to just go straight to the point. "I'm a nun."

"A nun?" His gaze swept over her, from the top of her unruly dark hair down to her shoes, stained with blood spatters. "Jesus—I mean, Jeez," he corrected quickly, "talk about a waste."

This was not the first time Molly had heard that statement. She understood that much of the world found women who'd chosen to sacrifice worldly pleasures mysterious. What she'd never figured out was why so many men seemed to take a woman's decision to live a celibate life personally.

"I'm afraid we're in disagreement about that, Mr. Nelson." She patted his arm. "Have a happy holiday."

Two hours later, the shift had finally come to an end. After assuring Reece that she'd be at their house for Christmas dinner, Molly retrieved her coat from the nurses' locker room and left the building.

Unlike the previous night, the street was quiet and empty in the midnight hour. A huge white galleon of a moon soared high in the sky, illuminating the men wrapped in sleeping bags, blankets or newspapers, sleeping in doorways, all their worldly possessions piled into purloined shopping carts.

Molly stopped in front of the crèche. As she'd feared, the towels intended to represent the baby Jesus had been stolen. One of the lambs and an angel were also missing and someone had painted gang signs on Joseph in seasonal red and green paint. A lingering scent of spray enamel blended with the aroma of garbage from the overstuffed Dumpsters and diesel fuel from the trucks that roared by overhead on the freeway.

As she continued walking to the bus stop, Molly thought it sad that those truckers were having to work on Christmas, the one day of the year they should be home with their families.

Families. As content as she was with her life, there were times Molly found herself wondering what would have happened if things had been different? If the police could have convinced her father to surrender, that long-ago Christmas Eve? Or if Tessa hadn't been taken away from them and adopted by some unknown family. Not a day went by that Molly didn't think about—and pray for—her missing sister.

She was standing on the corner, waiting for the light to change so she could cross the deserted street, when she became aware of someone coming up behind her.

She reached into her coat pocket, intending to give the poor beggar her usual referral to the mission, when a gloved hand came over her mouth and she was dragged backward, toward the alley.

She fought the man, flailing out with her arms, digging her heels into the sidewalk, trying to slow him down long enough to allow someone to come to her rescue. But he was strong. And so determined.

Her breath was trapped in her lungs, blood drummed deafeningly in her ears. Molly tried going limp, but all that did was earn a vicious curse and cause her hips to hit the pavement with a painful thump.

Her assailant tossed her onto a pile of boxes as if she were a rag doll.

Molly lay on her back, the man standing over her. She couldn't see his face because of his garish black-and-purple ski mask. His clothes—camouflage printed shirt and pants topped by an faded army denim jacket—were ragged and filthy. His hair was long and stringy and unkempt.

She grabbed hold of the nearest box and flung it at him, but he knocked it away as if it was no more than a fly. And, to her amazement, he laughed. A rich roar of pleasure that was such a contrast to the menace in those black eyes that she almost believed she must be imagining it.

A nearby sound suddenly caused him to stiffen, as alert as an infantryman on reconnaissance. Taking advantage of his momentary shift in attention, she scrambled to her knees and on a half crawl, half stag-

ger, tried to make her way over the tumbling, shifting
pile of cardboard.

Unfortunately, he proved faster and, grabbing hold
of her hair, yanked her back as the cat, who'd made
the distracting noise, shot out of the alley.

He held her down with a booted foot that threatened to crush her chest. "What's the hurry, honey?"
His deep voice vibrated through her, sending icy fingers of fear zipping up her spine.

"You don't want to do this." She tried for a calm,
reasonable voice, but the tremulous tone gave her
away. "I can help you. I can help you find someplace
to stay, some food—"

He struck her, a vicious blow to the face, cutting
her off in midsentence. Seeming pleased with himself,
he hit her again, with a backhanded slap that made
her ears ring.

"Please." Molly was not above begging, if that's
what it took to stay alive. "I'm a nun."

Even as she said the words, Molly was infused with
guilt. As if a nun was better than any other woman?
More deserving to be spared the horror of rape? Yet
she couldn't help hoping that deep down inside this
monster was a man who might respect her vocation.

She'd thought wrong.

"Even better." As if to please himself, he hit her
again. Harder. Her head was still spinning as she
heard the sound of bone breaking and felt her cheekbone shatter beneath his fist.

A memory flashed through her mind, a memory of
her father slapping her mother. Right before he'd put
that gun to her head. Refusing to die as Karla Mc-
Bride had, Molly managed to curl her fingers around

a beer bottle and pushing herself up, slammed the bottle against the front of the mask.

"Bitch!" Her attacker roared like a wounded lion and swung his arm at her, sending her tumbling back into the boxes. She heard the beer bottle rattling as it rolled away.

He ripped off the mask and pressed the back of his gloved hand against his nostrils. When he took his hand away and viewed the black leather copiously stained with dark wine-colored blood, he screamed, "Fucking cunt!"

Molly felt him ripping away her clothes, exposing her to the chilly December air. But there was no longer anything she could do to stop him.

Through the swirling bloodred haze filling her head, she watched the heavily booted foot swing forward, then moaned as it landed with a bone-shuddering strength between her lax thighs.

His heavy demonic weight came crashing down on top of her, crushing her lungs, stealing her breath. Molly tried to scream as he battered his entry into her tight, dry virginal body, but the pained sound caught in her throat, choking her.

The back of her head kept banging against the asphalt as he pounded away violently at her defenseless body. Sometime during the seemingly endless assault, Molly vomited violently. Over herself and over the monster.

And then, as the crimson haze spread and she prayed silently to a god that seemed to have abandoned her, Molly finally surrendered to the enveloping darkness.

Chapter Three

Reece was almost home free. His grueling shift was over, he'd showered, shampooed the smell of disinfectant, disease and death out of his hair, shaved and changed into a pair of jeans and a T-shirt that didn't have a single bloodstain on it. He took the poinsettia he'd remembered to buy for Lena, and was headed toward the door when he saw a ragged man arguing with the security guard.

He considered trying to sneak out another exit, but recognizing Thomas and knowing that Molly would never forgive him if he turned his back on whatever problem was plaguing the former priest this time, Reece cursed beneath his breath and waded into the breach.

"What's wrong, Thomas?"

"It's Molly." The eyes beneath the filthy hair were wild with distress. "I tried carrying her here, but—"

"Where is she?" Reece interrupted, tossing the poinsettia toward the nearby counter. It missed and landed on the floor, spilling dirt and breaking stems, but no one noticed.

"Out there." He pointed a filthy finger. "She's in bad shape, Doc."

That was, Reece discovered, an understatement. Her face was bruised and battered, her eyes were swollen shut, she was stripped nearly naked, allowing him to see the bite marks on her breasts and the vaginal bleeding. She was also unconscious.

"Jesus Christ." He knelt down and felt her thready pulse.

"Christ has nothing to do with this, Doc. Whoever did this to Saint Molly was a devil."

Reece couldn't argue with that. As he scooped her from the pile of trash, he understood the impetus behind crimes of passion. He was not, by nature, a violent man. But he could easily kill with his bare hands whoever had done this to Molly.

Thomas followed him to the hospital door. "Is she going to die?"

Reece looked at the distress on the man's haggard face, and for the first time since Molly had introduced them, felt a kinship with this man whose life had gone so tragically wrong.

"Not on my watch," Reece promised. The doors hissed open and he carried her into the light. And to safety.

A few miles away, a young woman cursed beneath her breath as she viewed the flashing lights in her rearview mirror.

"Terrific," Tessa Davis thought as she pulled her

Mustang convertible over at the corner of Hollywood Boulevard and Vine.

The days when movie stars, bathed in the dazzling glow of klieg lights, arrived in limousines to attend premieres at Grauman's Chinese Theatre were long past. And the fabled glitter surrounding the walk of fame had given way to junky tourist traps. Even so, as she'd driven into the city last week, Tessa had gazed in awe at the Hollywood sign gleaming like a beacon in the rising sun and imagined she could breathe in the scent of glamour and success.

Unfortunately, she was finding out what generations of beautiful women before her had discovered the hard way: success was not instantaneous. As she watched the cop climb off his motorcycle and come walking toward her, Tessa could envision additional hard-earned savings flying away.

She rolled down her window and flashed her most dazzling smile. The one that never failed to bring boys to their knees.

"Is something wrong, Officer?" Her eyes were wide and innocent.

"I don't suppose you happened to notice that red light you just went through."

"Was it red?" She chewed on her bottom lip. "I was certain it was still yellow."

"It was red." He pulled off his black leather gloves. "May I see your driver's license?"

Damn. He appeared immune to feminine charms. Sighing, Tessa took her billfold out of her purse and held it toward him.

"If you wouldn't mind taking it out of the folder, ma'am," he said politely.

Of all the cops in the city, she had to get Mr. Play-by-the-Book. Hadn't anyone told him this was sup-posed to be the season of goodwill?

"I really am sorry." She tried again as he perused the license.

"You're from Oregon?" He looked up from the photo to her face.

"Portland."

"And now you've come to Hollywood to be a movie star."

He didn't have to make it sound so impossible. When Tessa chose not to answer what she took to be a sarcastic question, he glanced across the street, where two women clad in fishnet stockings and short shorts leaned against a storefront.

"You know, this isn't the safest neighborhood any-more," he warned her. "Not even in the daytime."

"Now you sound like my dad."

"He didn't want you to come to Lotusland," the cop guessed.

"That's putting it mildly." Tessa sighed, thinking how General Marshall Patton Davis had her life all mapped out for her.

"Let me guess." He folded his arms across the front of his leather jacket and rocked back on the heels of his boots. "You were supposed to get your teaching degree from the local college."

"Actually, I was majoring in fine arts at the Uni-versity of Portland."

"Close enough." His smile revealed appealing dimples. "Then, after graduation, you'd settle down with the boy next door—"

"The air force aviator next door."

"Ah." He grinned at that. A broad flash of white that held considerable charm. "So you were destined to be Mrs. Top Gun."

"Mrs. Tom Kelly." Despite the circumstances, Tessa was beginning to enjoy herself.

He gave her a quick, unthreatening perusal. "I can't see you spending your life playing the role of a loyal, supportive military wife while your husband played war games with his macho pals."

"Neither could I. Which is why I'm here." It might not have been a bad life, being married to Tommy and having his babies. If she hadn't had other plans.

Big plans. Like becoming a famous actress. And someday earning her own star on Hollywood's Walk of Fame.

"And now you're going to be the next Demi Moore."

Tessa lifted her chin. "The first Tessa Starr." Tessa Davis, she'd decided long ago, was too boring for the woman she intended to be.

He laughed at that. A rich, bold sound that slipped beneath her skin and warmed her in a way that Tommy never had. "You've definitely got the right attitude. And the looks. If you've got even a smidgen of talent—"

"I have a lot of talent."

"Sounds like you're on your way. So, have you found a place to stay yet?"

"I've rented a room in West Hollywood." At first she'd been a bit taken aback by the red-haired trans-vestite dressed in a marabou-trimmed dressing gown who owned the house, but the room in the funky bungalow was the most affordable she'd been able to find that didn't remind her of the Bates Motel.

"Sounds like you did okay," he said when she told him about her landlord and gave him her address. "But I think I'll run the guy through the computer, just to make sure he doesn't have a record."

"Oh, I'm sure he's perfectly safe."

"Probably is. But I'd never forgive myself if he turns out to be a serial killer and I end up investigating the disappearance of the first Tessa Starr. Protect And Serve, that's our motto." He dimpled again in a way that made her feel warm all the way to her toes. "So, do you have any plans for Christmas dinner?"

"I saw a sign in the window at Denny's advertising the turkey special." She refrained from admitting she'd been there applying for a job after discovering that waitress positions at all the trendy eateries were filled by equally gorgeous women who'd gotten to Los Angeles before her.

"Denny's?" He shook his head. "That's no way to spend your first Christmas in Tinseltown. How would you like to have dinner with me?"

"With you?" As a policeman, he was undoubtedly safe. But Tessa didn't think it wise to allow herself to be picked up by the first handsome stranger she met.

"I should have mentioned that I'm eating at my brother's house. My mother will be there. She can properly introduce us."

Even her overprotective air force general father couldn't complain about that, Tessa decided. "If you're sure your brother won't mind last-minute company."

He laughed. "Miles always throws a bash on Christmas Day. So many people show up, you could probably invite the entire Dodgers team—and their families—and he wouldn't notice. Although," he said on afterthought, "I doubt if anyone would miss your appearance."

The masculine appreciation in his friendly blue eyes was all it took to overcome Tessa's last lingering concern. "It sounds wonderful."

"Terrific. Why don't you go home and change into something a bit more festive while I finish up my shift. Then I'll pick you up about two this afternoon."

Although Tessa hadn't wanted to admit it, even to herself, the idea of spending her first holiday alone had been more than a little depressing.

There was just one more little thing. "What about my ticket?"

He shrugged. "It's Christmas. I suppose I can let you get away with a warning." His eyes sparkled with laughter. "This time."

As she watched him walk back toward his motorcycle, Tessa took this serendipitous meeting as a sign that her dreams really would come true.

It was only after the cycle had roared away that Tessa realized she'd never thought to ask his name.

She was flying. From her bird's-eye vantage point, high in the stunningly clear sky, Molly could see the vast cobalt expanse of the Pacific Ocean, edged by ribbons of sparkling, diamond-bright sand. The tide was ebbing, leaving pastel pink and ivory shells in its frothy wake. She soared higher, taking in the lush green hills, the unmistakable Los Angeles skyline, the crescent-shaped bay off Catalina Island. The sun was a gleaming ball, sinking toward the water, casting a ruby-and-copper glow over the landscape, giving it an otherworldly appearance.

It was so quiet up here, with only the sound of the air rushing over her outstretched arms. So peaceful. Looking down at the idyllic-appearing landscape, one would never imagine that the city could harbor so much cruelty, pain and suffering. She began to soar even higher, toward the vast firmament with its sparkling stars and Milky Way glittering like gold dust scattered over midnight blue velvet.

As she flew past the sun, her flowing silver sleeves suddenly went up in flames, engulfing her in a blazing fireball. She came crashing back to earth, hitting the ground with a bone-rattling thud that made her moan.

"Reece! She's coming to!"

Lena's familiar voice sounded as if it was coming from the bottom of the sea. Molly thought she heard Reece answer, but she could not make out the words. She struggled to regain consciousness, tried to open her eyes, but they were so heavy and her mind was so fogged, she gave up the attempt and drifted back into the mists.

The next time she woke, the sun was streaming in through the window, and Molly wondered what she was doing in bed in the middle of the day. She must be ill, she decided. But that was odd because she never got sick. The nuns at the Good Shepherd Home for Girls had always said she had the constitution of a horse. And the personality of a mule.

Concentrating mightily, Molly managed to rouse herself, then immediately wished she hadn't. Her muscles were screaming with pain, there was a bone-deep throbbing between her legs, her breasts felt as if someone had touched a torch to them and her face ached horribly. So horribly, Molly wondered if her dream of burning up hadn't been a dream at all.

It took a herculean effort, but she managed to pry her eyes open. The first thing she saw was Reece, slouched in a plastic chair across the room. He was asleep.

She opened her mouth to say his name, but her lips were too dry to form the words. Her faint moan snapped him from his light sleep.

"It's about time you decided to wake up and join the living." As a doctor, Reece had thought he'd become immune to suffering and death. Until he'd seen Molly lying amidst all that garbage, valiantly clinging to life.

He held out a plastic glass, encouraging her to take a sip of water from the straw. "Not too much." He took the glass away too soon. It seemed she'd barely had a chance to wet her lips.

"I'm...so...thirsty." It was not Molly's nature to complain. But she felt as if all the sand on the Los Angeles coastline had somehow ended up in her mouth.

"I know. But you've been on IV's for the past eight hours, so you're in no danger of dehydration—"

"Eight hours?"

"Thomas found you when I was going off shift."

Thomas? She shook her head, then wished she hadn't, when lightning flashed behind her eyes and boulders inside her head shifted.

"Was I—" she had to struggle to get the words

out "—in an accident?" Molly felt as if she'd been run over by a bus.

"There's plenty of time to get into details later." He reached down and brushed her dark hair away from her forehead with a soothing touch. "Lena's been going out of her mind with worry. She's in the cafeteria. Let me go get her."

He left the room, leaving her question unanswered.

Molly was staring up at the ceiling, trying to focus her mind, which she realized was fogged with some heavy-duty painkiller—Demerol?—when she became aware of the sound of footfalls on the tile floor.

The sight of the blue uniform took her back suddenly to that terrifying night when the house had been surrounded by police. She could hear the unforgettable sound of the front door being kicked in, and she gasped involuntarily. The sudden intake of breath was incredibly painful.

"The doc said your ribs are cracked," a baritone voice rumbled. "You probably should avoid any deep breaths." Ignoring hospital rules, he sat down on the bed. "How are you feeling?"

His face bore a striking resemblance to Alex Kovaleski. But this was not the man who'd tried for so many hours to talk her father out of murder. It was his son, Dan, who had, over the intervening years, become almost like a brother to Molly.

"Thirsty," she managed.

He glanced over at the pink plastic glass. "Did Reece say you're allowed to drink anything?"

"Since when did you become a stickler for rules and procedure?"

He laughed at that and held out the glass to her.

"Welcome back. I told Lena that low-life slimeball couldn't beat the spunk out of you."

"Beat?" After taking a long wonderful drink, she tried to blink away the fog clouding her memory. "I was beaten?"

"Aw, hell. Reece didn't tell you?"

"No." But Dan Kovaleski's frown spoke volumes. "I guess it's up to you."

He looked as if he'd rather try to serve a speeding ticket on Zsa Zsa Gabor. "How about we wait and see what the doc thinks you're ready to hear?"

"I never would have taken you for a coward, Daniel Kovaleski."

He cursed ripely. "Anyone ever tell you that you've got to be the most stubborn female God ever made?"

"All the time." The familiar sparring helped clear her head and take her mind momentarily off her pain. "Personally, I've always taken it as a compliment."

"You would." He cursed again, softer this time as he linked their fingers together. "There weren't any witnesses, Molly. At least none that we could find, which doesn't mean anything.

"Right now, all we know is that you left the hospital a little before midnight. Six hours later, Thomas showed up at the ER door, frantic because he'd found you lying unconscious in the alley a few blocks away."

Her fingers tightened on his. "Is he all right?"

Dan shrugged. He had never liked Molly's dangerous predilection for picking up strays. "Thomas is Thomas. He's the same as he always is. Nuts."

"He's in emotional pain," she managed to argue. "But he still managed to get help for me."

"Point taken." His gaze drifted out the window toward the mean streets. "It's also a possibility that he's the one who did this to you in the first place, then suffered a sudden case of remorse. Or fear."

"Thomas would never hurt anyone."

Dan's expression was cop hard. "You can't be sure of that, Molly."

"I'd stake my life on it."

"When all that Demerol wears off and you can think rationally again, you might just realize that may be exactly what you've done."

Although the brief conversation had exhausted her, she had to stand up for a man she knew didn't have the strength to stand up for himself. "Thomas isn't responsible."

"Actually, you're probably right," he agreed with obvious reluctance. Two strong-willed people, they'd argued often over the years and neither was fond of losing. "Since the test results came back negative."

"Test results?"

A reluctant smile hovered at the corner of his grimly set lips. "From what we could tell, you bopped the guy a good one, kiddo. Not all that blood in the alley was yours."

"Nor Thomas's."

"No." He gave her a long look as if judging whether or not to say more.

Belatedly understanding his dilemma, Molly decided to help him out. "I was raped, wasn't I?"

He closed his eyes, briefly. When he opened them,

Molly saw regret and embarrassment. "Yeah." He exhaled a long breath. "Hell, Molly, I'm so sorry."

She thought of all the rape victims who'd come through the doors of the ER and realized that in some way, she might be fortunate her memory had blocked out the assault. "You and Reece don't need to tiptoe around the subject. I'm no different than any other rape victim."

"Yes you are," Dan shot back. "The fact of your being a nun—and a virgin—should put you off-limits to creeps like that."

Jacob's daughter, Dinah, had been raped, Molly remembered. When she also recalled that Dinah's brothers had massacred all the men in the rapist's city to avenge the defilement of their sister, she decided not to share that particular Bible story with this grim-faced man.

"Virgins get raped every day. Some of them are children." Although her eyes were barely slits, she managed to meet his frustrated gaze. "And I've seen you deal with that."

"True." This time it was his fingers that tightened on hers. "But what you don't see is me throwing up afterward."

Molly tried to smile, then flinched when the attempt pulled the stitches Reece had sewn in her top and bottom lips. "You're a good man, Dan. And you're definitely your father's son."

His grip loosened, his smile brightened his brown eyes. "Speaking of Pop, he's been driving everyone nuts waiting to get in to see you."

Amazingly, Alex Kovaleski had taken an interest in the orphaned McBride sisters after that fateful night fourteen years ago. He'd even tried to adopt them, only to be informed that divorced men were not suitable fathers for little girls.

The bureaucrats were wrong. Molly didn't want to think about how much worse their rocky childhoods would have been without Alex Kovaleski in their corner.

He'd attended her Profession Day, his chest puffed up with pride as she'd repeated her vows and had the slender gold ring of Christ slipped onto her finger. And although he was a man given to wearing plaid shirts and jeans while off duty, he'd willingly donned a morning coat to give Lena away at her wedding to Reece. Her unconscious smile tugging at the stitches returned Molly's mind to her reason for being a patient in her own hospital, but before she had a chance to think about that, Lena rushed into the room and threw her arms around her older sister.

"Do you have any idea how much you frightened us?" she asked on a sob as tears streamed down her delicate cheeks. "I was so afraid I'd lose you. Just like..."

Lena didn't finish the sentence. There was no need. Molly knew they were both thinking of their mother. And Tessa.

"I know." Although the tight embrace was making her ribs feel as if they were on fire, Molly hugged her sister back. "It's okay. I'm going to be fine."

"Of course you will," Lena agreed. Belatedly remembering Molly's injuries, she released her. "And as soon as Reece lets you out of here, we're going to have the biggest celebration in history." She gave Dan a watery smile. "You and your dad are invited."

He grinned back. "We wouldn't miss it for the world."

They might not be a Norman Rockwell painting, Molly admitted. But she and Lena and Reece, along with Dan and Alex, made one pretty terrific family. And even as her head throbbed and her body ached, she felt the warmth of love in the room and knew everything was going to be all right.

Chapter Four

Elaine Mathison was a stunning woman with a lion's mane of tawny hair that tumbled over her shoulders. She was tall and slender, and wore a simple tube of ivory silk designed to showcase a figure toned from hours spent with a personal trainer.

"Hello. And aren't you lovely!" she welcomed Tessa. She exchanged a look with Jason—that was the handsome policeman's name, Tessa had learned. "Darling, you've outdone yourself this time."

"Tessa was afraid she'd be crashing the party," Jason revealed.

"Nonsense." Elaine smiled. "A party can never have too many beautiful women. Believe me, darling, with your fresh, innocent looks, you're going to be a hit." That stated, she linked arms with the young woman and led her across the sea of white marble in the entry hall.

A massive crystal chandelier dominated the hall, showering sparkling light on a towering sculpture of two lovers in an intimate embrace. Palm trees framed the arched doorway of a living room shimmering in silver and white.

Set high in the hills of Bel Air, the house boasted stunning views of the glittering city below and the dazzling waters of the Pacific Ocean. The scene reminded Tessa of something from the *Arabian Nights.* Just gazing out over the scene was like being on a magic carpet ride above Los Angeles.

Although there weren't as many big-name movie stars as Tessa might have wished for, she did recognize several guests. All the women, she noted with a tinge of envy were young and ravishingly beautiful, and the men older, but still handsome. And those who weren't handsome looked as if they had so much money, it didn't matter. Expensive perfumes filled the air, mingling with the seasonal scents of juniper, fir and pine.

Tessa was not overly intimidated by the unfamiliar splendor. Having grown up on air force bases all over the world, she'd acquired the instincts of a natural chameleon. By the time she was ten years old she'd attended seven schools and had developed the ability to adapt her behavior to immediately fit in to her new landscape. She'd worn Izod polo shirts and khaki shorts in New England, flowery cotton summer dresses in Georgia, faded jeans and eelskin boots in Wyoming.

She'd hiked the Grand Canyon, donned Gore-Tex against the unrelenting rains of the Pacific Northwest to ride a racing bike along thirty miles of Mount Rainier's Wonderland Trail, and had, in what she would always consider the ultimate endurance test, sat through Wagner's famed Ring Opera with fellow senior year drama students in Germany. Of course, the fact that she'd been having a secret, passionate affair with her teacher, a self-professed Ring fanatic, made the experience more palatable.

She'd no sooner sat down beside the pool with Jason when Elaine approached.

"Darling," she said to her son, "I hate to bother you with business, when you've just arrived, but Jeremy Stone insists on speaking with you in the library. It seems he's in desperate need for someone to serve as a police consultant on his new movie and of course you immediately came to mind."

"I've already got a job, Elaine," Jason said equably.

"Of course you do. But if you'd only talk with him."

He sighed as if this was a familiar argument, and turned toward Tessa. "I won't be long."

She smiled up at him. "I'll be fine."

He laughed at that and ran a finger down the slope of her nose. "Oh, you're a lot better than fine, Tessa Starr."

Still glowing from that tender touch, Tessa was watching a stunning blonde clad in a thong bikini playing a spirited game of Marco Polo with an aging television comic when a handsome man wearing obviously expensive linen slacks and a collarless shirt approached. If Jason hadn't just left, Tessa would have sworn it was him.

"My baby brother tells me you're an actress," he said, handing her a slender crystal flute of champagne.

"Jason's your younger brother?" She took a sip. The pale gold wine tasted like sunshine on water.

"By eight minutes. And I do my best not to let him forget it." His grin might have been a replica of his brother's, but the devils in his dark eyes were all his own. "But I have to admit this time the kid has definitely demonstrated terrific taste."

Tessa took another sip of champagne. "Thank you," she murmured into her glass.

"Don't thank me. Thank whatever magnificent gene pool you were spawned in." He rocked back on his heels. "I assume you have photos?"

"Of course." She was pleased for a chance to demonstrate that she wasn't as naive as he thought her to be. She pulled the photos from her oversize purse.

Although Tessa thought them flattering, Miles's frown was not encouraging. "These look like high school graduation shots."

"Your brother thought they were good."

"My brother's a cop. All he saw was a drop-dead gorgeous female. While I, on the other hand, see the unflattering shadow beneath your eyes, and the way whoever was behind the lens didn't even try to show off your cheekbones."

He reached out and ran his fingertips along the bones in question. "You could cut crystal with these," he murmured. "But that hack made you look like a chipmunk-cheeked farmer's daughter."

That stung. "I suppose you're an expert on photography?"

"Actually, I am." Rather than appearing fatally wounded by her attempt at hauteur, he seemed amused. He cupped her elbow in his palm. "Come with me and I'll show you what a real photographer can do with a face like yours."

Tessa didn't think she liked him. She knew she didn't trust him. However, now that he'd pointed out the flaws in the photographs, she could see that he was right.

She was trying to decide what to do when Jason returned. "You keep manhandling my women, Miles," he said mildly, "and I'll have to throw you in the slammer."

"I was just going to show Tessa my rogue's gallery."

"I think she'd rather see my Wanted posters." He put his arm around her bare shoulders. "Wouldn't you, sweetheart?"

She looked back and forth between the two brothers, trying to figure out whether or not their rivalry was real or a longtime game they enjoyed playing.

"You're scaring her," Miles complained. The smile he bestowed on Tessa was absolutely harmless. "Would you feel better if Officer Friendly here came along with us?"

Tessa reminded herself that a faint heart never achieved anything. "I think I'd like to see your photographs."

"Terrific." He nodded with satisfaction. "I've shot some of the most stunning faces in the business. And believe me, very few of them can hold a candle to you."

Exchanging a look with his brother over the top of her head, he led Tessa back into the house.

* * *

The next time Molly woke, she found another familiar face sitting in the chair beside the bed.

"You realize, of course, that you scared us all to death," the elderly nun, who was the closest thing Molly had to a mother, scolded.

"Next time I'm raped and beaten, I'll try to be more discreet about it."

A frown furrowed the forehead that, when Molly had first met her, had been covered by a starched wimple. "This isn't a joking matter."

"On that we're in full agreement." Molly scooted up in bed, wincing at the pain in her hips. Obviously Reece had cut back on his orders for drugs. "How's Lena?"

"Your sister's going to be fine." The nun fingered her rosary beads absently. "Thanks to her husband. The man appears to be a rock."

"He is that."

"Father Murphy said a mass for you this morning," Sister Benvenuto announced. "And the congregation is praying for you. As are all the members of the order, of course."

"Tell everyone I appreciate their prayers." Molly glanced around the room. "It looks as if someone threw a hand grenade into the middle of the Rose Parade."

"You have a great many friends. The red and white carnations in that plastic Santa Claus vase are from Thomas. I have every suspicion that he stole them from a supermarket."

Molly figured Sister Benvenuto was undoubtedly correct in her assumption. "It's the thought that counts."

The older woman shook her head. "You're too easy on him. With the proper motivation he could return to the work he was called to do."

"If God can't provide the impetus, I'm not about to try." Molly sighed as she thought about Thomas. "Besides, if he hadn't given up the priesthood, he wouldn't have been there to help me."

"I suppose we'll just have to write it off as another case of the Lord working in mysterious ways." The older woman's gaze sharpened as she studied Molly. "I was afraid we were going to lose you."

"There was a moment I thought that, too."

Molly knew the nun was not talking about her leaving the order, something they'd discussed on more than one occasion. Each time Molly had dared to profess doubts about a true vocation, Sister Benvenuto had assured her that such thoughts were not only normal, but expected. That such reflection would ultimately make her even more committed to her religious calling.

"It's going to be difficult to deal with," the nun predicted. "But you've always been strong, Molly. And with God's help, you'll survive this test of faith just as you've survived every other trial in your life."

Although she didn't believe that God would have deliberately caused her to be brutally attacked, to test her as he had Job, Molly saw no point in arguing. Even during her teens, when she'd been an angry young girl, rebelling against the myriad rules the sisters who ran the Good Shepherd Home for Girls had expected her to obey without question, Molly had admired the nun's seemingly unwavering faith. So unlike her own, which always seemed to question everything.

"What would I ever have done without you?"

"God only knows. Although there's always the possibility you could have ended up on the street, like those poor girls I pass every day," the no-nonsense nun said briskly.

"Being sent to Good Shepherd was the best thing that ever happened to me." What at first had seemed to be punishment, had, in the end proven a blessing. The home for girls had been a sanctuary, the first Molly had ever experienced. "I wish Lena could have had the same security."

Molly had often thought it ironic that Lena, who'd tried so desperately to fit in, was the one who'd suffered the most by being constantly shuffled from foster home to foster home.

"Lena is going to have to learn that true strength comes from within," Sister Benvenuto said sagely.

Unable to argue with that, Molly was grateful for Yolanda's interruption.

"I vant to suck your blood," she said in a ghoulish voice. The sight of the gag store fangs gleaming white and red in the nurse's dark face made Molly laugh. When you worked in a world where the bizarre and horrific were commonplace, sometimes laughter truly was the best medicine. And the only way to stay sane.

"This is the first in the series of HIV tests, isn't it?"

"Now, aren't you a clever girl. Anybody'd think you were a health-care professional, or something." Yolanda took the fangs out of her wide mouth, put them in her pocket and pulled out a rubber tourniquet. "Hold out your arm."

Molly did as instructed.

"Lordy," Yolanda complained, shaking her head as she studied Molly's freckled arm. "You call those veins? Those are purely pitiful, girl." She wrapped the tourniquet around Molly's upper arm.

"Lucky thing you're in the hands of an expert. Health services tried sending up one of their lab vampires, but I cut him off at the pass. They tend to spatter the stuff all over, and with that pale white skin, I figured you didn't have any blood to spare."

When she took a needle out of another pocket and uncapped it, Sister Benvenuto rose. "I believe it's time I let you get some rest, dear."

Molly didn't blame the nun for escaping. Hating having blood drawn even more than she disliked drawing it, Molly would have left if she could.

"I'll return during visiting hours," Sister Benvenuto assured her. "Sister Joseph is making those fudge brownies you used to enjoy. She's making enough to bribe the medical staff into giving you preferential treatment."

"As if anyone would have to bribe us to take care of our own," Yolanda muttered after the older nun had left the room.

"She means well."

"I suppose so. Although she reminds me an awful lot of that harridan who used to rap my knuckles whenever she caught me chewing gum at Sacred Heart Academy."

The needle slipped into the vein as smoothly as a hot knife through butter. Although accustomed to the sight of blood, seeing her own filling the cylinder was an entirely different matter.

"All done." Yolanda capped the cylinder and released the tourniquet. "I have to ask you if you do IV drugs."

"You know I don't."

"Just following procedure. So, how about safe sex?"

Molly laughed at that, but the sound held no humor. "Before or after Christmas Eve?"

"Point taken. I'll have the lab rush this and either Reece or I will let you know as soon as the results come in. You've got three more of these over the next nine months. When you test negative on the third one, you'll be home free."

"Thank you for saying *when* and not *if*."

"Positive thinking is a powerful thing. Sister Crack-the-Whip who just left might call it praying, and existentialists might call it meditating, but the way I see it, it's all the same thing."

Although she knew Sister Benvenuto would probably have her down on her knees saying an Act of Contrition and countless rosaries for such heresy, Molly decided she'd be willing to pray to God, all the saints, Mohammed, Buddha, the Dalai Lama, even some ancient druidic pagan oak tree if only she could dodge this deadly bullet.

"If I get AIDS, I'll just die," she muttered, more to herself than to Yolanda.

She and her longtime friend exchanged a gloomy look. Then burst into laughter.

"She's going to be all right," Reece assured Lena once again as they drove home from the hospital together. Although he never would have wished such horror on Molly, he couldn't deny being grateful for the change seeing her sister victimized seemed to have made on his wife these past days.

"I know." She put her hand on his leg. "Thanks to you. If you hadn't done all that you did..."

Her voice drifted off and she stared out at the brilliant lights of the city as they drove up the curving road to their Pacific Palisades home. The house, situated on a cliff overlooking the Pacific Coast Highway and the ocean beyond was more expensive than a resident could afford, but Reece was independently wealthy. He'd inherited a generous trust from his parents, who'd died in a plane crash when he was a boy.

He slanted her a sideways glance. "How are you with all this?"

"Strangely, although I was panic-stricken when you first called, I'm doing pretty well." Lena shook her head. "All my life, even when we were separated, I knew that Molly would be there for me if I ever needed her."

"In a heartbeat," he agreed.

"I think, although she meant well, her protective behavior kept me from growing up."

Since there was no way he was going to get trapped into agreeing that the woman he adored was immature, Reece didn't say anything.

"Then, of course, I married you, who took over where Molly left off."

He laid a hand over hers. "I think it's only natural for a man to want to protect his wife."

"I suppose."

Lena thought back to the tarot card reading. Amazingly, the destiny foretold that night seemed to be coming true. *Out of apparent evil,* she remembered the young woman saying sagely, *much good can come.*

"What happened to Molly made me realize I can't always count on other people taking care of me. It's time I learned to stand on my own two feet."

Something inside Reece went still. And cold. "Are you saying you want a divorce?"

"A divorce?" Shocked, she looked over at him. "Of course not." Turning her hand, she linked their fingers together. "You're the most wonderful thing that's ever happened to me, Reece. I just think it might be a nice change if you were to discover that you were married to a woman. And not a girl."

Reece thought about that and decided she was right. As much as he adored his bride, there were times when he found being the sole focus of her life—along with her desperate desire for a child—more than a little wearying.

"You certainly don't have to change on my account. I love you just the way you are."

"I know. And I thank God for that every day. And I'm not changing for you. I'm doing it for me." Lena smiled, pleased with the plan she'd come up with while drinking far too many cups of that toxic waste the hospital cafeteria tried to pass off as coffee. "Although I think you'll find some side benefits."

There was something in her voice. Something lush and sensual, an impression that was heightened by the way she'd begun trailing her fingernail up his thigh.

"Why, Mrs. Longworth," he murmured, "are you trying to seduce me?"

She laughed at that. A silky, womanly laugh designed to get beneath a man's skin. "I *am* going to seduce you, Dr. Longworth." Her fingers trailed higher. "And you're going to love it."

The sound of his zipper lowering was the sexiest thing Reece had ever heard. Or felt. When she freed his erection from his jeans, blood rushed from his head straight into his groin.

"Jesus, Lena." The words clogged in his throat, his breath was trapped in his lungs. "If you're not careful, you're going to make me run off the road."

"Don't worry, darling." She bent her head and pressed her lips against the tip of his penis. "I promise to be very, very careful."

Her breath was like the Santa Ana winds that blew in from the desert, fanning flames he'd banked for too long. From the first night of their honeymoon, wanting to prove himself different from all the users she'd gotten involved with before him, Reece had gone out of his way to treat his bride with consideration and respect. Their lovemaking, while enjoyable, had remained restrained.

After she'd become obsessed with having a child, the only times they made love were on those days when she was most likely to conceive. And although he adored her to pieces, lately he'd begun to feel more like a stud bull than a husband.

"Lord, Lena," he groaned as she took him fully into her ripe wet mouth. "You're going to get us both killed.... Let me..." He managed, just barely, to turn into the half-moon driveway and cut the engine.

On the verge of exploding, Reece grabbed hold of a fistful of thick silky hair and yanked her head up.

"Let's go in the house." His voice was harsh and guttural. "I want to take my time. And do this right."

The silvery moonlight streaming through the windshield illuminated her face, letting him see the sexual fever burning in Lena's eyes.

"You can take all the time you want." She unfastened her seat belt and straddled him. "Later."

"What the hell did you do with your panties?" he gasped as she teased the tip of his throbbing cock with hot female flesh.

"I tucked them away in my purse before we left the hospital." She put her hands on his shoulders, her mouth on his.

That she'd planned this seduction made it even more exciting. Reece's fingers delved beneath her sweater, digging deeply into the bare skin of her waist as he forced her down on him at the same time he slammed up to meet her.

Their teeth clashed as their mouths ate into one another's, their tongues tangled. The ride was hard and fast, their slick damp bodies slapping against each other in a ruthless need for release. When she cried out his name, then shuddered violently, Reece gave in to his own white-hot, explosive climax.

He stayed deep inside her as they enjoyed the aftermaths of passion. "I can feel you," he murmured against her throat as the rhythmic tightening of her inner muscles continued to caress him like silken gloves.

"Mmm." She tilted her head and outlined his mouth with the tip of her tongue. "I can feel you, too. And you feel so good inside me, I don't think I'll ever move."

"We'd get arrested for indecent exposure."

"I'm willing to risk it if you are. Besides, we have friends on the police force who'll vouch for us."

Reece felt his body beginning to warm again, but became aware of the chill of the December night. "I want you again." Shoving her sweater up, he took her breast in his mouth, suckling deeply in a way that made her body involuntarily clutch at his. "But this time I want to do it with all our clothes off. Inside, where no one can hear you scream."

As she felt him growing hard again inside her, Lena shivered with anticipation. And just a touch of erotic fear. "Are you really going to make me scream?"

He bit her nipple, not harshly, but with a dark sensual intent that caused excitement to curl in her belly. "You bet." His tongue soothed the tingling flesh. "And you're going to love it."

Reece proved to be a man of his word. He did wonderful, wicked things to her. And then, when she was positive there couldn't be more, he'd proven her wrong.

But this time it was different, Lena mused as she lay wrapped in her husband's arms, luxuriating in the feel of him still buried deep inside her. Because for the first time since they'd been married, she'd given him more than her body. She'd given him her heart.

And that, she thought with a soft smile as she drifted off on gentle wavelets of sleep, made all the difference.

Chapter Five

Molly had always suspected she wouldn't make a very good patient; she was too restless to lie in bed all day. Daytime television was a revelation, filled with programs about women who loved men who murdered, mothers who slept with their daughter's boyfriends, husbands who got their wives' best friends pregnant. Since her work had given her an up-close and personal look at society's ills, none of the subjects shocked her. What was surprising was that viewers would be interested in watching all these depressingly dysfunctional relationships.

She tried to read, but every time an ambulance cut its siren outside the ER doors, or a code came over the loudspeakers, she wanted to jump up and return to the battle. If her days were boring, her nights were anything but. Her sleep was interrupted at regular intervals by horrifying nightmares in which she was forced to suffer the rape, which she now remembered, over and over again.

From her talks with the psych resident, Alan Bernstein, Molly understood the night terrors were her subconscious mind's way of struggling to deal with the trauma she'd suffered. She also became convinced that as soon as she was allowed to return to the routine of normal daily life, the nightmares would stop.

Yolanda remained sympathetic, but refused to do anything to help Molly escape what she'd come to view as her imprisonment.

"Reece says if you're a good girl he may sign you out tomorrow."

"I've already been here five days."

"So, you'll be here six."

Molly muttered something that while not exactly a curse, wasn't exactly nunlike, either. "At least tell me what's happening down in The Pit. I never thought I'd miss that place, but I do."

"Taking religious vows doesn't prevent you from becoming hooked on the adrenaline rush, just like the rest of us."

Molly couldn't argue with that. She'd be the first to admit that the impatient streak that had once resulted in her being disciplined as a child with depressing regularity, now made her a natural ER nurse.

"Oh, there is some news," Yolanda said. "About Benny."

Molly's own petty frustration was instantly forgotten. Benny Johnson was a five-year-old boy who'd suffered more than any child should have to. He'd been born a crack baby on Molly's first day in the ER. His near-fatal withdrawal had been excruciatingly painful, making more than one battle-hardened ER nurse cry.

Social Services had taken Benny from his mother. Unfortunately, they'd turned him over to his grandmother, who was no model of maternal expertise, either. By the time he was six months old, Benny had suffered a broken arm and possible head injuries from being shaken.

He'd been put in a crisis nursery, only to be released to his mother again when she was released from a drug-abuse treatment program. Two days later, Benny was back with mysterious burns.

The cycle had continued for five years. And each time Benny showed up in The Pit for treatment after another one of his *accidents,* Molly was more tempted just to take the poor little boy and run away.

"What now?"

"He came in this morning all bruised, with cracked ribs. The court's toughened up. He's going to be released for adoption over his mother's consent."

That should have been good news, but unfortunately, Molly knew better.

"Older children are difficult to place," she murmured. She also recalled, with vivid clarity that long ago day when she'd eavesdropped on a conversation between the Mother Superior who ran the orphanage and prospective parents.

The well-dressed couple who thought Lena "sweet" and were prepared to overlook the fact that Molly could be "a bit of a handful," had been reluctant to adopt the sisters because of their background.

"How can anyone know about genetics, really?" the man had asked. "What if one of the girls harbors some impulse that might cause her to violently explode with rage? As her father did?"

"That's highly unlikely," the nun had assured him.

"Unlikely perhaps. But you can't guarantee it's not a possibility."

"There are no guarantees in life, Mr. Howard," the nun had tried again. "Even if the Lord were to bless you with your own children—"

"That's just it. They'd be our own. And believe me, Sister, there are no murderous alcoholics in either my wife's or my family. No." Molly, who was standing with her ear against the door, had heard a deep sigh. "I'm afraid it's just not worth the risk."

Over the years the faces in that office had changed. But the argument had remained the same. Molly and Lena McBride were damaged goods.

"Benny has a lot of strikes working against him when it comes to adoption," Molly murmured, thinking back on those lonely, frustrating days when she and Lena had been forced to watch other children leave the orphanage with their new families.

"That's sure true. But you know Dr. Moore?"

"In pediatrics?"

"That's him. He and his wife have been trying to have kids for ages with no luck. I overheard him talking to the social worker about getting the paperwork started."

"Oh, that is good news." Sometimes God did answer prayers. "Is Benny still downstairs?"

Yolanda's sharp look revealed that she knew Molly all too well. "Yes, but you're not—"

"I promise not to do any work. I just want to keep a little boy company for a while."

"Reece will kill me."

"Reece is too much of a sweetheart to kill anyone. Especially these days."

"You noticed that the doc's been floating up somewhere on cloud nine, too?"

Molly returned Yolanda's grin with one of her own. "You'd have to be blind not to notice."

"He's got the look of a man who's getting laid regular. And your sister's looking like a kitten who discovered a saucer of cream. I swear, if I hadn't sworn off marriage after my third divorce, I'd almost be willing to give it a try again."

Molly laughed. She didn't know what had happened between Lena and Reece. But whatever it was, she was definitely more than a little relieved at the change.

"If you could just get me some scrubs," Molly coaxed, returning to their previous subject.

Yolanda folded her arms across her ample breasts. "If you tell anyone where you got them…"

"I won't say a word. Cross my heart."

Muttering to herself, Yolanda left the room, but returned a few minutes later with a pair of green surgical scrubs. "I didn't see a thing," she said. Then left again.

Molly found Benny in one of the waiting rooms, seated at a small table. Someone had given him a box of crayons and a coloring book, but he hadn't touched them, and sat staring out into space. Molly didn't want to know what the child was seeing. What he'd already seen. She also hoped that Dr. Moore and his wife had an immense store of patience.

"Hi, Benny," she said cheerily.

He looked up, his expression flat until he saw her bruises. "Somebody hit you, too, Sister?"

"I'm afraid so, Benny."

He thought about that for a minute. "People aren't supposed to hit nuns."

"People aren't supposed to hit children, either. But sometimes people do."

"Yeah." He looked down at the backs of his small hands, which had circular scars that could only have been made from cigarette burns.

"Have you had lunch yet?"

"Yeah. One of the nurses brought me a peanut-butter-and-jelly sandwich from the cafeteria. And some chocolate milk."

"That was nice."

"I like chocolate milk." Despite his words, his eyes had gone flat again.

"How about popcorn?"

He shrugged. "It's okay, I guess. I only ever had it once. When the lady at one of the places I was staying took a bunch of us to see *An American Tail*."

"That was a cool movie."

Another shrug.

"I was sitting upstairs feeling a little sorry for myself when I decided popcorn might cheer me up." Molly decided a white lie in this case was definitely one of the more venial sins she'd committed. "But I hate snacking alone and can't eat the entire bag anyway. So, I was kind of hoping you'd help me out."

She watched the flicker of interest in the depths of his dark eyes.

"I guess that'd be okay. Since I have to hang

around here, anyway, until the social worker shows up.''

"Thanks, Benny. I really appreciate your helping me out.''

She took him into the nurses' lounge, retrieved a bag of popcorn from her secret hiding place and put it in the microwave.

Five minutes later, they were working their way through the plump white kernels.

"I heard the nurses talking,'' Benny volunteered. "One of them said that Dr. Moore wants to be my dad.''

"How do you feel about that?'' Molly asked, popping the top on a soft drink can and handing it to him.

"I guess that'd be okay. I never had a dad.''

"I lost mine when I was little, too,'' Molly volunteered.

He gave her a long look, but didn't ask any questions. Molly knew all too well how children from violent homes learned the importance of keeping secrets.

"Johnny Brown has a dad. He hits him. A lot.''

"Dr. Moore would never hit you, Benny.''

"You don't think so?''

"I know so.''

He fell silent, mulling that over.

"I guess it'd be okay, then.''

"I think it would be even better than okay,'' Molly agreed mildly.

That little worrisome matter settled, neither Molly nor Benny said anything else. There was no need to. For both of them, the quiet companionship was enough.

* * *

Molly was packing away the last of her toiletries. She was finally being allowed to return home to her own apartment. At least that's where she had thought she'd be going. Until Lena had shown up, determined that she come and stay with her.

"You and Reece have been acting like you're newlyweds. The last thing you need is me hanging around your house." Molly returned to the adjoining bathroom for the shampoo. "What if you want to make love, hanging from the dining room chandelier while I'm in the room eating my microwave dinner?"

"Molly!" Lena appeared shocked that her sister would even think of such a thing. "You're a nun!" Then color flooded into her cheeks as she thought of the fantasy game she and Reece had played last night. The one where he'd been a ruthless Norman plundering the Saxon countryside. And dear Lord, how wonderfully he'd plundered!

"All this is beside the point," she insisted, shaking off the sensual memory. "Because we're not going to be alone anyway." Her shoulders slumped beneath her pale blue angora sweater. "Reece's aunt called last night. She's arriving in town this evening."

"Theo's coming here?" Molly had met Theodora Longworth at Reece and Lena's wedding. A successful writer, she was a bold, larger-than-life character who could have stepped from one of the pages of her romance novels.

"She's gotten an offer to be head writer for some soap opera," Lena said glumly.

"Wouldn't that mean she'd have to settle down?"

"I don't know. I suppose so. I do know that if the

woman is going to be living under my roof, I need someone in my corner.''

"Why? She seemed genuinely fond of you at the wedding.''

"She's filthy rich, Molly.''

"So's Reece. And that's never seemed to bother you.''

"Because he's never acted rich. Theo is just so…'' Lena's voice trailed off.

"Like Rosalind Russell's portrayal of Auntie Mame?''

"With a lot of Bette Midler thrown in.'' Lena sighed. "I'll really feel better if you're staying at the house, too. Heaven knows we've plenty of room.'' Rooms she'd planned to fill with children.

Molly suspected that the invitation was more than a little due to Reece and Lena's concern about her returning home alone to her apartment, which was in a neighborhood not much better than the area surrounding the hospital. However, whether or not they'd done it intentionally, they'd managed to come up with a situation she couldn't refuse.

"Just for the next week or so,'' Molly insisted. "But as soon as I come back to work, I'm returning to my own place.''

"Oh, thank you!'' Lena rushed forward to hug Molly, remembering the cracked ribs just in time. "I promise, Molly, I'll make this up to you.''

"There's certainly nothing to make up to me. Lounging around your house is not exactly on par with doing missionary work in Zaire.''

"Wait until you spend a few days with Theo.'' Lena's expression of impending doom echoed her glum tone. "I hate this time of year, anyway." She sighed and began picking at her fingernail polish. "Do you ever think about that night?"

"Of course." Molly knew Lena was not referring to the recent Christmas attack, but the earlier one.

"I used to think about it all the time. It's gotten better, but it never goes away. Like a scab I can't resist picking."

"May's almost as bad," Molly murmured.

"When you walk in the drugstore to buy some aspirin or tampons and get attacked by all those aisles of flowery Mother's Day cards," Lena agreed. "I didn't think it bothered you. That once you became a nun—"

"God automatically took away the pain on my Profession Day?"

"Something like that."

It was Molly's turn to sigh. "Unfortunately, it doesn't work that way."

"I guess not." Lena walked over to the window and stared down at the parking lot, but Molly suspected it was not the cars she was seeing, but that long-ago scene that had been imprinted indelibly on both their minds. "Do you ever hear Mama's voice?"

"No. I stopped being able to hear her about the third year after Daddy...after it happened."

"I do." Lena glanced back over her shoulder. "Every once in a while, I imagine I hear her singing. Remember how she used to love to sing?"

The memory was bittersweet. "Just like Patsy Cline."

"Yeah. I remember her once telling me how tragic

it was that Patsy had died so young in that plane crash. And then she died too young, as well....

"I think that's why I turned wild for a while, until I met Reece," Lena admitted. "Because I have this terrible fear I'm going to die young, too." She dragged her hand through her thick auburn hair. "I look just like her, don't I?"

Molly didn't like where this conversation was going. "I suppose there's some resemblance," she hedged.

"I stole a picture the day the social worker took us away," Lena revealed. "It was a snapshot of Mama in a bathing suit at the beach. I've kept it all these years. I look at that picture and it's like looking in a mirror....

"Then I look in the mirror and it's as if Mama's ghost is looking back at me. As if she's reminding me that I could die anytime, just like she did. Like Patsy did...

"Did you know that I'd planned my funeral when I was twelve?"

"You never said anything."

"I wrote it all down. So you'd find it after I died. I still update it every year, but I'm always a little surprised when I don't make all that many changes. I've planned your funeral, too. And Reece's."

"I didn't know that, either." Molly reminded herself that she'd only been a child herself, that she'd done the best she could for her sister under the circumstances. Nevertheless she felt a familiar stab of guilt that she hadn't managed to provide Lena with the security she'd needed growing up.

"Of course you didn't. Because I never told you.

But it seems as if I've spent my entire life waiting to die. Waiting for people I love to die. Which was why I was so terrified of loving Reece.

"If he was ten minutes late coming home, I knew he'd had an accident on the freeway. If I called here and he didn't answer his page, I was certain some crazed homicidal junkie had taken him hostage and was going to kill him. I was so fixated on all those morbid thoughts that I was too afraid to enjoy life."

"And now?" Molly asked carefully.

"I think it's finally sunk in that the secret to life may be living for the moment, but it's also important to make certain that the moment's worth living for."

"And that's where Reece comes in."

The thought of her husband was like a bright and comforting sun, burning away the gloomy clouds in Lena's mind. Her smile literally lit up the room. "Absolutely."

Tessa was having no difficulty enjoying life.

"Well?" She twirled around, arms held out, showing off the beaded evening gown as a child might show off a new party dress. "What do you think?"

Jason Mathison sat in a gray suede chair, a pilsner of imported Australian beer in his hand as he gave her a slow, judicious look. "It's red."

"Well, of course it is." Tessa grinned. "You said you wanted me to look sexy for New Year's Eve. And this is definitely the sexiest dress so far."

The strapless scarlet gown fit like a glove, plunged to below the waist in back and was slit high on both thighs.

"It's overkill." He frowned and pulled a cigar out

of the pocket of one of the Armani jackets he favored when off duty. Tessa still hadn't decided which look she found sexier—the starched blue uniform of authority or this aura of casual money.

The chic blond saleswoman clad in Armani gray herself, immediately leaned forward to light the cigar. "I tried to suggest something a bit more subdued," she murmured. "But your friend had her own ideas."

"You should have explained my preferences."

Tessa didn't like the way they were talking about her as if she wasn't there. "You said you liked my Christmas dress."

"It had a certain gut-level masculine appeal." The glint in his eyes made her think he was remembering the short skirt and low-scooped neckline. "But if you want to break into the business, we need to upgrade your image."

"This is Hollywood." If there was one thing the general had taught Tessa, it was not to surrender without a fight.

"Actually, it's Beverly Hills." He puffed on the cigar, and although the noxious smell was bound to get into the fabric of the exquisite gowns displayed around the showroom of the famed Rodeo Drive boutique, Tessa noted the saleswoman didn't utter a word of complaint.

He turned to the statuesque blonde. "I want to see her in the Bill Blass."

"Not that one?" Tessa had rejected the dark unadorned gown at first glance. "Why don't you just see if there's a nun's habit hidden away in the back room? Or perhaps some sackcloth and ashes?"

Jason laughed at that. "I'm beginning to understand how Henry Higgins must have felt when trying to turn Eliza Doolittle into a lady."

When the saleswoman laughed, as well, Tessa became irritated again. "I *am* a lady."

Although the smile didn't fade, his eyes suddenly turned as hard as blue stones. "Then you should dress like one," he said reasonably.

Realizing that she'd just run up against his professional cop intransigence, Tessa exhaled a deep dramatic sigh, snatched the dress from the woman's arms and stomped back into the marble-walled dressing room.

Damn him! The change was so dramatic, it took Tessa's breath away. She stared at her reflection in the three-way mirror, stunned by the sleek, sophisticated woman looking back at her. The black halter-necked gown, which had appeared so drab on the padded silk hanger, skimmed over her body like a jet waterfall and proved a startling foil for her fiery hair. Although she'd always regretted her pale skin, the unadorned black dress made it gleam like porcelain.

Jason instantly confirmed her appraisal. "Perfect. There won't be a woman in the room who'll be able to hold a candle to you." He turned to the saleswoman. "She'll need gloves. Above the elbows. And those black silk pumps in the window."

By the time he dropped her off at her apartment, Tessa was floating on air. "I feel like a fairy-tale princess. But it was all so expensive, and I know policemen don't make all that much money..."

"I told you not to worry about that." He skimmed the back of his hand down her face. "Miles and I both inherited money from our grandfather."

"But you still work."

"Although I enjoy the ability to make a beautiful woman happy, I've never found the life of the idle rich to be appealing. I like being rich. And I like being a cop. This way I have the best of both worlds."

He was leaning closer, his lips a whisper away from hers. All she'd have to do would be to go up on her toes, just the least little bit...

"Would you like to come in?" Her heart was in her voice. And in her wide green eyes.

"I'd love to. But duty calls." As if reading her mind, he tipped forward and brushed his lips against hers in a light, friendly kiss that created a flare of heat that only left her wanting more. Much, much more. "I'll pick you up tomorrow night at seven."

She tamped down her disappointment that the first kiss he'd given her was over so soon. She knew he found her attractive. Even an independently wealthy man didn't spend so much money on a woman unless he was interested. Telling herself that she should be grateful that he was proving to be the kind of gentleman she could actually take home to her strict father, Tessa vowed that it was time for things to change.

"I'll be ready," she promised.

As she watched him walk back to the black Porsche, she pressed her fingers against her lips and decided that no matter how ladylike she looked tomorrow night, she was going to pull out all the stops to seduce this man she was falling in love with.

Chapter Six

Theodora Longworth hit Los Angeles like a hurricane. To Lena's vast relief, Reece's aunt insisted on staying at her favorite bungalow at the Beverly Hills Hotel. She did, however, manage to make her presence known, and although Lena was obviously intimidated by the fifty-year-old woman's powerful life force, Molly found her a welcome diversion from her own problems.

"Gin," Theo announced as she put her cards on the table with a flourish. She'd ostensibly come over to the house to keep Molly company while Reece and Lena went out to a New Year's party with the hospital staff.

Although Molly had assured them that she was more than capable of spending the evening alone, she'd gotten the feeling that were it not for Theo's presence, Lena, who'd continued to hover over her like a mother hen, would have refused to go.

As she'd cut the new deck of playing cards earlier

in the evening, Theo had informed Molly that she never played for penny ante stakes, not in any part of her life, including card games. "However," she'd stated, "given your unfortunate vow of poverty, I suppose I'd be willing—just this once—to play for chump change. So, how much can you afford to lose?"

"Twenty dollars." Surely that should last all night.

After spending the next two hours getting thoroughly trounced, Molly decided she'd definitely been overly optimistic. "Did anyone ever happen to mention that cheating is a sin?"

Molly's dry tone flew right over Theo's head. "Good thing I'm a Baptist," the older woman shot back as she deftly palmed a queen of hearts. "And for your information, Sister Molly, I was taught in the Healing Waters Sunday school that the Lord helps those who help themselves."

"Then He should be extremely proud of you," Molly muttered as she glared at the miserable hand Theo had dealt her.

"I have no doubt about it," Theo said cheerfully as she laid down a five card straight of hearts.

Secretly, Molly was grateful Theo hadn't reined in her typically outrageous behavior on her account. Ever since the rape, everyone had been treating her with kid gloves. It was definitely a relief to have someone finally behaving as if Molly were a normal person.

Five minutes later, she'd lost another hand. "The Lord does love a cheerful giver," Theo said encouragingly as Molly counted out the dimes and quarters.

"Well, you've cleaned me out. So I guess that

leaves us no choice but to tune in to Dick Clark's New Year's countdown at Times Square.''

"Now, let's not be in such a hurry." Theo swept the change into her gold leather duffel bag. "How about I advance you a stake?"

"So I can lose even more?"

"You never know." Theo shuffled the cards with a flair that would have put an old-time Mississippi riverboat gambler to shame. "Maybe you're about to get lucky."

Molly knew, without a single doubt, that Theo was about to start cheating to let her win. Since that held scant appeal, she was trying to figure out a way to turn Reece's aunt down when the doorbell chimed.

Theo left the room and returned two minutes later with Alex Kovaleski in tow. "You're off the hook, kiddo," she told Molly. "Gorgeous here has offered to take your place at the table."

"Why do I feel like Wild Bill Hickok just before he drew that deadman's hand," Alex drawled. He bent down and kissed Molly's cheek, kindly ignoring the way she involuntarily flinched at the male touch. "How you doin', sweetheart?"

Embarrassed by her behavior, Molly managed to smile up at him. "I'm a lot poorer than I was two hours ago. Theo cheats."

"Hell, if the woman tries it with me, I'll arrest her. After all, gambling's still illegal in California."

His gunmetal gray eyes sparkled with the amusement Molly had first seen directed Theodora's way at Lena and Reece's wedding. Although they were two totally dissimilar individuals, it was obvious they found each other more than a little entertaining.

"It figures you'd threaten me with that." Theo folded her arms over her breasts. "Did I ever tell you that I'm not overly fond of authority figures?"

"Several times." He folded his own arms. "Did I happen to mention that one of these days I'll win you over with my unrelenting charm?"

Theo snorted. "You did. And I recall telling you that better men have tried."

"Other men perhaps," he said with that same unshakable confidence that had once made him a good hostage negotiator. "But not better."

His eyes warmed to pewter as they skimmed over her. Although she was staying home, she'd dressed for the evening in a colorful full skirt, white satin blouse and glittering beaded vest. Molly half expected her to break out a pair of castanets and start dancing at any moment.

"You really are looking better than ever, Theodora," Alex said. "And although you looked great as a blonde, your new hairdo is dynamite. You remind me of Rita Hayworth in her prime."

To Molly's amazement, Theo blushed to the roots of her newly dyed red hair like a schoolgirl. "Compliments like that will get you anywhere you like, Officer."

Molly decided it was time to give the couple some privacy. "Well," she said, pretending to stifle a yawn, "it's been a long day. I think I'll go upstairs to my room."

"Don't you want to watch Dick Clark bring in the New Year?" Theo asked a bit too quickly.

Molly was greatly amused by the way she seemed

suddenly nervous at the idea of being alone with Alex.

"Why bother? He's not going to look any different. And the ball will come down on time, the same way it always does. No, I'd rather get some sleep and be fresh to watch the parade tomorrow morning."

"We haven't even popped the champagne yet. It's Cristal," Theo coaxed.

"I'm not supposed to be drinking while I'm on medication," Molly reminded her. "Why don't you share it with Alex?"

"I'd rather have a beer," he said. "If you have one."

Theo tossed her head in a way reminiscent of Hayworth's famed Gilda. "There you go, with that Mr. Macho routine again."

"It's not a routine." His grin was quick and wicked, and even Molly, who'd always considered this man the closest thing she'd ever known to a loving father, couldn't help noticing that it held considerable masculine charm. "And believe me, sweetheart, I'm just getting started."

When Theo shot back that she hadn't left a glorious beach on Thebes to come all the way to California just to be hit on by some beer-drinking civil servant, Molly decided it was definitely time to call it a night.

She was not surprised when neither Alex nor Theodora noticed her departure.

High atop the Westin Bonaventure hotel, Lena swayed in her husband's arms, trying to get up her nerve for the conversation to come. She'd made the decision to put the past behind her, to begin the New

Year with a clean slate, and that meant it was time—past time—to tell Reece about that long-ago Christmas Eve night.

His arms were wrapped loosely around her waist, his lips were nuzzling the sensitive flesh behind her ear. "You are," he murmured, "the most beautiful woman in the room."

"Flatterer." She tilted her head back to allow his mouth access to her neck.

Reece readily obliged. "It's the truth."

"What about her?" Lena asked as a vision in black swirled by.

Reece paid no attention to the stunning redhead. "She can't hold a candle to you."

Even as she knew that wasn't the truth, Lena laughed softly with delight. "You're prejudiced."

"You bet." He drew her closer. "I'm mad about you, Lena Longworth. And if it wasn't for the unfortunate fact that the Chief of Staff of Mercy Sam just happens to be dancing five feet away, I'd drag you beneath the dessert table and ravish you."

The idea was deliciously wicked. And inviting. Tempted to put off the carefully planned conversation until tomorrow, Lena reluctantly reminded herself that she'd already waited far too long.

"Being ravished by the sexiest man in the room sounds wonderful," she admitted breathlessly as he dragged her against him, inviting her to feel his erection. Her body warmed and softened in automatic feminine response. "But there are a few things I need to tell you."

Although he'd been fantasizing about unzipping the froth of gilt-threaded ivory chiffon, then running his lips down her delicate spine, kissing each vertebrae in turn, something in his wife's tone garnered Reece's unwilling attention.

"Are you all right?" He knew she'd had an appointment with her gynecologist. "You told me that your exam went well."

"I'm fine." That was the truth, so far as it went. Yet another thing they'd have to discuss tonight, Lena thought. "Really," she insisted when she viewed something that looked amazingly like fear in his eyes. "But we really do need to talk. I was hoping we could go downstairs to our room."

Reece had been hoping the same thing. The irony was that when he'd booked the suite, he'd had a much more romantic scenario than talking in mind. "Whatever you want, darling."

It was what he always said. But as they walked hand in hand across the dance floor, Lena wondered if Reece would still want her. Once he'd heard her story.

Tessa watched the attractive couple leave the ballroom. Although it was more than obvious that they were madly in love, something told her that the reason for their early departure was not a midnight tryst, but something far more serious. She'd watched their discussion, witnessed the concern, followed by resolve move across the man's handsome features.

"I'm beginning to feel ignored," Jason murmured in her ear. "You've been watching that guy all night."

"I'm sorry." She smiled up at him. "Actually, I've been watching his date. She looks so familiar." Of course that couldn't be, Tessa had been telling herself. After all, she'd only been in Los Angeles a week. "Do you know either of them?"

"I've never seen them before in my life." He watched the sway of the woman's hips in the full short skirt and knew he'd remember those long, wrap-around legs.

"Perhaps she's an actress." She was certainly attractive enough, Tessa thought. Her dark auburn hair glowed like autumn leaves highlighted by a benevolent sun and her green eyes tilted upward, catlike, at the corners. Perhaps the woman had been a bit player in some movie or television program she'd seen.

"She's good-looking enough to get work," Jason agreed. He drew his head back and gave her a long assessing look. "But you are, without a doubt, the most ravishingly beautiful woman here tonight."

The way he was looking down at her, as if she was a raw piece of clay he'd molded to his own personal preference, made her feel a bit uneasy. However, Tessa couldn't deny that the analogy definitely fit. Not only had he chosen her dress, he'd selected her jewelry—borrowed from Fred Hayman—her hairstyle and even her makeup, which had been applied by a woman who was alleged to have done Susan Sarandon's makeup in the movie *The Witches of Eastwick*.

The dramatic makeover had not been in vain. From the looks she'd been getting all night, it was obvious his creation had met with instant approval.

"Hey, kid," a voice behind her said, "how about giving me an opportunity to show Tessa which brother inherited the dancing talent?"

Jason grinned down at Tessa. "Whatever you do,

don't flatter him. His head's already big enough.''
Without asking if she wanted to change partners, he
handed her over to his brother, leaving Tessa feeling
once again like a piece of property.

It was a night made for romance. The glass wall in
the hotel room provided a dazzling view of the city
lights. A late-afternoon rain had washed away the
smog, and the stars shone like diamonds in the midnight black sky.

"Would you like some champagne?" Reece had
ordered a bottle of Dom Pérignon and caviar to be
waiting when they arrived back at the suite. A splen-
did bouquet of long-stemmed red roses had been delivered, as well.

The story Lena was determined to tell Reese wasn't
exactly a cause for celebration and she debated turning down the offer of champagne. Then decided that
a little bottled courage might be in order, after all.

"Thank you. That sounds wonderful."

Although the words fit the occasion, her expression
reminded Reece of a condemned prisoner on the way
to the electric chair. The fear he'd felt earlier rose
again. Again he tamped it back down and concentrated on opening the wine. The cork came out of the
dark green bottle with a discreet pop and a hiss of
vapor.

"You do that very well," Lena murmured. She
looked at Reece, so handsome in his custom-tailored
tux, marveled not for the first time at the easy so-
phistication of this man she'd married, and wondered
why he hadn't chosen a sleek, elegant woman from
his own world for his wife.

"It's all in the wrist." He had no idea if that was the case. But he felt the need to say something to ease the strain building between them. He poured the sparkling wine into the flutes, then handed one to her.

"To the best wife any man could ever wish for," he said, lifting his glass in a toast.

"To the best husband," she corrected quietly.

Reece wished to hell she'd smiled when she'd said that. "How about a compromise? To us. And a New Year filled with love and laughter."

Reece swore inwardly when he watched the suspicious sheen of moisture suddenly appear in her eyes.

"To us." It was little more than a whisper. Lena took a sip. Although the sparkling wine danced like laughter on her tongue, her mood remained bleak. When the suffocating silence settled over them again, she began nervously rubbing a crimson rose petal between her thumb and index finger, releasing the blossom's sweet fragrance.

Never having been one for game playing, Reece decided that as much as he wanted to let Lena take her time with whatever it was she wanted to say, he'd go nuts if they didn't just cut to the chase.

"Is this about your visit to Dr. Carstairs?"

"No." She abandoned plucking petals from the roses and began running her finger nervously up the crystal stem of the champagne flute. "Yes." She shook her head. "No."

Reece forced a smile he was a very long way from feeling. Happy goddamn New Year. He wondered what magic it would take to make his wife happy.

"Which is it, sweetheart?" Not wanting to make

things worse than they already appeared to be, he managed, just barely, to keep his building frustration from his voice.

Her bare shoulders slumped. "Dr. Carstairs only confirmed what all the other doctors have already told me. That there's no way I can ever conceive a child."

She'd already shared the unhappy news with Molly, who'd assured her that her infertility, possibly due to a sexually transmitted pelvic infection acquired before her marriage, had not been punishment from God for her promiscuous behavior. But still, having been brought up under the stern guidance of the St. Joseph nuns, Lena couldn't help wondering.

"I always wanted children," she murmured, looking out over the city, wondering how many people were sitting home alone, wishing they had someone— anyone—to love them. New Year's, she knew from personal experience, could be one of the loneliest nights of the year. That thought reminded her of all the strangers she'd gone to bed with, just to avoid being alone. "I always dreamed of becoming the mother I never had."

"I know how important having a child is to you, sweetheart," Reece said carefully, feeling as if he were making his way across a deadly conversational minefield. "But I've never felt any great need to perpetuate the Longworth name. And we could adopt."

"I suppose that's one possibility."

She sighed and sat down in the suede chair across the room. Although he longed to take her in his arms, Reece took the fact that she'd chosen not to sit next to him on the sofa as a sign she needed her own space to tell him what was bothering her.

"You never asked how my mother and father died."

"I figured you'd tell me. When you were ready."

She smiled at that. A soft sad smile that tore at something elemental inside Reece. "You are so incredible. I've never known anyone with such patience."

For some reason, her words rankled. "Dammit, Lena, don't make me into any kind of saint. Because I'm not. I'm just a man. Who loves you with a depth I never would have imagined possible. I've tried to come up with a word for how I feel. *Obsession* comes close. But it's still not enough."

She felt the traitorous tears overbrimming her eyes. "I'm never going to make it through this if you keep making me cry."

Reece managed, just barely, to remain where he was, watching with admiration as she drew in a deep, calming breath. She'd changed since Molly's attack, the emotionally frail young bride he'd married had begun to show signs of becoming an independent woman.

Lena turned her gaze away from him and looked back out the window at the lights of the city below them. "I can't remember a time when my parents weren't fighting." Her voice was soft, little more than a whisper, but Reece had no difficulty hearing it in the hushed room. "About everything. And anything. My father was a big man. With a big hairy belly that always stuck out from beneath his sweat-stained undershirt. And big hands that loved to hit little girls. But of course, I was very little, so perhaps he wasn't so big at all. Perhaps he just seemed that way...

"Did I ever tell you I had a kitten?"

"No," Reece said carefully, feeling like he'd just entered one of those dark carnival fun houses that weren't really any fun at all but filled with monsters who'd gleefully leap out and scare the piss out of little kids.

"Her name was Miss Puss in Boots." She turned toward him, her eyes as flat as her voice. "Because she had white paws. Like little boots. I found her in the alley and brought her home. Molly helped me hide her in our bedroom closet and every night I'd let her out of her box and she'd sneak beneath the blanket and curl up next to me and purr. I used to listen to that sound, like a small warm little engine, and it helped me block out the sound of the fighting."

She fell silent. Reece waited.

"One night he came in to drag us out of bed for some perceived misbehavior. I can't remember what, and it probably wasn't anything at all. Drinking always made him paranoid and he'd imagine all sorts of things we might have done. Or even thought.

"Anyway, he found Miss Puss. He pulled her out of the bed, and Molly tried to stop him. He knocked her away and she hit her head on the corner of the metal bed frame. If I live to be a hundred, I'll never forget that sound.

"She still has the scar on her temple. It's faint, but if you know it's there, you can see it. There was so much blood, I thought she was going to die. But of course she didn't....

"Then he strangled Miss Puss with his big hairy hands. And threatened to do the same to us if we ever brought another animal into his house."

As an ER doctor, Reece thought he'd seen all the evils humans could do to one another. But never had such horror hit so close to home.

"My God, Lena—"

"No." She held up a hand. "Please, just let me get this all out. Because it's taken me years to get up the nerve to say it out loud, and if I stop, I may never be able to do it again."

Reece tamped down his building fury and nodded.

"I think he raped our mother that night. I didn't understand the sounds coming through the wall from their bedroom at the time. But now I believe that's what happened. Then he left the house to go out drinking.

"Molly and I tried to see if Mama was all right— we could hear her crying—but she wouldn't open her bedroom door. She told us to go to bed and everything would be all right in the morning.... She always said that. But of course it never was."

Lena shook her head and dragged her hand through her hair. In the moonlight streaming in through the window, the diamonds in her wedding band glistened like ice.

"Molly put a Band-Aid on her head to stop the bleeding, which it really didn't do, but it finally slowed down. At least it wasn't streaming down her face anymore.

"Once Mama seemed to be all right, Molly wrapped Miss Puss in a clean nightgown. Then, when we knew he wasn't coming back that night, when it was safe, she got a flashlight and we went out in the backyard and Molly dug a hole and we buried Miss Puss.

"Our house was by Dodger Stadium and Molly had just finished saying a prayer, when the game ended and suddenly the sky lit up with the most wonderful fireworks."

She closed her eyes. "I can still see them today. They were so beautiful. The most beautiful thing I'd ever seen. And Molly told me they were in celebration of Miss Puss's arrival in heaven, where all the angels would love her and she'd have all the cream and kibble she'd ever want."

Reece had always known what a special person Molly was, but for the first time he was getting a sense of the burden she'd had put on her young shoulders, and he finally began to understand her seemingly limitless capacity for caring.

As if in a trance, Lena continued to relate the story of the lives and times of Lena and Molly McBride. Reece had been sickened by the saga of Miss Puss, but he was horrified by his wife's tale of the murder/suicide of her parents.

When she was finally finished, when she'd unburdened her heart and her soul, including the self-destructive sexual behavior that may have left her unable to have children, she turned to him, her eyes wide and dark in her too-pale face.

"So now you know the truth. And I'll understand if you decide you can't love me any longer."

A complicated rage burned through Reece. He wanted to beat her dead father to a pulp for having inflicted such terrible pain on his family. His feelings for Lena's mother wavered somewhere between fury and pity.

But since there was nothing he could do to correct

past sins, at this moment Reece's overriding urge was to shake his wife. To shout at her. To ask her what the hell kind of man she thought he was that he could ever hold her responsible for any of those horrors she'd described. But understanding that his anger was directed toward the injustice of what had been done to her, he managed, just barely, to hold his tongue.

"I told you—" He had to force the words past the massive lump of anguished fury that had taken up residence in his throat. "I love you, Lena." Needing to touch her, to hold her, he crossed the room and drew her into his arms. "More than life itself."

"But…"

"Shh." He pressed a finger against her trembling lips. She was like a block of ice in his arms. "You've had your say. Now it's my turn, okay?"

She nodded, her shimmering wet eyes on his.

"If I could go back in time and erase all those things that happened, I would. Unfortunately, life doesn't work that way, so I can't change the past. But the one thing I can do is to vow to spend the rest of my life helping you to feel happy. And safe."

Relief flooded through Lena, like a cool crystal river.

"You've already done that," she said on a deep, shuddering breath. "I realize I don't say it enough, but I've been happier since meeting you than I ever thought possible. And I've never felt so safe." Wrapping her arms around his waist, Lena hung on for dear life.

Reece kissed her then. A deep, heartfelt kiss filled with love and promise. And then he carried her into the bedroom, where he made love to her with a tenderness that made her cry all over again.

But this time, Lena's tears were not born of sorrow, but joy.

Chapter Seven

"**Y**ou're very good," Miles said with apparent surprise as he led Tessa through a sophisticated tango.

She tilted her head back and gave him a coolly dismissive look that fit the style of the dance to perfection. "For a 'chipmunk-cheeked farmer's daughter'?"

He had the grace to laugh at that. "Thanks to my brother's expert eye, no one would ever know you weren't born with a fistful of gilt-edged stock certificates in your lily-white hands."

He slipped his fingers beneath her hair, brushing at the suddenly ultrasensitive skin at the back of her neck in a way that created little tremors. "I think you should pose for me."

"Really?" Her pulse quickened. The photographs lining the trophy wall in his Bel Air home looked like a promo for "Lifestyles of the Rich and Famous."

"You're a gorgeous woman, Tessa. With the right photographs you could end up owning this town."

"Right now I'd settle for a part in a feminine hygiene product commercial," she muttered.

Although Jason had told her that it would be almost impossible to make an appointment with an agent during the holidays, she was admittedly impatient. And there was also the salient fact that her traveler's checks were disappearing a great deal faster than expected.

His hand warmed her back as he bent her into a low dip. Tessa could feel each of his long fingers against the pale flesh bared by the halter-style dress. "Oh, I think we can do a great deal better than that."

There was something in his eyes—something that promised more than a photography sitting—that caused a frisson of fear to skim up her spine. But before she could dwell on it, the music stopped.

"You can let me up now," she suggested.

"I suppose you're right." His smile was slow and unnervingly intimate as he kept her bent backward over his arm. If he suddenly let go of her, she'd fall to the floor.

"Miles—" Her heart was hammering in her throat. From fear. And something else. An emotion darker and more dangerous than she'd ever felt before. And strangely, more enticing.

They'd become frozen in some sort of strange tableau, Miles's hooded eyes looking down at her, while she stared back up at him, when a familiar deep voice shattered the spell.

"Dammit, Miles," Jason complained, "quit playing your cat-and-mouse games with Tessa. She's not one of your usual women. She's a nice girl."

"So you keep telling me." His eyes not moving

from hers, Miles lifted her back to an upright position. But as he did so, his fingers dipped even lower beneath the black silk, creating a flare of sparks. "Such a pity," he murmured as he trailed the back of his other hand down the side of her face. Tessa could feel the heat, the bane of a true redhead, rising in her cheeks.

"Don't pay any attention to my brother." Jason knocked Miles's hand from her face in a fraternal, nonaggressive way that suggested this was not the first time he'd had to come to the rescue of one of his dates. "Anyone in town can tell you that Miles is the evil twin."

"It's a dirty job." Miles's insolent eyes settled on her lips in a way that made Tessa's mouth go dry. "But someone's got to do it…. So, when are we going to do it?"

"Do it?" she echoed blankly.

"Your photos. As it happens, I have some time next Wednesday afternoon about five."

Tessa couldn't help glancing over at Jason, who laughed in response. "You've gotten her spooked, Miles." He put his arm around her waist and drew her against his side in a possessive gesture that made Tessa feel immediately safe. "I'll go with you and stand guard to make certain my evil twin doesn't get any kinky ideas, then afterward we'll go out on the town."

"That sounds wonderful." There was one more thing to be considered. She didn't want to be obligated in any way to Miles. "It's not that I don't appreciate your fitting me into your busy schedule, but I'm not certain I can afford—"

"Why don't you let me worry about that," Jason broke in smoothly.

"But you've already done so much."

"And had a dandy time, too." His smile, in contrast to his brother's, was warm and absolutely harmless. "Why hoard money when you can use it to make people feel good?"

He was such a good man. Such a generous one. Tessa was instantly reassured. "I don't know how I can ever repay you."

He winked in a sexy, seductive way she suspected very few women could resist. "I'm sure we'll come up with something. If we put our heads together."

He then turned to Miles. "Five o'clock it is. And don't forget, my partner, Dan Kovaleski, just got transferred to the vice squad. You try to use my girl for any of those dirty pictures you like to take, and I'll turn you in."

"The kid always was the family snitch," Miles told Tessa in a light, easygoing way that almost made her think she'd imagined his earlier dark edge. "I suppose that's why he became a cop."

As the twin brothers shared a laugh, Tessa's mind was not on a joke she suspected they'd shared before, but on what Jason had called her.

My girl.

As the words warmed her, thrilled her, Tessa decided that they were the sweetest she'd ever heard.

While Lena slept in Reece's arms and Tessa rang in the New Year on the dance floor, Molly was tangling the sheets of the queen-size bed in the Longworth guest room.

Caught up in the grips of a nightmare, she tossed and turned, tortured by images that shifted in and out of focus like a fun-house mirror, tossing back reflections that altered reality.

She was struggling up the side of a steep, rocky cliff. Although it was raining, she was clad in a flowing white nightgown so sheer, the streaming white moonlight rendered it nearly transparent. Icy raindrops stung her bare flesh like needles; her hands and knees became scraped and bloody as she crawled over the sharp stones of the path.

Behind her, she could hear the heavy footfalls belonging to the man who'd forced her into this dangerous flight. A man more than capable of chasing her to hell and back.

In the distance, the sun had begun to set into a vast expanse of ocean. Although the wind was blowing at gale force, she managed to stand up. She found herself teetering on the rocky edge of the precipice.

There was, finally, absolutely nowhere to go.

A gust of wind swirled upward from the cove below, threatening to blow her off the face of the earth. As she held out her arms in an attempt to balance herself, the man caught up with her.

He was dressed all in black; dark shadows obscured his face. As if conjured out of the air, a jeweled chalice appeared in his hand. He held it out to her, the gold skull ring on his left hand flashing in the slanting silver moonlight.

As if he'd stolen her will, Molly took the chalice between her palms and took a tentative sip. The bloodred wine tasted like vinegar in her mouth. She closed her eyes, swallowed and felt her stomach roil.

When she opened her eyes again, she found herself looking into the face of pure evil.

"Holy Mary, Mother of God, pray for us." Her words were whipped away by the cold swirling winds. "Now, and at the hour of our death..."

It's too late to seek intercession. Although he hadn't spoken the words out loud, they tolled in her head like a funeral knell. *Too late.* Knowing she was lost, she had no choice but to cling to her captor as he flew off the cliff, taking her with him to his dark kingdom beneath the sea.

As desperately as she struggled to wake up, Molly remained locked in the grips of the nightmare. The creature dragged her through a dark dank labyrinth, stopped before a granite slab and forced her to gaze down at the ghostly waxen face of a young woman lying dead on the cold damp stone.

"No!" Molly screamed as she recognized her sister.

Magic. That was all Tessa could think of as Jason drew her into his arms and finally kissed her the way she'd been yearning to be kissed.

"Happy New Year," he murmured against her mouth.

"Happy New Year," she whispered back. Twining her fingers together behind his neck, she smiled up at him as the band broke into a juiced-up rendition of "Auld Lang Syne."

He grinned back down at her. "How about we blow this place and go downstairs to our room?"

"You got us a room?"

"I've always believed in planning ahead." He put

his hand on her bare back and began leading her through the crowd. As they rode down in one of the glass elevators, they could hear horns and the voices of merrymakers welcoming the New Year. But Tessa could barely hear them over the wild pounding of her heart.

The room was as spectacular as the rest of the hotel, but she scarcely noticed. Every atom in her body was focused solely on Jason.

"You have the most expressive eyes." He drew her into his arms and brushed his lips against hers. His kiss teased, tantalized, tormented. When he finally drew the moan he'd been seeking, he pulled back, leaving her shaking in her high heels.

"Turn around."

Tessa did as instructed.

He lifted up her hair and brushed his lips against the nape of her neck. "Did you know you have a little mole? Right here?"

Her heart hammered against her ribs when he touched the tip of his tongue to that small brown spot. "When I have enough money, I'm going to get it removed, but—"

"Don't. It's unique. And it draws a man's eyes— and his mouth—to your neck." He began slowly lowering the zipper on the dress. "I think, as luscious as your hair is, we'll have to cut it short."

The air conditioner was blowing on the exposed flesh of her back, making her shiver. "Don't I have a say in the matter?" she challenged, striving for some balance in this fledgling relationship.

"No," he said simply. With a flick of the wrist, he sent the dress skimming over her body to land at her feet like a black silk pool. "You can turn around again."

Unable to deny this man anything, she complied. He stood there, for a very long time, studying her as if she were some exotic piece of art he was considering buying.

Her long-line black lace strapless bra dipped to the dimples at the base of her spine in back. With the bra, she was wearing a pair of thong bikini underpants and black nylons that ended at the top of her thighs.

"Your skin is like porcelain," he murmured, tracing a finger along the top of the nylons, seeming entranced by the contrast between the ebony lace and her pale thighs. "But you're cold." He made a slow, lazy figure eight up the flesh on the inside of her right thigh, and repeated the gesture on her left leg. "Do I frighten you?"

His treacherous touch enervated even as it excited. "No." Tessa didn't tell him that it was his brother she found threatening. "It's the air-conditioning."

"I could turn it off." He lifted his hand to his mouth, touched his tongue to his fingers, then skimmed the wet tips along the high-cut leg on her panties. "Or, perhaps we could find some other way to warm you up."

A hot heavy moisture had gathered between her legs, soaking the jet silk crotch of the skimpy panties. "Oh, yes."

Jason smiled at her breathless answer. Framing her flushed face between his palms, he kissed her again, a slow deep, drugging kiss that stole the breath from her lungs.

Using his body, he nudged Tessa toward the bed

until the backs of her knees were pressed against the mattress. From there it took only the slightest nudge to send her tumbling.

"Absolutely exquisite," he murmured with approval, standing there, looking down at her.

The satin spread was cool against her back, but his heated gaze warmed her breasts, her stomach, her thighs. She realized how wanton she must look, sprawled on her back, the white mounds of her breasts provocatively displayed in the long black push-up bra, her legs spread, her mound barely covered by the minuscule triangle of silk. But instead of feeling embarrassed, Tessa felt a surge of feminine power that such a handsome, rich man—a man who could have any woman he wanted—wanted her.

There was also something extremely erotic about being nearly naked while he remained dressed.

As her nerves heightened with anticipation, waiting for his next move, a foreign sound captured her attention. She turned her head, saw the police helicopter passing by, and the erotic mood threatened to shatter.

"We forgot to close the curtains."

"I didn't forget. It's more exciting this way. Knowing that anywhere in the city, someone with a telescope, or binoculars, or even a helicopter can watch us."

Tessa had never considered herself an exhibitionist. But his words, crooned in that deep, almost hypnotic tone proved thrillingly seductive.

"Perhaps a television news helicopter will fly by," he suggested as he reached down and ripped the scanty underpants away. "By this time tomorrow, bootleg videotapes of me ravishing you will be circulating all over town....

"I told Miles you were a natural redhead," he murmured as he viewed the fiery curls that were glistening with diamond-bright drops of moisture.

"You talked about me that way? With your brother?"

"Of course." He knelt down beside the bed, put his palms against her inner thighs and pushed her legs farther apart. "You're so pink. And wet. Like a ripe piece of fruit." He seemed to delight in the way she shuddered at his intimate touch. "Good enough to eat."

His hands cupping her bare bottom, he lifted her up to his mouth. It was wonderful. Better than wonderful, Tessa thought as her eyelids, too heavy to stay open any longer, fluttered closed and her hands grabbed fistfuls of satin bedspread. It was sublime.

As his wickedly clever tongue delved deep into her hot core, and his teeth scraped at her clitoris, Tessa willingly, blissfully surrendered to Jason. Body, mind and soul.

Chapter Eight

Tessa frowned into the mirror surrounded by light bulbs. Her lips were decidedly too full, her nose slanted just a bit to one side, and her skin, in this land of tanned bodies, looked as pale and translucent as skim milk.

"Or a ghost," she muttered.

"Come on, sweetheart," Miles called in to her, his sarcasm making a mockery of the endearment, "I don't have all night."

Exhaling a frustrated sigh that ruffled the artfully tousled bangs created by the hairdresser, Tessa exited the dressing room. Miles had already set up the lights. She narrowed her eyes against the glare, but was unable to see Jason standing in the shadows behind his brother. As a primal Latin salsa beat poured out of speakers set around the room, Miles came over to stand in front of her. His long, critical look stretched her nerves almost to the breaking point.

"Not bad," he said finally.

Tessa let out a breath she'd been unaware of holding. "I'm so pleased you approve."

"It's not my approval you need to worry about." That said, he began barking orders, having her move to the music, positioning her body in uncomfortable, unnatural ways.

Thirty minutes later, he was obviously as frustrated as Tessa.

"Christ, loosen up, will you? You're as stiff as a sixteen-year-old virgin."

"Perhaps if you'd stop yelling at me and insulting me, I wouldn't be so nervous," she shot back.

"Tessa's got a point, Miles," Jason said, coming to her defense for the first time since they'd arrived at the studio. "If you went a little easier on her, she might be able to relax. And maybe some wine might help. How would you like some champagne, sweetheart?"

"We don't have time for a party," Miles ground out, his impatience shimmering around him like a force field.

"You've already wasted half an hour. What could ten minutes matter?" Jason coaxed.

"Ten minutes," Miles snapped. "Then, if we don't get some halfway decent shots, your girlfriend can just get her portfolio done at the portrait studio at Sears."

Although she welcomed the champagne, Tessa balked at the pill Jason held out to her. "I don't do drugs."

"This isn't really a drug."

When she arched a disbelieving brow, he shrugged. "All right. But it's not anything I bought off the street, sweetheart.'' He refrained from mentioning that he'd obtained it from the police evidence room. ''One little pill isn't going to get you hooked. It's just going to relax you enough that you can enjoy this experience.''

''It'd take a truckload of Valium to do that,'' she muttered.

''Take the fucking pill, Tessa,'' Miles snapped. ''I have a dinner engagement and I'd like to see the lady sometime before the sun rises tomorrow morning.''

Tessa was still hesitant. But then she looked at the photographs lining the wall and realized that this was a once-in-a-lifetime opportunity. She couldn't allow herself to miss out just because, having a girlfriend who'd fried her brain on Ecstasy, she'd always been afraid to do drugs.

It was just one little pill, Tessa told herself as she took the scored tablet from Jason's outstretched palm. She swallowed it with the last of the champagne, and didn't protest when Jason refilled her glass.

Fifteen minutes later, as Miles positioned her on a black leather sofa in front of the camera, Tessa felt herself beginning to relax.

''Is that better?'' Jason asked from the shadows as Miles cupped her chin and tilted her face.

''Much better.'' Feeling wonderfully loose, she smiled up at the man who'd been tormenting her. ''Are you happy now?''

''Not yet.'' He turned her shoulders away from the camera. ''But we're getting there.''

''Good.'' Her bones were turning to water. ''When we're finished, I want more champagne.''

"Lord, she's already turning into a prima donna."

Feeling more relaxed than she'd ever felt in her life, Tessa smiled up at him.

"Amazing," Miles murmured. "One pill and you're floating." He moved back behind the camera lens. "Lick your lips."

Tessa licked her lips and tasted Vaseline.

"Good girl. Now, think of something sexy."

Tessa thought of Jason. Her body warmed, humming in all those hidden erogenous zones she hadn't even known she possessed until he'd discovered them.

"Now *that's* what I was looking for," Miles said approvingly. "Whatever you're thinking, sweetheart, don't stop." Tessa heard the shutter click several times, imagined Jason watching from the shadows, pretended the lens was him, lowered her eyes and looked up at him through her thick fringe of lashes.

"Oh, baby," Miles crooned seductively, "you're looking so fine. And hot."

He continued to encourage her, his voice deep and husky, like a lover. Aided by the pill and the champagne, Tessa found her inhibitions disappearing like a sand castle at high tide. She flirted with the camera, determined to break through Miles's sardonic reserve.

As his voice grew progressively deeper and rougher, she knew she was getting to him. Tessa couldn't remember ever feeling sexier. Or more powerful. Knowing that she could arouse a man who'd photographed the sexiest women of this Hollywood era went straight to her head. And that hot, dampening place between her legs.

"Okay," Miles said, his abrupt tone shattering her

forbidden fantasy of making love to both twin brothers at the same time, "that should do it."

Brought back to earth with a painful thud, Tessa blinked. "What?"

"I've got enough." He began turning off the photographic lights. "They're going to be dynamite."

"If you do say so yourself."

He laughed at her sarcasm. "You shouldn't try hauteur, sweetheart. It doesn't suit you." He moved closer, brushed the crest of one breast with his fingertips and made her tremble. "Looks as if you're going to get lucky tonight," he said over his shoulder to Jason. "You owe me for warming your girlfriend up for you."

"The day I need your help to bed a woman is the day I throw myself off the Santa Monica pier with my wrists and ankles handcuffed," Jason shot back. He moved out of the shadows and put his arm around Tessa's shoulders. "Get your clothes on, sweetheart," he said. "I've got some plans for this evening I think you're going to really get a kick out of."

Molly was not surprised when three weeks after her attack, there were still no leads on her rapist. The area was home to countless transients; he'd undoubtedly moved on. As Thomas seemed to have done. She was disappointed not to be able to thank the former priest for saving her life.

The part of her that had locked that horrific night away in some dark box in her mind was grateful her attacker hadn't been captured. Molly couldn't bear the thought of ever having to encounter the monster again. On the other hand, she was terribly concerned for the other helpless women he would undoubtedly attack.

She was relieved to be back to work. Although she hated the sideways glances and whispers that ceased whenever she passed by, at least when things got hectic in the ER, she was too busy to think about her own problems. Which were looming larger with each passing day.

She was standing at the desk charting medications, when an orderly approached. "The lab sent up these results, Molly." The young man handed her a manila folder. "I'm supposed to give them to you personally."

"Thank you, Peter." Molly put the folder under the metal charts.

"Is that the diabetic mother's test results?" Yolanda asked. "Because Reece was waiting—"

"No, it's not Mrs. Gannon's." She felt uncomfortable keeping secrets from her friend. But then again, Molly reminded herself, she'd always been an expert at keeping secrets.

"It can't be the junkie in treatment room B, because there's no way the lab could get the blood work up this fast," Yolanda said.

Molly didn't answer.

"So, you gonna tell me?"

Molly turned toward her. "Of course. But not just now." She finished her charting, then picked up the file. "I'll be in the nurses' lounge if anyone needs me." That said, she took the folder and walked away.

Yolanda watched her go, wrinkles marring her broad brown forehead. "Aw, hell," she muttered as a possible answer occurred to her.

Molly briefly closed her eyes—*Dear Lord, have mercy on me*—then opened the file. The words swam on the page, but she'd just managed to bring them into focus when the loudspeaker overhead clicked on.

"Trauma," the disembodied voice announced. "ETA four minutes."

Her own concerns forgotten, Molly dropped the folder and rushed back to the emergency room that had immediately sprung to life.

"A police car was broadsided by an unknown vehicle and went over a cliff in Laurel Canyon," the clerk who'd been monitoring the emergency band radio announced. "It took emergency crews two hours to reach the car. Another forty-five minutes to cut the driver out of the wreckage. He's arriving here by copter. Emergent, with multiple trauma to his lower extremities."

"Page Dr. Wagner, stat," Reece instructed. "Then get the rest of the team up here. We'll probably need a microsurgeon, so call Dr. Goldberg. He should be home. And notify the lab, X ray and Ortho—tell them to stand by."

He turned toward Molly. "You up to this?"

"I wouldn't be here if I wasn't."

He gave her a deep, probing look, then made his decision. "Let's go, then."

A familiar rush of adrenaline shot through her as they ran up the stairs together. When they opened the door leading out onto the roof, they were hit with a blast of chilly night air.

"Look at that," he said, pointing up into the night sky at the blinking lights of the helicopter heading toward them. On that copter was a man who, through an inexplicable twist of fate, was about to have his life placed in their hands. "Call me insane, but I freaking love this job!"

Although the noise from the rotors prevented her from answering, Molly silently agreed as she watched the helicopter touch down.

Before the pilot had cut the engines, the door burst open. Molly took one end of the gurney, Reece the other. Then they ran toward the helicopter, ducking their heads to avoid the still-rotating blades.

The patient had been wrapped in blankets and strapped onto the stretcher with nylon restraints. "We've got a fifty-two-year-old male suffering multiple trauma to his lower extremities," the medic shouted to be heard over the noise of the rotors.

He and the flight nurse helped Molly and Reece lift the patient down onto the gurney and they began running back toward the door.

"Driver's license lists him as Captain Alexander Kovaleski, LAPD."

"Kovaleski?" It couldn't be! Without missing a step Molly took a look at the patient. Heaven help her, it was!

"The patient has been unconscious and unresponsive since we cut him out of the car," the paramedic continued as they rushed the gurney into the rooftop elevator. "Bilateral femur fractures to both legs, along with copious bleeding from the femoral arteries. No known medical history.

"We applied tourniquet, Mast trousers and started Ringers lactate for replacement of lost blood," he continued. "BP is catastrophic—fifty over ten."

"No burns?" Reece asked.

"No. The guy lucked out. The gas tank didn't blow."

Not many people would consider anyone with such grave injuries lucky. But Molly had witnessed her share of gas-tank-explosion victims and knew, that as bad as things sounded, they could have been a great deal worse.

Even so, if they didn't get Alex's pressure up quickly, not only would he be at risk of kidney failure, his heart and brain would be in critical danger.

The team was waiting at trauma room A, known as the Doom Room. The X-ray and lab technicians formed an outer ring, just outside the door, allowing them to be out of the way, but instantly available.

Nurses and residents formed the inner core, with Dr. Wagner on one side of the steel table, Reece on the other and Dr. Paul Fong, the anesthesiologist, at the head. Overhead video cameras and microphones began recording the action for any interns and junior residents who'd gathered in the adjoining staff lounge. The cameras also allowed the team to view their actions afterward, much like a football team watching game films on Monday morning.

Despite the need to hurry, Reece looked at her over the gurney. "Are you going to have trouble with this?"

"No." When her usually self-assured voice proved little more than a whisper, Molly took a deep breath and tried again. "No. I'm fine."

Reece nodded, satisfied.

While Yolanda began cutting away Alex's shirt, Molly set the automatic blood-pressure machine to take readings every thirty seconds.

"BP sixty-five over twenty," she announced as Reece placed the EKG leads. On some distant level she noted that the hairs covering Alex's broad chest were gray. It was difficult to think of the man who'd always been there for her getting old; impossible to think of him dying.

Thy will be done. The familiar words of absolute faith tolled in her head, but Molly couldn't—wouldn't—accept them. Not when they were talking about someone she loved so dearly.

"Looks like the IV raised it some," Reece said. "Let's get the blood started."

Molly waited with a bag of highly concentrated O-negative cells while Reece deftly inserted the large bore intravenous line.

Alex's eyes fluttered when Reece drew an arterial blood sample, but he failed to rouse. "Unresponsive to painful stimuli," Molly reported to a floater RN who'd been assigned to the ER from the medical floor. The young man logged the information on a flow chart.

"There's no internal bleeding," Dr. Wagner, the senior ER resident decided after a cursory examination.

"We don't know that for sure," Reece argued.

Molly glanced up just in time to see Wagner glare across the supine body. "Are you challenging my diagnosis, Doctor?"

"Of course not," Reece responded mildly. "But it wouldn't hurt to do an abdominal tap. After all, it'd be a real bitch if the guy codes on the surgery table for something we've missed down here. Especially since he's a cop. You know how the TV guys love showing the pomp and circumstance of cop funerals on the six o'clock news.''

There was a slight hesitation as the senior surgical resident considered how such an event could sidetrack his career. The room became unnaturally silent, the only sound the steady *beep beep beep* of the heart monitor. When Wagner shrugged, Molly knew Reece had won this professional skirmish.

She handed Wagner a scalpel, which he used to make an incision just below the navel. Without looking at her, he held out his hand. Molly immediately placed the small catheter into it.

Then Reece took over. He let a liter of fluid flow slowly into the abdomen. While everyone watched, he gently rocked it, then siphoned the fluid out again. It came out as clear as it had gone in, a sign there was no internal bleeding. Wagner's smirk suggested he'd never expected any other outcome.

"Satisfied, Doctor?" he snapped at Reece.

"Actually, I am," Reece responded mildly.

The monitor sounded a shrill alarm. Molly looked up at the screen and saw the lines—like worms wiggling every which way—revealing a heart that had lost its rhythmic memory. She forced the green plastic airway into Alex's mouth, applied the mask, tilted his head back and began forcing oxygen into his lungs.

At the same time Reece began chest compressions in sync with the forced respirations, while Yolanda applied electrolyte gel to prevent burning from the defibrillator paddles.

"We'll start at two-fifty," Wagner barked.

"Charging," Yolanda called out as she turned on

comfort the young woman. However, these were far from usual circumstances. It was her first day back on the job, she'd stayed hours past the end of her shift and was physically, mentally, not to mention emotionally, exhausted.

The man she'd come to love like a father was upstairs struggling to hold on to life. And then, of course, there was her other little problem.

She dipped her fingers into the holy water at the font by the door and made a sign of the cross, then slipped into the back pew, knelt with her hands clasped together, and gazed up at the stained-glass window depicting a colorful portrait of Christ healing the leper.

The window reminded her of the one that had dominated the chapel at the Good Shepherd Home for Girls, which had depicted Jesus carrying a sheep on his shoulders.

Feeling a great deal like that allegorical lost lamb, Molly began to pray. For Alex. And for all the other people of the world who would be needing strength in the days ahead.

Including herself.

Her eyes were closed, but that didn't stop her from sensing the person who'd joined her.

"You should be at home in bed," Reece scolded quietly. "If I'd known you were going to overdo like this, I would never have let you come back to work so soon."

"I'm all right."

"Are you?" He paused, as if choosing his words. "It wasn't just my idea to come find you."

Her eyes flew open. "Alex, is he—"

the machine. The seconds it took to charge to two hundred and fifty watts seemed an eternity.

Wagner placed one paddle under and to the left of Alex's left nipple and the other to the right of the sternum. "Clear!" He squeezed the trigger for the asynchronous shock.

The body lifted off the table. Nothing.

"Three-hundred."

This time the line snaked violently, then settled to a weak, but steady rhythm. Everyone breathed a collective sigh of relief.

"The injuries to lower extremities must explain the blood loss and shock," Wagner said. The heart problem settled, at least for now, he withdrew the catheter and sutured the wound closed. "Let's get these MAST trousers off the guy and see what we've got."

The antishock trousers were designed to help stabilize patients with massive blood loss in the abdomen, pelvis or lower extremities. Once inflated, they maintained blood pressure by keeping blood in the more vital central parts of the body. The debate over whether the trousers were helpful or dangerous continued to rage in medical circles. However, since this emergency rescue crew had protocol orders to use them, the ER team had to be prepared to deal with any possible negative consequences.

Alex's left foot looked gray and felt cold to Molly's touch. That could either be a result of the trousers keeping blood from it, or a sign that the sharp edges of the broken femur had torn the large artery. If that were the case, deflating them could result in hemorrhaging.

"Both IV lines are in place and working, Doctor,"

she said after checking them one more time. The scary part about deflating MAST trousers was at the beginning.

Reece took a deep breath. In no way did he reveal his personal dislike of the trousers. "Okay, boys and girls. Here goes nothing." He undid the valve on the left leg, released the pressure slightly, then closed the valve again.

Molly grasped the left foot. "The pulse seems stronger."

At that moment, Alex's blood pressure, which had risen to a weak, but life-supporting eighty, dived to seventy-two.

"Shit," Wagner muttered.

Reece remained silent, his eyes, like everyone else's in the room, on the blood-pressure monitor.

"Reading stabilized," he said as the numbers crept back up to eighty.

He opened the valve again. There was another pause as they all watched the blood pressure dip, then slowly rise.

Reece repeated the technique a third time. The team relaxed a bit. He finished deflating the trousers, then unfastened them.

Molly had to bite her lip to restrain an involuntary gasp. Both legs were hanging by shreds of skin and small strands of tendons. The left leg was clearly too crushed to be saved. And the right was horribly mangled.

Dr. Fong whistled softly. Then began administering anesthesia in preparation for the lengthy surgery that would take place upstairs, where a microsurgery and

reimplantation team, orthopedic surgeons   to
constructive plastic surgeon had already gat   fa
                                                    o
And then Alex was whisked away.   s

Seven hours later, he had been moved to   e
on the recovery wing of the surgical floor.

Molly sat beside the bed for a time, watch
vital signs. "You may as well go home and ge
sleep," the recovery nurse said. "We'll call you
he's awake and functioning."

Molly knew Reece had made the decision to
until he could break the news to Lena in person.
since Dan was transporting an extradited drug dea
back from Tennessee, he still hadn't been notifie
There was no way she was going to leave until she'd
talked to Alex and could assure them both that he
was going to be all right. But there was something
else...

"I'll be in the chapel," she said.

The nurse shrugged. Molly bent down and brushed
a kiss against Alex's ashen cheek. "I'll be back," she
promised.

She took the elevator down to the first-floor chap
located around the corner from the gift shop. At
hour of the morning it was nearly deserted. Sunsl
was streaming through the stained-glass window,
ating dancing red, yellow and purple jewels or
white walls.

An elderly man was lighting a white votive
at the front of the chapel; in a pew midway do
aisle, a young woman knelt, her fingers workin
way through a set of dark brown rosary bea
tracks in her makeup suggesting she'd been
Under usual circumstances, Molly would h

"He's fine," Reece said quickly. "At least there's been no change."

Cool relief flooded through her.

"But Yolanda told me you might need to talk to a friend."

Molly sighed. She'd suspected she hadn't put anything over on the eagle-eyed nurse. "She's right." She turned toward him, viewed the calm, unwavering reassurance in his eyes and understood, not for the first time, why Lena had married this wonderful rock of a man.

She took a deep breath, wanting to phrase her remarks carefully. Then Molly, who'd never been known for beating around the bush, decided it would be best just to say the words straight out.

"I'm pregnant."

Chapter Nine

"Pregnant?" Reece stared at Molly as if she'd suddenly begun speaking some arcane language. "What the hell do you mean, you're pregnant?"

Molly understood Reece's inability to immediately grasp her dilemma. She had, after all, had more time to get used to the idea. From the time she'd missed her period ten days ago, she'd suspected this possibility.

At first, she'd reacted as she had in childhood, when her prayers had more often than not consisted of deals with her Maker: If he'd only let her get an A on her spelling test, she'd never talk back to Sister Celestine again; if he'd find a home where she and Lena could live with a real family, she'd dedicate herself to being a shining example of his goodness on earth. If only...

There had been hundreds, thousands of them. And whenever things had worked out as she'd hoped, Molly had believed God had come through for her. When they hadn't, she'd struggled to believe the nuns when they'd assured her that God always answered prayers. But sometimes the answer wasn't the one you were seeking.

She'd had Saint Augustine's assurance to the faithful quoted to her so many times, she still knew it by heart: "Do not be troubled if you do not immediately receive from God what you ask of him, for he desires to do something even greater for you, while you cling to him in prayer."

And so, although this time she'd been tempted to ask God not to give her such a trial, Molly was trying to focus on becoming emotionally strong enough to survive this ordeal.

"I'm going to have a child," she said quietly.

"You can't be pregnant. You're a nun."

"I'm a woman first," she reminded him gently.

Molly could practically see the wheels turning in Reece's head as he processed this unexpected bit of information.

"Are you sure about this? I mean, you've had a huge shock to your system. It wouldn't be unexpected for you to miss a period or two."

"The test came back positive."

"Test results have been wrong before."

"True. Which is why I made an appointment for an exam tomorrow. But I don't have any doubt, Reece. Because, although I know it sounds medically impossible, I can feel the new life growing inside me."

"What are you going to do?"

"I don't have any choice in the matter."

"Of course you do," he insisted. "This isn't the

Dark Ages, Molly. My God, you've been raped. No one would expect you to carry the fetus to term.''

"I'm afraid this is one case where I'm going to have to disagree with you, Reece.'' Molly covered her still-flat stomach with her hands in an unconscious gesture of maternal protection. The plain gold ring she'd received on her Profession Day gleamed symbolically in the sunlight streaming through the stained-glass window. "I could never—ever—forgive myself if I aborted this child."

"But you're a nun,'' he repeated.

"Unfortunately not the first one to get pregnant from a rape,'' Molly said, thinking of the various sisters around the world who'd found themselves in similar conditions due to war or urban violence. "There are ways of handling this. I'll carry the baby to term, then it will be given up for adoption to a good home."

She made it sound so cut-and-dried. But knowing Molly well, having witnessed countless examples of her warm and caring heart, Reece wondered if such a solution would prove as uncomplicated as she was making it sound. However, he decided this was no time to argue the point. "Well, one thing's for certain,'' he said, "you're not going back to your apartment. You're going to move in with us."

"But—''

"I'm not giving in on this one, Molly.'' His tone was as firm as she'd ever heard it. "Your neighborhood is too dangerous.''

It was a familiar argument. "The Vatican doesn't write support checks anymore.''

"I understand that. But you have Lena and I who

want you to stay with us. Lena couldn't bear it if anything else happened to you. Hell, neither could I."

"All right," she agreed reluctantly, too exhausted to argue. "But just for a little while. Until I can find another, more secure place to live."

"Why don't we jump off that bridge when we come to it?" Reece suggested, smiling for the first time since he'd sat down beside her. Then he hugged her.

Molly had always known that Reece was a physically strong man. But now, as she felt his arms wrap around her in a gesture of protection that seemed as natural as breathing, she realized that he was emotionally strong, as well. His shoulder, upon which she rested her head, was wide, capable of carrying the strongest of burdens.

She could have stayed there forever, in that hushed place, in Reece's comforting embrace. For the first time since entering the chapel, indeed, since she'd first read those fatal words on the lab report, Molly felt warmed. Inside and out.

Was this how Lena felt when Reece took her in his arms? she wondered, as her mind drifted on soft waves of serenity. Did they share many such moments of pure and perfect harmony?

Molly almost found herself envying what her sister shared with this very special man. Then, realizing that she was coming horribly close to breaking the ninth commandment, she firmly closed her mind to the dangerous idea and moved away from Reece. But as she did so, Molly experienced a strange, undefinable sense of loss.

* * *

Sister Benvenuto had always been the most pragmatic person Molly had ever known. In this case, she did not disappoint.

"It's obvious you can't continue to work at Mercy Sam," she declared upon hearing Molly's news.

"You can't make me stop work for eight months," Molly argued, once again conveniently forgetting her vow of obedience. "I'd go crazy."

The elderly nun gave her a scolding look from beneath beetled white brows. "Did I say anything about making you stop work?"

"No, but—"

"You've always had a regrettable flaw of jumping to conclusions, Molly McBride. I'd hoped that you'd outgrow such behavior, but I fear that the good Lord has His work cut out for Him when it comes to your impulsiveness.

"Of course you'll continue to work—the order needs you. However, everyone here knows of your vocation. How would it look, having a pregnant nun on staff?"

"I don't recall that you were ever overly concerned about appearances."

"True enough. But the Church has received enough negative publicity lately. And short of a sign around your neck, explaining the circumstances of your condition, I fear that you'd just contribute to unpleasant gossip.

"No, the best thing to do is to transfer you to another hospital. Or, perhaps one of our grossly understaffed inner-city clinics."

"And conveniently forget to mention I'm a Sister

of Mercy?'' Molly challenged dryly. The idea of such subterfuge made her decidedly uncomfortable.

Molly's mentor chose not to answer the question directly. ''After Vatican II, I recall several members of various orders being concerned that without their habits, they would no longer feel like sisters in Christ. But in all the years since abandoning our traditional garb, I've never found a single sister who felt less of a calling now that she's wearing street clothes instead of those heavy, restrictive habits.''

''So clothes don't make the nun,'' Molly said. ''What exactly, does that have to do with keeping my vocation a secret for months?''

''If our vocations truly come from our hearts and souls, there's no need to wear them on our sleeves, so to speak.''

Although she hated to challenge authority yet again, Molly was convinced that this ordeal facing her would be much easier to bear if she were surrounded by friends.

''I really would prefer to stay on at Mercy Sam,'' she said quietly but firmly.

Sister Benvenuto gave her a long look. Then sighed her surrender. ''I suppose we could give it a try.''

''Thank you.''

The nun's lips quirked. ''You're welcome.'' She reached out and touched Molly's still-flat stomach. ''As much of a problem as this might seem at the moment, the creation of a new life is always a miracle. Of course it's never our prerogative to question God's plan for our lives. But I can't help but believe that this child, admittedly conceived under such horrendous circumstances, is a very special gift meant to bring joy to a great many lives.''

Since Molly had begun experiencing morning sickness, joy was not precisely the term she would have chosen. However, she hoped that Sister Benvenuto was right. To believe that something good could come out of something so evil would make the coming months a great deal easier to bear.

Tessa had just turned off the shower when she heard the phone ringing. Since her money was almost gone, she couldn't afford an answering service. Nor could she afford to miss a call.

She raced into the adjoining bedroom and scooped up the phone. "Hello?"

"I like that breathless tone," a familiar voice drawled. "It reminds me a bit of Marilyn in her heyday.''

Depressed it wasn't one of the agents she'd been hoping to hear from and unnerved as she always was whenever she had occasion to speak with Miles, Tessa sank down onto the lumpy mattress.

"Were you calling for some reason, Miles? Because I was in the shower and I'm dripping all over the bed.''

"You naked and wet on a bed. This is getting better and better. I don't suppose you'd be willing to re-create the scenario in my studio?"

"Not in this lifetime," she shot back, embarrassed as she thought about the Polaroid shots she'd allowed Jason to take after her photo shoot.

"Too bad," Miles said. "But I suppose having naughty photos in circulation might hinder your chances of winning a part in Darren Sands' new series."

"Darren Sands?" What was Miles talking about? She had no chance of landing a part in a Sands' production under any circumstances.

Darren Sands was a Hollywood legend, known for his ability to conceive high-ratings television. That his critics regarded his programs as little more than tits and ass seemed to bother him not in the least. He laughed all the way to the bank. Then proceeded to build a mansion high in Beverly Hills that was remarkably ostentatious even by Tinseltown standards.

"We had dinner last night," Miles said. "He happened to see your proofs and decided you'd be perfect for a part in his new series, 'Country Roads.'"

"Darren Sands wants me to be in one of his series?" The idea was too incredible to be taken seriously.

"Actually, it's a pivotal role. You'd play a naive young country singer seduced, then corrupted by her evil, manipulating manager."

"So help me, Miles, if you're lying, just to get a rise out of me—"

"Actually, literally speaking, you're the one who gets a rise out of me," he shot back wickedly. "However, I'm absolutely on the level. I also promised Darren I'd call him back tomorrow with the name of your agent."

Tessa knew there had to be a catch. "I don't have an agent."

"Any girl Sands declares a star of the future won't have any trouble getting an agent. In fact, I took the

liberty of making an appointment for you with Terrance Quinn. It's for eleven."

This was too much! Terrance Quinn was not only
the premier agent in Hollywood, he'd recently been
listed by *Cosmo* magazine as one of the top ten bachelors in the country.

Tessa glanced over at the clock on the bedside table, saw it was already almost ten and suffered an
instant panic attack. "You'd better get cracking,"
Miles advised. "Terry hates for people to be late."

He rattled off the address, which she already knew,
having dropped off her portfolio at his office her first
week in town. Needless to say, she hadn't received
an answer.

"Oh, and although it's an intriguing way to make
a first impression, I'd advise getting dressed before
your meeting."

Before she could thank him, he hung up, leaving
her staring down at the receiver. Then she laughed
out loud.

Things were definitely looking up.

Three weeks after learning of her sister's pregnancy, Lena entered a church for the first time since
her marriage. Unlike Molly, who'd embraced her religion, Lena had always held the Church responsible
for having broken up what had remained of their family.

Tessa had been adopted, and the nuns had stead-
fastly refused to discuss the matter, except to assure
the girls that their baby sister had been placed with a
fine, upstanding, churchgoing Catholic family out of
state.

With their mother and baby sister gone—Lena had never shed any tears for her father and never expected to—she and Molly had clung to each other in the orphanage. But even this was not to last. After it was decided that Molly was unable to fit into foster homes, she had become a virtual prisoner in the Good Shepherd Home for Girls, and Lena had been left all alone at the mercy of various foster families, some kinder than others, but none capable of providing the love and emotional support she'd needed so badly.

But since learning of Molly's condition, guilt had been grinding away at Lena's heart until she knew that there was only one way to free herself of her burden. Having committed a grievous sin, she was desperate for absolution.

The church, designated a basilica during a visit by Pope John Paul II to Los Angeles, was in a predominantly Hispanic section of the city, far from her own wealthy neighborhood. The crucified Christ hanging above the linen-draped altar was not the usual unlikely Caucasian version, but a modern, stylized wrought-iron figure that seemed jarringly out of place with the fat-cheeked, gilt-winged cherubs on the arched ceiling.

The marble statue of Our Lady of Guadalupe atop a pedestal at the side of the altar appeared to be pregnant, reminding Lena of her reason for having come here today. A sanctuary lamp glowed dimly in front of the tabernacle that had been placed in an arched-wall niche.

Glancing around, she realized that she was the only person of her age in the church on this Saturday afternoon. All the others were either elderly women,

uniformly dressed in black, wearing lace mantillas
and clicking their way through their rosary beads, or
children obviously impatient to get the weekly chore
over with so they could run outside to play in the
California sunshine.

Lena chose a pew near the back of the church, knelt
down and folded her hands. Although she appeared
to be praying—contemplating her sins in order to
make a good and truthful confession was how it had
been put to her in her school days—she was resorting
to a juvenile trick taught to her by a younger, unrepentant Molly.

Although she kept her eyes downcast, she was able
to watch the lines of people on either side of the
church. Before long, she'd determined which priest
was more lenient. The dual lines to the right moved
swiftly; penitents entering the red velvet-draped confessional remained only a brief time, after which
they'd return to a pew, kneel down, make the sign of
the cross, speed through the required prayers and be
on their way again.

In contrast, the line on the left side of the church,
beneath the stained-glass window depicting the Sacred Heart, inched along at a snail's pace. Not only
was this line moving much more slowly than the line
on the other side, the exiting penitents did not look
the least bit overjoyed to be resolved of whatever sins
they'd committed, and spent a much longer time on
their knees.

No fool she, Lena immediately joined the right line,
but by the time the ancient woman in front of her
entered the confessional, her heart was in her throat
and she was wondering how a sweating hand could

be ice-cold. Nervous perspiration slid down her sides; she could smell its acrid aroma over the scent of incense, melting tallow and the cloying fragrance of the overblown pink and white roses on the altar.

The elderly woman, who must have lived a sin-free life, exited the confessional in less than three minutes. And although she'd been taught by a rigid third-grade teacher that looking back in church would turn you to salt, like Lot's wife, Lena dared to glance back over her shoulder and desperately considered escape.

But she'd come too far to run now.

Dread hanging over her like a shroud, she entered the small booth that at first seemed as dark as a coffin. Over the pounding of her heart in her ears, she could hear the priest murmuring something to the person in the confessional on the other side of him. And then there was the sound of the wooden slide between them opening and she was facing a dark shadow on the other side of the screen.

He said something her troubled mind could not process. But when the indiscernible words stopped she realized it was her turn. Old habits, not easily forgotten, came back.

"Bless me, Father, for I have sinned," Lena whispered in the hushed sanctity. "It has been—" she paused, trying to recall the last time she'd taken part in this ancient sacrament "—a very long time since my last confession," she finally said.

"And your heart is heavy," the calm male voice suggested.

"Oh, Father." She leaned her forehead against the screen and closed her eyes. Tears welled up behind her closed lids. "You have no idea."

Silence settled over them. Lena waited for him to speak, to pressure her to come clean, but he seemed willing to wait until doomsday, if that's what it took. So much for getting out of here swiftly.

"I've committed a grievous sin."

"And you've come here seeking absolution."

"Yes." Lena swallowed painfully. "But I'm not sure I deserve it."

"Our Lord died for all of us sinners, my child," the deep voice echoed in the private darkness. "There is nothing He will not forgive. And you must believe the fact that you've come here today has already gladdened many hearts in heaven."

His words, meant to reassure, brought to mind her mother, causing Lena's tears to flow. Once again, with a patience that reminded her of Reece, the priest waited her out.

And then, feeling a need to fill that lingering silence, Lena began to talk. The words poured out of her, like an out-of-control river bursting through an ancient dam. She told him everything, about the night her father had murdered her mother, then killed himself, about losing Tessa, and finally Molly.

She told him about her previous promiscuous lifestyle and how she'd married a man she'd respected but did not love.

"But I do now, more than anything in this world," she assured him.

She went on to describe her desire for children, and her inability to conceive. She related Molly's horrendous experience and told about the resultant pregnancy, then took a deep, shuddering breath. Finally she had come to her reason for being there today.

"And, although I know this has to be a horribly painful time for her, I can't help being jealous." There. It was finally out in the open, in all its dark ugliness.

"Because she's carrying the child you want so badly," the priest surmised accurately.

"Yes." Lena literally hung her head in shame.

"That's not unexpected," the priest surprised her by saying.

"It's not?"

"God may have created us in His image, but He made us human. Envy, even jealousy, is a very human emotion. It's how we act on that emotion that's important."

"I'd never wish Molly any harm," Lena insisted with a burst of heartfelt emotion. "She's my sister. I love her."

"Which is why these feelings are proving so painful for you," he suggested. "Surely you've felt envy when you've seen other expectant women in the supermarkets, or mothers playing with their children on the beach."

"All the time," Lena admitted.

"Yet you didn't feel the need for absolution then."

"I didn't think those feelings were all that sinful." As the contrast sunk in, she realized exactly how right she'd been to come here today. "You're a very wise man, Father."

He chuckled at that. "Believe me, my dear, I'm not so wise at all. But I receive a great deal of help in this job. Otherwise I doubt I would have lasted a week."

While she was still stunned at that admission—so

unlike the unyielding priests she remembered from childhood—he said, "Now, as for your penance...can you cook?"

"Cook?" Lena stared at the screen, wishing she could see his face. "Of course. Why do you ask?"

"Because not all women do in this modern age." He sighed. "Even we priests no longer have house-keepers to tend to such things. I, myself, can manage a meat loaf that's heavy as a stone, but filling, none-theless....

"But I'm getting off the point. For your penance, I want you to go home, hug your sister and assure her that she'll have all your support during this dif-ficult time.

"And then I want you to cook a romantic dinner for your husband. Candles are a nice touch, too, I believe. And assure him that you'll always love him, even if it's God's will that you spend your lives to-gether without children."

It was the absolute truth, Lena realized. "Are you saying my penance is to make a romantic dinner for Reece?"

"Exactly. Your feelings have undoubtedly hurt him, as well. It would behoove you to make amends."

Once again he was so, so right. "Thank you, Fa-ther," she said, grateful to be spared the Our Fathers and the Hail Marys of her childhood Saturday con-fessions.

"Well, then, let's make a good Act of Contrition, shall we?"

He had to help her through it, but by the end, the words, committed to memory so many years ago began coming back and as she received absolution, Lena felt the burdens lift from her shoulders.

Although the young girl who'd been standing behind her in line gave Lena a curious look as she exited the confessional—she had, after all, taken far more time than the others—Lena barely noticed. The formerly faint glow from the sanctuary lamp suddenly seemed to gleam brighter—like a gilded promise from on high.

As she walked out of the basilica into the bright sunshine that was streaming down on the City of Angels that warm winter day, her heart felt so featherlight, she was amazed it didn't float out of her body into the clear blue sky.

Everything would be all right, Lena assured herself. Her marriage, which had strengthened in the past months, would grow more solid now that she was focused on celebrating the love she had been given, rather than bemoaning the fact that she might never be a mother.

With warm feelings of joy flowing through her veins like liquid gold, Lena realized that, as horrible as Molly's situation was, there was even a positive side to that. Because now, for the first time in their lives, she had the opportunity and the inner strength to help her sister.

She'd be there for Molly these next four months, providing whatever emotional—and even financial assistance—she required. And in doing so, she'd finally repay her older sister for all those years of undying devotion.

Chapter Ten

Days, weeks, then months passed in a blur as Molly struggled to balance the demands of work with her advancing pregnancy. Fortunately, Lena and Reece provided support in ways she never would have guessed she'd need. Molly didn't know what she would have done without them. Indeed, after a time she even stopped looking for an affordable apartment and allowed herself the luxury of being pampered in their oceanfront home after a long day.

At the end of May, although summer was still nearly a month away, Los Angeles was hit with a blast of heat that caused suffering all over the city. Everyone—from the privileged glitterati of Beverly Hills to the hookers strolling Sunset Boulevard on their stiletto-heeled sandals—was sweating.

Unsurprisingly, business in the ER boomed as the staff dealt with numerous cases of heat exhaustion, a dozen cases of bona fide heatstroke and varying degrees of sunburn ranging from uncomfortable to serious.

Shortly before Molly's shift ended, she noticed Tina Alvarez, a floater sent down from the surgical floor to assist with the overload, arguing in Spanish with a young Chicana who couldn't be more than seventeen. The girl, known on the street as Rubia— for her dyed blond hair—was a prostitute who hadn't let her pregnancy get in the way of her work.

Although Molly had done her best to talk the girl into leaving the dangerous life on the streets, her arguments had fallen on deaf ears. And the police, who had enough serious crime to deal with without trying to settle the social problem of runaway children, hadn't been all that interested, either.

"What's the matter?" Molly asked.

"I'm handling it," the nurse snapped.

"I'm hurting real bad, Sister," the young prostitute complained to Molly in English. "I think I'm having my baby. I need something for the pain."

Tina scowled darkly. "The baby's not due for another three months. She's trying to con us out of drugs."

"That's not true!" Rubia's face was wet with perspiration. Just like Molly's own. Unfortunately, a city-wide brownout had caused Mercy Sam's ancient air-conditioning to all but shut down. "I really hurt, dammit. And this bitch—"

Tina broke in with a stream of furious Spanish as fast as a round of bullets from the automatic rifles that were all too common in the area. Although Molly was fairly fluent in the language, the nurse was speaking too rapidly for her to keep up.

"This isn't getting us anywhere," she interrupted calmly. She glanced down at her watch and sighed, realizing that it was too late to call Lena—who insisted on picking her up every afternoon—and let her know she'd be running late. "Let's take a look at what's going on."

She'd no sooner gotten Rubia onto the examination table than the girl began to bleed copiously.

"Oh, my God," the young prostitute wailed in a voice choked with pain and fear. "What's happening?"

"This is your lucky day," Tina answered before Molly could. "You're miscarrying."

"I'm losing my baby?"

Even Molly was surprised by Rubia's obvious distress. Considering her age and life-style, she would have suspected this pregnancy would be less than welcome. She came around from the end of the table and brushed some lank wet hair off the girl's clammy forehead. "I'm afraid it appears you might."

"But I want it." Fake fingernails painted the reddish black hue of old dried blood, dug painfully into Molly's arm. The needle tracks running up the thin arms told their own tragic story. "She's going to be the first thing in my life I've ever had that was all mine." Tears began to overflow doe brown eyes rimmed with kohl liner. Mascara streaks made dark tracks down her gaunt face. "And I'm going to love her so much."

Molly had heard this too many times to count. She also knew that Rubia was naively counting on her baby to automatically love her back. Unfortunately, if the fetus survived, and managed to escape being born drug addicted, the too-young mother would soon discover that adorable sweet-smelling babies also messed their diapers, demanded constant attention and cried when they didn't get it. Such maternal disillusionment was often the reason for the battered children she was forced to treat on an almost daily basis. Children like Benny who, according to the hospital grapevine, was flourishing in his new home with the Moores.

"We'll try our best," she said, prying the fingernails from her arm and patting the girl's thin shoulder. Even though Dr. Muchnick, the resident on duty was a very good doctor, Molly wished Reece was there.

"The doctor at the free clinic gave me one of those ultrasound exams. She's a little girl. I'm going to name her Eden."

"That's lovely." Since her own ultrasound had revealed that she, too, was carrying a daughter, Molly experienced a tug of maternal bonding.

No one in the ER was surprised when Dr. Muchnick couldn't save the premature baby girl. The horrible thing was that the negative Tina may have been right. Miscarriage might have been the best thing for the young drug-addicted prostitute. And for the child.

Feeling horribly depressed, Molly signed out, then went to find Lena.

"I'm sorry to have kept you waiting all this time," she greeted her sister, who was seated in the outer waiting room looking disgustingly clean and cool in a white linen dress. "By the time I realized we had a problem, it was too late to call."

"I didn't mind waiting. I've been sitting here reading all your pamphlets."

"You're probably the first person who's ever bothered." A defeated tone crept into Molly's voice.

"Bad day?"

"Let's just say it wasn't exactly a stellar one."

"Since Reece is at that medical conference in New York, I was going to suggest the two of us have a girls' night out on the town. Dinner, then a movie perhaps. But if you'd rather go straight home..."

"If you don't mind, I think that is what I'd rather do." Even discounting her exhaustion, Molly knew she'd feel guilty enjoying herself after another expectant mother—no matter how ill prepared—had just lost her own child.

"Terrific." Lena changed gears with alacrity. "We'll call out for pizza and have a slumber party. That sounds like a lot more fun, anyway."

Molly agreed. Especially since she couldn't remember them ever sharing any innocent childhood pleasure as prosaic as a slumber party.

As they walked out of the hospital, Molly wondered when, exactly, the tables had turned. She'd always been the strong sister. These days, Lena had definitely taken over the supportive role in their relationship.

"I don't know what I'd do without you," she said honestly.

"Oh, Molly." Lena stopped in the act of opening the car door, turned and hugged her. "Believe me, anything I've done is nothing compared to what you've done for me over the years."

Before Molly could answer, they both felt it. A faint fluttering inside Molly's expanding stomach.

"Oh, my God," Lena breathed, leaning back to look up at her older sister. "Is that...?"

"The baby." Molly's exhaustion vaporized as she

felt another faint, fluttery movement like butterfly wings. "Here." She took Lena's hand and splayed it across the front of her blouse. "Feel."

This time they both felt a definite kick. "It's a miracle," Lena said, her eyes misting.

Molly's own eyes were suspiciously wet. "Yes," she said with a sense of wonder that expunged the last of her painful feelings about how the child she'd been carrying for the past five months had been conceived. "It is."

Later that night the two sisters were stretched out on Reece and Lena's wide bed watching a videotape of *Peggy Sue Got Married*. The comedy about a woman's second chance at love was just what Molly needed to take her mind off the exhausting and depressing day at work.

"I have a confession to make," Lena said suddenly, after the movie was over. She pressed the remote, darkening the screen. "I've been trying to get up the nerve to tell you for months."

Molly looked at her sister in surprise. "If I'm in your way here—"

"Oh, no. That's not it. Reece and I love having you stay with us. It makes us seem even more like a real family," Lena said. "It's just that when I first discovered you were pregnant, despite the terrible way it happened, I couldn't help being horribly jealous of you." She was so eager to get the words out, they tumbled over one another.

"Jealous?" The moment she heard herself repeat the word, comprehension dawned on Molly. "Oh, honey, I've been so wrapped up in my own worries, I didn't take time to think about yours. I never real-

ized how my having a child, and your not being able
to…"

Her voice drifted off as a thought flashed through
her mind, so clear and bright Molly was amazed she'd
never thought of it before.

"Lena." Her fingers tightened on her sister's. "I'm
going to suggest something, but I don't want you to
answer yet. Not until you've had lots of time to think
it over. And discuss it with Reece… You know I've
been planning to give the baby up for adoption."

"Of course. It's the only thing you could do."
Lena's heart took off on a series of somersaults as
she began to follow Molly's train of thought. "Are
you saying…?"

"I'm saying that I think, if you're both willing, that
you and Reece should adopt this baby."

"Are you certain that's what you want?"

"Only if you both do. I've understood from the
beginning that there was no way I could keep this
child, but that hasn't stopped me from worrying about
what kind of family she might end up with. And all
the time, the perfect parents were right in front of
me."

Having witnessed Lena and Reece's strengthened
marriage, having seen firsthand all the little signs of
how much the couple loved each other, Molly knew
they'd provide not only a comfortable, but a loving,
caring home. Something neither Lena nor Molly had
ever known.

"Oh, Molly, I don't have to think about it." Lena's
beatific smile could have lit up the entire Los Angeles
county. "And I don't have to ask Reece. Because I
know he'll love the idea as much as I do. And I prom-

ise that no one would ever love your daughter more than we will."

"I know that."

Laughing and crying all at the same time, the two sisters who'd been through so much together, hugged. As if casting her own vote of approval, the baby chose that moment to turn another somersault.

"Are you certain this is what you want to do?" Reece asked Molly over lunch in Mercy Sam's cafeteria.

They'd spent the first ten minutes of the lunch hour discussing the paper on ER triage and Fast Track treatment he'd presented at the medical conference he'd attended. Understanding that he was deliberately avoiding a discussion of he and Lena adopting her baby, Molly forced herself to bide her time and let him bring the subject up. Which he eventually did. Abruptly and with a great deal less enthusiasm than Lena had predicted.

"Only if you think you'd like being a father," she said carefully. Nervously, she pressed the back of her spoon against a bloodred gelatin square on her plate that had to be three days old. "I certainly didn't intend to put any pressure on you, Reece."

"Hell, Molly, that's not the problem. I love the idea of being a father. Even more, I love the idea of Lena being a mother. We've both wanted a child. But Lena isn't the only McBride sister I have strong feelings for, and I'm worried this might prove too hard on you."

"I've thought about that," Molly admitted. After her impetuous offer, she'd spent a long and mostly sleepless night considering all the aspects of the decision. "And I've come to the conclusion that it would be easier watching my baby growing up with two loving parents than spending the rest of my life wondering what happened to her."

Reece remained silent for a time, fiddling with his cutlery, lining up the edges of the stainless-steel knife, fork and spoon as if he were preparing to do surgery. "You said 'my baby,'" he pointed out quietly.

She got his point immediately. Loud and clear. "It was just a phrase, Reece. I'm well aware that if you agree, she'll be yours and Lena's child."

He gave her a long look rife with both tenderness and concern. And, she felt, lingering questions. "I'm tempted to jump at the opportunity to have a daughter. But I'm still worried—"

"You needn't be." Molly reached out and covered his hand with hers. "I'll admit that I blurted the idea out to Lena when I should have given it more thought. But I *have* thought about it almost constantly since then and I'm extremely comfortable with this solution."

He gave her another long look, then turned his hand, linking their fingers together. "You're a helluva woman, Saint Molly."

Strangely affected by the warmth in his husky tone, Molly lowered her eyes to the table and didn't, as she'd always done in the past, protest the nickname he'd teased her with for so many years.

She truly had made the right decision, Molly told herself a week after signing the preadoption papers at the attorney's office. So why did she feel strangely let down?

"You've obviously bonded emotionally with your unborn child," Sister Benvenuto assured her. "It's only natural to suffer misgivings."

Molly's gaze drifted to a print of an oil painting depicting the Assumption. "It crossed my mind, in the middle of the night, that perhaps, I could keep the baby. After all, I do have a good career, and—"

"Impossible." Sister Benvenuto looked at her with the same stunned amazement she might reveal were Molly to suddenly announce that she'd taken up strip-tease dancing at one of the nudie clubs on Hollywood Boulevard. "Nuns cannot have children."

"But if I were to leave the order—"

"You don't want to do that, Molly."

For not the first time, Molly admired—and envied—the nun's unwavering belief that she knew what was right not only for herself, but for the younger members of the order, as well.

"Sometimes I do." Molly dragged her attention away from the romantic portrait of the Mother of God floating up to heaven on that gilt-edged, puffy white cloud and forced herself to meet her superior's hawk-like gaze with a level look. "There's a little boy who used to be a Frequent Flyer in the ER—"

"Benny."

"Yes." Molly belatedly recalled fretting about the young boy's plight in this very office on more than one occasion. "I used to fantasize about running away with him."

"Fantasies are normal. So long as they don't get out of hand," Sister Benvenuto tacked on. "Anyone who knew that unfortunate child might briefly imagine doing exactly the same thing.''

"I imagined being his mother.''

"Again, not unusual.''

"The same way I imagine being a mother to this baby.''

The nun's expression didn't change, but Molly detected the faint gray cast that moved like a warning shadow over the remarkably unlined olive complexion.

"It's merely hormones,'' the nun said finally. "I'm neither a nurse nor a mother, but I do know pregnant women are famous for their mood swings. Factor in the little matter of your working too hard, and it would only stand to reason that your mind might indulge itself in harmless daydreams.''

She folded her hands atop the desk, drawing Molly's attention to the slender gold ring that was a twin to Molly's own. "So long as you understand that these are fantasies, and not a viable alternative, I can't see that any harm's been done.''

"It doesn't feel like mood swings. It feels like something primal. Something deep in the bone.'' And, heaven help her, in her flesh, which seemed to have become too warm and painfully sensitive lately. Just yesterday Reece had accidently brushed against her in the cubicle in treatment room B, leaving her feeling as if he'd taken a torch to her ultrasensitive breast.

"You've always had difficulty surrendering yourself to the desire of God. You must pray for relief from your doubts. And for guidance. Believe me,

Molly, if you open your heart, Our Lord will not abandon you.''

Sister Benvenuto stood up, signaling that in her mind, at least, this interview was over. Not having the strength nor the inclination to argue any longer, Molly pushed herself out of the too-soft chair and left the book-lined office of the Mother House.

Although it was her day off, she returned to Mercy Sam for her daily visit with Alex, arriving during his physical therapy. Although he'd regrettably ended up losing both legs in the accident, the wonders of modern prostheses had him up on his feet again. Now all he had to do was work out the glitches.

She stood in the doorway, watching as he held on to the parallel bars on either side of his still-strong body, each step an obvious effort. His pain and frustration were evident—sweat had beaded on his brow and above his top lip and he was cursing beneath his breath—but Molly was not at all surprised when he refused to stop until he'd reached the end of the bars.

"That's wonderful," she said, clapping her approval.

He glanced back over his wide shoulder, his grimace instantly turning into a grin. "I'm not exactly ready to take on Michael Jordan in a game of one-on-one, but it's coming along."

"You've improved so much since the last time I watched," she assured him as she entered the room.

"Anything to get out of this damn chair." He glared at the electric wheelchair the therapist was helping him into.

Molly couldn't think of any man who'd be more frustrated being confined by such a chair. In her mind,

Alex Kovaleski had always epitomized the great American West's outdoorsman. When he wasn't working, he was hiking, camping, hunting, and shortly before his accident, he'd even terrified Molly, Lena and Theo by taking up rock climbing during a vacation in Yosemite.

She took a tissue from a nearby box and wiped his damp forehead. "You'll be walking again before you know it," she assured him.

"Don't forget dancing," a throaty voice from behind the pair offered.

Molly turned to see Theo standing in the door, dressed in a bright cotton dress emblazoned with giant red poppies. Molly didn't believe that the dress, cut nearly to the waist in back, and ending high on Theo's still-firm thighs, had been designed for a woman of her years. But she had to admit that it worked.

Her hair was blond again this month—"My summer shade," she'd announced when she'd shown up for Sunday dinner at Reece and Lena's last weekend—and bounced on her tanned shoulders as she walked into the therapy room with a familiarity that suggested she'd spent a great deal of time here.

Ignoring Molly, or, more to the point, Molly decided, unconcerned about any audience, she bent down, held Alex's face between her hands and gave him a long deep kiss that demonstrated their relationship had definitely flowered since New Year's Eve.

"Lucky guy," the male therapist standing beside Molly murmured as the kiss went on and on in a way that had her mutinous skin beginning to burn again.

Although she felt uncomfortable witnessing such open sensuality, Molly thought Alex and Theo were extremely fortunate to have found each other. Since they were two of her favorite people, she was thrilled by their romance.

"I'm sorry, Molly," Theo said when the couple finally came up for air. "I didn't mean to ignore you. It's just that whenever I get within kissing distance of this big teddy bear, my heart just runs away with my head."

Theo seemed more than comfortable with their situation, but to Molly's amusement, Alex blushed furiously. His face looked every bit as warm as Molly's felt.

"Dammit, woman, if you'd only learn to use a modicum of restraint—"

"You'd be miserable." Theo cut him off cheerfully. "We both know the reason you're working overtime to get back on your feet is so you can take me dancing." She glanced over at Molly. "He gets so jealous thinking about all my other male admirers."

"You haven't wanted any other men since the day I waltzed into your life," he growled.

Theo sighed dramatically and pressed her hand against her chest. "Heaven help me, I have no idea why I'm so fatally attracted to overly confident macho men."

"Man," Alex corrected firmly. But with a gentleness that Molly found endearing.

Theodora's expression softened. Her eyes, accented by a sweep of sea green shadow, warmed. "Man," she agreed.

They exchanged a long look that spoke volumes and had Molly suddenly feeling like the third wheel at a junior high school dance. "Well," she said, clearing her throat, "it's getting late and—"

"Oh, dear, now we've embarrassed you," Theo said.

"Actually, I think you're both sweet."

"Sweet?" Alex looked aghast at the suggestion.

"Sweet," Molly repeated with a grin. She turned to Theo. "By the way, I'm glad to see you. I've been meaning to tell you that was a dynamite article about you in last week's *TV Guide*."

"It was nice, wasn't it?" Theo agreed.

"They even gave her the cover," Alex pointed out. "And called her the Diva of Daytime Drama."

"Which may have been a bit of an exaggeration." Theo's false modesty almost made Molly laugh.

"Not if what they said about you increasing ratings is true. And the story line you've created sounded fascinating." Fascinating and convoluted. Molly had lost track of the cast of characters' layered relationships halfway through the flattering cover article.

"Don't tell a soul, but it gets even better," Theo confided. "Poor Allison's going to discover that the man she's fallen madly, passionately in love with is her brother."

"That *is* a complication."

"A rather touchy one, I thought. I still haven't figured out how she's going to respond. I was considering having her join a convent, but I discovered that's already been done by 'Days of Our Lives' back in the seventies and I hate the idea of being derivative."

"I'm also not certain a failed love affair is a valid

reason to embrace a religious life,'' Molly couldn't resist adding.

Alex laughed, a rich bold laugh that triggered countless warm memories of all the times he'd been there for Molly and Lena while they were growing up.

''You're in trouble if you're looking for reason in a soap opera, sweetheart. From what I've noticed, it's all storm and drama and incest—''

''And don't forget murder,'' Theo added with gusto. ''And the secret babies, and...'' Her voice drifted as she realized what she'd said. ''Aw, hell. I'm sorry, Molly, dear.''

''It's okay.'' Molly smiled. ''I'm well aware that if you wrote my life story, no one would believe it. Especially with this latest twist.''

''Oh?'' Theo gave her a sharp look. ''Have you been holding back on us, darling?''

Molly decided that since it had been her idea in the first place, and neither Lena nor Reece had asked her to keep it a secret, she may as well confide in the other two members of her small family group.

She paused for a heartbeat, decided she was behaving as dramatically as Theo, then said, ''Reece and Lena are going to adopt my baby.''

There was a moment of stunned silence. Theo was the first to break it. ''Why, isn't that wonderful!''

As hugs were exchanged, Molly failed to see the concerned look Theo and Alex exchanged over the top of her head.

Chapter Eleven

Unfortunately, Tessa's opportunity to become television's newest star fell through when she discovered that auditioning for the part involved a lot more than reading lines.

Her agent, the legendary Terrance Quinn, who had signed her after the meeting Miles had arranged, proved nonchalant about the incident.

"Sleeping with Sands is part of the deal," he said with a shrug. "Some girls find it worth their while."

"Not me. I'd rather dress up in a gorilla suit and deliver singing telegrams."

His lips quirked in an almost smile. "I doubt if it will come to that. You're getting commercials. And you still have a shot at that new sitcom."

She'd recently had a first reading for two guys who'd graduated from the UCLA film school, professed to be bored with L.A. faces and were searching for a new look. After numerous callbacks, Tessa—and more importantly Terrance—began to realize that she was at the top of a very short list for the role of the star's man-hungry sidekick.

"Meanwhile, you're not a vegetarian, are you?"

"No."

"Good." He made a notation on the back of a business card and handed it to her. "You've got a commercial for a new hamburger chain that shoots tomorrow night in Westwood. Think you can look as if you're experiencing an orgasm from a cheeseburger?"

"You bet."

The hamburger shoot was quick and fast, paid the rent and definitely beat screwing Darren Sands, who'd appeared about as old as dirt and just as inviting.

Even better was the commercial for a Porsche dealer who turned out to be impossibly rich, good-looking enough to be an actor himself and made her feel like the sexiest, most desirable woman on the planet during the shoot.

Wallowing in guilt instilled from her Catholic upbringing, the morning after her impulsive tryst Tessa was waiting for Jason when he arrived home from night-shift patrol.

"So you slept with the guy," he said with a shrug after she'd confessed.

He took his police pistol, laid it on the kitchen table, opened the refrigerator and pulled out a beer. He offered Tessa orange juice which she refused. But when he offered a pill he promised would cure her pounding hangover headache, she accepted.

"Jesus, Tessa, I don't own you. You don't owe me any apologies. Or explanations."

Tessa couldn't quite make up her mind about how

his nonchalant attitude made her feel. On the one hand, she was relieved that he wasn't angry. Or hurt. On the other hand, she was disappointed that he wasn't at least a little bit jealous.

"Was it good?" he surprised her by asking.

"Not as good as with you," she said truthfully. She took another sip of the orange juice.

Although he hadn't moved, she felt a shift in the air. Dressed in his dark blue uniform, with the metallic badge of authority pinned to his starched shirt, he seemed larger, more powerful.

With his eyes still on hers, he took a long pull on the dark brown beer bottle as he waited for the pill he'd given her to click in. The roofie was related to Valium, but ten times stronger. One of the side effects was blackouts with a complete loss of memory. After busting a street dealer for what was becoming known, in police circles, as the "date rape drug," he'd kept a bit of the merchandise for his own personal use.

"But not bad, either?" he coaxed.

He moved closer. So close, Tessa had to tilt her head back to look into his face. "I don't think we should be talking about this."

His hand cupped her cheek. "I do." She could feel the imprint of each of his long fingers against her skin. "Did you bathe before coming over here?"

"I took a shower." There was no way she was going to come here smelling of sin and sex.

"Too bad."

"Why?"

He shrugged. "No reason. Just an idle thought.... I want to hear all the details."

"Why?"

"Because it'll turn me on."

"I thought *I* turned you on."

"You do." His fingers trailed down her face, then curled around the base of her throat where her pulse had begun to hammer. "But a little variety is always nice."

"I don't understand." But she did. Too well.

His fingers tightened, ever so slightly. "Are you afraid of me?"

"No," she lied.

The pressure on her skin increased. "You should be, you know." He kept his tone conversational even as his vaguely threatening demeanor made Tessa wonder why she'd ever believed Miles to be the more dangerous of the twins.

"I think I am," she admitted on a whisper.

"Afraid of what I'll do to you?"

Tessa nodded, knots of fear, and, dammit, need, tangling in her stomach.

After putting the beer bottle down on the table, he tangled his hand in her hair and pulled her head back, forcing her to look up into his eyes. "Say it."

"I'm afraid of what you'll do to me."

"Afraid you'll like it."

"Yes."

"Believe me, baby, you will." He leaned forward, close enough for her to feel the heat emanating from his body. "Tell me everything the guy did to you." Although his voice was rough and raw, it possessed the confident tone of a man assured of getting his own way. "And I'll do exactly the same thing." The hand circling her throat moved down to cup her breast. "And then you can make a real comparison."

Tessa felt guilty about her impetuous night of passion with the Malibu car dealer. Now she felt embarrassed, as well. But his touch was beginning to make her head spin and she felt inexorably drawn into the sexual fantasy.

"First he made me strip for him. Then, when I was naked, he had me kneel down on all fours in the middle of the bed."

"That's a start." He backed away. "Do it for me, Tessa. Just like you did for him."

"I'd been drinking," she demurred.

Somehow, last night, drifting on a soft haze of alcohol, submitting to the sensual demands of a total stranger hadn't seemed so wrong. Now, in Jason's kitchen, with the buttery yellow morning light of a spring day streaming through the window, his suggestion seemed vulgar and offensive.

As if deciding to change tactics, he softened his stance. And his voice. "I can open some champagne," he suggested helpfully. "And get you another pill. Just to take the edge off."

Tessa knew instinctively that to say no to Jason would be to lose him. And she wasn't prepared to do that. Not when there were so many gorgeous, willing substitutes waiting in the wings. "Maybe a mimosa."

His smile, as he heard the capitulation in her tone, reminded her of the gold stars the nuns used to put on her spelling papers. "And a pill."

The last of her resistance ebbed. Tessa knew she was lost. She had to do whatever Jason wanted. Everything he wanted. Because she had no choice. "Perhaps, just a half."

In the end, she ended up drinking nearly half the

bottle of champagne. And taking at least two of the pills.

When she woke up hours later, Jason had gone back on duty, leaving a hastily scrawled note on the pillow assuring her that it was the hottest, best sex he'd ever had.

A maniac was banging away with a sledgehammer behind her eyes and although Tessa had no memory of what they'd done, the bruises he'd left on her body told their own story.

The pains came shortly after midnight. Lying in bed, her hands splayed across the hard expanse of her swollen abdomen, Molly assured herself that she was experiencing false labor.

Beneath her fingers, her muscles tightened. The hardening began above her pubis, spread toward her groin, and encompassed her entire uterus, then softened like the ebbing of the tide. Indeed, the feeling reminded Molly of the ocean waves she could hear outside the bedroom window of the cliffside home—gathering, breaking, subsiding.

By the time a soft, silvery pink predawn glow had settled over the room, Molly knew these were not false contractions. The baby she'd carried all these months was about to be born.

She waited for the wave—stronger than any so far—to crest, then pushed herself into a sitting position and picked up the telephone beside the bed.

Five minutes later, she was tapping on Reece and Lena's bedroom door. Seconds later it opened.

Although she'd certainly seen Reece wearing less out by the pool and on the beach, there was something uncomfortably intimate about viewing him standing in the open door to his bedroom, clad in a pair of royal blue silk boxer shorts. She dragged her gaze from his tanned chest to a point just beyond his left shoulder.

"I hate to bother you, but I think I'd better get to the hospital."

"How close together are the contractions?"

"About ten minutes apart."

"Ten minutes?" His voice held a very undoctor-like panic. "How long have you been in labor?"

"Since about midnight."

"Midnight? And you waited until now to let me know?"

"There wasn't any point in waking you up earlier." She decided, since he wasn't technically her physician, not to add that her water had just broken.

Lena was now out of bed, as well, looking beautifully ethereal with her sleep-tousled auburn hair floating around her shoulders. She was wearing an exquisite, lace-trimmed white cotton gown that made Molly feel vaguely like a pregnant street urchin in the oversize Kermit the Frog nightshirt Yolanda had given her as a gag gift.

"Oh, Molly!" She reached out and took both her older sister's hands in hers. "How wonderful." Her smile belonged on one of the angels that had been painted on the ceiling above the altar at the Good Shepherd Home. "It'll only take me a couple minutes to get into some clothes. Meanwhile, you should probably put on a robe. No point in getting dressed, since they'll undoubtedly make you put on one of those ugly old hospital gowns as soon as we arrive."

She turned to Reece. "You'd better call Dr. Carstairs."

Amusement at his wife's take-charge attitude seemed to make Reece relax. He grinned. "Yes, ma'am."

"I've already called Dr. Carstairs," Molly revealed. "She said she'll meet us at the hospital."

"Well, then." Even though her expression stayed calm, anticipation and excitement were more than a little evident in Lena's tone. "What are we waiting for?"

After they'd arrived at the hospital and Molly had been checked into a labor room, Lena, who'd been her coach during her birthing classes, remained by the bedside, holding her hand, reminding her to relax, massaging her back and stomach, timing her contractions, wiping her forehead with cool cloths and providing the same constant moral support and encouragement she had during the long months of Molly's pregnancy.

To the amusement of both of them, Reece proved to be a basket case. By the time Molly had reached transition, her obstetrician, Dr. Carstairs, fed up with his continually second-guessing her treatment, sent Reece downstairs to the cafeteria for coffee.

"I liked it a lot better when prospective fathers were kept outside," she muttered. "Where they could pace, smoke and worry to their heart's content without getting in the way."

Molly managed to laugh even through a contraction so hard and lasting so long, it literally took her breath away. The pain increased, sucking red tides that seemed endless.

When the doctor finally declared her eight centi-
meters dilated and gave her a paracervical injection,
Molly could have wept with relief. She was moved
to the delivery room, lifted onto the table, her legs
put in stirrups and draped.

Through the exhaustion clouding her mind, Molly
vaguely heard the doctor telling her to push.

"Okay, the baby's crowned. The hard part's over
now, so you can lie back for a minute, Molly," Janet
Carstairs said. "You're doing great."

"Better than great." Lena smiled a bright, watery
smile of encouragement as she pushed the damp,
stringy hair off Molly's forehead. "You're spectacular, Molly. Just like I knew you'd be."

Molly, who was panting, huffing and puffing like
a blowfish, couldn't answer.

And then she was pushing again and heard the doctor say, "Just one more now, Molly." A moment
later, Molly felt something wet and slippery slide ef-
fortlessly from her body.

"You've got yourself a little girl," Dr. Carstairs
announced.

"A beautiful little girl," Lena echoed.

"Do you want to hold her?" the doctor, who knew
all about the adoption arrangement, asked Molly.

While she hesitated, the baby began to cry. At first
the sound was faint and ragged and stuttering. But as
it grew stronger, Molly felt something unbidden stir
in her heart. The pull was deep and private, as old as
the earth and every bit as strong.

"Molly?" Lena was smiling down at her. Happy
tears were streaming down her cheeks. "Whatever

you want, honey. You did all the work, it's your call.''

The crying had escalated to a scream. ''Perhaps if she could just nurse, for a minute or two, it might comfort her,'' Molly said finally.

Reece, who'd missed out on the actual delivery, arrived just in time to see the still-wet infant placed on Molly's stomach, where it instinctively nuzzled its head against her breast, rooting for her nipple. With each tug of the tiny rosebud mouth, as the baby suckled the clear fluid from her breast, Molly felt a corresponding pull deep in her uterus.

Mine. The reckless thought reverberated dangerously in her head. *My daughter. My heart.*

''Isn't she beautiful, darling?'' Lena asked Reece as they stood beside the bed, hand in hand, watching the baby nurse.

''Gorgeous,'' Reece murmured, running his finger down the satin cheek. ''She's got hair.''

''Of course she does,'' Molly countered on a voice choked with unshed tears. She ran her own fingers over the wet black strands. ''You didn't think I'd give birth to a bald baby?''

''It'll fall out,'' the nurse advised. ''It usually does.''

''Is that true?'' Lena asked.

''Sometimes.'' Even as he answered his wife, Reece was looking down at Molly. ''You did good, kid.'' Although he was smiling, she could see the questions in his eyes. Questions she didn't dare answer. Not even to herself.

''I did, didn't I?'' Molly murmured with maternal

pride as she gazed down in wonder at this child she'd carried beneath her heart for so many months.

Although she suspected every mother was prejudiced, she knew this was truly the most beautiful baby she'd ever seen. And, like so many other new mothers, she couldn't resist counting fingers and toes. She was also vastly relieved that her final AIDS test had come up negative, meaning she couldn't have passed the fatal disease on to her child.

Later, as she'd watched her blue-eyed, black-haired daughter—now cleaned up and dressed—placed into Lena's arms, Molly suffered a jolt of loss so wrenching, she almost cried out. As she watched the blissful new parents ooh and aah over their darling daughter, her heart lay stonelike in her chest.

"Have you decided on a name?" the attending nurse asked.

Lena was smiling down at her daughter as if the entire world had just been handed to her on a silver platter. "Grace," she said as she lifted her gaze to Molly. "Grace Margaret Longworth."

Molly was moved by her sister using her name as the baby's middle name. As for Grace, she realized that Lena had chosen well. This innocent infant, the result of a heinous crime, was, indeed a very special gift from God.

Thy will be done, Molly prayed mentally. And struggled not to weep.

Six weeks later, Molly was back in Sister Benvenuto's office, waiting to hear her superior's response to her written, formal request for a transfer.

"I think you've made a wise decision," the nun

said. "It's not surprising you'd continue to have strong emotional ties to the child. As it is, it can't be easy, living in the same house with your sister and brother-in-law and daughter."

"Grace isn't my daughter," Molly corrected softly. "She's my niece."

"Or soon will be, legally," the older nun agreed. "But matters of the law are often at odds with matters of the heart."

"That's true." Molly was twisting a tissue into little pieces. Although she'd blamed her recent depression on a case of postpartum blues, she feared the reason for her melancholy went far deeper.

"The assignment you've requested is not an easy one," Sister Benvenuto told Molly, a fact she already knew. "Are you certain you're up to the work?"

"Dr. Carstairs says that I'm physically fit."

"And emotionally?"

Molly met the nun's questioning gaze with an unflinching one of her own. "I will be. As soon as I can get away from here."

Away from her daughter. The words were not spoken, but both women heard them over the roar of the cars on the nearby freeway. Sister Benvenuto played with her pen for a time and continued to study Molly intently. "I've never believed that running away from a problem is the answer."

"I'm not running away," Molly said, not quite truthfully. "I prefer to think of it as running *to* something. And you've often stated that our missions on the Native American reservations are in dire need of nurses."

"True. As is Mercy Samaritan."

Molly couldn't argue with that.

"I assume you've prayed about this matter," the elder nun said after another long pause.

"Of course." Constantly. "And I know this is the right answer."

"Well, then." Sister Benvenuto nodded. Then signed the papers in front of her. "Who am I to question God's plan?"

Having expected resistance from her sister, Molly was surprised when Lena instantly accepted the idea.

"We're going to miss you," she said, giving Molly a hug. "But I understand that there are others in the world who need you even more than we do." They both looked up instinctively toward the door as they heard Grace suddenly begin to cry in the nursery. The nursery Lena had decorated for a princess. "Fortunately, Arizona and New Mexico aren't that far away."

The baby's cries increased. "Not far at all," Molly agreed. It was a cry of hunger. Over the past weeks she'd learned to distinguish them.

"You'll be able to come home often," Lena said, obviously distracted.

"Yes." Molly was no less distracted.

Even with baby Grace's wails now reaching ear-splitting decibel level, both sisters studiously pretended to ignore them. "But you will stay for the baptism?" Lena asked.

"Absolutely," Molly said.

"Good." Lena nodded. That settled, she left the room.

As she remained behind, listening to her daughter's

plaintive cries dwindle away, Molly realized why her plan had met with no resistance from her sister.

It was obvious that Grace could only have one mother.

Just as it was obvious that Lena was that mother.

Once again, Molly assured herself that her decision was for the best. For everyone. So why did she want to cry?

Hormones, she told herself as she stubbornly blinked away the threatening tears. That's all it was. That's all she would allow it to be.

One week after her decision to leave Los Angeles, seven weeks after her daughter's birth, Molly was alone with Reece in the vestibule of our Lady of Perpetual Help Church.

"Are you certain you want to go through with this?" Reece asked gently.

"Of course." Molly flashed him a bright, feigned smile. "I'm thrilled that Lena asked me to be Grace's godmother."

"I tried to talk her out of it, but—"

"Why?"

"Because it puts you in an uncomfortable position."

Molly heard the question in his tone and chose to ignore it. "Grace is Lena's daughter," she said firmly, wondering who she was trying to convince, Reece, or herself. "And yours."

"Still, there's time to change your mind. I know Theo would love to fill in...."

"Theo's a fallen-away Southern Baptist," Molly reminded him. "And, although the Catholic Church has embraced the ecumenical movement since Vatican II, I doubt they're ready for Baptist godmothers.''

He sighed. "You're right, of course. It's just that...." He shook his head, jammed his hands deep in his pockets and looked away. "After you made your announcement to go and work with the Indians—"

"Native Americans."

"Whatever." He turned back to her. "When I first heard about your decision, I realized that Lena and I had been so wrapped up in our own happiness, we hadn't really given enough thought to the one individual who made it all possible."

"You've been wonderful to me. You've given me a place to stay, Lena bought me more maternity clothes than any self-respecting nun who's taken a vow of poverty should possess, you paid for the best obstetrician in town. I don't know what I would have done without you."

"All those things are peripheral. I was talking about our insensitivity to your feelings."

It was Molly's turn to look away. "I don't know what you're talking about."

"Don't you?" he challenged quietly.

There were three people Molly had never been able to lie to: Alex, Sister Benvenuto and Reece. However, unable to be perfectly open with him—since he was an integral part of her problem—she opted to hedge.

"It's a difficult situation for all of us."

"I warned you that it could be."

"Yes." She took a deep breath. "So, once again you were right. But I've given this a great deal of thought, Reece. And I've prayed over it. And everything will be fine. Once I've removed myself from the scene.''

"And your daughter?"

"*Your* daughter."

They exchanged a long look. "Yes," he said finally. Shoulders slumped, he did not exactly look like a happy father about to witness the baptism of his child. "We'd better go. Before they come looking for us."

"Yes." Because she hated seeing him look so disturbed, Molly reached out and put her hand on his arm. "It really will all work out, Reece."

He covered her hand with his own. "I sure as hell hope you're right, Molly. Because if you're not—"

"I am," she said quickly, refusing to believe otherwise.

Choosing Lena and Reece to be her baby's parents was the right thing to do. Just as leaving them alone to raise their daughter without worrying about her feelings or her possible interference was equally the right—and only—thing to do.

Molly continued to tell herself this as she held baby Grace, clad in a long flowing white lace christening gown that Theo proudly told them had been worn by three generations of Longworth babies, including Reece. Beside her, sitting erect and proud in the wheelchair he vowed to soon discard, Alex Kovaleski, the sleeping infant's godfather, accepted responsibility for the development and safeguarding of the grace given at the holy sacrament.

Afterward, while Grace continued to sleep blissfully, Molly exchanged polite conversation with Father O'Connor, the parish priest, managed to force down a piece of too-sweet white cake, and toast the occasion with strawberry punch.

Then she slipped away from the festivities, climbed into the medical van the order had equipped for her and drove away, headed for Arizona.

Molly hoped that in the wide-open spaces of the Navajo reservation, she'd be able to throw herself into a new medical mission that would renew her faith and strengthen her wavering commitment to the religious life.

And, although she knew the request to be self-centered, she also desperately prayed that somehow she'd manage to overcome the suffocating guilt that had been eating away at her ever since she'd abandoned her child.

Part Two

Chapter Twelve

The vast Navajo Indian reservation, stretching across parts of three states, was always in need of additional medical facilities. Those Native Americans willing to accept western medical care often had to drive miles for treatment. Which was why, when Father Francis Pius Casey inherited several acres of prime Arizona ranch land and donated the proceeds of the sale of the property to the Church—which were used to build a clinic/hospital in the remote area north of Canyon de Chelly—the event was much celebrated. In reward for his generosity, the bishop promptly upgraded Father Casey's status to Monsignor.

Molly always enjoyed her stops at the hospital. Dr. Joseph Salvatore, not long out of a ER residency, was working a three-year stint for the National Health Service and Bureau of Indian Affairs to pay off his extensive medical school bills. He was experienced enough to provide excellent care, yet the ink on his degree still wet enough that he hadn't grown disenchanted with his medical career.

He'd been with the Navajos for the past nine months, and although at first he'd been greeted with the suspicion always accorded outsiders—especially those connected with the government—his unfailing good humor and genuine concern for the people's well-being had eventually overcome most of the skeptic's doubts and now, Dr. Joe, as he was called by his patients, had been accepted by the community.

He was a good doctor and a nice man. In many ways, he reminded Molly of Reece. It had also not escaped her attention that his thick-lidded dark eyes, which gave him a sexy, perpetually sleepy look, thick black hair and lean muscular physique earned by running five miles a day had captured the interest of the young women in the area. And older ones looking for a husband for their daughters, as well.

"Welcome back to God's country," he greeted her when she arrived at the hospital one snowy autumn day after a recent visit to Los Angeles. "How was Lotusland?"

"Still there."

"Damn. I keep waiting for it to fall into the sea." A native New Yorker, he was no fan of Los Angeles.

"It's a lovely city," Molly defended her hometown. "And the people are friendly."

Lena and Reece had been particularly friendly, but had treated her more like a guest than a member of the family. Although the vacation had gone well, and heaven help her, Molly lived for these brief visits with

Grace, it seemed as if the adults had all been walking around on eggshells.

"Except when they start gunning each other on the freeways during rush hour," Joe countered. "Whoever named that place the City of Angels definitely had one screwed-up sense of humor."

"At least the weather was definitely better." She looked out at the swirling snow that had escalated to blizzard conditions, and found it difficult to believe that only two days ago she'd been basking in the warmth of the California sunshine.

"Constant sunshine would get boring."

Molly didn't hear him. She was still thinking back on her visit to the Longworth home. Although Grace, fortunately, hadn't picked up on the occasional tension between her mother and her aunt, Alex and Theo had. Separately, they had questioned Molly. To both of them, she'd insisted everything was fine.

Molly hadn't admitted that lately she'd begun to feel as if she were trapped inside a cage. A cage she couldn't escape because she'd built the unyielding iron bars herself.

The strident sound of a horn blared from outside the hospital, yanking her from her depressing thoughts. Through the driving snow, Molly viewed the familiar sight of a pickup truck.

The driver, a Navajo sheepherder she remembered trying—and failing—to talk into getting a flu shot, leapt out of the driver's seat and came rushing into the emergency room.

"Dr. Joe, Sister Molly, you've got to come help my boy."

Joe already had his jacket on and was headed out

the door. Molly was close behind him. "What happened?"

"His horse spooked in the storm and fell on him. He's unconscious. And he looks bad, Doc. Real bad."

John Chee had refused a flu shot because he was suspicious of white medicine; he preferred the ancient, traditional healing ways of the *ha tathli,* or medicine man. That he'd bring his only son here for treatment suggested a potentially fatal injury.

David Chee lay in the back of the truck, strapped to a board. The traditional Navajo blanket covering him held a thick coating of snow. Fortunately, the wool, even wet, proved a good insulator.

The last time Molly had seen the eight-year-old boy had been six weeks ago when she'd played a pickup game of baseball with a bunch of reservation kids. David had been the pitcher.

At the time she'd been impressed by the strength of his arm and the sturdy, robust body that came from hard work and miles of daily walking herding his family's sheep. Right now, unfortunately, David looked anything but robust.

Together the three of them managed to get the boy out of the truck and into the clinic. There were, Molly realized immediately, the expected broken bones. But there were also the unmistakable signs of internal bleeding.

"His blood pressure's dropping like a rock," Joe said grimly. "There's no chance of getting a helicopter from Winslow or Flagstaff in this storm. We're going to have to cut him open here."

"Here?"

During her three years on the reservation, Molly

had witnessed procedures that, under normal conditions, should have been done in a fully equipped trauma center. Unfortunately, in an area as remotely populated as the vast Navajo reservation, such a hospital was out of the question.

"The kid's a goner if we don't," he said, as if reading her mind. "It's the only chance we've got."

"What will we do for an anesthesiologist?"

"Actually, we're in luck. Peter Nelson dropped by on his way from Winslow to Window Rock. He didn't want to drive in this storm, so he's staying out at my place. I'll call him right now."

Joe placed the call and quickly announced that Dr. Nelson was on his way. "So you see," he said with a bravado Molly suspected was intended to reassure himself as well as the other two adults in the room, "we don't have any problem.

"John, as much as I hate to kick you out of here, I'm going to have to ask you to wait in the reception area. I can't vouch for the coffee—made it myself, and I tend to like it as thick as mud—but there's lots of it."

Although John Chee's impassive face revealed not a hint of what he was thinking, Molly could see the unmistakable seeds of fear in his eyes.

"You'll take care of my boy, Dr. Joe?"

"Molly and I will do our best."

Molly had never respected him more than she did at that moment, when he'd opted for the truth instead of hedging his bets. They would do their best. Of that there was no question. But so many doctors might have been tempted to assure a worried parent of a positive outcome.

The man's dark eyes went from Joe to Molly, then back to Joe again. Knowing how she'd feel if it were Grace lying unconscious on the stainless-steel examining table, Molly suspected she knew exactly what David's father was thinking.

"Where there's life, there's hope," she assured the older man. "And, if you have no objection, I'll pray for him, as well." Molly knew that just as he preferred traditional medicine, he followed the ways of his ancient religion.

He didn't hesitate. "Thank you, Sister." That said, he gave his son one last look, as if memorizing his features, then walked out of the room. Leaving David in the hands of the experts and all the ancient gods, including Sister Molly's Christian one.

"I wish Naomi was here," Molly murmured as they scrubbed up. The nurse had called earlier to inform them that the storm was making it impossible for her to get to the hospital. Naomi Begay had once told Molly that becoming a nurse had been a lifelong dream. Unfortunately, her parents, possessing the traditional abhorrence of anything to do with the dead, had refused to allow her to attend nursing school.

Naomi had honored her parents' feelings. And, after her mother died three years ago, she'd taken on the role of caretaker for her aging father. The morning after *his* death, having fulfilled her daughterly duty, she left the reservation and headed off to school to realize her dream. She was, without a doubt, the most dedicated nurse Molly had ever met.

"We'll do fine," Joe assured her easily as Peter

Nelson, the visiting anesthesiologist, arrived at the clinic.

They dried their hands on sterile towels, put on their sterile robes and gloves, adjusted the fingers of the gloves, washed off the powder necessary to put them on in the first place, then went into the operating room. An IV bag of intravenous fluids hung from a stand beside the stainless-steel table. A blood-pressure cuff had been wrapped around David's other arm.

"Okay, David," Dr. Nelson announced to the now barely conscious boy, "we're going to put you to sleep now."

It didn't take long for David to go under. His young body stilled.

"Okay." Joe drew in a deep breath. His eyes, above the green mask, were coolly determined as he studied the boy's belly, framed in the sterile blue drapes, like a painter studying a bare canvas. The skin had been swabbed with brown antiseptic.

"Let's get this show on the road."

He held out his hand. Molly immediately slapped a scalpel into it, watching as, with one quick, decisive motion, he sliced through the tough nut-brown skin into the layer of fat beneath. Under optimum operating conditions, Molly would be in charge of handing the assisting doctor scissors and clamps and threading needles. Since these were far from normal conditions, both worked quickly together to clamp and tie the bleeders.

"Well," Joe said with some satisfaction, "that went well. Let's go a little deeper."

Molly immediately handed him another knife, which he used to cut open the body wall. She was more than a little impressed when he quickly, deftly divided the blood vessels and tied them off with silk thread.

"How's the pressure doing?" he asked.

"Only eight-five systolic. But holding," the anesthesiologist answered. "And the pulse is stable at one hundred ten."

"Let's run half a unit of blood," Joe decided. "See if we can bring the pressure up a little bit." One thing he wanted to avoid at all costs was the kid crashing on them. "So far, so good," he said, once the blood had been started. "Let's go for it."

One more cut and David Chee's body lay open. After an examination of the intestines, the liver and the pancreas, Joe got down to the spleen.

"Bingo," he murmured, his words slightly muffled by the mask. "Looks like we found our bleeder."

He turned and dipped his gloved hands into the basin of sterile water he'd instructed Molly to set up beforehand. It wasn't really necessary; it was more of a stalling tactic to calm his hands and steady his nerves. As he watched the water turn from clear to pink, Joe debated about what to do next.

The spleen was obviously ruptured; blood was draining out of it like air from a bright red balloon. Spleens were tricky, with a tendency to hemorrhage. He decided he had no choice.

"It has to come out."

Molly nodded. Her eyes moved from the portable EEG, which showed the patient remained stable, to Joe's confident eyes, to David Chee's opened body, then back to Joe again.

"You're the doctor," she said, trying for humor

even though she was as nervous as she'd ever been in a medical condition.

In contrast, as Joe worked, old habits returned to unwind the knot in his stomach and as he felt himself getting into the groove, he discovered he was enjoying himself.

He removed the spleen quickly, tying off and cauterizing the new bleeders as Molly clamped and sponged.

"Closing," he announced when he was finished.

Molly immediately handed him the monofilament nylon suture, which while more difficult to tie off, would prevent against infection better than old-fashioned silk.

Once the surgery was completed, Joe pulled off his bloody gloves and dropped them into the plastic-lined wastebasket. Then set the broken bones.

"Well, I've done all I can," he said to Molly as the anesthesiologist began slowly bringing David up. "Now it's your turn."

"My turn?" Molly paused in the act of taking off her own gloves.

"To pray. Like you've never prayed before. Because believe me, Molly, for the next few hours this kid's going to need all the help he can get."

The four adults sat by David's bedside, keeping a vigil throughout the day and long into the night. Molly and Joe checked their patient's vital signs regularly and kept in touch with the Flagstaff hospital by phone, but the clinic did not have the computer network that would allow more professional support.

Around midnight, David developed a fever, and although Joe remained outwardly encouraging when speaking with John Chee, Molly knew that if they couldn't get his temperature and his white count down, the riding accident could ultimately prove fatal.

"He's not going to die," Joe assured Molly quietly during a brief time when the father had gone into an adjoining office to call a combination gas station/trading post near his home to ask someone to pass the news of his son's condition on to the rest of the family. Peter Nelson had gone off to sleep on a cot in the closet-size room laughingly referred to as a doctors' lounge. "We've worked too hard to lose him now."

Molly hoped he was right. And continued to pray.

By the time the sun rose on the eastern horizon the following morning, she'd gone through several mental rosaries, had recited the beatitudes more times than she could count, and had asked God in every way she knew how to spare this boy who'd come to mean so much to them.

"Hot damn," Joe said, just after John Chee had gone outside to sprinkle corn pollen in the crisp clear air to greet the return of Father Sun. "The fever's broken, Molly. And the storm's stopped, so we can get the kid out of here and into a proper hospital."

He wrapped his arms around her and, to her surprise and shock, planted a big kiss right on her mouth. When he appeared totally unrepentant about his enthusiastic behavior, Molly assured herself that he didn't mean anything by the kiss. Not really. It had been an extemporaneous act of celebration. Nothing more.

Two hours later, David Chee, in pain, but conscious and encouragingly alert, and been placed aboard a Medevac helicopter. John Chee accompanied his son on the trip to Flagstaff, and as the copter took to the sky, Naomi arrived on the scene, apologizing for missing a day's work.

"It didn't matter," Joe assured the young woman. "The storm kept everyone away. We only had one customer."

"I should have been here," she repeated firmly. Her warm dark eyes flicked over their faces. "You two look exhausted."

Joe grinned. "Never felt better in my life." He looped a friendly, unthreatening arm around Molly. "Sister Molly and I made a great team, Naomi. Too bad you missed the show."

Putting aside her earlier ridiculous misgivings, Molly smiled and basked in the satisfaction of a job well-done. And, more importantly, a life saved.

Chapter Thirteen

Lena could not believe it was possible for any one woman to be so happy. When she'd first agreed to adopt Molly's baby, she'd secretly worried that she wouldn't know how to be a mother. There had been times, during her sister's pregnancy, when she'd wake up in the middle of the night, drenched in sweat after dreaming of her child drowning in the pool, or getting run over by a car. In the worst nightmares she momentarily forgot she even had a child, and leaving the stroller in the mall, wandered off window shopping, only to return to that very same spot and discover that her baby had been kidnapped. The subsequent search through the mall—or in other versions, the beach—was always the same: frantic and fruitless.

She must have told herself a hundred times a day that she wasn't a good enough person to be a mother. Even after she'd first brought Grace home, and worried continually about whether the baby was getting enough milk, if she was changing her diaper often enough, if her cries meant she was hungry, wet or simply bored, and what to do about that strawberry rash on Grace's face, some nagging little voice in a far distant corner of her mind would point out that Molly would know exactly what to do.

But gradually, as her maternal instincts developed, assisted by a mountain of child-care books, Lena began to relax. And to enjoy being a mother. So much so, that by the time Grace was three years old, she couldn't imagine a life without her bright, beautiful child in it.

There were a few moments of self-doubt, like last week, when she'd watched Grace and Molly having a pretend tea party together and wondered, deep down inside, if she and Reece had deprived the pair of having an honest mother-daughter relationship.

But it wouldn't have worked, Lena reminded herself yet again. After all, Molly was a nun. Whoever heard of a nun raising a child?

The courts had decreed that Lena was Grace's mother, Reece her daddy and Molly her aunt. Despite Reece's initial concerns, the situation had worked out for everyone involved.

But sometimes, late at night, while she was lying in bed unable to sleep, listening to the sound of the waves outside and Reece's breathing inside, Lena worried about what she'd do if Molly ever decided to leave the order and claim her child.

But she wasn't going to worry about such an unlikely scenario on such a picture-perfect day, she vowed as she carried the bag of peat moss into the backyard.

The sun was shining, making the ocean beyond the

cliffs shimmer like glass. A few white clouds drifted by in a dazzlingly clear blue sky. Lena and Grace had decided that the largest one definitely looked like a cocker spaniel.

They were planting bulbs in the rock garden beside the house. "Tulips have always been my favorite flower," Lena confessed to her daughter. She did not mention that this was the first time in her life she'd ever actually planted any. Always before, obsessed with the idea of dying young like her mother, she'd always stuck to annuals. It had seemed safer that way.

Grace looked up from patting the dirt over a newly planted bulb. "Why?"

"Because they're a happy flower."

Grace's smooth brow furrowed. "Flowers can't be happy or sad," she argued, reminding Lena of Molly. "They're just flowers."

"I was talking about the way they make you feel." Lena smiled down at her daughter. "They're so bright and cheery, just like crayons. You can't help but smile when you see them."

Grace thought about that. "Is that true?"

"Absolutely."

"Everyone smiles when they see tulips?"

"It's impossible not to."

"Then I think we should give some to Uncle Alex," she decided. "Because he's been really grouchy lately."

Lena laughed. "Good idea. But he'll feel better when he and your aunt Theo get married."

The clear bright blue eyes widened with obvious delight. "Uncle Alex and Aunt Theo are getting married? Really?"

"Absolutely." Lena grinned conspiratorially down at her daughter. "But don't tell your uncle Alex. Because he doesn't know yet."

"It's a girl thing, right, Mama?" It was what her mommy and her aunt Theo always told her when they were having lunch together here at the house, laughing about Daddy and Uncle Alex.

"Absolutely." Unable to resist touching her daughter's black curls that fell nearly to her waist, Lena pulled off her gloves and ruffled Grace's hair. "Come here, you," she said, pulling the little girl into her arms, "I need a hug."

As she felt Grace's slender little-girl arms wrap around her, Lena closed her eyes and said a brief prayer of thanksgiving. Then wished that it were possible to freeze time.

"Well?" Alex glared over at the woman who'd been driving him up a wall for weeks.

Theo stretched with feline satisfaction. "It was wonderful," she all but purred. Turning over onto her side, she ran her hand over the chest that remained rock hard from daily workouts on the Soloflex machine. The pewter hairs sprinkled among the darker chestnut ones reminded her that no matter how young she felt inside, they didn't have all the time in the world. "But you've always been a wonderful lover, Alex."

"That's not what I'm talking about. And you know it."

"Oh?" She arched a russet brow. She was a redhead this week, but had been considering a rich sable she thought might make her look a bit like Jackie O during the former First Lady's editorial days.

"Don't play dumb with me, sweetheart. In case you've forgotten, I used to have the best confession rate on the force. I can play this game better than you."

Although she truly doubted that, Theo decided this was not the time to argue the point. "I assume we're back to my offer."

Back-to-back Emmys for best Daytime Drama, as well as others for writing, and several cast awards, had earned Theo a highly lucrative offer from "The Guiding Light."

"What else?" he grumbled, reminding Theo of a grumpy old bear just emerging from hibernation.

"Believe me, darling, the day I take my work to bed, is the day I retire. Especially when I'm in bed with you." She pressed a wet kiss against his navel.

"Dammit, woman, I'm trying to have a serious conversation here." He grabbed hold of her hair and jerked her head up, not gently. "The least you could do is cooperate."

"I'm sorry." The ability to empathize had made her a very wealthy woman. Looking at the honest frustration on his face, Theo realized that the time for teasing was over. "I promise to be on my best behavior, Officer."

Although her tone was as sweet as spun sugar and her gaze guileless, Alex looked at her sharply, as if trying to decide whether or not she was laughing at him.

"All right," he said. "We're long overdue for a talk. But first, there's something I need you to do."

"Anything," she answered promptly, meaning it.

"Put something on. There's no way I can talk business while you're sitting there with your gorgeous tits in my face."

The complaint, which Theo decided to take as a rather backhanded compliment, made her reconsider her recent decision to have her ample breasts "fluffed up" a bit.

"Whatever you say, sweetie." She reached down, picked up the gauze swim cover-up from the floor and pulled it over her head. "Is that better?"

Alex shook his head. "Not much." The damn top was nearly see-through. "But it'll have to do." Using his hands, he pushed himself up to a sitting position beside her. "First of all, I want you to know that I understand what a coup this job would be."

"Not every writer gets a chance to be a producer," she agreed.

"I know. And you deserve it. And I'm damn proud of you."

Theo, who'd never lacked self-confidence, found his gruff compliment more pleasing than all the gilt statues she had won. "Thank you."

"And I realize the money they're offering could set you up for the rest of your life."

"It's quite a lucrative offer. Of course," Theo added, "it does cost more to live in New York."

"Yeah."

Theo wanted to assure him that she didn't want to go to New York. That she hated the idea of leaving him. But since they were playing for higher stakes here—the most important she'd ever played for in her life—she resisted showing her hand.

Alex took a deep breath. "We've been together now four years. And as Dan keeps telling me, a relationship is like a shark. It's gotta keep moving. Or die."

For a fleeting, horrifying moment, Theo wondered if Alex was trying to tell her it was over. While she waited for her heartbeat to settle, she pretended sudden interest in the watercolor of a vineyard, across the room. She and Alex had bought the painting on a recent trip to Napa Valley where they'd sampled wines, had picnics overlooking lush green sunlit valleys and made love for three glorious days and nights.

"Interesting, Daniel should know so much about relationships," she murmured. "Since I doubt if he's managed to make one last more than ten days."

"That's his point. He says that when a guy finds the right woman, he'll know it right off. If the woman you're dating isn't the right one, you move on. If she is, you move hell and high water to keep her."

"I see." Growing more and more nervous, Theo began plucking at the sheet. What was he thinking of, asking his son—who couldn't be more than thirty—for romance advice? She'd thought for sure that Alex had fallen in love with her, as she had with him. Surely she couldn't have misjudged him so badly?

He reached out and took hold of her hand. Theo watched, momentarily intrigued as it disappeared between his much larger ones.

"I don't know what I would have done without you, these past few years," he said. "I'll admit when we first met, I didn't take you all that seriously. I mean, you were a lot of fun to play cards with, and even more fun in bed, but I never imagined any kind of future with a woman like you.''

A woman like you. The words did not strike her as exactly complimentary. Theo reminded herself that she should be paying attention to her feelings right now. After all, they'd prove invaluable in her work. Hadn't her very own mother, a brilliant, manic-depressive poet once told her, ''Everything's grist for the literary mill, darling.'' Including, it seemed, Theo thought miserably, a broken heart.

''But then I had that accident. And amazingly, you stuck around, encouraging me, daring me, cussing at me when I didn't want to get out of bed. Comforting me when I needed it.'' His hand tightened, squeezing hers. ''I honestly don't know if I ever would have had the guts or fortitude to walk again if I hadn't had you in my life at the time.''

''That's me,'' she quipped flatly. ''Florence Nightingale to the lame and stubborn.''

He tilted his head and looked at her curiously, surprised by her shaky attempt at humor. ''Are those tears?''

''Of course not.'' Furious with her atypical lack of self-control, she blinked furiously. ''Go ahead, Alex,'' she said with a brittle brightness, ''this little tour down memory lane is fascinating.''

A tear escaped. He brushed it away with a fingertip. ''You *are* crying.''

''It's allergies,'' she sniffled.

''Bullshit.'' He gave her another long, puzzled look. ''I don't understand.''

''Of course you don't!'' Frustrated and embarrassed, Theo pulled away and jumped out of the bed.

"And you know why? Because you're a fucking man. And like all men, you don't have a clue about how to conduct a relationship."

"I believe I already admitted to that."

Theo, who was on a roll, didn't hear him. "Oh, you all think, so long as you give a woman at least one orgasm every time you make love and pretend to listen to her when she's gossiping about something you find excruciatingly boring, give up a few basketball games on ESPN in order to go to the theater, and assure her she doesn't look fat in her new dress, you're being the perfect nineties male." She stopped pacing long enough to glare down at him. "But you still don't get it, do you, hotshot?"

"Get what?"

"I give up!" She threw her arms in the air and resumed pacing.

Fascinated, and a little afraid of her, Alex watched. And waited. He did not have to wait long.

"Do you realize how hard it was on me to spend all that time at the rehabilitation clinic while I was trying to establish a new career?" she demanded, her hands splayed on her hips in a way that pulled the transparent material taut against her body, momentarily distracting him. "Do you have any idea how many scripts I wrote while stuck in traffic on the Santa Monica Freeway? Did you have any idea that I was operating on less than four hours' sleep a night during the first six months after your accident?"

"I said I appreciated it. You don't have to shout."

"Dammit, I'm not shouting," she shouted. "I'm not telling you this because I want your appreciation!" She spat the word out of her mouth as if it had a bitter aftertaste. "I didn't hang around after the accident because I had any martyr complex, Alex Kovaleski. I stayed with you because I realized that I'd already fallen in love with you. Serious, once in a lifetime, forever-after kind of love, goddammit!"

"You love me?"

"Of course I do, you big boob. And it's coming as a definitely unpleasant revelation to discover that it's got me feeling every bit as bad as when I was fifteen and had a gigantic crush on Jeremy Parcell. So, why don't you just get it over with?"

"What over with?" Alex was more confused than ever.

"Aaagh!" She closed her eyes and took a deep breath that once again drew his eyes to her magnificent breasts. Despite the disastrous way this conversation he'd planned so carefully was turning out, Alex experienced a renewed stirring of desire.

"I categorically refuse to make this easy on you, Alex. After all we've been through, all we've shared, I'm not letting you off the hook that easy. If you want to break up with me, you're going to have to damn well say the words."

"Break up with you?"

He'd always thought of her as the strongest, bravest, sexiest woman he'd ever met. Now, realizing how badly she needed comforting, he damned the artificial legs that were lying beside the bed, cursed the stumps that kept him from leaping out of bed and taking her into his arms.

"Isn't that what all this is about?" she asked.

"Hell, no. Actually, what I was trying to do, in my own admittedly clueless way, was to propose."

"Propose?"

"As in, ask you to marry me." He sighed, thinking of how badly he'd screwed this up. Dan would laugh his fool head off if he knew what a fuck-up his dad was. "I was also going to ask you—beg you, if necessary—to stay here in California with me, but I realize now how important this new job offer is, so I was thinking, there's no reason we can't have one of those commuter marriages—"

"No." She flung herself back onto the bed so hard the mattress bounced, threw her arms around his neck and kissed him. Hard.

"No?" he asked when the blissful kiss finally ended.

"No, I'm not going to New York. And yes, yes, yes, I'll marry you."

She kissed him again. Harder, longer. And as the kisses deepened and the afternoon shadows grew longer, Alex decided that while he might have screwed up the actual proposal, there were some romantic things he did pretty damn well. If he did say so himself.

"You don't understand." Tessa sighed as she refilled her champagne glass. It crossed her mind that she'd been drinking a bit too much lately. But who wouldn't? With all the stress she had in her life. "I don't have the money."

Jason laughed at that. "Hell, baby, don't give me that." He was lying on his back, floating in the pool. With his tanned, buffed-up body, Tessa thought he looked a lot more like a soap opera hunk than a cop. "You've got it made. A house in Beverly Hills—"

"On the flats, not in the Hills," she pointed out. "And it's rented."

"It's still a long way from that dive in West Hollywood. A shiny red Porsche sitting in the driveway—"

"Leased."

"Dammit, Tessa, would you quit interrupting me." Although the mirrored sunglasses kept her from seeing his eyes, from the warning edge to his tone, Tessa knew they'd be as hard as granite.

"I'm sorry." She took another long drink and willed her nerves to calm.

She didn't need this. Not now. Not with the rumors circulating about Terrance Quinn being in Mexico, hidden away at some secret clinic in Guaymas, receiving an esoteric cure for liver cancer.

Although she'd worked in Hollywood long enough not to believe every rumor, she'd been worried for days that this story just might be true. *Terrific.* That's all she needed. Her agent dying just when it was time to renegotiate her contract.

"My point," he said, "is that you're a supporting cast member in a top ten-rated sitcom. You're getting fifteen thou a week, baby. Even a dopehead wino like you can't spend all that."

"I wish you wouldn't talk to me like that."

She'd tried for a flash of fire and ended up sounding pitiful. Dammit, if they were going to argue like this, she'd have to take another Xanax. Besides, it wasn't true. She hardly ever drank while working. As for drugs, she managed to get along just fine without them during the week. It was on the weekends, or during the program's hiatus, that she'd get in trouble.

What she needed, she told herself for the umpteenth time, was to get back to work.

So, where the hell was Terrance?

"Then quit holding out on me." He rolled off the float and came out of the pool to stand over her. Drops of water fell onto her hot oiled flesh. "You seem to be forgetting who made all this possible, sweetheart. If I hadn't discovered you that day on Sunset Boulevard and introduced you to Miles, you'd have ended up slinging hash at that Denny's where you were going to eat Christmas dinner. Or making porno movies for the mail-order video market."

"I really don't have any money." It was the truth. Her expenses were ridiculous. Not to mention the checks she kept writing out to him. She'd discovered early in their relationship that Jason was a gambler; unfortunately, he was a chronically unlucky one. "And I won't until I sign the new contract."

"Then sign it."

He made it sound so simple. "Terrance says it isn't in my best interest. He says I should hold out for a movie of the week to be part of the deal. He also says that their demand for approval on any commercial endorsement contracts—"

"Terrance says this. Terrance says that." His acid tone mocked her concerns. "For your information, sweetheart, your agent is currently puking his guts out in Mexico. And not because of any Montezuma's revenge he might have picked up while deep-sea fishing. I wouldn't hold my breath waiting for him to come back. Because it isn't going to happen."

"You don't know that."

"Believe me, I do. Don't forget, I've got contacts

south of the border. And they tell me that Quinn's ticket on planet earth is about to get punched.''

Her head whirling with the horrible reality of her situation, Tessa downed the rest of her champagne and rose unsteadily to her feet.

"Where do you think you're going? We're not finished here."

"I have to pee."

"You need a downer."

She didn't deny it. "You don't understand, dammit—"

"Of course I do." Even though she knew this sudden show of concern was an act, Tessa didn't resist as he gathered her into his strong arms. "I understand your career is at a crossroads right now, baby. I also understand that it's got to be scary, thinking about losing your agent."

Tessa wrapped her arms around his waist. "I don't know what I'd do without Terrance," she mumbled into his chest.

"We'll figure out something." He ran his hand down her hair. "Meanwhile, since there's no way either one of us can come up with a cure for liver cancer in the next twenty-four hours, we may as well find something to take our mind off our problems." His hand slid slowly, past her waist, cupped her bottom and lifted her against him.

"You always think sex is the answer to everything."

"Not everything." He leaned back and grinned down at her. "Did I happen to mention that I busted a guy selling coke at a dance club last night?"

Against her will, she felt that little trip of her heart.

"I don't suppose you happened to miscount how many Baggies he had on him?"

His smile widened. "What do you think?"

"I shouldn't. Not with all the champagne I've drunk."

"You haven't had that much." His lips plucked at hers. "Come on, sweetheart. We'll get a little high, have some mind-blowing sex and in the morning everything will be coming up roses."

Anything would be better than this constant arguing. If only Terrance were here.

But he wasn't. And if Jason was telling the truth—and about this, there was no reason to doubt him—he wouldn't be coming back. Tessa couldn't imagine what she was going to do without the man who'd so skillfully guided her career through the rough white water that was Hollywood dealmaking.

"Perhaps I should call Miles." Miles had set her up with Terrance in the first place. Maybe he'd know what to do.

"You don't need to call my damn brother. When are you going to get it through that gorgeous red head that I'm all you need?"

Before she could respond, Jason had picked her up and was carrying her into the house. The very same house on which she owed two months' back rent.

There had to be an answer, Tessa assured herself. After all, she'd already had more than her share of luck. She was a successful actress. Her publicist had called last week to set up interviews with "ET" and *TV Guide,* and there was even talk of her making the cover as one of three upcoming stars of the future.

As Jason had pointed out, she lived in Beverly Hills

and drove a Porsche. And not just any bottom-of-the-line model, either, but a Targa that screamed success. Okay, so they were both leased, but the majority of wannabe actresses in town wouldn't even be able to afford a fraction of the payments.

Something would work out, she assured herself as Jason dropped her onto the bed. It always did.

"One day Coyote came across some otters playing a game of nanzoz," Molly read to the children who'd gathered at her motor home. Today was inoculation day in Canyon de Chelly and now that all the shots had been given and tears dried, she was entertaining her young patients by reading from a book of Navajo legends. "He asked if he could play with them."

"But the otters knew he was a rascal," a little girl about Grace's age volunteered.

Molly rewarded her with a smile. "They certainly did, Helen. They told him to go away, but he begged and begged and finally they agreed to let him join the game. So long as he bet his skin, the way they did."

"But when they lost their skins, they just jumped in the water and got new ones," a little boy said.

"Exactly. And, of course, Coyote, who didn't know how to play the game nearly as well as the otters, lost his skin. But when he jumped in the water—"

"He didn't get a new skin," the children shouted the familiar story line in unison.

"He jumped into the creek again and again, but his skin didn't come back," Molly agreed. "Finally he was so exhausted, the otters took pity on him and

pulled him out of the creek, dragged him to a badger
hole, threw him in and covered him up with earth.

"Well, before he got into all this trouble, Coyote
had had a beautiful smooth coat, just like the otters.
But by the time he dug his way out of that badger
hole, he was covered with fur again, but it was a
coarse, rough fur, like badger fur. And this is the coat
Coyote has had to wear ever since."

"Tell us about Coyote fighting the spiders and
swallows," Helen Redhouse said. "That's my favorite one." Her smile lit up her dark face and her eyes,
like polished brown stones, looked up at Molly with
something bordering on adoration.

"I want to hear about Bear Woman," a boy called
out, prompting an argument as the various camps took
up sides.

Molly glanced out the window, to where the sun
was setting in the west behind them. Following Navajo tradition, she'd parked the motor home so her
door faced the east, and the rising Father Sun.

"I think, if we don't waste time arguing, we just
may have time for both before your parents have to
take you home."

Since the adults in question were enjoying themselves at the trading post, bartering, pawning, selling,
buying and gossiping, Molly knew they would not
mind her keeping their children a little longer.

The truth was, although she worked each day until
she was exhausted, and had put thousands of miles
on the motor home driving from outpost to outpost,
she hadn't been able to entirely shake her depression.
The only times she ever felt truly happy—and fulfilled—were times like now, when after a day's work,

she was surrounded by children. Children she could pretend, for a brief time, were her own.

When the cheers settled down, she turned the page and began to read another of the beloved stories they all knew by heart.

"I feel like a damn fool." Theo stood in front of the full-length mirror, staring grimly at her reflection.

"What on earth do you mean?" Lena asked.

"Surely you're not having doubts?" Molly asked at the same time, exchanging a concerned look with her sister.

"Not about marrying Alex." Never about that. "It's just this getup." Theo ran her hands down the front of the ivory lace jacket topping a chiffon tealength skirt that swirled around her ankles.

"You look beautiful," both sisters said in unison. The subsequent smiles they traded held none of the tension that had hovered between them for days.

"Like a blushing bride," Molly tacked on.

"That's just the point. I've already been married—"

"Only for two weeks," Lena pointed out. "Thirty years ago."

"I never would have suspected George was gay," Theo mused. "I mean, back in those days, they didn't have TV talk shows. I was so damn innocent, I figured I must be the only woman in the world to come home and discover her new groom makin' whoopie with the pool boy."

"That must have been a shock," Lena said sympathetically. Theo had told her the story two days ago over a long lunch.

"Well, you certainly don't have to worry about that with Alex," Molly said.

"No." To both sisters' amusement, Theo blushed like a girl at the thought of her fiancé's lovemaking. "That's for sure. But I still think I should have just worn my purple satin. Alex likes that one a lot."

"The purple looks gorgeous on you. But this makes you look as if you stepped from the pages of a bride magazine," Molly said.

"When you tried it on last night, Grace said you looked like a fairy queen," Lena reminded her.

"Nah." Theo turned this way and that, her frown softening as she studied the uncharacteristically feminine dress sprinkled with seed pearls. "George was queen of the fairies."

As she laughed along with Molly and Lena, Theo began to feel more like herself again. Maybe it was a ridiculous dress for a woman in her fifties to wear. But dammit, she felt pretty. And for someone who'd worked overtime all her life striving for over-the-top glamour, she was discovering that pretty and feminine could feel nice, too.

"What about my hair?" She patted it nervously.

"Perfect. I love the new shade," Molly said reassuringly.

"You look just like Jackie O," Lena seconded.

Theo leaned closer to the glass. "I think my nose is shiny."

"Your nose is perfect." As they heard the harpist downstairs begin to play, Molly put her hands on Theo's lace-clad shoulders and turned her toward the bedroom door. "You don't want to keep your groom waiting."

The wedding was being held in the Longworths' garden. From the upstairs window, the women could see Alex, standing beside Dan—who he'd asked to be his best man—beneath the rose-covered arbor. A green-and-white striped tent had been erected beside the pool for the reception; a buffet fit for royalty had been set up on the damask-draped tables, and silver urns held nuggets of sparkling ice and dark green bottles of champagne.

"No." Theo squared her shoulders and reminded herself that not many women were fortunate enough to be so loved. "We've both waited too long as it is." She scooped up her bouquet, a tasteful arrangement of white orchids. "Let's get this show on the road."

"So," Joe Salvatore asked Molly two weeks later as they were preparing to leave the hospital, "how was the wedding of the year?"

"Absolutely perfect. The bride was beautiful and the groom was a wreck." Molly grinned as she thought back on the obvious nervousness of the man who'd risked his life so many times during his years on the L.A. police force.

"Sounds like the situation was normal. Although in my family, Uncle Thomas always gets drunk, tries to give the bridesmaids hickeys and grabs the microphone sometime during the evening to sing 'Volaré.' I don't suppose anything like that happened?"

"Everyone was a model of decorum."

"The average Californian is obviously too laid-back to have any flair for the dramatic. I suppose you brought pictures?"

"Tons." She pulled the snapshots out of her purse and handed them over. He flipped through the stack, making appropriate comments, pausing when he got to the one of Alex awaiting the arrival of his bride.

"Looks as if he's getting along pretty well with those artificial legs." Molly had told him the story of Alex's accident, and what he'd endured on the way to recovery.

"He plays in a police veteran's basketball league," she informed him. "And not one of those wheelchair leagues for disabled cops."

"That's terrific." He nodded his medical approval and moved on to the next photograph, which happened to be of Grace, standing in the garden, holding her flower-girl basket of snowy rose petals. "Jeez, that's a gorgeous child!"

"She is, isn't she?"

Molly experienced that same unbidden surge of maternal pride she'd felt when she'd first seen her daughter—Lena's daughter—in a powder pink lace dress that was a perfect foil for her gleaming jet hair. As she'd done all the other times, she'd firmly tamped it down. Still, as hard as she tried, she knew she'd never forget the musical sound of Grace's childish laughter as Reece scooped her up into his arms after the wedding and began dancing across the wooden platform that had been laid beneath the tent.

"She's definitely going to break a lot of hearts." He turned to a family photo of Grace, Lena, Reece and Molly. "Although they're both good-looking, she doesn't seem to resemble either of her parents," he murmured.

"Not all children do," Molly said quickly. A bit

too quickly, she realized, when he looked up at her, a tinge of curiosity in his expression.

"Now that you mention it, my brother, Dominic, takes after my mother, my sister, Ann, resembles my dad, but except for the same coloring, I don't look like anyone else in the family." He studied the photo again. "Actually, you know who she looks like?"

Molly's blood went cold. Although no one had said anything, she'd been aware that several of the wedding guests—and everyone in the family—had noticed the remarkable resemblance. "Who?" she asked in a voice that was not as strong as she would have liked.

"The kid's a dead ringer for you."

Molly turned to gaze out the window, pretending a sudden interest in the towering red-rock formation in the distance. "Do you really think so?"

"Don't you? She's got the same wavy black hair, the same blue eyes, the same stubborn chin. And her nose tilts to the left, exactly like yours."

"My nose isn't crooked," she argued in an attempt to change the subject.

"Of course it is." He took her hand and led her over to the mirror above the white pedestal sink in the doctors' lounge. "See?" He ran a finger down the slope of her nose. "Right here, it takes just the slightest turn."

"It does not."

"Anyone ever tell you that you're real cute when you get your back up, Sister Molly?"

"And to think I was about to offer to cook you dinner."

"Really? Honest-to-God food that doesn't come in

a cardboard box and has to be nuked in a microwave?''

''Actually, now that you bring it up, I *was* planning to reheat it in the microwave. I made too much lasagna last night and will never be able to eat it all by myself.''

''Brains, beauty, and the woman can cook.'' He sighed, and stretched, working out the kinks earned from a long day treating everything from cold sores to arthritis to a broken elbow, to an emergency C-section. ''I think I'm in love.''

Accustomed to his teasing attitude, which reminded her of Reece, Molly didn't take him seriously. ''You probably say that to all the nurse practitioners you work with.''

''Nah. Just the drop-dead gorgeous ones.''

Something flickered in the depths of his dark brown eyes. Some unnamed emotion that came and went so quickly, if Molly hadn't met his gaze at that precise moment, she might have missed it. Something that seemed strangely close to a masculine appreciation that had nothing to do with her medical skills.

Deciding that notion was ridiculously fanciful, she put the idea away. ''Such a tongue you have on you, Dr. Salvatore. Are you certain you're Italian, and not Irish? I have the feeling you must have kissed the Blarney stone.''

''Perhaps in some other life,'' he agreed, his mood lightening to match hers as they left the hospital and crossed the parking lot to the motor home that had served as her home for nearly four years. Since so much of the space had been converted to a portable clinic, her living quarters were little more than a kitchen, a propane stove, a table, two wooden chairs and a narrow bed. Although it wasn't spacious, compared to some cloistered nun's cells Molly had heard the older nuns describe, it was downright homey.

But it wasn't home. Not really. A home was what Reece, Lena and Grace shared. And now Theo and Alex. And even as she tried to remind herself that God had never promised that the road she'd chosen would be free of bumps, Molly could no longer ignore the haunting thoughts of what might have been. And the even more tempting thoughts about what, if she were brave enough, could still be.

A silence settled over them as she took the lasagna from the refrigerator and put it into the microwave. While the dinner warmed, Joe opened the bottle of wine he'd retrieved from a hiding place in the doctors' lounge.

"This is damn near close to perfection," he said with a warm, satisfied smile. He was a remarkably good-looking man, making Molly wonder, not for the first time, how he'd managed to get all the way through medical school, an internship and a residency without some woman staking her claim on him.

Telling herself that Joe Salvatore's love life was absolutely none of her business, she began buttering some French bread to serve with the lasagna.

"Would you like a glass of wine?"

Molly paused. Although she'd drunk a bit of illegal beer during her rebellious teenage years and wine on special occasions, like the champagne at Alex and Theo's wedding, she'd always worried that her father's tragic tendency for alcoholism might run in her veins.

"Would you feel safer if I promise not to get you drunk and have my way with you?"

His teasing tone made Molly realize he'd misunderstood her ambivalence and concern. "Just a bit," she said. "I'm really not much of a drinker."

"Just a bit." True to his word, he poured a scant few inches of the ruby red burgundy into her glass.

After complimenting her on the lasagna, assuring her it was every bit as delicious as his grandmother used to make, Joe didn't say another word. Sitting across the narrow table from him, Molly realized he was deep in thought and decided he was undoubtedly running through today's C-section in his head. During her tenure at Mercy Sam, she'd seen Reece sitting silently reviewing a patient's treatment countless times.

A comfortable silence settled over them as they finished the simple meal. Molly cleared the table, then settled back, not complaining when he topped off her wine.

"You are, you know," Joe said suddenly, his words shattering the stillness inside the van.

"Am what?"

"Drop-dead gorgeous." He leaned toward her, his forearms on the table between them. "I love what you've done to your hair."

She tensed slightly as he reached out and ran his palm down the rippling waves that had suddenly appeared when she'd had her straight, nearly waist-length hair cut to a more stylish shoulder length for the wedding.

"Joe—"

"It looks like obsidian, all black and shiny," he

said, ignoring her murmured warning. "But it feels like silk. And your eyes. Lord, if you only knew how many nights I've lain awake thinking about your eyes."

"I don't think—"

"That's right." His hand curved around her jaw, his long fingers holding her face to his. "Don't think. Not until I've had my say. Please?"

There was something remarkably close to torment in his expression. Something that rendered Molly temporarily mute. She could only nod, slowly, in response.

"They're such a clear pale hue, almost like Irish crystal at the center, but they get darker and darker with each ring outward, from the blue of the Celtic sea to a dark, moonless midnight sky at the outer rims. A man could drown in those incredible, magical eyes, Molly McBride. And welcome the experience with open arms."

Never had any man ever spoken to her this way. Sensual intent swirled in his own dark eyes, which had deepened to a jet nearly as dark as his hair.

"And, of course, we've already discussed your endearingly crooked nose. Which brings me to your mouth. And your lovely, luscious lips."

His gaze had settled on her mouth, which suddenly went as dry as the red desert dust. Molly knew she should tell him to stop. Knew she must remind him that he must not talk this way. But she could not make the words that were swirling around and around in her head come out of the mouth that seemed to enthrall him so.

Before she could utter a single word, he was on his

feet. His chair teetered, then clattered to the floor but went ignored. And then he was pulling her out of her own chair and his arms were around her and his fingers were tangled in her hair and his firm hard masculine mouth was pressing hard against hers with a passion she'd never, ever experienced.

Chapter Fourteen

When Joe's tongue slipped wickedly past the barrier of her lips and teeth, in some far distant corner of her whirling mind, Molly vaguely remembered having been taught that French kissing was a mortal sin. But how, she wondered as his tongue swept the moist dark interior of her mouth, could anything so thrillingly perfect be wrong?

"Do you have any idea how long I've waited to taste you?" he rasped. As his lips plucked at hers, those same deft fingers that had cut a woman open to deliver a baby, then sewed her back up again, began to unbutton Molly's blouse. When she didn't—couldn't—respond, he answered his own question. "Forever."

Considering the passion underlying his kiss, his touch was remarkably gentle. But when she felt his hands on her breasts, a vision flashed through Molly's mind, an image of a man kneeling over her in the alley.

"No!" She cried out, pushing against his chest.

Joe's response was instantaneous. He released her and backed away, his hands in the air. "Christ, Molly, I'm sorry. I didn't mean to do that...well, actually, to tell the truth, I did. I've been wanting to kiss you, to touch you, to love you, for months. But I certainly never intended to frighten you. Or hurt you in any way."

Terror that she thought she'd put behind her, disoriented Molly. She sank down onto the bed and stared up at him, trying to understand where she was. And more importantly, with whom. Frightening images continued to flash before her open eyes like strobe lights.

Finally, the handsome face, stark with guilt and concern gradually settled into focus.

"Joe?"

"I'm so sorry," he repeated as he sat down beside her. His clever fingers fumbled as he began rebuttoning her blouse.

"It wasn't you." Reality sank in, swiftly replaced by embarrassment. "I thought I'd put it behind me. But when you touched me, it all came flooding back."

As her complexion colored, his paled. "Are you saying—"

"I was raped and brutally beaten."

His curse was ripe, vicious and directed inward. "I guess I really screwed things up, didn't I?"

"It wasn't your fault."

"Wasn't it?" Molly had never seen him look so bleak. "If I hadn't talked you into drinking that wine, if I hadn't taken advantage of your innocence—"

"You didn't take advantage of me, Joe." It was a difficult admission, but Molly knew this was a case when honesty was more important than her own shame. "Oh, I wasn't expecting you to kiss me. But I could have asked you to stop. And you would have." Of that she had not a single doubt.

"I would have," he agreed huskily. He sat there, looking down at her for what seemed like forever. "I'm sorry I was the cause of painful memories, but I'm not going to apologize for wanting to make love to you."

"I suppose it's not that surprising," she admitted reluctantly. In a way, it was almost a relief, after years of locking her emotions tightly away, to realize she could feel something as powerful as the edgy desire created by Joe's kiss. "After all, we shared a tremendously intimate experience together, today, Joe. We brought a new life into the world. Factor in the alcohol, and it was probably inevitable that we'd feel a bond—"

"I've delivered other babies, Molly. I've worked for thirty-six hours straight with nurses before. And never once have I wanted to drag any of them off to the nearest bed."

Molly couldn't help smiling at that. "Not ever?"

Joe smiled a bit sheepishly. "Well, perhaps there were a couple occasions…. But, dammit, what I felt a few minutes ago, what I've been feeling for months, is different. It's not just sex. I love you, Molly McBride," he finished up on a burst of heartfelt passion.

Molly stared up at him. "You can't."

"Why not? You're an incredibly lovable person.

Even discounting your beauty, you're warmhearted, you have the most generous nature of any woman I've ever met, you're loyal, hardworking..."

Humor rose to soothe her tangled nerves. "Now you make me sound like a German shepherd police dog."

"I was just about to mention your sense of humor." He grinned down at her and combed his fingers through her tousled dark hair. "I really am head over heels in love with you, Molly. And nothing you can say is going to change that."

Perhaps not. But she had to try. "I'm a nun."

"You're a woman first," he said, unknowingly repeating what she'd told Reece four years ago when he'd resisted the possibility of her pregnancy. "And I love you. I want to marry you, Molly. And have children with you."

His words moved her in ways too complex to unravel while she was so physically tired and emotionally unsettled. They also forced her to wonder if, perhaps, some deep-seated, hidden feelings for Joe were part of the reason she'd decided to ask to be released from her vows.

"That's the most wonderful compliment anyone's ever given me, Joe. And I'll treasure it forever."

"That sounds suspiciously like a rejection."

"I'm afraid it is."

He gave her a long regretful look. "You realize that you're not just rejecting me. But you're cheating yourself, as well."

"What do you mean?"

"You're too passionate a woman to devote your life to some lonely, cold, celibate existence," he argued. "Whether you want to admit it or not, your uninhibited response to me proved that. And don't forget, I've watched you with the kids that come into the clinic. You're a natural-born mother, Molly. You deserve children of your own."

Once again, he'd hit too close to home. When Molly flinched at that statement, his eyes widened.

"My God." He stared at her as if seeing her for the first time. "Grace doesn't look like her parents because she's not their child.... She's yours, isn't she?"

Molly closed her eyes briefly, which was all the answer he needed. "She's Lena's."

"Perhaps legally. But she'll always be the child of your heart." He shook his head and trailed the back of his hand down the side of her face. "Poor, poor Molly," he murmured. "Don't you realize how difficult it's going to be? Going through life, watching some other woman play mother to your daughter?"

"Lena's not just some other woman. She's my sister."

"That's got to make it even harder." He shook his head. "I realize you've already made your decision, and changing your mind and claiming Grace now would destroy too many lives. But there's still a chance for you to have a family, Molly. You could have more children. With me."

"It wouldn't work, Joe. I like you. And respect you. And I do love you. But not in the way a woman should love a husband." Even as she said the words, Molly realized, with some relief, that they were true.

"Besides," she said, belatedly recalling the true reason she couldn't accept his out-of-the-blue proposal, "it's a moot point. Because I'm a nun." She felt a prick of guilt using her vocation for an excuse at a time when her religious status could be about to change, but this wasn't the time for a lengthy discussion regarding her future plans.

"You've said that before. And believe me, sweetheart, having a second cousin who left the convent and eventually ended up an assistant D.A. in Queens, I happen to know that it doesn't have to be a permanent condition.

"However," he said, when he realized she was about to argue, "you're right about it having been a long day. And since you have to leave at first light for your meeting with Sister Benvenuto tomorrow in Flagstaff, I should be going. But I know damn well that I'm going to dream of you. Just as you'll dream of me."

He gave her another quick kiss, just a peck on the lips that created a brief flare of heat. "We'll talk about this when you get back."

With those words ringing in her ears, he was gone.

Molly flopped back onto the mattress and covered her eyes with her forearm. She knew she should be down on her knees, begging God's forgiveness for her sinful behavior, but her mind kept rerunning her undeniably passionate response to his forbidden kisses.

She remembered, just before she'd had that flashback, how warm his hands had felt on her breasts. But strangely, his intimate touch hadn't made them tingle the way they had when she'd arrived at LAX for the wedding and Reece had hugged her, pressing her against his hard chest.

"No." She shook her head, refusing to think about

her mutinous body's unbidden response. She had no business feeling desire for anyone, least of all her very own brother-in-law.

Molly's mind, seemingly determined to plague her, turned next to Grace who, although she struggled against it, she adored in a way that only a mother could love a child. Each time she visited Los Angeles, hearing her daughter calling Lena *Mommy* hurt. But even though such occasions were painful she could no more stay away than she could turn back time to the day she'd made the decision to give her child to her sister.

She'd made her choice, Molly reminded herself firmly. The only choice she could have made. The best choice for everyone concerned, especially Grace, who may have been conceived in violence, but had been born in love.

That settled once more in her mind, Molly forced herself to stay awake long enough for the obligatory prayers of repentance. Then, finally, she allowed sleep to claim her.

And when she did, indeed, dream the sensual dreams Joe had predicted, the face of the man making such slow, exquisite love to her was not that of Dr. Joseph Salvatore, but Reece Longworth.

Molly grew increasingly uncomfortable as she met with her superior, who was visiting a group of Sisters of Mercy in Flagstaff. The painting on the wall behind the desk where Sister Benvenuto sat was a romanticized print of the adoration of the savior by the shepherds, with a host of gilt-winged angels hovering overhead. Although the pink seventeenth-century-

style dress did not at all resemble anything Mary
might have worn, Molly had no trouble recognizing
the expression of unconditional maternal love on the
Madonna's face. She wondered if that was how she
looked at her daughter, reluctantly decided it probably
was, and understood all too well why Reece seemed
worried and Lena uncomfortable and nervous whenever she visited Los Angeles.

The elderly nun had been silent for a very long
time. She was looking out the window at the small
garden, seemingly deep in contemplation. Molly suspected that her request was more disappointing to her
superior than surprising.

When she turned back to Molly, her expression was
grave, her eyes shadowed with regret. "I cannot let
you do this, Margaret."

It was the first time in years Molly could remember
the nun using her full name. "No disrespect intended,
Sister, but it's not really your decision to make."

"I realize that. Yet I have an obligation to protect
you from making a mistake, and I would not be living
up to my duty if I allowed you to leave the order
without trying to change your mind."

"But I've been questioning my vocation for a very
long time," Molly argued.

"We all question." A trace of irritation sharpened
Sister Benvenuto's tone. "Teresa of Avalon wrote of
her battles with herself. And you can't have forgotten
Christ's agony in the garden of Gethsemane, when he
kept asking his Father to take the cup away."

"Of course not, but—"

"But Mark tells us in his gospel that Jesus finally

accepted his fate. 'Let it be as you would have it, not as I.' This is a powerful lesson for us all.''

"It's not a lesson I can personally live up to," Molly said quietly. "Although I love the order, and everyone in it, my heart needs more."

"You must pray—"

"I do!" Molly leapt to her feet, hectic spots of color marring her cheeks. "But prayers don't change the way I feel, deep inside. They don't take away my need for a child."

"You have many children," the nun pointed out. "I've had reports about how good you are with the reservation children, how much they love and look up to you."

"I love them, too. But at the end of the day they go home to their families. I want my own child, Sister."

"That's distressingly self-indulgent, Molly," the nun chided gently.

Her legs were trembling; Molly sat back down. "I realize that. But it's how I feel."

"Trying to reclaim your child would cause terrible heartbreak."

"I wasn't talking about taking Grace away from Lena and Reece!" Molly was shocked that after all these years the nun would think her capable of such a thing. "No, Grace is Lena's daughter. Not mine. But that doesn't mean I can't have another child. After all, I'm young and healthy, and—"

"And have you, perhaps, found a man to father this child you seem to need so badly?"

"No." Memories of the wicked, sensual dream starring her brother-in-law flickered in her mind, and she recalled with vivid detail the power of Joe's kiss. "But, I have to admit, that there have been times lately, when I've found myself tempted to break my vow of celibacy."

"Again, that's not surprising," the nun stated briskly. "As you said, you're young and healthy and perhaps we made a mistake allowing you to stay out there alone on the reservation, so far from the companionship of other members of the order. If you were to return to Los Angeles—"

"I don't think that's such a good idea," Molly said quickly.

"You took a vow of obedience."

"That becomes a moot point if I leave the order." The nun sighed. "And now we're back to that?"

"Yes." Molly forced herself to meet the look of disapproval head-on. "I've tried my best to overcome my doubts for years. But it's not going to happen."

"God works in His own time," Sister Benvenuto advised sagely. "And His time is often not our time." Her smile—the first she'd managed since Molly had arrived for her meeting—did not touch her eyes. "Why don't we attempt a compromise?"

Molly had suspected this wouldn't be easy. "What kind of compromise?"

"You have three months left on the contract we signed with the BIA. I could, of course, replace you with another nurse practitioner, but you've already established yourself as part of the community, so you may as well finish your work there.

"Then, after you've returned to Los Angeles, allow yourself another three months to spend time with the other sisters. Help me with the postulate training, which may put you back in touch with all those feelings that you first had when you chose to join us."

"I'm not certain it really was a choice made of free will."

Sister Benvenuto's brow creased in a frown. "I never realized you'd felt obligated to join us."

"I'm sorry, I didn't mean it the way it sounded." Molly clasped her hands together tighter. "It's just that the order was the only safe home I'd ever known. You and the others offered me a haven and I'll always be appreciative. But it's occurred to me lately that what I believed to be a vocation was instead, a crutch."

Sister Benvenuto gave her another long look. "Yet something else to pray on during these upcoming months of contemplation," she murmured. "If, after that time, you still feel the need to leave, I'll be the first to wish you well and Godspeed."

Six months. It seemed like a lifetime. Then again, Molly knew it was a fair suggestion. Not that she had any intention of changing her mind.

"I suppose I could agree to that."

"Fine." This time the nun's satisfied smile brightened her eyes. "That is all I can ask."

Two days after Molly's meeting with Sister Benvenuto, Lena woke early and spent several enjoyable moments watching Reece sleep. How fortunate she was to have found this wonderful man! Growing up in the revolving door of the Los Angeles County foster care system, she'd never, in a million years, dared dream of such a perfect family. In Reece, she had the most caring, handsome, sexiest husband on earth. And

there wasn't a day that went by she didn't thank God
for Grace.

But Lena wasn't thinking of her daughter at the
moment.

No, the thought filling her mind as she drank in the
sight of him, sprawled on his stomach, was what a
magnificent body her husband had. Sunlight streaming in through the slanted slats of the blinds danced
on his bare skin like laughter. The smooth play of
muscles in his back fascinated her and created a familiar ache deep inside her.

Unable to resist touching him, she reached out and
trailed her fingers down his back, slipping them beneath the sheet below his waist. He murmured something inarticulate, but his steady breathing revealed
he was still asleep.

Enjoying herself immensely, she leaned forward
and pressed her lips against the tanned flesh.

His resultant moan reminded her of a deep-throated
lion's growl. He rolled over, kicking off the sheet. He
was fully, rampantly erect.

Reece woke as she curled her fingers around his
heavy warmth. "I was hoping that was you."

"Who else would be in your bed?" His penis
stirred in her hand as she stroked it from base to
straining tip. "Were you dreaming of some sexy
woman?"

His lips quirked. "You caught me."

"What?" She was about to release him, but he
covered her hand with his and resumed the slow,
stroking caress.

He flashed her a sexy grin she knew would have

the power to thrill her when she was a hundred. "I was dreaming of you."

"Oh." It was her turn to smile. "That's nice."

"It's the truth."

Since he'd never lied to her, Lena believed him. "Happy birthday."

This time his groan had nothing to do with desire. "Boy, do you know how to ruin a great start to a day."

Laughing, she rolled over on top of him. "You're just lucky I'm attracted to older men."

"Older men?" His long fingers wrapped around her waist and lifted her up, then lowered her onto him. Their bodies fit together with a warm silky ease that was more perfect than anything Lena had ever known.

"You *are* thirty-one," she reminded him as she began to move her hips in a slow, sensual rhythm.

"There you go, reminding me again." He cupped both her breasts in his hands. "Guess I'll just have to prove I'm not over the hill." He raised one aching breast to his mouth.

All it took was the tug of his teeth, the wet touch of a tongue against a nipple to make her climax. She cried out as she felt herself shattering like fine crystal shattering at high C.

"That doesn't count," she gasped as she collapsed on top of him after her shimmering implosion. "I had a head start because I was fantasizing about your making love to me while you were still asleep."

He laughed, a rich bold laugh of masculine pleasure that vibrated from deep in his chest. "I'm just getting started."

He deftly rolled them over without slipping out of

her. Indeed, as her pulsating body continued to clutch at him, Lena felt him growing even fuller. Harder.

"Lord, you feel good," he groaned.

Lena shivered as he lifted her hips to meet him. She wanted to tell him that he felt better than good. That he was perfect and she loved him more than life itself and always would.

But instead, as he thrust deeper, touching her in places he knew she liked to be touched, kissing the breath out of her, all she could do was moan and whimper and gasp and beg him never to stop. Which it seemed he had no intention of doing.

Only after she'd lost track of how many times she'd come, did he finally give in to his own explosive release, shouting out her name as he emptied into her, filling her. Loving her.

As they lay entwined, moist bodies cooling in the golden aftermath of pleasure, he kissed her. A kiss so soft and sweet and so different from the earlier passion they'd shared, it seemed a benediction.

"May I ask a favor?"

Lena smiled up at him. "Anything." It was the absolute truth. There was nothing she wouldn't do for this man she adored.

"Can we make this a birthday tradition?"

She laughed, her heart practically bubbling over with joy. "Absolutely."

He grinned back, his eyes shining with shared humor. "Then I guess I won't mind getting older." He ran his hand down her back, from her shoulder to her bottom. "Although this might get a bit dangerous when I'm a hundred."

His words caused a sudden chill to skip up her

spine. There were times when she feared that this glorious oneness she'd found with Reece was too perfect. That it was dangerous for any two people to be so happy. That they were risking the jealousy of the gods. Deciding that she was being ridiculously superstitious, she firmly closed her mind to the icy fear.

"Don't worry." She pressed a kiss against his stubbled cheek that had scraped against every inch of her burning skin like the finest grade of sandpaper. "After you turn ninety, I promise to do all the work."

He pretended to consider that. "You've got yourself a deal, sweetheart."

Later, as she recalled their uninhibited lovemaking in vivid detail, Lena decided that making love to Reece that morning had been like drowning, over and over again, then being reborn in joy. Although their lovemaking was always wonderful, this had been different. She knew she would remember this birthday for the rest of her life.

"How's this, Mommy?"

"What, dear?" Realizing that her mind had been drifting, Lena turned away from the cookbook and observed the flowers Grace had just finished arranging. They'd cut the bright blooms together, Grace selecting the flowers, Lena wielding the scissors.

The tulips had been jammed into the vase. Grace had chosen too many, but Lena had no intention of throwing cold water on her childish enthusiasm. "They're perfect."

"I picked the tulips because you said that they're the happy flower. I thought it would make Daddy not feel so bad."

"Daddy doesn't feel bad," Lena assured her daughter as she took the vase into the dining room and placed it in the center of the table that was already draped in the ivory lace that had belonged to three generations of Longworth brides. Theo had given her the tablecloth to welcome her into the family, and as exquisite as the hand-tatted Irish lace was, it was the meaning of the gift that had meant so much to her.

"I was watching him shave this morning and he said he didn't like birthdays because it meant he was getting old."

"Your daddy says that every year." Lena ran a reassuring hand down the springy jet curls. "But he's not old at all."

"That's what I told him. I told him that Mary Beth thinks he's handsome."

"She does?" Lena glanced down at her daughter with surprise.

Mary Beth Williams, the little girl next door, was only a year older than Grace. Surely they wouldn't have to start worrying about boys so soon?

Grace misunderstood her frown. "Daddy *is* handsome. You tell him that all the time."

"That's true. I just didn't realize Mary Beth would have noticed."

Grace shrugged. "Mary Beth is boy-crazy. She kissed Jimmy Young last week on the playground." She giggled. "He was wiping his mouth all day."

Dear Lord, Reece would undoubtedly want to lock his little girl in a closet until *her* thirty-first birthday. Not that it was such a bad idea, Lena considered as she imagined some pimply faced lothario trying to talk Grace into the back seat of his car.

Lena returned to the kitchen a bit shaken by the conversation, and was trying to decide whether or not she should have a little talk with Mrs. Williams, when she realized she was missing a vital ingredient for tonight's birthday celebration.

"Damn."

Grace, who'd returned to coloring at the kitchen table, looked up. "What's wrong, Mommy?"

"I forgot to buy the buttermilk for your daddy's cake." German chocolate was Reece's favorite and Lena knew he'd be expecting it. "We'll have to run to the store."

"Maybe we can get Daddy a balloon while we're there," Grace suggested. "In case the tulips don't make him smile."

Lena's irritation eased as she gazed down into her daughter's beautiful, earnest face. "Want to know a secret?"

"What?"

"Daddy doesn't need tulips or balloons to make him smile. All he has to do is look at you." Something moved over her heart, a cold shadow of premonition, much like this morning's chill, that shook her to the bone. She knelt down and gathered her daughter into her arms, holding her close.

Please God, she prayed, as she did so often, *don't let anything ever happen to this perfect miracle.*

"Mommy?" Grace was wiggling. "You're hurting me."

Realizing that she was practically crushing her daughter, Lena loosened her hold. "Sorry, sweetie." Her voice was bright, her smile feigned. "Sometimes Mommy forgets how strong she is."

She laughed, trying to make a joke out of what had been a moment of icy fear. Unfortunately not the first. Ever since Theo's wedding, when she'd seen the unmasked yearning on Molly's face when she'd looked at Grace, Lena's fears about losing her daughter had returned to haunt her.

Grace looked up at her. "You look like you need tulips, too, Mommy."

This time Lena's laughter was genuine. "You may be right, darling. When we get home, maybe we'll just pick some more." She stood up and clapped her hands. "Now, run get your shoes so we can get back to creating the best birthday party your daddy's ever had."

As she watched her daughter run from the room, Lena reminded herself that such grim thoughts were foolish. They were nothing more than a psychological fear left over from having lost her parents—and her baby sister—at such a tender age.

Just because you loved someone didn't mean you were going to lose them, she reminded herself. She'd never been happier than she'd been these past years with Grace and Reece. There was no way she was going to let old knee-jerk feelings take hold of her.

Her spirits renewed, Lena strapped her daughter into the passenger seat, then backed the family minivan—that had replaced the Jaguar—out of the garage.

Chapter Fifteen

As Lena maneuvered the minivan around the curves leading down from the cliffside home, her mind was on tonight's party. Did Reece have any idea? She'd only let Grace in on the preparations a few days ago, and except for a few suspicious giggles, she didn't think her daughter had let the cat out of the bag.

No, she decided, he didn't know.

Would he be upset when he found out? After all, he had insisted that he wanted to ignore the event. As if thirty-one was over the hill. He'd certainly proved this morning that wasn't the case. Just remembering all the things he'd done to her, all the things they'd done to each other, warmed her blood and turned her cheeks red.

Lena laughed. Imagine, an old married woman—a mother, for heaven's sake—blushing.

She turned a corner and was treated to a dazzling view of the sun-gilded ocean. A plane, taking off from LAX, left a puffy white vapor cloud in the clear blue sky. The sight of the jetliner caused a faint stirring of memory. Then suddenly, Lena understood all too well why her husband was reluctant to celebrate his thirty-first birthday.

The senior Reece Longworth had been only thirty when he'd died, along with Reece's mother, in that plane crash when Reece was only a child. Obviously he was having problems with the fact that today he'd outlived his own father.

"I should have figured it out." She hit the steering wheel, frustrated with herself. "I'll make it up to him," she vowed. "After the party."

Her thoughts focused on what she could do to ease this difficult time for Reece, she didn't notice the approaching car until it had crossed the center line.

Lena had no time to react. There was the sickening sound of metal slamming into metal, glass shattering.

And then...nothing.

It was turning out to be just another typical day in the ER. There were the usual drunks, crackheads, minor traumas, shooting victims, sprained joints, lacerations and homeless, but nothing to really get the blood pumping. By early afternoon, the patient flow had dwindled to a trickle.

Although Reece had insisted he didn't want anyone to make a big deal about his birthday, he was not overly surprised when he was called into the doctors' lounge near the end of his shift for a consult with the senior resident and discovered all the trappings of a party about to happen.

Latex gloves filled with helium bounced against the ceiling, he was hit with a cloud of metallic confetti he knew he'd be brushing out of his hair for weeks, and in the center of the table was a cake in the shape of a woman's torso, the white frosting hospital gown open to reveal rounded breasts topped with maraschino cherry nipples and a skimpy, coconut G-string.

"It's a good thing Lena's not here," he said with a grin. "Because I'd hate to try to explain this to my wife."

"Who do you think found the dirty cake baker in the first place?" Yolanda challenged, drawing more laughter.

Reece looked at the nurse who'd been off the schedule today. "I assume there's a reason you're dressed up like Big Bird."

"Why, Dr. Reece," she drawled, looking out through the eye holes in the oversize hood covered with bright yellow feathers, "surely the memo about the hospital blood drive didn't escape your attention?"

"I seem to remember reading something about it." Since becoming attending physician three months earlier, Reece spent his days dodging a virtual blizzard of memos from the suits upstairs in Administration. He was vastly grateful the powers that be hadn't yet mastered the intricacies of e-mail.

"Well, I've been out drumming up business." She flapped her wings. "Don't be a chicken." She squawked. "Donate blood."

Even as Reece joined in the laughter, he thought about the dedication it took for a single working mother to spend her day off making a fool of herself in order to save lives. He was suddenly deeply moved. By Yolanda's sacrifice, which she'd never consider extraordinary, and the party.

"There's not a service at any hospital in the state as special as Mercy Sam's ER team," he said with feeling. "I really love you guys."

A sudden silence fell over the room as everyone seemed embarrassed by his emotional response. Reece was wishing he'd just kept his mouth shut when Yolanda came to his rescue.

"Why, Dr. Longworth, we all love you, too," she said. Knowing how to milk a performance, she gathered him up in her yellow wings and with her beak, gave him a big peck right on the mouth.

Everyone roared with laughter, the moment passed and the party began.

Reece had just cut into the cake when the trauma radio squawked from the other room. "Squad 64, Code Three, auto accident, severe head trauma, full arrest. Female patient comatose, blood pressure sixty, two large-bore needles going full speed, clean abdominal tap. ETA two minutes."

The trauma team began to assemble. The junior resident donned a lead jacket to protect against the X rays he'd be taking. The senior resident prepared the ventilator. Reece, as attending physician, stood by to ensure that everything was done according to procedure. In a teaching hospital, the adage was Watch A Procedure, Do A Procedure, Teach A Procedure.

And, although it wasn't as simple as that, he was of the belief that the only way to learn was by doing. Which was why he allowed his residents more practical experience than they'd get at some hospitals. At least when a doctor left Mercy Sam, he'd be prepared to tackle real emergencies, not just textbook cases.

He glanced up at the clock on the wall and sighed, wishing the hapless victim had waited another fifteen minutes to have her accident. No telling how late he'd be now. Which would, of course, screw up the surprise party Lena had planned for him at home. He smiled inwardly, thinking back on all the whispering that had been going on between his wife and daughter the past few days.

With any luck, the incoming accident case would be cut-and-dried. They'd either stabilize the patient, then send her up to surgery or the neurological ICU, or, she'd flatline and he could go home on time.

Reece was wondering if he should have the clerk call Lena and warn her that he might be late, when the ambulance suddenly pulled to a stop, the pneumatic doors hissed open and the paramedics ran into the ER with a gurney, one holding the IV bags in the air, another pumping away at the patient's heart. She was, Reece noted, already on a ventilator.

They rushed her into trauma room A. Not wanting to crowd the team, Reece stood in the doorway, watching as they performed as they'd been trained.

"Christ," the senior resident said, "the back of her head is nothing but a spongy mass." That explained the blood all over her head and face, Reece decided. The blood that continued to flow, despite the large bandage the paramedics had wrapped around her crushed skull.

"Pupils fixed and dilated," the resident called out. "Skull unstable." He lifted the supine body up and reached a gloved hand behind her. "I can feel the bone fragments."

While more IVs were begun and blood started, a nurse took a towel and wiped her face. "Facial fractures on the right cheekbone," the resident said as he continued his examination.

"Oh, my God," the nurse suddenly gasped.

"What?" the senior resident asked, obviously irritated by her outburst.

"What?" Reece demanded when she didn't immediately answer. He entered the room, then stopped in disbelief as he viewed the patient on the gurney.

"No." He shook his head. "It can't be." Looking at how beautifully serene his wife looked in the midst of all the turmoil, Reece told himself that this had to be a mistake. She couldn't be hurt. Not really.

"What the hell?" the senior resident demanded.

"It's Lena," the nurse said in a voice that sounded like a robot.

"Lena?" The young doctor looked down at his patient, as if seeing her as a human being for the first time. "Christ."

Later, looking back on this, it seemed to Reece that everyone in the room froze, presenting a nightmarish tableau of the most horrifying moment of his life. Time seemed to have frozen, as well.

And then, suddenly, the EEG monitor screeched.

"She's crashing!" While the first-year resident began pumping away at her chest, the senior resident prepared the paddles.

"No!" There was a brief struggle as Reece grabbed them away.

"Goddamn it, Reece," the younger man yelled, heedless of rank, "you shouldn't even be in here."

"She's my wife." He turned toward the nurse, barking out the setting. "I'm not going to let her die... One-fifty... Clear!"

The first-year resident backed away to avoid getting shocked. Lena's body was literally lifted off the table.

Nothing.

"Again," Reece barked. "Clear!"

It took two more tries. After her heart was successfully restarted, they began pumping blood in as fast as they could, even as it poured out of the massive wound in her head.

Her heart stopped again. And again. But Reece refused to give up as he dragged his wife back and forth along that ragged razor's edge between life and death. With each shock, the smell of burning flesh increased.

"This is crazy," the resident complained after they'd been at it for an hour, twice the normal length of time for a Code Blue.

"Shut up," Yolanda, who'd changed from her Big Bird outfit into scrubs—now soaked with blood—shouted into his face. Reece, concentrating on keeping Lena alive, didn't notice.

"You realize," Joe said at the end of another grueling day after Molly had returned to the reservation clinic, "we're going to have to talk about it."

"There's nothing to talk about."

"Excuse me for arguing with you, Sister Molly," he corrected, an edge of sarcasm she'd never heard in his voice before sharpening his tone, "but I don't consider falling in love nothing."

"I'm sorry." Unreasonably nervous, she began straightening the small cabinet, lining up the jars of tongue depressors, cotton balls, a box of latex surgical gloves. "You're right, of course. It's just that I don't know what to say."

"How about we just agree to forget what happened? And start over again?"

"I'm not certain that's possible."

"Okay. Then how about we just talk about the usual things people talk about when one of them has humiliated himself and the other one's feeling vastly uncomfortable within a six-foot radius of such an idiot."

She couldn't help smiling, just a little, at that. "You're not an idiot."

"True. The idiots are all the men who let you get away long enough to run off to the convent in the first place."

"Joe..."

"I'm sorry," he said again, responding to her soft warning. "But I have to admit, it's been driving me crazy, wondering how a woman like you ended up a nun."

"A woman like me?"

"I'd cite your attributes again, beginning with your naturally passionate nature, but I believe you've already put them in the off-limits category.

"I really would like to know about you, Molly. What kind of little girl you were, where you grew up, what your favorite subjects in school were, all those normal conversational, getting-to-know-you kinds of things.''

"Like men and women discuss on dates?" Her renewed attack of nerves at the mention of her childhood made her tone sharp.

"No." He'd returned to his usual calm, reassuring demeanor. "Like two friends."

Molly had to ask. "Will that be enough for you? That we stay only friends? And not lovers?"

"I don't know," he answered honestly. "But we'll never know if we don't try. And I do know that there's no way we're going to be able to work together if we don't come to grips with this, Molly. Running away from a problem only puts off the inevitable."

Molly marveled at the way Joe had of unconsciously hitting all her hot buttons, forcing her to take a long hard look at herself. She'd obviously run away after Grace was born, when she'd found watching her daughter and sister beginning to bond too painful. Had she also run away from her forbidden feelings for Reece?

Molly sighed. "It's a long story."

"I'm not going anywhere."

Which was how they ended up back in her motor home, alone together once again. Wisely forgoing any more alcohol, Molly made a pot of coffee and they sat down to talk.

She was surprised that despite her initial reluctance, the words began to come easily, and before she knew it, she'd told him about her parents and that horrible Christmas when she, Lena and Tessa had been orphaned.

"So you never saw Tessa again after that night?" he asked.

She shook her head. It was one of the major sorrows of her life.

"Ever think to look for her?"

"Of course." Molly took a sip of lukewarm coffee. "I even tried once, a few months before my Profession Day, but the adoption records were sealed."

"There are ways of getting around that these days."

"I know. But she was too young to know what went on in that house, Joe. I'm not certain the woman she'd have become by now needs anything triggering possibly deep-seated memories."

Although he didn't completely agree, Joe was in no mood to argue. In truth, after his outrageous display of raging hormones, he'd feared when she drove off to her meeting with Sister Benvenuto in Flagstaff that he'd never see Molly again. Encouraged by her willingness to be open with him now, he was not about to do anything to screw things up.

"So," he said, folding his fingers—which were itching to touch her—behind his head, "you and Lena ended up in the foster-care system. How in the world did you get from there to the convent?"

"I'd just turned fifteen." Strange how it seemed like yesterday, she thought as she stared deep into the depths of her milk-lightened coffee. "I'd been placed with a Catholic family who had five kids of their own. The oldest son was a senior in high school and a star athlete. He was quarterback of the football team, star center for the basketball team—"

"Pitcher for the baseball team," Joe broke in dryly,

knowing the type. He'd always been too busy working after school, saving for college and later cracking the books to keep his grades up in med school to go out for the sports that seemed to attract all the prettiest girls.

"First baseman," Molly corrected with a faint smile. "Needless to say I had a major crush on him. His name was—" she paused, stunned when she drew a blank. "I can't remember."

"It doesn't matter. He's obviously bald with a beer gut and spends his weekends lying on the couch watching ESPN, bossing the little woman around while reliving his old high school glory days in his mind."

"You paint such an attractive picture. If I didn't know better, I'd think you were jealous of an eighteen-year-old from my past."

"You bet I am. I'm jealous of any guy you ever looked at twice," Joe said without rancor. "So, did the jock return your interest?"

"I didn't think so, at first. But apparently he'd noticed me mooning over him, which wasn't all that surprising, considering the fact that I wasn't at all subtle about my girlish crush. Anyway, one night, after I'd been living in the house about three months, he slipped into my room after everyone had gone to sleep. I was dreaming of him, as I did every night..." Her voice drifted off as she recalled Joe's prediction of sexual dreams.

"Don't stop now," he drawled. "Not when it's just getting interesting."

Once again she felt the color rise in her cheeks. "I was dreaming that he was kissing me. Holding me.

Then, when his hand touched my breasts, I realized that I wasn't dreaming at all.'' She sighed. ''Before I could kiss him back, the door suddenly opened and the light came on and his parents were yelling about the slut of a seductress who was trying to ruin their perfect son's life.

''Since I already had a reputation for being difficult, the next day I was shipped off to the Good Shepherd Home for Girls. Wayward girls.''

''That little nighttime petting session doesn't sound very wayward. In fact, it sounds downright normal.''

''I realize that now. However, at the time, I was convinced I was headed straight to hell.'' Molly thought of all the days she'd spent kneeling in the school chapel doing penance for her carnal sin. ''Naturally, that was enough to turn me off romantic relationships.''

''You mean you gave up boys? Entirely?''

The idea was preposterous. Like so many other teenagers, Joe had experienced a similar situation himself. While parked in a car on a Long Island beach late one night, he'd been discovering the delights to be found in the pillowy softness of Teresa Magionne's lushly feminine body when they were caught by a patrolling cop. As humiliating as it was to have been literally caught with his pants down, Joe had never considered joining an order of Trappist monks.

''That was my only sexual encounter,'' she admitted. ''Until that night—''

''That doesn't count.'' His tone was rough and firm. His expression could have been carved from the red rocks that made Arizona so scenic. Then, as Molly watched, it softened.

"Has it ever occurred to you, Molly," he said gently, "that your only two sexual experiences have had either a forbidden or painful aspect about them?"

"I've never thought about it that way," she admitted. But, of course, once again, he was right. Even her feelings for Reece...

Before Joe could respond, the cellular phone in the motor home rang. A frisson of fear skimmed up Molly's spine. Not many people knew this number. Only Sister Benvenuto, the coordinator of the mobile health services program and her family.

Her mind immediately flashed to her daughter. If anything had happened to Grace... *Please,* she prayed, *let it be work.*

"Hello?"

"Molly?" Theo's voice sounded strange. Almost as if she'd been crying. "Thank God I got you."

Later, when Molly tried to reconstruct the conversation she realized that only bits and pieces of it had sunk in. She'd been too stunned. And terrified.

"I'll be there as soon as I can," she heard herself saying, her voice flat with shock. She hung up the receiver, but continued to stare down at it, wondering if the call had been real.

Perhaps she was merely suffering another nightmare. As she had so often in the past.

"Molly?" The sharp male voice filtered through the shock reverberating through her mind, proving that it was no nightmare. "What the hell is wrong?"

She turned toward him slowly. Her eyes were vague and unseeing. "I have to go." She glanced around, as if having no idea how to accomplish that feat.

"Go where? Back to Los Angeles?"

"Yes." Her skin had turned to ice. Joe began rubbing her arms to stimulate circulation. Molly didn't seem to notice. "There's been an accident... Oh, God."

As her uncharacteristically frail voice drifted off, Joe realized she'd be leaving him again. "Don't worry." In an attempt to comfort, rather than arouse, he drew her to him. "I'll take care of everything."

The team finally got Lena stable enough to survive a CT scan. They wheeled her out of the trauma room, leaving behind a floor strewn with needle caps, IV bag wrappers, gauze pads and pools of blood. The room, which had been enveloped in the controlled chaos of a Code was suddenly, eerily silent.

"Shit," Yolanda said as she stripped off her bloody gloves and dropped them uncaringly onto the floor with the rest of the mess. "Did anyone think to ask those paramedics if she was alone in the car?"

Joe proved to be as good as his word. A mere two hours after Molly received the phone call from Theo, she was waiting in the gate to board a commuter plane headed for Flagstaff. From there she'd fly to Phoenix, and catch a connecting flight to Los Angeles.

Although Molly had been holding his hand since their arrival at the small remote air terminal, Joe suspected she was unaware of his presence. He guessed that what slender part of her mind was still managing to function, was focused solely on her sister.

She was so deep in thought, Molly failed to hear the boarding announcement come over the loudspeaker.

He touched his fingers to her cheek. "It's time."

She blinked, then took a deep breath. Then hugged him. "I don't know how to thank you." She knew there was no way she would have been able to take care of the details of her travel plans herself.

"You don't have to thank me, Molly. That's what friends are for."

Thinking again how much this kind, caring man reminded her of Reece, Molly threw her arms around him. "I'll call you as soon as I know anything."

He hugged her back and felt guilty when his body responded as it always seemed to do when Molly was in the vicinity. His reaction might be inappropriate, but he could no more prevent himself from becoming aroused than he could stop the sun from rising over the vast red earth each morning.

Unaware of his thoughts, Molly kissed him on the cheek, then boarded the small jet, where she tried to pray. Unfortunately, the words wouldn't come.

Instead, images of her sister lying in the tangled mass of steel that had been Lena's beloved new minivan, flashed in Molly's dazed mind like scenes from some late-night horror movie.

Chapter Sixteen

By the time Molly arrived at Mercy Sam, Lena had been moved to the neurological intensive-care unit. Yolanda was waiting for her, and although Molly was desperate to see her sister, the nurse insisted she first talk with the neurosurgeon.

"The CT scan shows no brain activity," Dr. James Parker told Molly, speaking to her more like to a nurse than to a concerned relative. "Which confirmed our worst suspicions. But Reece refused to accept that diagnosis and insisted she'd be all right if we relieved the pressure on her brain. So we did."

Molly closed her eyes, knowing that the procedure meant inserting a tube into the ventricle of her sister's brain.

"And?" she asked weakly, reaching out to grasp the arm of a nearby chair when her legs began to feel a bit wobbly. Yolanda, who never missed a thing, pushed the chair over so Molly could lower herself into it.

"Instead of a clear cerebrospinal fluid, we got chunks of brain," he said flatly. Brutally. "If I may be frank, given the fact that you've been an ER nurse yourself, at this point diagnosing death is only a formality."

His words hit home. Hard. Stars began to dance in front of Molly's eyes like fireflies.

Then everything went black.

Reece sat beside his wife, holding her hand. "Hey, sweetheart," he coaxed, "don't you think it's time you woke up? We've got a surprise party to go to."

He smoothed his hand over the bandage on her head, wishing they hadn't had to cut her hair. Lena had never liked short hair, and although he knew it was horribly chauvinistic, Reece had always been glad that she'd never wanted to cut those long waves that felt so good draped across his chest. Had it been only this morning they'd driven each other crazy making love? It seemed a lifetime ago.

"You're going to be madder than hell when you find out what we did." He traced his fingers over her lips. "But don't worry, honey, it'll grow back. Just think of it as a really bad hair day."

He kept his voice upbeat and reassuring. Despite the negative diagnosis from James Parker, Reece knew Lena could hear him, and he didn't want her to be afraid or depressed. She had to realize that she was going to make it. That they would have years and years of love and laughter yet together.

"You don't have to worry about Grace. Theo's taking great care of her." He thanked God that Theo had shown up at the house just as Lena had been leaving, saving Grace from being in the minivan. "She's coloring me another birthday card and is impatient for her mommy to get home so we can get on with the festivities."

He leaned down and touched his mouth to her cool dry lips in a brief kiss meant to reassure them both.

Standing in the doorway, observing the intimate kiss, Molly felt as if her heart would shatter into a million pieces. Her initial relief at learning Grace had escaped the tragic accident had been offset by her sister's critical injuries.

Outside the room, the stark fluorescent lights in the hallway created the illusion of day. Inside, Reece had obviously turned them down to spare his wife the harsh, shadowless glare. Not that Lena would notice, Molly thought miserably.

Although her sister's head was wrapped in a bandage, the doctor had assured Molly that her sister's body, and all her internal organs, had remained undamaged.

Looking at her lying on the narrow criblike bed reminded Molly of an ancient sarcophagus she'd once seen in a cathedral crypt in Rome. On the lid of the marble coffin had been carved the likeness of the young princess who lay within. Her pale skin was unmarred, her features unscarred by pain or worry. Which was exactly how Lena looked.

"Oh, Reece."

He turned. "You came." His grim parody of a welcoming smile did not reach his unnervingly blank eyes.

"Of course." Molly crossed the room, knelt down

in front of Reece and gathered him in her arms. "How could I not?"

He didn't hug her back. His arms hung limply at his sides. "She's going to be all right." Reece turned back to his wife. In her presence, they kept their voices soft, respectful. He reached out and laced his fingers with Lena's pale slender ones. "We've seen this a thousand times before, a patient in a coma who suddenly makes a miraculous recovery."

"It does happen." It was true she'd witnessed such events. But certainly not as frequently as he was suggesting.

"And you're in the miracle business." He flashed her another of those strange horror-movie smiles. "You can pray for her. God's bound to listen to Saint Molly."

Molly decided there was nothing to be gained in pointing out, as she always used to, that she was far from being a saint. "I've been praying since Theo first called with the news."

"See." He lifted Lena's hand to his lips. "Did you hear that, darling? Molly's been praying for you. We've got it made in the shade."

Dr. Parker had been right. After she'd revived from her embarrassing faint, he had warned her that Reece had removed himself from any realm of medical reality. After a consultation with Alan Bernstein, they'd come to the conclusion that it wouldn't hurt to allow him his little fantasy, for a time, if it helped ease the pain.

"But," the neurosurgeon had warned Molly, "we can't wait forever. The harvest coordinator's already been notified. Your sister's driver's license stated she was an organ donor," he'd added somewhat defensively when Molly had given him a sharp look.

She'd sighed at the time, reminding herself not to take Lena's tragedy out on him. After all, hadn't she been forced to ask grieving families for transplant permission more times than she could count? Now as she sat beside her silent sister she thought about how careful Lena had been about details like signing the human tissue consent section on her license, about how she'd long ago planned her own funeral in detail because she'd been so afraid of dying young....

Molly felt the sting of salty tears at the back of her lids but willed them away. "Why don't you go get something to eat?" she suggested in that same hushed tone they'd been using. Except when Reece spoke to Lena. Then, his false enthusiasm reminded her of a television weatherman. "I'll stay with her." Expecting resistance, Molly was surprised when Reece didn't argue.

"All right," he said. "If you don't mind."

"Not at all."

He paused, looking down at Lena. An expression of grim determination moved across his face like a sudden storm cloud. "I won't be long."

"Take your time." She forced a smile she feared was as horribly fake as his had been. "We'll be fine."

Reece left the room, taking the elevator down to the first floor. But instead of going to the cafeteria, he walked out the front door to where his car was parked in the staff parking lot.

He was on his way to Cedars-Sinai Hospital, where

he'd learned they'd taken the drunk driver who'd hit Lena's minivan head-on.

Reece had a desperate need to see this evil man who had, in that single horrible moment, tried to destroy his family.

He was going to look him right in the face. He was going to make certain the bastard knew exactly what he'd done.

And then he was going to kill him.

"When's Mommy going to be home?"

Theo exchanged a quick look with her husband. "We don't know, darling."

"We told you," Alex reminded Grace gently, "your mommy had an accident. She's in the hospital."

"I know that. But Daddy's taking care of her, right?"

"Right," the two adults confirmed in unison.

The little girl took another crayon from the box and began filling in a picture of Monument Valley in the coloring book her aunt Molly had brought her from Arizona. "Then Mommy will get better." She concentrated on filling in the towering red rocks. Sometimes it was very hard to stay inside the lines. "Because Daddy's the best doctor ever."

Alex and Theo exchanged another worried look. Then Theo turned away and began picking the dead leaves off a pothos plant hanging in front of the picture window; she was trying to keep Lena's daughter from seeing the sheen of tears in her eyes.

From the reports they'd received from Yolanda, despite Reece's unwavering optimism, she knew all they could do now was wait for the inevitable.

As heartsick as she was over Lena, Theo couldn't help worrying about Molly's reaction to all this. She'd received some unnerving vibes when Grace's birth mother had visited for the wedding. If Molly were to try to claim her daughter...

No, Theo decided, she was creating problems where none existed. There was no way Molly could consider raising Grace in that motor home out in the middle of an Indian reservation.

Somehow, this horrible time would pass. Somehow, Reece and Grace would find the strength to get on with their lives. But in the meantime, Theo dreaded the moment when the adults who loved her to distraction would have to shatter a little girl's safe, comfortable existence.

As Alex watched Grace laboring intently over her drawing, he was reminded of another little dark-haired girl, not so much older, who had struggled with the same fierce determination to protect her little sisters. First from their brutal, alcoholic father, then from the system.

He knew, from their many discussions over the years, that deep down inside, Molly believed she'd failed Lena and Tessa. She was, of course, mistaken, but Alex had never been able to convince her that her unwavering support may have been the one thing that had kept Lena from going completely over the edge during those early rocky years. Molly had been the single fixed star in Lena's firmament. These past years that role had been taken over by Reece, but he knew, without a doubt, that Lena gave full credit to her older sister for having saved her life innumerable times.

Alex thought about the vibrant young wife and mother lying in that hospital bed, now kept alive only by the intrusion of medical machinery, and he realized that it would inevitably fall to Molly to break the news of her mother's death to Grace.

It wasn't fair. Molly had already overcome so damn much. It wasn't right that she'd have to take responsibility yet again. But he knew she'd have it no other way. He also knew, from all the years on the force, that life wasn't always fair.

As he'd expected, Reece encountered no difficulty discovering the whereabouts of the drunk driver. As soon as he flashed his Mercy Sam ID card at the clerk on duty, she began tapping away on her computer keyboard, and presto, the name of the patient and room number flashed on the screen. He didn't even have to use his cover story about being called in for a consult by the patient's personal physician.

He exited the elevator and was prepared to show his ID again. But it didn't prove necessary. The nurses at the desk were too busy charting to pay any attention to him. Obviously, in these lofty environs, security issues weren't as vital as they were in Mercy Sam's neighborhood.

Cedars-Sinai was the hospital of choice for the Los Angeles elite—caretaker to the stars. Reece was not surprised to discover that the man—who he'd learned from one of the paramedics, was a hotshot criminal defense attorney with penthouse law offices at Century City—had a private room.

His eyes were closed, but his rough, uneven snores revealed that he was not unconscious, but merely sleeping off the effects of too-much alcohol. A system of pulleys had been erected over the bed; the man's left leg was suspended in traction. From what Reece could see without looking at the chart, the broken leg was the only sign of injury.

He took the vial from his jacket pocket. He'd stolen the procaine, a local anesthetic, from the ER drug cabinet while Lena had been undergoing her CT scan. The plan, when he'd first come up with it, had seemed so simple. But now, as he looked down at this snoring drunk, Reece no longer felt rage. What he felt was empty.

Reece told himself that it didn't matter. The man deserved to die. An eye for an eye. A life for a life. His fingers tightened around the vial as he realized this was the first time he'd allowed himself to think that Lena might not survive.

Determined to keep this criminal from ever driving drunk again, Reece pulled the syringe and twenty-five gauge needle from his pocket. He removed the cap from the needle and drew the clear liquid into the syringe, then walked over to the bed, his fingers holding onto the deadly dose with a vise grip.

He took hold of the man's limp wrist and turned the arm to expose the vein. At the same time, he heard the soft footfalls of rubber-soled shoes pause in the doorway.

"Can I help you, Doctor?" the female voice asked.

He turned and forced an everything's-just-fine-and-dandy expression onto his face. "I didn't want to bother you, Nurse. I was asked for a consult, and—"

"It figures he'd get top-notch care."

Something in her voice alerted him. "Isn't that what Cedars is acclaimed for?"

"Of course. It's just sometimes I wish our mortality rate was a bit higher." She glared down at the man who was snoring away. "In this case, a lot higher." She glanced over at Reece as if expecting a reprimand. "I realize that doesn't exactly sound like Florence Nightingale, but I lost a daughter to a drunk driver five years ago."

"I'm sorry." Reece thought how, if Theo hadn't shown up when she had, Grace would have been in the van with Lena.

"It was prom night. She and her boyfriend were driving home. The woman never stopped, but fortunately there were witnesses. When the police showed up at her house to arrest her hours later, her alcohol level was still above the legal limit.

"Losing a child is the worst thing that can happen to a parent," she said. "My husband couldn't take it. He kept wanting to kill the woman. He even bought a gun and kept it loaded, but fortunately, I suppose, he never had the nerve to use it. But our marriage disintegrated under the stress. He lives in Ohio now. With a new wife. She's pregnant."

"I'm sorry," Reece said again. The words seemed so horribly inadequate.

"Like I said, it was five years ago. But I still can't bring myself to treat a bastard like that."

When Reece didn't immediately respond, she took another deep breath. "I'm sorry, Doctor. I didn't mean to dump on you. My only excuse is that being a survivor of a violent death is like a boil you think

has healed, and suddenly, something triggers a rein-
fection and all that pus just pours out.''

Reece realized she was forecasting his life. Not just
his future, but Grace's, as well. And even if Molly
was able to pray up a miracle, it would be a very long
time before Lena would be ready to return home and
pick up her life as they all knew it. Their daughter
would need him to be strong. How much help could
he be in prison?

"There's no reason to apologize. Your daughter
was a very fortunate girl to have you for a mother.
And your husband was lucky, as well. Even if he
didn't know it."

She smiled at that, a quick pleased smile that banished the remnants of cold anger from her expression.
"His loss," she agreed as she left the room.

Reece stood beside the bed, staring down at the
man for a long silent time. Then made his decision.

It was not easy, but he managed to rouse the sleeping drunk. "What d'ya want?" the man grumbled,
his words slurred.

"I want you to wake up."

"Go 'way, Doc." He tried to roll over and found
his movement stifled by the leg pulleys. "What the
hell?"

"Look at me." Reece shook him by the shoulder.

Bleary eyes stared up at him.

"See this needle?"

The man nodded. "Good. I could use a little shot
of painkiller, Doc."

"This isn't painkiller. Oh, I suppose in a way you
could consider it that, since believe me, it'll stop your
pain." He proceeded, on a brisk, no-nonsense tone to

describe exactly what would happen to the man before death. "You're lucky I'm going to inject it," he said. "Otherwise, even with all the booze in your system, it could take a lot longer to work. You'd suffer dizziness, cyanosis, tremors, convulsions, bronchial spasm.

"But in your case, the reaction will be immediate. As soon as I inject this procaine into your vein, you'll go into immediate cardiac arrest.

"Then, that's that." He picked up the limp arm and touched the tip of the needle to the thin blue line at the inner bend of the elbow. "You're finished. Flatlined."

"What the hell?" The man tried to jerk his arm away. "Who are you? What the hell do you think you're doing?"

Even without the icy rage flowing through his veins, Reece would have been stronger. His fingers tightened around the man's arm. He pricked the skin. Both men watched the faint red dot of blood rise beneath the shiny sharpened steel.

"You were driving drunk." Reece's fingers were a tourniquet, causing blood to begin to trickle down the bare arm. "You crossed the center line and ran into my wife's minivan."

He squeezed harder. The trickle became a flow. "Do you understand what I'm saying?"

The man's eyes were round with panic. "I don't unnerstand anything."

The needle tip was sparkling with deadly sharpness. All it would take was a quick spearing flick for revenge to be delivered. But even as Reece imagined driving the needle deep into the vein, tearing away at flesh and muscle, breaking into the bone, he knew he couldn't do it.

For years he had fought the dark angel, Death. Ultimately, of course, Death won, but Reece had sworn a sacred oath to put off that victory for as long as possible. He could not join forces now.

He recapped the needle and returned the syringe to his pocket. "This is your lucky day," he told the gray-faced man. "I'm going to let you live."

Then he took out his billfold and retrieved a snapshot of Lena he'd taken during their Maui honeymoon. She was standing up to her knees in an unbelievably blue lagoon, her hair gleaming like copper in the bright Hawaiian sun. She was laughing, blissfully unaware that only a few years later her life would be cut tragically short by this drunken killer.

"This is my wife." He placed the picture on the man's chest. "Her name is Lena." He took another photo. This one depicted Grace at Disneyland, enthusiastically hugging Goofy. "This is our daughter, Grace. The little girl who's going to grow up without her mother."

He placed this photo beside the first. "I hope you live a very long time, you worthless son of a bitch. And I hope, for every day of your miserable useless life, you're haunted by these faces."

That said, he left the room. And the hospital.

Molly had never felt so helpless or so useless as she sat beside Lena, holding her hand. Dr. Parker had been kind, but brutal in his assessment. There was nothing medically that could be done. Which left Molly to pray for a miracle as the ventilator went rhythmically up and down, breathing for her sister who could no longer breathe for herself.

From time to time she couldn't resist pinching her sister's limp arm, which had been tanned to a golden California Girl hue when Molly had arrived for Alex and Theo's wedding, but now resembled porcelain. Had the wedding been only a couple of weeks ago? It seemed an eternity.

She tried talking to her sister and singing old familiar lullabies that dated back from their childhood days when a terrified Lena would crawl into Molly's bed, seeking shelter from their father's alcoholic rampages.

But there was no response. Lena's pupils remained dilated, her lungs lifting and falling in response to the respirator. The only interruption was when one of the ICU nurses would briefly disconnect Lena from the machine to suction clean the tubes. The squat, multi-dialed aluminum-and-plastic box was infinitely, obscenely patient.

Unfortunately, the harvest team was less so. Dr. Parker had contacted the transplant donor network as soon as brain death had been verified. When they entered the room to rate her body for the harvest of usable—healthy—parts, Molly was immensely grateful that Reece was not there to witness the necessary, but ghoulish procedure.

Which brought to mind another concern. Where was he? Yolanda had filled Molly in on the details, so far as anyone knew about the accident. Including the fact that the driver of the other car, suspected to have been drunk, had been taken to Cedars-Sinai. Surely, Molly tried to assure herself as the day dragged on and there was still no sign of Reece, he wouldn't try to take revenge into his own hands?

"If he's anywhere in the hospital, he isn't answering his pages," Yolanda told Molly when she shared her fears. "But I think you're overreacting. He adores Lena, but there's no way he'd do anything that would cause Grace to lose her father as well as her mother."

"It's not always possible to predict what people will do in times of stress," Molly reminded her.

"True. But Reece doesn't have it in him to kill anyone. No matter how much such an act would be justified." Yolanda shook her head as she looked down at the woman who, were it not for the machines and tubing, could have been merely sleeping.

"The word's gotten out. Security had to turn away some of those slimeball tabloid reporters. Turns out the guy driving the car was some hotshot legal eagle. Karin, at Admissions, said one of them told her he was the same guy who got that action hero hunk an acquittal in that drunk-driving manslaughter case a few years ago."

Molly remembered the case. As well she should, since she was one of the medical team who'd tried to save the eleven-year-old Little League player who'd been dragged two hundred yards beneath the bumper of the actor's Mercedes convertible. She also recalled that Reece had been the doctor on duty when the fatally broken child had been brought into the ER.

"If Reece realizes that—"

"You don't have to worry," a deep voice interrupted from the doorway. "I didn't do it." Reece took the syringe from his pocket and held it out to Yolanda. "I think you'll find the med cabinet short one vial of procaine. I must have slipped it into my pocket earlier when I was treating that jogger with the blown knee, then forgot about it.''

Yolanda didn't so much as blink at the outrageous lie. "I'll see it's accounted for," she replied smoothly.

"How is she?" Reece asked Molly when they were alone again.

At this moment, looking up at his haggard face, Molly didn't know who she felt sorrier for. At least, if James Parker could be believed, Lena was beyond pain.

"Nothing's changed."

He didn't immediately respond. Instead, he opened a nearby cupboard and took out a blanket. "She gets cold feet," he explained. "I always kid her—warm heart, cold feet."

"I was worried about you," Molly admitted quietly. "About what you might do."

"I went over to Cedars to kill the bastard," Reece said in a matter-of-fact tone that frightened her.

"But you couldn't do it."

"No." He dragged his hand down his face and sat down beside Lena on the other side of the bed. "But Lord, how I wanted to."

"I can understand that."

"Really?"

"She's my sister. I've loved her all of her life. How can you even ask that question?"

"Touché. So, even you can understand my motives, Saint Molly. But can God?"

"I have to believe that since He made us human in the first place, He understands our frailties.''

"Ah, now we're back to free will."

Molly wasn't prepared to enter into a theological debate. She didn't have the strength. Not when her heart was aching for these two people she loved so very much.

"What about the other guy?" Reece pressed his case when she didn't respond. "Wasn't he demonstrating free will when he chose to get into that car and drive drunk? Or was it God's will that he ram that fucking one-hundred-thousand-dollar car into Lena's minivan, and in an act of pure selfish disregard for human life, turned a vibrant, laughing, loving wife and mother into a vegetable?"

"Reece." She reached across the blanket and covered his fisted hand with hers. "This doesn't solve anything."

"I should have killed him." Reece had been second-guessing his behavior all the way back to the hospital.

"No." Molly's voice was firm, revealing that on this, at least, she was on firm ground. "I can't claim to understand God's plan for any of us." She thought about all the painful twists and turns in her own life. "But I do know we've moved beyond the Old Testament belief of an eye for an eye."

"Perhaps that was a mistake."

"Murdering the man who did this terrible thing probably would have made you feel better for a moment or two," she allowed. "But think how you would have felt saying goodbye to Grace as they hauled you off to prison."

"There isn't a jury in the state who'd convict me."

"You can't be certain of that. And even if you were

eventually acquitted, think what it would do to Grace.'' Molly felt his fingers clenching and loosening beneath hers. "Lena knew what it was to grow up under a violent cloud. There's no way she'd want that for her daughter.''

Reece didn't immediately answer, but from the way his harsh expression softened as he looked down into Lena's too-still face, Molly knew he was giving serious consideration to her words.

Chapter Seventeen

While Reece and Molly maintained a silent vigil at Lena's bedside, Tessa was sunning herself beside Miles's sparkling blue pool.

"So," he said, as he leaned back in the chaise, "Jason tells me he's asked you to help him out of this latest fix."

"He had no right to tell you that."

"We're brothers, sweetcakes. More than brothers, we're twins. We've always shared everything."

His eyes were hidden behind the mirrored lens of his glasses, but Tessa could feel his gaze crawling over every tanned and oiled inch of her, and although the day was typically hot and sunny, her flesh turned ice-cold.

"Well, almost everything," he tacked on.

His meaning was implicit. Tessa knew that Miles had wanted to make love to her—no, she corrected with brutal honesty—he'd wanted to *fuck* her since their first meeting over four years ago. He'd made that more than clear.

But he'd also held off pressing her, which should have made her feel relieved, but didn't, because he reminded her of a patient spider sitting in the center of a glittering web, waiting for his hapless prey to stumble into the imprisoning silk.

"Sleeping with Jason's bookie to get him off the hook would have been prostitution. I may as well go to work for your mother." Tessa had not been all that surprised to discover Jason's mother was the premier madam for the Hollywood elite.

They were a perfect team. Jason's job as a traffic cop working the Sunset beat and Miles's work as a photographer offered access to beautiful former beauty queen MAWs—model/actress/waitresses— new to town, all trying to break into show business. After realizing the odds stacked against them, a high percentage were eager to join Elaine's privileged stable of working girls.

"That's not such a bad idea."

"Not on a bet."

"You're overreacting again. You slept with that car dealer."

Obviously, Jason did tell him everything, Tessa thought grimly. "Afterward."

"Before, after, what's the difference?"

It was the same thing Jason had said. "I didn't come to Hollywood to become a whore," Tessa repeated firmly. "I haven't worked hard at my craft to sink to selling my body."

"What a lovely speech. It almost reminds me of a young Bergman playing St. Joan." He lifted his frosty mint-hued margarita to her in a mocking salute. "But the truth of the matter, Tessa, dear, is that you haven't been working all that much these days.''

"It's just a lull.''

One that had been going on for too long. The agent she'd hired after Terrance Quinn's death, the same one who'd lost her the job on the sitcom by advising her to hold out for double the weekly salary, which resulted in her being written out of the show, was having trouble even getting her commercials. He'd recently warned her that she was developing a reputation for being unreliable. Which, Tessa supposed with a sigh, was true.

If only she hadn't missed that audition last week. But Jason had had a party at the house and naturally, drugs had been readily available, along with constantly flowing liquor, and before she'd known it, it was the next afternoon and she'd completely forgotten all about her ten o'clock meeting with the casting director looking for a female costar for a new Western series.

"It was just as well,'' Jason had reassured her during her crying jag. "It'd be a damn stupid move to cover that magnificent body in homespun.''

Having learned the hard way that Jason was not at his best after partying, and not wanting to trigger his hot quick temper, Tessa had refrained from mentioning that dressing up in a body-concealing prairie wardrobe certainly hadn't hurt Jane Seymour's career.

"Something will turn up,'' she said now, wishing she believed that.

"It always does,'' Miles agreed mildly. "In the meantime, why don't you be a good girl and help Jason out? You do owe the guy a lot, Tessa.''

That might have been true in the beginning. But the way Tessa figured it, she'd paid for everything Jason had done for her. In spades.

"If you're so worried about your brother, why don't you pay off his debts?"

"Because Benny doesn't want to sleep with me, darling," Miles countered patiently. "It's you he wants. And he has a reputation for being generous to pretty girls. Play your cards right, and you might even cover the overdraft at the bank and keep your car from being repossessed."

Tessa was not an actress for nothing. She tossed her head and gave him a steady cool look that gave nothing away. "I don't know what you're talking about."

"Of course you do. And perhaps, before you get up on your high horse, someone ought to remind you that writing bad checks is a felony." The smile he flashed at her over the salted rim of the glass, held not an iota of warmth. "It would be a crying shame if Jason had to arrest you."

"He wouldn't."

The man she'd mistakenly thought she loved was many things. He was a thief, a liar; she had every suspicion he was a drug dealer, and if she gave in to the pressure he'd been putting on her lately, he'd also be a pimp. On top of all that, he was undoubtedly the most crooked cop on the L.A. police force. But to turn her in, he could end up implicating himself and she knew he'd never risk that.

"You're probably right," Miles allowed. "However, did you ever think that if that bookie's thugs kill my brother, you might find yourself in the middle of a murder investigation?'' He reached out and ran his hand down the red-gold slide of her hair. Against Jason's instructions, she'd begun growing it long again, and it now reached her shoulders.

''Which, considering your affection for illegal drugs, could well land you in prison.'' His fingers traced a trail of ice along her bare collarbone. ''Do you have any idea what a woman's prison is really like, Tessa?'' Those treacherous fingers continued down to the crest of her breast. ''You'd undoubtedly end up down on your knees in a broom closet, giving cunnilingus to some dyke guard.''

Her nipples were visible through the white bikini top. He pinched one, hard enough to cause her to draw in a sharp breath. ''And I don't even want to get into what the other prisoners would do to you. But I have heard tales of young women being raped with everything, from pipes ripped from beneath sinks to butcher knives stolen from the prison cafeteria.''

His words, meant to frighten, did exactly that. Despite the warmth of the day, Tessa shivered. ''I can't do what he wants.''

''Sure you can,'' Miles said encouragingly. ''I'll help you.''

''Ah.'' Tessa might be unnerved, but she hadn't lost her wits. ''This is where you offer to give me lessons.''

''Exactly.'' This time his smile held more warmth. ''You can't deny you've been wondering how we'd be together since that first night we met. Would fucking me be just like fucking Jason? Are twins alike in every way? Or do I know things my brother is too self-centered to ever dream of doing? He can make a woman scream in pain. But have you ever been made love to for hours and hours until you were screaming in ecstasy, Tessa?"

She didn't answer. But she felt the red rise in her cheeks, like mercury in the glass tube of a thermometer.

Radiating a superbly masculine self-satisfaction, Miles put his empty glass down on the wrought-iron table beside the lounge, then stood up in a lithe, smooth movement that reminded her of a panther and held a hand down to her.

Although she'd never admit it, Miles was right about her having wondered how they'd be together. He'd always stirred something uncontrollably primal in her. Something dark and dangerous that caused a disturbing, discordant hum of anticipation in her veins.

"What about Jason?" Her hesitant tone revealed that she was on the verge of capitulation.

"Jason's otherwise occupied." He tilted his dark head toward the Jacuzzi, where his brother seemed to be engaged in foreplay with a former *Playboy* centerfold who'd discarded the top to her bikini shortly after arriving at the party. "He won't notice."

Worse yet, he wouldn't care. When hot adolescent jealousy flashed through her, Tessa stood up and put her hand in Miles's.

She expected him to say something smugly obscene. But instead, he surprised her by lifting her hand to his lips. Then he linked their fingers and together they walked into the house and down the hall to his bedroom.

Although she'd fought against it, Tessa had fantasized about this room more times than she cared to count. She'd imagined it as a sybaritic pleasure palace, a place of leopard-skin bedspreads, mirrors on the ceiling and undoubtedly a large-screen television for viewing pornographic movies.

But Miles's bedroom was nothing like her fantasy. The moment she entered, she felt as if she'd walked through a shift in time and space and ended up in the Far East.

The floors were bleached hardwood that added a sense of space and light. Sheer white screens separated different areas of the huge room. An antique Chinese altar table stood at the far end of the room, topped with a small bronze Japanese bull and a trio of black vases, each holding a single white lily.

The one thing she had not guessed wrong about was that the bed, indeed, did dominate the room. But rather than the tacky round water bed she'd envisioned, the wide bed draped in white linen seemed to float on its black lacquer pedestal, its four posts looking like jet lacquer arrows reaching for the white arched cathedral ceiling. The view from the bed looked out on to a Japanese rock garden so perfect that the grains of sparkling gray sand appeared to have been put in place with a pair of tweezers.

As spartan and bare as it admittedly was, Tessa found it surprisingly sensual. "It's exquisite." As the serenity of the room worked its magic on her nerve endings, Tessa began to relax.

"I'm glad you approve." His eyes, usually so cool and mocking, seemed to observe her with warmth and gentle humor. "Would you care for a drink? I have some white wine on ice."

She'd had two strawberry daiquiris out by the pool and a line of coke. Since her head was already spinning because of what she was about to do, Tessa decided against adding any more alcohol to an already-combustible situation.

"Thank you," she said, as politely as a sorority girl attending a rush tea party. "But I believe I'd better not."

"Fine." His voice remained equally polite, but the dark, unblinking eyes looking into hers reminded Tessa of a predator all too certain of its prey. She tried telling herself that the sudden chill causing goose bumps to rise on her skin was merely due to the artificially cooled air blowing through the air-conditioner vents, but knew that was a lie.

She risked a cautious glance downward, to his groin, where his erection was pressing against the silky black material of his brief, European-style swim trunks in a blatantly erotic way he didn't attempt to conceal.

"See something you like?" he asked mildly.

Tessa didn't answer. But she couldn't take her eyes away as he hooked his long dark fingers into the low-slung waistband and lowered the trunks, freeing his penis that jutted out of the curly black hair.

He stood in front of her, boldly, proudly naked, studying her for a long silent time that made her more and more uncomfortable. Tessa wondered if he meant for her to take off her bikini, as well, and was strangely reluctant to dispense with what little protection it provided.

"You can still change your mind, Tessa." His tone was mocking, his eyes cool and sardonic as he watched her for a reaction. "I'm not into raping women." His smug smile suggested he didn't need to.

Tessa swallowed and resisted, just barely, licking her arid lips. "I'm not going anywhere."

He nodded, satisfied. "Good girl."

"If I was a good girl," she shot back recklessly, "I wouldn't be here."

His smile was a slash of white in his dark face. "Point taken." He tilted his head and studied her for another of those seemingly endless times that made her flesh hot and cold all at the same time. "Are you afraid of me?"

"No." It was not quite the truth.

"You should be. You're not a schoolgirl anymore, Tessa. You're playing with the grown-ups now. And sometimes a girl can get hurt."

"You wouldn't hurt me."

He laughed at that. A low, rich sound that slipped beneath her skin and into her blood and went coursing straight to the secret place that was growing increasingly wet and warm.

"Ah, but that's where you're wrong." He wrapped his fingers around his rampant penis and held it toward her, like an offering. Or a weapon.

"I am going to hurt you. I'm going to take you hard and rough and you're going to love it. I'm going to teach you all the things men secretly want women to do to them. And then I'm going to do wicked things to you that you could have never imagined. Things that will shock you. And thrill you. And have you crying out for more."

Heaven help her, the crotch of her bikini bottom

was drenched with need. So much so, that when he told her to get down on her knees, she was powerless to resist.

"Crawl over here."

Even the violence she'd come to accept as a prelude to lovemaking had never been so demeaning. Tessa realized that was because Jason's behavior was born of his flash-fire, wicked temper. While Miles's grew out of a calculating need to dominate.

"Now, Tessa." His voice was soft, with a razor-sharp edge that excited even as it frightened.

The throbbing between her legs became almost painful as she obeyed him.

"I'm going to teach you how to suck a man. When you do it right, you'll be rewarded. When you do something wrong, you'll be punished. So you'll never make that mistake again."

His hands tangled in her hair as he pulled her head back and forced himself between her lips. Deeper and deeper he pushed himself into her mouth, but every time she gagged, he yanked on her hair, hard enough to bring tears to her eyes.

He seemed capable of lasting forever. Eventually she learned how to open her throat muscles to take him deeper than she'd ever swallowed any man. Including, and especially, his brother. As she accepted the hot explosion of jism that came with his release, she experienced a surge of feminine power that she'd finally caused him to surrender his own rigid control.

When his hips stopped thrusting and his penis deflated, he took her by the shoulders and lifted her to her feet. He ripped off the bikini, leaving her standing naked and trembling with desire in front of him.

He smiled. A smile edged with sexuality and menace. "Now it's your turn."

Before she realized what he was doing, he'd fastened a set of silver handcuffs around each of her wrists, then snapped the other end of each cuff to the bedpost.

As he tied a black silk mask over her eyes, Tessa reminded herself that she was not the kind of girl who did these kinds of things. The Tessa Davis who'd been taught by her general father that people should treat one another with respect and honor was not the kind of girl who allowed such things to be done to her.

She tugged against the cuffs, but the cold metal chafed her wrists. She felt helpless and afraid, and she'd just opened her mouth to tell Miles that she'd changed her mind after all, when he dipped his tongue into the very heat of her and wiped her mind as clean as glass.

He feasted on her savagely, using his lips and tongue and teeth to stir deep-seated urges she'd never suspected dwelt inside her. Writhing on the cool white sheets, Tessa Starr forced thoughts of that old Tessa Davis away.

She screamed when she came against his mouth, just as he'd predicted she would. And that was just the beginning.

Tessa had no idea how long she stayed in that cool, serene-appearing bedroom. It could have been hours. Or days. At some point, Jason joined them in the room as well and, treating her as if she were nothing more than a mannequin designed for their own carnal pleasures, both brothers bent her body to their liking,

sucking, biting, fondling, probing. Gradually they
broke down all her inhibitions and Tessa surrendered
to them totally. Their most outrageous fantasies became her own, and with them she went crashing
through every sexual boundary.

Molly spent the night in Lena's hospital room with
Reece. The time passed so slowly, she glanced down
at her watch several times to make certain the clock
on the wall hadn't stopped. Finally, when the bustle
outside in the hallway revealed it was time for morning rounds, Dr. Parker entered the room, examined
his patient and turned to Reece.

"She's developed a fever. And it sounds as if she's
got a low-grade pneumonia in her right lung."

"Then put her on antibiotics."

The physician exchanged a glance with Molly who,
reading the finality in his somber gaze, walked over
to the window and looked down at the parking lot.

"It won't do any good. She's dead, Reece. The
only thing keeping her alive are those machines."

"You don't know that."

"There's a way to find out."

Molly closed her eyes and pressed her forehead
against the cooling glass of the window.

"I'm not going to do that," Reece insisted. "Goddammit, James, we don't have any right to play God
with my wife."

"We do it every day with other patients," the neu-
rologist reminded him.

"Not Lena."

"You know that legally, it's my decision to
make."

"She's my wife. And I'm a physician."

"You're not Lena's physician. You can't make the decision, Reece. It would be too hard to live with."

"I couldn't live with myself if I didn't fight to keep her alive."

"We'll disconnect the respirator. If there's any life in your wife's brain, she'll breathe for herself. If not, the rest of her will die, too."

"She won't die. She just needs more time."

The older physician turned to Molly. "Talk to him," he told her. "Because if something isn't done to resolve this situation soon, I'm going to have to take it up with the ethics board." That said, he left the room.

"Don't say a thing," Reece warned as soon as they were alone again. "Not a goddamn word."

Knowing he had to come to this decision on his own, Molly obliged. The only sounds in the room were the beeping of the cardiac monitor and the steady swish of the respirator, its mechanical sigh an echo of the grief they were feeling.

Finally, at Reece's insistence, another electroencephalogram was taken. The test was examined by four doctors at three hospitals. All four proclaimed the patient irreversibly brain dead.

Chapter Eighteen

It was when the results were given to Reece that Molly finally felt she had to say something.

"They're right." Her voice was little more than a whisper, but easily heard in the hush of the room where the deathwatch was now entering into its thirtieth hour.

The look Reece shot her over Lena's still body was as sharp and lethal as a scalpel. "When did you get your medical degree?"

"Reece." Understanding that the sarcastic remark was born of deep pain, Molly didn't take offense. "Look at her."

"She's beautiful," he said doggedly.

"She's always been beautiful," Molly agreed. "Inside as well as out. But it's obvious that her spirit, or her soul, or whatever it was that made Lena the warm, sweet, loving wife, mother, sister and friend she was, isn't there any longer."

"She wouldn't leave me. Not alone. You don't

know her like I do. You couldn't possibly understand what we have together.... She can't be dead. She's the most alive woman I've ever known. She's my life. If she were dead, I'd be dead. And I'm not, dammit!''

He dragged both hands down his face. When he took them away, his eyes were those of a man who'd visited hell and had unfortunately lived to tell about it.

''I can't let her go, Molly. I don't know what I'd do without her. I don't know what Grace would do without her.''

''She'll be with us, in spirit,'' Molly assured him.

''Ah, I was waiting for Sister Molly to make an appearance. This is where I get the lecture about all souls going to heaven, right?''

''Actually, I was going to say that I don't believe we truly lose the ones we love. That as long as we're alive, the people we love live on in our hearts.''

''A helluva lot of good that's going to do me when I have to send Grace off on her first day of school without her mother.''

Even though he continued to resist her efforts to comfort, Molly could feel Reece beginning to accept the inevitable. But that didn't make things any less painful. At last he agreed to speak with Mercy Sam's procurement coordinator and signed the organ donor consent form.

A priest was called to give Lena last rites. He entered the room vested in a violet stole, carrying his holy water and the sacred oils. Molly listened as he absolved her sister of her sins—how few and insignificant they must be—and watched as he dipped the tip of his thumb in the oil and anointed Lena's eyes, ears, nostrils, lips, hands and feet with the sign of the cross.

"Lord have mercy," he said.

"Christ have mercy." Molly murmured the familiar response. Reece, standing grim-faced beside her, was rigid as stone. And remained as mute as marble when the priest asked the Lord Jesus to take the purified soul of his servant Lena into his loving arms.

"It's such a goddamn depressing shame," Yolanda whispered to Molly a short time later as they left the room to allow Reece to prepare his wife for death in private.

He lovingly bathed her with scented French milled soap, then rubbed perfumed oil into her skin and finished up with a dusting of the Anaïs Anaïs powder she favored. Theo had sent Alex with the powder and oil earlier that day.

All the time, he continued to talk to her in low tones, husband to wife, assuring her that he loved her. That he'd always love her.

And then it was time. Dr. Parker joined Reece and Molly in the room. Molly watched as Reece whispered a private goodbye into her ear.

"No," he said, when the older physician reached for the machine. "I need to do this."

"It's against policy."

"Then take me up before the fucking hospital board, because it's going to take every security guard in the damn hospital to stop me."

When the neurosurgeon only lifted his hands in a gesture of surrender, Reece slowly, deliberately went around the side of the bed and disconnected the tube between Lena and the machine. Then he sat down and took her hand.

Looking at her, Reece recalled all the times he'd watched her sleeping. He thought of how fortunate he was that she'd agreed to marry him. How beautiful she was. How perfect.

He was struck with a sudden, almost overwhelming impulse to reconnect her to the machine. If only he could have her with him for a little longer!

Molly drew in a sharp breath as Reece reached up, his hand near the machine. But instead, he merely turned off the respirator, silencing the steady *swish swish swish*. They all waited. And watched. But there was no sound, no motion from the still figure on the bed that had only days ago been a laughing, loving woman planning her husband's surprise birthday party.

"I fell in love with her the minute I saw her," Reece murmured, his voice as quiet as if he were in a cathedral. "Do you remember, Molly? We were in the cafeteria. I'd ordered that sawdust they try to pass off as meat loaf, and a baked potato. And apple pie."

"À la mode."

"You remember, too."

She didn't, not really. But since he always liked ice cream on his pie, it was an educated guess.

"And then, she came into the room, her face lit up like a Christmas tree."

"She'd just gotten a job teaching kindergarten," Molly recalled. It hadn't been easy for Lena, with all her insecurities to get through college; her diploma, and later, her job, had meant so much to her.

"She couldn't stop talking about how much she

loved children and how this was like a dream come true. Her enthusiasm was so contagious, I knew right away I'd just met the woman I was destined to spend the rest of my life with.'' He sighed and lifted a limp hand to his lips. ''Oh, God, I'm going to miss her so much.''

The room was hushed, save for the tiny click of the electrocardiogram attached to Lena's chest. The noise remained regular and strong.

Then it missed a beat. And another. The three people in the room leaned forward, as if transfixed by the suddenly jerking waves on the screen.

The clicks, each a heart beat, became less frequent. And slower. Then slower still. Until finally they stopped. And there was only silence.

After what seemed an eternity, but was only fifteen minutes, Dr. Parker slowly reached into his white coat, brought out his stethoscope and placed the bell on Lena's stilled chest.

His face professionally impassive, he wound the stethoscope up and replaced it in his pocket. Then he took a flashlight from another pocket, lifted each lid, one at a time, and directed its thin yellow beam into her eyes. Each was a still deep pool.

Finally, he took the silver end of the flashlight and held it in front of her porcelain pale lips, a mirror to catch a vapor of breath. The mirror remained as dry as Molly's mouth.

After the attending physician called the death for the record, Reece leaned down once again and touched his lips to his wife's.

Molly, who couldn't hear what final words he whispered, watched as he slipped the wide gold band from her finger and put it on the little finger of his left hand, then placed his own wedding band on her slender finger and turned away from this woman he'd loved at first sight.

She saw him hesitate, as if waging some internal struggle with himself. Then, with tracks of tears on his ashen cheeks, he walked out of the room.

Although she knew better, Molly glanced up, half expecting to see Lena's soul floating over them.

The organ transplant team, who'd been waiting outside the room, entered. Molly was surprised at the quiet professionalism they displayed as they lifted Lena's lifeless body onto the gurney. Usually transfers were noisy and confused, with all the teams from various hospitals around the country jockeying for position. She suspected the respect being shown this donor was due, in large part, to the fondness and respect everyone at Mercy Sam had for Reece.

Molly stopped the gurney on the way out of the room and touched her sister's satiny smooth cheek, saying a final goodbye of her own.

Then, with a heavy heart, she went to find Reece.

She located him in the bar across the street appropriately named The ER because so many off-duty medical personnel hung out there. He'd just ordered a double Scotch when she approached.

"I was looking for you." She climbed onto the stool beside him.

"Well, now you've found me." He tossed the Scotch back and held the glass out for a refill.

The bartender hesitated.

"Hit me again, dammit," Reece demanded.

The bartender exchanged a look with Molly. "Are

you driving? The doc's already had two doubles."
His expression revealed this was definitely not a usual
occurrence.

"I'm driving." Molly put her hand on Reece's
arm. "Are you sure you want to do this? Grace is
going to need you tonight."

"Grace is going to need her mother every night.
But that doesn't seem to make a goddamn difference,
does it?"

He polished off the refilled drink the bartender
placed before him. The third drink did the trick; even
as the whiskey burned his throat and gut going down,
Reece felt a cool pure white glacier moving over his
mind that only moments ago had felt as if it were
teeming with writhing, poisonous snakes.

Understanding how deeply he was hurting, Molly
prayed silently for strength and managed, just barely,
to resist reminding him that she'd just lost a sister.
She took his arm and was more than a little grateful
when he didn't resist her leading him out of the bar
and across the street to the hospital parking lot.

When they arrived home, Theo and Alex were
there to greet them. Theo embraced Reece, who remained as stiff and straight as a rod of cold steel.
When it was her turn to be hugged, Molly felt as if
she were sinking into the comforting warmth of a
feather bed. It was more than the fact that Theo's
voluptuous curves had begun to soften with the years.
It was the absolute love the older woman offered that
was such a comfort.

Later, as the four adults sat in the cozy kitchen,
arguing over how to tell Grace, who was sleeping

upstairs, Theo was not as gentle with Reece as Molly had been.

"You can't permit yourself the luxury of wallowing helplessly in grief," she reminded him. "You have to think of your daughter."

Reece shook his head and poured another drink from the bottle he'd retrieved from the library. The earlier alcohol had begun to wear off and he could feel the pain trying to break through the cold white ice fields in his mind.

"I *am* thinking of Grace," he argued. "I'm wondering how she's going to learn to do all those mysterious women things—like using a tampon, shopping for bras, getting perms and prom dresses. And how the hell is she going to get married without Lena to take care of all the details and give her all that motherly advice women need before they become wives?"

"It's not as if you and the child live at the North Pole," Theo argued. "I'm not going anywhere. I can fill in on the day-to-day details like tampons and perms. And Molly can help whenever she visits. As for the wedding advice, may I point out that Lena didn't have a mother to share those intimate little details with before she married you."

"That's my point. Lena was a basket case when we got married."

"Grace is stronger than Lena was," Alex said, entering into the argument that had been going on for nearly two hours. "She has you and Lena to thank for that."

"Listen to the man," Theo advised, her voice softening to match the fond gaze she bestowed upon her husband. "He knows of what he speaks. A tragic thing has happened, Reece, and it would be wonderful if we could go back and change things, but we can't. So, the only thing you can do now is go on and be the best person—the best father—to Grace you can be.''

"I don't think I can do it alone." He closed his eyes, wishing he could crawl into some dark cave and suffer his grief in private.

"Ah, baby." Theo got up from her chair and pressed his head against the pillowed softness of her breasts. "I promise, you're not ever going to be alone."

It was, Reece remembered with a flash of unwelcome clarity, the same thing she'd said the day she'd shown up at his family home, where he'd been left in the care of servants, to inform him that his parents had not survived that plane crash. He remembered clinging to her while he bawled his eyes out.

As the glacier continued its steady pace, engulfing him in ice, the part of Reece's mind that was still functioning wished he was seven years old again, when the horrors of the world could be solved with a hug, a good cry and the hot fudge sundae Theo had fixed them both, bravely daring to invade the Longworth kitchen despite the harridan of a cook that had declared it off bounds for as long as Reece could remember.

Although Molly was not overly fond of platitudes and clichés, because of Grace's tender age, she went along with Theo's romanticized explanation that God must have needed an angel up in heaven to help take care of the little children whose mommies hadn't arrived there yet.

If the adults had thought that would satisfy the precocious child, they were wrong. "But I need her, too," Grace argued. She turned toward Molly. "Why couldn't God pick someone else's mother to help those children?"

Her daughter's morning glory eyes, dark with confusion, broke Molly's heart. "I don't know," she answered honestly.

"But you told me that you talk to God all the time. You can ask him to send Mommy home again."

"I wish I could, sweetheart, but—"

"He'll listen to you, Aunt Molly," Grace interrupted. "Mommy said that you don't have a husband because you're married to God. So if you ask him real nice, he'll have to give in. Like Daddy always does to Mommy."

"God isn't going to send your mommy back." Reece's slurred voice suggested either he'd begun drinking early this morning or hadn't stopped last night. "Not even for Saint Molly."

The acid he heaped onto what had once been a term of fondness stung, but Molly wasn't about to get into an argument with her brother-in-law in front of Grace.

"I have an idea, honeybun," Alex said with the calm reassurance that had once made him such a successful police negotiator. "Why don't you and I go out and water your mama's garden? I always found that a garden is a real good place to talk to people in heaven."

"Really?" Grace turned toward the older man with obvious confidence in his veracity.

"Absolutely." Despite his artificial legs, he picked her up as easily as if she were a feather. "And sometimes, if you listen real closely, you can hear the butterflies and the honeybees passing along messages."

"Do you think my mommy will send me a message from heaven?" Molly heard Grace ask as Alex carried her out of the room.

"Absolutely," he said with the same certainty as when, so many years ago, he'd assured two terrified little girls who'd just witnessed a double murder that everything would be okay.

Since Reece refused, it was left to Molly and Theo to choose Lena's clothing for the funeral home.

"I never would have imagined how difficult this is," Molly murmured to Theo as they stood in Lena's walk-in closet later that day.

"It's definitely one sad chore," Theo agreed, pausing to admire a garnet knit suit with gold braid epaulets. The color, which could have clashed with Lena's auburn hair, had suited her perfectly, making her look like a slender scarlet candle topped by a brilliant flame.

"It's more than that. What if we choose wrong?" Molly imagined Lena's spirit haunting her forever, asking her why on earth she'd forced her to spend eternity in *that*.

"Lena looked wonderful in everything. This is nice." Theo fingered a short silk dress. The bright hues brought to mind the magnificent sunsets that so often turned the ocean outside the French doors of the bedroom to molten gold and copper. "She bought it to wear for Reece's surprise birthday party."

Molly noticed the price tag still hanging from the dress and decided that there was something too sad about burying her sister in a party dress she'd never had a chance to wear. Especially one she'd planned to wear on the night she was killed.

"What about this?" Theo said after Molly had revealed her feelings. "I suppose, in a way, it's appropriate."

Molly shook her head as she studied the tasteful Chanel dress. "It's too somber. This may be a funeral, but Lena loved life too much to be consigned to wear black for all eternity."

She moved on to another plastic bag. "Oh, I like this," she breathed. The dress in question was a full-skirted cloud of white silk, tea-length and embroidered with flowers.

"That was one of her favorites." Despite the sadness of their duty, Theo smiled. "Reece loved it, too. He said it made her look like the gardens at Versailles come to life."

Molly made her decision. "It's this one."

"Good choice," Theo agreed robustly. "I couldn't have done better myself."

While Alex and Theo took the dress, shoes and shimmery stockings to the funeral parlor, Molly busied herself in the kitchen, putting into the freezer the various casseroles, cakes and pies that had begun arriving from friends and neighbors. Reece was holed up in the library and Grace was next door at a neighbor's. Although at first Molly had worried that the little girl should stay at home, the mood in the house was so somber, she and Theo had decided that it might be good for her to play dolls with her best friend.

Molly was grateful to have some time to be alone, but before a half hour had passed, a phone call came from the neighbor saying that the girls had been playing when Grace had suddenly run out of the house in tears. Molly had no sooner hung up the receiver when Grace burst in through the kitchen door.

"What's wrong?" Molly asked, then inwardly cringed at the stupid question. What wasn't wrong?

"You and T-T-Theo told me that M-M-Mommy was an angel." Grace's face was as white as paper and hectic red flags flew in her pale cheeks.

"That's right." Molly squatted down and gathered the stiff, miserable little girl into her arms, mindful of the time when Alex had held her close and buried her face against his broad strong chest to keep her from looking at her parents' blood splattered all over the living room wall. "She's in heaven."

"Mary Beth's crummy b-b-brother Kenny told me that she isn't really going to go to heaven," Grace sobbed into Molly's shoulder. "He said that my m-m-mommy's going to be put in the ground."

The wail of anguish, emanating from the very core of that delicate young body caused scalding fury to flood through Molly. Although she knew it was an uncharitable thought, she would have dearly loved to smack the nasty little boy who could tell a child such a horrid thing. The anger burning through her veins and throbbing deep in her bones made her legs unsteady. She managed to sit down on one of the antique Windsor kitchen chairs Lena had lovingly refinished, holding Grace on her lap. *Please Lord,* she begged silently, as she rested her cheek atop her daughter's ebony head, *help me through this one.*

"Remember a few weeks ago, right before Aunt Theo and Uncle Alex's wedding, when we all went to Disneyland?"

Grace didn't answer. But she managed a faint, almost imperceptible nod as she hiccuped.

"Remember we passed that pretty place with the velvety green lawns and flowers and those tall white stone angels?"

Another nod.

Encouraged, Molly continued. "And remember when you asked if it was a park where you could play?"

"Uncle Alex said we couldn't because it was a cem…cemtry…or something like that," she said in a small dead voice.

"A cemetery, that's right." Molly forced into her tone encouragement she was a long way from feeling. "It's a place where people's bodies rest after they die. But their souls, which God put inside them before they were even born, go up to heaven and become angels."

Grace said nothing. The only sounds in the room were the hum of the refrigerator motor, the steady *tick tick tick* of the kitchen clock, a little girl's sniffling and the occasional hitch of her breath.

"Is it like the tulips?" she asked finally.

"The tulips?"

"When Mommy and I planted tulips, we put them in the ground, then covered them up with dirt." Her young face, surrounded by hair that shone blue-black in the bright light flooding into the kitchen, was thoughtful beyond her years.

"Mommy said that they needed to sleep for a while and the dirt was like a warm blanket. Then, when spring came, they'd wake up and make everyone happy when they bloomed."

"It's just like that. I just know everyone in heaven will be happy because your mommy's with them."

"I still wish Mommy was here with me." Grace's eyes, fringed with thick sooty lashes, overbrimmed with tears again.

Having run out of pithy explanations and ineffectual excuses, Molly could only hold her close while she wept.

The vigil the evening before the scheduled mass was held in the funeral home. Wanting—needing—to be alone with his wife, Reece remained behind. Looking down at Lena, lying in her casket, he wondered how so much wonderful wit, beauty and sweetness could be reduced to something that appeared like wax in the subdued lighting.

Someone, he supposed either Molly or Theo, had chosen his favorite dress—the flowered one he'd loved to see Lena wearing and loved even more to take off. Had it only been last month when she'd laughingly warned him that if he didn't slow down he'd rip it to shreds? It seemed as if that night was an aeon ago, light-years away in another world.

He reached out and cupped her breasts with his palms, as he'd done so many times before. But it wasn't the same; he imagined he could feel Lena's body turning to dust beneath his impotent caress.

Molly had been right, Reece realized. Whatever life force had flowed through Lena's veins was gone, making it impossible to connect her with this frozen, waxy-faced mannequin.

Although he couldn't recall the last time he'd prayed, he knelt beside the gleaming white casket and begged God to make his beloved wife alive again.

Hours later, when He still hadn't answered the desperate prayers, Reece cursed God's cold black heart in words he knew would shock Molly and unfortunately didn't make him feel any better.

There was a gaping hole in the pit of his soul. His entire world had turned as cold and black as an arctic winter's midnight, and as he sat beside his wife's lifeless body, Reece wished that he'd die, as well.

He considered going to the nearest gun store, buying a shotgun and ending it all. But then he recalled Grace. And how Lena had been orphaned, and the subsequent pain it had caused her, and knew she'd never forgive him if he left their daughter with such a deadly legacy.

"I'll try to take care of her," he whispered into the artificially chilled air. He felt something hot splash onto his fisted hands and realized the moisture was from his own tears. "But goddammit, Lena, how do you expect me to handle this without you?"

And as the night grew longer, Reece, who already hated God and that drunk driver, found himself unable to forgive his wife for deserting him and the young daughter she'd wanted so desperately.

Chapter Nineteen

It was late—nearly ten o'clock, when the doorbell rang. Dreading the idea of making polite conversation, or accepting any more of the food that had filled the freezer or flowers that were already overflowing the house, Molly almost ignored it. But afraid of waking Grace, she sighed, pushed herself off the sofa and opened the door.

"Joe?" She stared up in disbelief at the man standing there.

"I know," he apologized, "I should have called. But I was afraid you'd tell me not to come. And you can send me away if you want, Molly, but I couldn't stand the idea of not being with you when you're in pain."

"Don't be foolish." She moved aside, inviting him into the house. "I can't think of anyone I'd rather see right now."

Joe brought a much welcome, palpable energy into the dark and quiet house of mourning. He was no sooner in the door than he put his bag down, turned toward her and gathered her into his strong secure arms.

Having been forced to remain strong for Grace's sake, Molly didn't think about the propriety of her behavior as she clung to him, immensely grateful for the comfort he was offering.

There were more arguments about whether Grace should be allowed to attend the funeral. Finally it was decided that she would attend the mass but skip the interment. Before they left for the church, the little girl picked a handful of crimson, saffron and purple tulips, and prior to the funeral mass, the sight of the solemn child placing the tulips on the white-draped coffin at the front of the church caused an outbreak of silent weeping among the mourners.

Although she'd been living under the same roof with Reece, Molly had been too preoccupied with comforting Grace and with her own grief to take much notice of him. Now that she did, she was shocked at the change. As they rode back to the house in the limousine after the interment, she took a good long look at him and was shocked by the change. He looked like a dead man himself, a mere shadow of the vibrant man who'd changed her sister's life. His eyes, ringed by deep purple shadows of sleeplessness, were sunken, and his handsome face was painfully haggard. And she knew he had been chewing gum to disguise the scent of whiskey on his breath.

When she'd introduced Joe to him earlier in the day, Reece had merely looked through her friend as if he were invisible. Another of the ghosts haunting him, perhaps. Molly began to worry that Reece was walking on a very ragged razor's edge.

When they reached home, Molly's head was throbbing from stress and sorrow, but her heart lifted slightly at the sight of Grace running out to meet them.

"Aunt Theo bought me new crayons, Daddy," she said, holding a piece of paper toward him. "I drew a picture of Mommy in heaven for you. So you'd feel better."

Molly caught a glimpse of a stick figure of a woman in a flowered dress with fiery hair and golden wings jutting from her shoulders. She was standing on a puffy white cloud and handing a bouquet of colorful tulips to a smiling bearded stick figure of a man obviously intended to be God.

As sorrow almost caused her knees to buckle, Molly was grateful for Joe's steadying hand on her waist.

Reece studied the drawing for what seemed like an eternity. Strangely, this primitive crayon picture seemed more real to him than the sight of his bride lying so still and as waxy as a gardenia in that overpriced white casket.

Reece shook his head to clear it, like a dog shaking off unwanted water after a bath. "It's beautiful, sweetheart." He reached down and, in a familiar, fatherly gesture, ruffled the ebony cloud of hair. "I'll treasure it forever."

He bent down and hugged her, as a loving father should, but it escaped no one's attention that although he'd said the right words, and acted appropriately, he'd emotionally distanced himself from the situation.

As soon as they'd entered the house, Reece disappeared into the library. Even as the rest of the adults did their best to keep Grace occupied with a seemingly endless game of Candyland, there was no escaping the pall of gloom that had settled over the house like a shroud.

A week after Lena's funeral, Joe, who was staying in a nearby hotel, finally talked Molly into leaving the house—and Grace—long enough to take a walk along the cliff. The morning was unnaturally still. With only the soft sigh of the distant surf washing up onto the golden sands, Molly imagined she could hear the feelings that Joe had been trying to put into words.

"This isn't going to work, you know," he said finally. He was standing beside her, his hands shoved deep into the pockets of his jeans, looking not at Molly, but out toward the horizon where fishing boats chugged along, laying their long orange nets.

Molly pretended ignorance. "What?"

"Your staying here indefinitely, pretending to be Grace's mother."

Although his tone was as gentle as ever, the words stung. "A week is not an indefinite stay. And I *am* her mother."

"No." He turned and looked at her and his eyes were sad. "Not really. Oh, biologically, you are. But Grace thinks of you as her aunt."

"An aunt who loves her."

"I'd never suggest otherwise." He took his left hand out of his pocket and linked his fingers with hers. "But you're not helping her, staying here, letting her hover next to you like some pale, ghost child.''

"That's not fair!" She tried to back away, but his fingers tightened, effectively holding her hostage. "I'm her closest relative. She needs support right now."

"Her father's her closest relative. She needs his support."

"He isn't capable of providing it right now."

"Because he doesn't have to. Because Saint Molly's here to pick up the pieces and keep everything running smoothly, so he can wallow in self-indulgent grief instead of trying to shore up the hole in his daughter's life."

Joe's tone, as he referred to her as Saint Molly, held none of the sarcasm Reece's had only last week. Although the words made her angry, she knew they were spoken with honest concern.

"That's not a very nice thing to say."

"No." He took a deep breath, turned toward her, framed her cheek with his free hand and looked down into her sad, mutinous face. "But it's the truth. You've kept her so busy with games and trips to the zoo and planting those damn flowers that she hasn't had any time to grieve the loss of her mother.

"And meanwhile, Reece is sinking deeper and deeper into depression because you're allowing him to abdicate his responsibility." His fingers were warm on her skin. His tone was warmer still. "You can't fix the world, sweetheart."

"I don't want to fix the world," she said in a small voice that sounded pitiful even to her own ears. "Just my little corner of it."

"Aw, Molly."

He fitted her face into the side of his neck and held her, wishing he could stumble across a bottle on the beach and release a magic genie who would make everything all right for her. And, Joe decided, since the genie would already be out of the bottle, it'd be nice if he could also make Molly fall in love with him. As he was, and always would be, with her.

As they stood there on the edge of the cliff, bathed in the clear bright light of a late-spring morning, neither Joe nor Molly saw Reece, standing at the library window, grim-faced as he observed their embrace.

Molly was disappointed, but not overly surprised, when the other adults in the house sided with Joe.

"Reece and Gracie have to figure out some way to be a family without Lena," Alex said gently. "And as much as we understand you're trying to prevent her from emotional pain, we can't continue to pretend her mother's just off frolicking with God in some fanciful tulip bed, and encourage her to stuff her feelings of loss beneath layers of denial. Because somewhere down the line, she has to deal with any painful emotions she's suppressed."

The way he was looking at her, as if he could see all the way inside her, gave Molly the feeling that Alex was no longer talking about Grace, but about her.

"Losing a loved one is a lot like breaking a bone." Joe entered into the conversation. "If the bone isn't set properly, it'll heal on its own, but it'll cause pain for the rest of the patient's life. If Grace isn't allowed to grieve for her mother, Molly, she'll never feel emotionally whole."

Like she'd never allowed herself to grieve for the loss of her daughter, Molly thought, angry and miserable at the way all of them were ganging up on her, seeming determined to separate her from Grace again, just when they were establishing a bond.

"We know you mean well, darling," Theo said. "But this can't be good for you, either. If you allow yourself to become too close to Grace, it could prove wrenching when you have to go back to your own life."

The quiet words hit home. They were right. Especially Theo. It would be hard enough to leave Grace now. If she stayed any longer, she might be tempted to destroy the comforting fabric of well-meant lies they'd wrapped around her daughter.

"I need to talk to Reece," she said after a long, thoughtful pause.

"That's a good idea," Alex agreed as the others nodded. The relief in the room was palpable.

When he didn't answer her light tap on the closed door, she gingerly entered the dimness of the library, feeling as if she were braving a lion in its den.

Unlike the rest of the house, which Lena had decorated in soft, shell-like colors of pink, ivory and sea mist, this room had been designed as a masculine retreat. The walls, lined with bookshelves, were paneled with a deep red mahogany, the furniture oversize and comfortable.

Reece was sitting in an oxblood leather wing chair, his back to the door, staring out over the vast sun-gilded waters.

"Go away." He had never thought of himself as rude. Oh, he could be brusque on occasion, but one thing he remembered from his childhood was his mother teaching him that politeness was a virtue all properly brought up Southern boys should acquire.

"I need to talk to you."

"There's nothing to say." He reached out, picked up the crystal decanter of brandy from the table beside him and refilled the Waterford balloon glass—one of a set he and Lena had received as a wedding gift from Mercy Samaritan's chief of staff and his wife. As he watched the level of amber liquor rise, Reece vaguely recalled the couple attending Lena's funeral, as well.

"Weddings and funerals," he muttered, thinking how they seemed to be the two occasions that brought people together. That and christenings.

Not wanting to think about that day when Lena had been so happy and their future had looked so golden, Reece downed the drink in long, thirsty swallows.

"Actually, I came to see what you'd think about me going back to Arizona."

"With that guy? Jim?"

"Joe." She wondered at the edge in his voice, then decided if she were Reece, she'd be angry at everyone right now. Including strangers. "And yes, I guess with him, although we don't really work together all that much—"

"So your relationship is mainly personal?"

He made what she and Joe had sound dirty. And wrong. "I didn't say that."

"I saw you." He pushed himself out of the chair. "Out on the cliff."

Although she had done nothing to feel ashamed of, unbidden color rose in Molly's cheeks. "It's not what you're implying."

"That's your story." His tone was gritty, his eyes as hard as stones. Where was the gentle, caring man who'd once been her best friend in the world? "I don't give a flying fuck what you do with the guy, Sister Molly."

He ignored her slight cringe at the uncharacteristic obscenity. "I also don't care if you break your vow of chastity and go to bed with every quack doctor in the BIA and the entire Navajo nation. But the one thing I don't want is having my daughter exposed to your blatant behavior."

He turned away, refusing to look at her shocked, pained face. "So, I think you're right. It's time for you to go."

Molly was stunned. By his condemnation and his coldly devastating anger that she couldn't understand. She was tempted, yet again, to remind him that Grace was her daughter, too, and she'd never do anything to hurt her in any way, but realized that it would be impossible to break through the icy shield he'd surrounded himself with.

Unwilling to leave things like this, she walked the few feet between them and touched his back lightly. His back became as rigid as marble.

"Take care of yourself." She swallowed past the lump of anguish and loss in her throat. "And be gentle with Grace. She'll need you now, more than ever."

He didn't answer. Nor did he turn around. Her heart heavy in her chest, she left the dark room. And the man she'd chosen—hopefully not mistakenly—to be the father of her child.

Reece waited until he heard the door click behind

her. Then cursing, he threw the empty glass into the fireplace, where it shattered into thousands of crystalline pieces.

Molly returned to the reservation and threw herself into her work with a dedication that was unheard of, even for her. When Sister Benvenuto professed concern about her eighteen and twenty-hour days, she reminded her superior that part of the reason she'd been assigned to the Navajo nation in the first place was that the BIA's health services were woefully understaffed.

When Joe complained about her obvious weight loss and the shadows beneath her tired eyes, she responded tartly that since she wasn't one of his patients, her health was none of his business. He'd shouted back, in front of an entire clinic of wide-eyed patients that it sure as hell was his business, "Because I'm in love with you, goddammit!"

But either he was more fickle than she would have believed, or he'd given up on a lost cause because when her schedule brought her back to his clinic three weeks later, he didn't say a personal word to her, other than to ask how Grace was doing.

"I don't know," Molly admitted, wishing that she hadn't caused such a gulf between them. Even though she knew she couldn't ever love Joe the way he'd professed to love her, she missed their easy friendship, the long conversations about everything and nothing.

She wanted to tell him about her dreams—dreams of her and Lena as children, holding each other tight as their parents screamed and fought, then, made wild, furious love on the other side of the thin wall. She wanted to share how even as she tried to keep from dwelling on the past, her mutinous mind had begun ticking off memories like rosary beads in the hands of the more devout old nuns.

There were days that the thoughts and words swelled up inside her head, crowding out the present, clamoring for release. She wanted to tell Joe all these things, but a chasm as wide and deep as the Grand Canyon loomed between her and the man their patients fondly referred to as Dr. Joe. He didn't seem eager to breach it and she didn't know how.

"I call her at least twice a week, and she seems all right. But Theo says the spark that always lit up a room is missing."

"That's not surprising," he offered as he put a tray of scalpels and tweezers into the autoclave. "Recovery takes time. It hasn't even been three months since she lost her mother. Perhaps she's not as proficient at denial as some people."

Well, they certainly weren't the comforting words she'd been hoping for. But at least it was the first personal thing he'd said to her since the embarrassingly public blowup a month after they'd returned from Los Angeles.

"I assume you're talking about me."

His gaze slid over her obliquely, giving nothing away. Molly realized she was holding her breath, but just when she thought he was going to say something, Naomi appeared at the door, announcing the arrival of a patient in the late stages of labor, and the opportunity to attempt to mend the charred bridges between them had passed.

* * *

In his wide lonely bed, Reece slept lightly, like a soldier in a far distant war zone expecting a heat-seeking missile to land in his bedroll.

Although he lived in what many would consider one of the most beautiful locations in the world, Reece's days and nights were spent in a howling black void as cold as a witch's heart. A vast empty darkness where Lena's bright, shimmering light had once shone like a beacon.

From time to time a white-hot rage would burn its way through the fog surrounding his brain, a fire quenched only by increasing quantities of whiskey and brandy.

Every night he'd go to bed and hope to die. Every morning he'd awake to the bleached white arid dawn of a new day. Another day in the years of aloneness stretching out before him like parched desert sands.

Some days after the funeral—he was not very accurate about passing time—he woke with a burning need to go to the site of the crash. Perhaps he'd merely dreamed his Lena's death. Perhaps, he thought, crazed with hope, the entire horrendous episode had merely been a figment of his alcohol-sodden mind.

But when he got to the tight narrow curve and saw some remnants of glass on the side of the road, Reece knew he'd not dreamed or imagined anything. It was frighteningly real.

Ignoring the blare of a horn and the raised middle finger of a driver speeding down the cliff, Reece squatted down beside the road and picked up a piece of glass that had once belonged to the minivan's headlights. He slipped the piece of glass into his pocket and took it home with him, where he continued to touch it several times each day, as if it were his own personal lodestone. His private, secret link to Lena.

Six weeks after the funeral, the prosecuting county attorney contacted Reece to tell him that the drunken driver had plea-bargained his way into a reckless driving and involuntary manslaughter plea. Under normal conditions that would have involved jail time. Unfortunately, the assistant D.A. who didn't sound old enough to shave yet, informed him, because of the crowded prisons throughout the state, they'd had no choice but to recommend probation and counseling.

"I understand," Reece managed. As he'd been doing for weeks, he willed his consciousness to a cold remote calm. There were times, when he actually managed to go for hours beneath this protective glacier without dwelling on his loss.

But invariably, like Jack the Ripper stalking his prey in the mists of London's deadly fog, it would sneak up behind him and waylay him with a force that took his breath away and left him literally doubled over with pain. And this, he thought, as he opened a new bottle of Chivas Regal, was definitely one of those times.

Theo fretted and Alex tried to talk reason into him, but Reece ignored their well-meaning efforts and continued his futile attempt to fill the gaping hole in his heart and in his life with alcohol, bitterness and self-pity.

Molly was about thirty miles outside of Window Rock, trying to see through a north country wind storm that filled the air with lightning and blinding red dust when the cellular phone in the motor home rang.

"Thank God I found you," Theo said when Molly answered.

Although the temperature outside the van was in the low hundreds, Molly's blood immediately turned to ice. "What happened? Is it Grace?"

"Oh, hell," Theo muttered with self-disgust. "I'm sorry, Molly. I should have realized after Lena's accident, you'd expect the worst.... Yes, I'm calling about Grace. She's all right physically."

"But not emotionally?"

"Emotionally, she's a mess. And Reece is impossible." Theo snorted. "He's refused to return to the hospital and spends all his time holed up in the library, drinking and creating imaginary scenarios of horrendously gruesome ways to kill that drunk driver...."

"But he's a grown man. He'll eventually come to grips with his own pain. It's Gracie that Alex and I are worried about."

"I read that children feel a period of disorganization and chaos after a parent's death," Molly said. "Perhaps she needs professional counseling."

"We tried that last week. And again today. She refuses to open up. She just smiled at the therapist and drew pretty pictures of her mommy in heaven planting those goddamn tulips. And meanwhile she's taken to wearing Lena's jewelry and burying her dolls in the garden."

"What?" Molly pulled off to the side of the empty road that trailed like an undulating black ribbon through the miles of deserted reservation land. "She's burying her dolls?"

"Alex caught her yesterday. Apparently she's been burying them in the morning, then digging them up again after dinner."

"Oh, Lord." Molly lowered her forehead to the steering wheel and closed her eyes against the pain gripping her heart. She took a deep breath and tried to focus, not on her own grief, but on what needed to be done. "I'll be there as soon as I can."

"Alex and I were hoping you'd say that." Theo's relief was so palpable, Molly felt as if it had ridden the air through the cellular signal to surround her.

"Should I call Reece?"

"No," Theo answered quickly. Too quickly, Molly thought. "I don't want to give him the opportunity to tell you not to come. I think it's better if we spring it on him."

Molly agreed. But after she'd hung up and turned the motor home around to head southwest to Los Angeles, she wondered if Theo's concerns had anything to do with the possibility that Reece might think she would try to take her daughter away from him.

He'd already lost so much, Molly didn't want to have to do that. On the other hand, she considered bleakly as she dialed the number of the Sister of Mercy's Mother House, she fully intended to do whatever it took to comfort and protect her child.

Chapter Twenty

"I'm so glad you've come," Theo said simply when she opened the door to Molly.

"How could I not?" Molly asked as she hugged the older woman. "I'm just glad you called me. After the last time I was here..."

"Alex and I think we may have made a mistake about that," Theo admitted. "But Reece has always been so strong, even when he was a little boy and his parents died, I believed he could handle losing Lena, as well."

Molly had never found it particularly strange that Reece seemed to have suffered no ill effects from being orphaned at such an early age. However, lately, she'd begun to wonder if perhaps they were both experts in denial.

Ever since Lena's death, there had been times when Molly feared she'd explode, allowing everything she'd been refusing to feel herself all these years to come hurtling to the surface.

"Reece is in the library," Theo said. "As usual. Alex and Dan took Grace to the movies and they're going to go out for ice cream later. That should give you at least three hours to knock some sense into his stubborn head."

Molly could only hope that would be enough.

The library shutters were closed, but enough natural light remained to allow her to see Reece clearly and even knowing how he'd cut himself off from the world, Molly was shocked at his appearance.

He'd lost a great deal of weight. His face was all harsh planes and shadows. The lines on either side of his mouth were so deep, they looked as if they'd been chiseled in granite, and the sunken flesh beneath his eyes was an ugly saffron color. She couldn't move. All she could do was stand in the doorway and stare at this haggard, tormented stranger.

Reece blinked at her from his dim and musty lair, unable to believe his eyes. He'd been prepared to tell Theo, or Alex, or even Dan, who'd recently joined the others in trying to coax him out of his hermitage, to leave him the hell alone. But the sight of Molly, standing there, backlit by the blinding California sun he'd been avoiding like some paranoid vampire, left him speechless.

For a long silent time they looked at each other across the abyss that had been inexorably widening between them ever since Molly had signed away all rights of maternity to her sister, ensuring that their relationship—indeed, the lives of all four people involved—would change forever.

Molly was the first to break the heavy silence. "I was in the neighborhood and thought I'd drop by."

Her calm tone, laced with her own wry humor and faint regret revealed none of the pain he knew she must still feel from those ugly, killing words he'd shot straight into her heart the last time they'd spoken. The words had been born of his anguish, but his intention had been to mortally wound. And yet here she was, back in his life like a breath of fresh air that promised to blow away the dark dank cloud that had been hovering over him for months.

Reece had missed Molly horribly without even realizing he'd been missing her. He'd needed her without admitting it, even to himself.

"It'd probably be easier for me to perform surgery in the middle of the San Diego Freeway at rush hour than to say I'm sorry." He took a deep harsh breath. "But I am."

She smiled at that. A soft smile that wrapped him in comforting warmth. "Stop the presses. Dr. Reece Longworth has just admitted to imperfection."

"I'm not a doctor anymore." He belatedly realized that she must have been contacted by a worried Theo and wondered exactly how much his aunt had told her.

"Nonsense." Her soft tone changed into the take-charge ER nurse he'd worked so well with for so many years. The woman who, in what seemed like another lifetime, had been his very best friend. "You took an oath, Reece. You can't just turn your back on the medical profession the way a sporting goods store owner can put a Gone Fishing sign on the door. You'll always be a doctor. Whether you're practicing or not."

"I'm not practicing. And I have no intention of ever walking into a hospital again."

"What a waste that would be." She entered the room and sat down on the leather sofa facing his chair. She was dressed in a pair of soft faded jeans and a blue chambray blouse. And cowboy boots. Reece almost smiled, thinking she looked more like a cowgirl than a nun. "And how self-indulgent of you."

What the hell did she want from him? He'd already apologized, dammit! What more did she expect?

"I'd forgotten how bossy you can be."

She crossed her legs with an angry swish of denim. "And I'd forgotten how stubborn you can be." His tenacity, which once had resulted in lives being saved, was at the moment proving to be a flaw. "I also never realized you were a coward."

The words struck home, just as she'd intended. Reece managed, just barely, to tamp down the anger. "Bull's-eye. Give the lady a Kewpie doll... If you've come all this way to insult me, Saint Molly, you're out of luck. There's nothing you can call me that I haven't already called myself."

Her own temper, which had kept her in hot water during so much of her childhood, flared. "Dammit, Reece, I understand you're hurting. Don't you think I am? We both lost someone we loved. But how do you think Lena would feel if she knew you were indulging in a maudlin drunken pity party while your daughter was left to fend for herself?"

He burrowed deeper into the chair, reached out, refilled his glass with Scotch, then, with his eyes locked on hers, took a long swallow. He'd die before he let her know that he was getting damn sick and tired of the taste of liquor.

"Obviously these past years on your own out in the wild West have hardened you. No more velvet gloves for Sister Molly. You've definitely taken up bare-knuckles fighting."

"I hate fighting. But I'll do it when it's important. Like to save two people I love."

"Don't waste your love on me, Molly." He turned away. "I'm not worth it." He reached for the bottle again, then seemed to reconsider and dropped his hand into his lap instead. "Hell, I couldn't save her. I'll never forgive myself for that."

"It wasn't your fault."

"I was a doctor," he said flatly. Stubbornly. "I was trained to save lives. But I couldn't save the single life that mattered most to me."

"No one could have saved her, Reece. Not you, not Dr. Parker—"

"Not even your precious, all-knowing, all-powerful God? You've always used your faith as a fucking shield to protect you from having to live a normal life like the rest of us. Well, what happened this time, Saint Molly? Aren't you ever haunted by the sight of Lena lying in that damn hospital bed, kept alive by those obscene tubes and machines? Don't you ever lie awake at night, wondering if you'd just prayed a little harder, Lena might still be alive?"

It was his turn to hit the mark. Of course those thoughts had occurred to her. They'd hovered at the back of her mind, but instead of hiding away in the dark like Reese, she'd thrown herself into her work to avoid dealing with what she feared would be devastating pain. The same wrenching emotional pain she'd successfully avoided all these years.

Lena's desperate need for love had been born out of that tragic, horrifying Christmas Eve night so many years ago. Although Molly had only been a child herself, she'd taken it upon herself to try to protect and comfort her younger sister. That was the night she'd begun building her parapets in earnest. Constructed stone by stone over the years, the barricade had grown as high and forbidding to the outside world as an old-time convent wall. She'd truly believed she could keep her childhood at bay, but now Molly realized she'd been lying to herself all these years.

Faced with the reality of her situation, frustrated by Reece's behavior and worried sick about Grace, she felt the gate come crashing down and the walls collapse.

The almost unbearable pain she'd managed to evade most of her life flooded over her. Clutching her stomach, she bent over and began to sob.

At first a shocked Reece couldn't believe what he was seeing. Molly, who'd always been the voice of wisdom, calm and order, had burst into a furious storm of weeping. Her face was buried in her hands and her slender shoulders were shaking like a willow in a hurricane as she rocked back and forth, bawling the deep, gut-wrenching sobs of a suffering child.

Reece had never seen Molly so abandoned; he'd never imagined she could experience such agony. Tears flowed from between her fingers, drenching her face, her neck, her chambray blouse.

He wanted to do something, anything, to stem this tide of anguish. To calm the violent seas that seemed to be storming inside her. The shock of seeing her terrible pain suddenly had Reece, for the first time in months, feeling stone-cold sober. He pushed himself out of the chair and made his way to the couch where he gathered her to him and buried his face into her drenched and matted hair.

"Aw, Molly." He brushed his cheek against the side of her wet face. "Hell, honey, I'm sorry." He touched his lips to her skin and tasted the salt of her tears. It was only later that he realized that part of the wetness on her face was from his own tears. "I'm so damn sorry. For everything."

They held each other for a long time, rocking and weeping in shared grief. Eventually, the tempest blew over, leaving behind a feeling of much-needed fresh air.

"I'm sorry." She swiped at her wet face with the backs of her hands, looking so much like Grace, Reece felt something move deep inside him. "I didn't mean to make such a fool of myself."

"There's nothing foolish about tears." He ran his hand down her tangled hair.

"I never cry." It was true. Not since... Molly shook her head, unable to think about that Christmas Eve night anymore. She knew she'd have to deal with it. But not right now. Not when her grief for the loss of her sister was still so fresh and raw.

"Then I'd say you're long overdue." He took out a handkerchief, handed it to her and once again, as she blew her nose, was reminded of Grace. "Besides, didn't Saint Augustine say something about a saint being a man willing to make a fool of himself to prove a point to fools?"

"I don't know." Reece's words reminded her of her theological contests with Thomas. Although she'd never seen him again after the rape, periodic notes from the former priest would arrive at the Mother House for her from all over the country, and she thought about him often.

"Well, if he didn't, he should have." Reece realized that for the first time in a very long while, he was actually almost smiling.

Then he sighed. "I miss her so damn much, Molly."

She sighed, as well. "I know. I do, too."

"I can't let her go. I keep playing the answering machine tape over and over again, pretending she's still here."

"I called here a couple weeks ago," Molly admitted. "And when I heard that recording, I tried to tell myself that it had all been a nightmare. That Lena was still alive." She didn't mention that her first startled thought was that she was hearing her sister's voice from the grave.

"I've been doing a lot of reading about death." Reece linked his fingers together between his knees. "Everyone keeps bringing me all these self-help books. Dan brought one by C. S. Lewis."

"I read that one," Molly said. Reece had not been the only one searching for answers. "At least part of it. I stopped when I got to the part where he decided that our loved ones don't watch us after their death because it'd be too painful for them to watch our lives continue without them in it."

"I wondered about that," Reece allowed. "About whether it would hurt Lena too much to watch Grace growing up without her mother." He shook his head. "But I can't believe Lewis is right. I need to believe that she can still see our daughter. And me."

"Which only makes you feel more guilty for being alive," Molly guessed. She'd felt the same way herself, many times.

"That's probably the understatement of the millennium." He'd stopped reading the damn books after that.

"Dan says I've been romanticizing my relationship with Lena," Reece divulged. "He says I'm idealizing the potential of my murdered marriage."

"Since from what Theo and Alex tell me, Dan's still into hit-and-run relationships, I'm not certain he's an expert on marriage," Molly said dryly.

The familiar tone made Reece grin. "That's pretty much what I told him."

They exchanged a smile. And both felt a little better.

"Are you going to stay?"

"For a while. If it's all right with you." Actually, it would take an entire team of Clydesdales to remove her from this house until she ensured her daughter's emotional well-being, but Molly wanted it to seem as if she was offering Reece a choice.

"I can't think of anyone I'd rather have here than you."

Hearing the honesty in his tone gave Molly the first hope she'd felt in a very long time.

Grace was obviously pleased to see the woman she knew as her aunt, but Molly was concerned by the change in the child. She appeared far too grown-up.

"It's not so surprising," Alan Bernstein told

Molly, Reece, Theo and Alex after she'd invited the
psychiatrist to dinner to surreptitiously watch Grace
in action. "Her mother's death has pushed her into
premature adulthood." He glanced over at Molly.
"You, more than most people, should understand
how that can happen."

"I do." Molly shook her head with regret. "But
understanding doesn't seem to help. She's like a
miniature Mary Poppins, fetching this, buzzing
around picking up after people, trying to anticipate
everyone's every need."

"I keep expecting her to burst out singing 'Chim-
Chim-Cheree' and fly over the rooftops," Theo muttered.

"She feels the need to be perfect," the psychiatrist
said. "She's already lost her mother. It's only natural
she'd develop an obsessive fear of her father abandoning her, as well."

"Lena didn't abandon her," Alex pointed out.

"I'd never do that," Reece said at the same time.

The psychiatrist took Alex's objection first. "She's
too young to distinguish the difference between death
and abandonment. One day her mother was there. The
next day she was gone. That's frightening for a little
girl. Especially one who'd bonded as closely with her
mother as Grace had with Lena."

As he turned toward Reece, Molly tried to ignore
the faint prick of painful envy his words caused. What
kind of person was she that she could feel jealous of
her dead sister?

"And, no offense intended, Reece, but you've already given indications of deserting her by your self-

imposed isolation. So, to protect herself, she's become like Antigone.''

"Don't you think that's reaching a bit far?'' Theo asked.

"Not really. Don't forget, after Oedipus realized he'd killed his father and married his mother, he stabbed himself in the eyes, then set off on a self-imposed exile—not unlike your retreat into the library, Reece.

"Antigone dutifully became his guide as they wandered the countryside. She was devoted, compliant, she never uttered a single word of complaint about her motherless state—remember, her mother killed herself after discovering her husband was really her son. The poor kid didn't stand a chance. She became the archetypal daughter of a helpless father.''

"Just like Grace.'' Reece accepted the unflattering analysis with a heavy heart. "I'm going to make that up to her.''

"I have no doubt you will.'' He smiled around the table. "Grace is fortunate to have so many loving adults in her life. Give her time, don't hover too much, but be there when she needs to talk about her mother. Which,'' he stressed, "she will. When she's ready.''

Having always respected Alan Bernstein, Molly was not surprised when he was proven right. As Reece began to emerge from his emotional cave, Grace, in turn, began to relax her vigil. The first time she walked past a newspaper left on the coffee table without hurrying to pick it up and put it in the recycling bin like a good little housewife, Molly felt like singing hosannas.

* * *

Two weeks after Molly had arrived at the house, she was sitting at the kitchen table, coloring in the Navajo book with Grace when the little girl suddenly put her crayon down and looked up at Molly, her young face sober.

"I wanted to go to the store with Mommy that day," she revealed.

"Oh?" Even as her nerves tangled with fear that she wouldn't handle this long-overdue conversation correctly, Molly managed a casual, but interested expression.

"There was a carnival at the grocery store parking lot. I wanted to ride the merry-go-round again. But Mommy said we didn't have time to play because of Daddy's party, and she left me with Aunt Theo instead."

Molly waited.

"I was really mad."

"I can understand that. Riding a merry-go-round is a special thing."

"There's this white horse with a black mane. He's the best. I named him Snowflake. The carnival was leaving the next day. I wanted to ride him one more time. But Mommy said they'd be back next year and I could ride him then."

"A year seems like a very long time."

"It is a long time." Grace looked down at the picture of a Navajo boy riding a pony she'd colored white with a black mane. "I told her I hated her."

Pansy blue eyes shimmering with moisture and worry lifted to Molly's. "Do you think Mommy knows I didn't mean it?" she asked in a frail, trembling little voice that made Molly feel as if her heart was shattering into a thousand little pieces.

"Of course she knows." She reached out and ran her hands down the wavy ebony curls and across the thin, slumped shoulders. "And she understands." Molly forced a smile. "You're not the only little girl that ever said hurtful things to her mother. Lena and I used to talk back to our mama, too."

They'd always gotten smacked and had their mouths washed out with soap for sassing, but Molly kept that unattractive little detail to herself.

"Really?"

"Really."

"I pray to my mommy every night," Grace admitted. "Because Alex told me that she's my guardian angel."

"Your uncle Alex is pretty smart."

"I know." A breath escaped soft pink lips that she'd been worrying with her teeth. "But I still wish I'd told her in person."

"Perhaps you can write her a note," Molly suggested.

"How can we get a note to heaven?"

Molly smiled. "I have an idea about that...."

Three hours later, they were standing on the beach below the cliff house. Hovering above them in a sky so blue and clear, it was almost blinding, was a huge red, yellow and purple kite. The colors, Grace had explained gravely as she'd carefully chosen the bright kite at the toy store, were the same as the tulips she'd planted with her mother.

"Okay," Molly said, "let's have the letter."

Grace reached into the pocket of her bright red

jeans and pulled out the folded note that she'd labored over with Molly's help.

Molly tore a slit in the letter, then folded it around the kite string. "Here it goes."

As soon as she let go of the letter, it skimmed up the string in a flash, as if carried aloft on angel wings. Molly and Grace watched and when it had reached the kite, Molly let go of the string and the kite sailed out over the water, higher and higher, like a brightly feathered seabird until it became a tiny spot that disappeared somewhere beyond the horizon.

"I think she got it," Molly said.

"I know she did." Grace put her hand against the front of her Aladdin T-shirt. "I can feel it in here."

Looking down into her daughter's rapt face, Molly experienced a surge of love so strong, it made her breath catch in her throat. As they walked hand in hand back up the stone steps leading to the house, she felt a weight lifting from her heart, soaring off into the cobalt blue sky, along with the tulip-colored kite.

Reece had refused to visit Lena's grave. He hadn't been able to bear to think of his sweet, beautiful wife lying in the ground. Especially when she'd been so afraid of the dark. The first night they'd spent together, she'd insisted on keeping a night-light on. That habit had continued all during their marriage.

Although they'd admittedly had their problems in the beginning, as she'd come to trust that he wasn't going to leave her—like all those other ill-suited men, and her own father had done—she'd changed. Indeed, during the years with Grace, the laughing woman he'd been clever enough to convince to marry him had reminded Reece of a butterfly, bright and seemingly lighter than air. Which was why, he considered as he walked through the heavy, wrought-iron gates of the cemetery, she didn't belong here surrounded by all these ubiquitous angels and lugubrious inscriptions.

He found the simple marble marker on which her name, the too-brief span of her life, and a single line—beloved wife, mother and sister—were carved.

Mindless of the wet grass, he knelt down on one knee and, reaching out, delicately ran his index finger around those insignificant words as a blind man might trace the facial features of his beloved.

He'd thought perhaps that by coming here today he'd achieve some comfort. But although he felt pleased that he'd overcome his dread of finally seeing the stone that Theo and Alex had insisted on ordering, the weight of grief remained heavy on his heart.

Not wanting to return home when he was in such a bleak mood, Reece drove along the Pacific Coast Highway. Although the day had dawned bright and clear, a sudden storm had blown in from the sea, bringing with it heavy rains that sheeted the windshield and hissed beneath the tires of his car.

He pulled over at Malibu's Surfrider's Beach, parked and sat in the car, watching the reckless surfers who'd rushed to the beach at the first sign of the storm.

During his days in the ER, he'd treated numerous surfers and had never understood why they would risk life and limb to ride the high-breaking tides into the rocky beach. But now he realized that there was something to be said for laughing in the face of Death.

Mindless of the wind and rain, he got out of the car and stormed along the cliff side, shaking his face in the face of that black-hearted dark angel. And at God. He cursed a Maker who could allow such a wonderful woman to die. He cursed himself for not knowing how to live without her. He swore and he shouted and he cried. Hot furious tears mingled with the icy autumn rain and ran down his cheeks; he didn't care. His clothes became drenched; he didn't notice.

Reece had no idea how long he was out on the cliffs. He was unaware of more than one curious look from a surfer who'd wisely given up when the tide crashed higher and harder as the day came to an end. A hazy red ball of sun, barely visible through the driving rain, dipped into the whitecapped water.

As the water appeared to flame, Reece lifted his arms to the darkening sky and turned his face upward so that the driving rain felt like needles against his skin.

"Lena!" he cried with a great primal howl of aloneness.

The single word, rife with grief and anger and regret, seemed to hover in the sky, like a seagull struggling to fly against the wind. And then it drifted away. And the water turned to a dark steel as the sun sank beneath the surface.

He stood there, a solitary figure on the edge of the western coastline, dragging huge drafts of rain-cleansed air into his lungs. The long-overdue release was cathartic, almost orgasmic.

And as he returned to the car, thinking that perhaps he'd take Molly and Grace out for a pizza tonight, for the first time since Lena's death, Reece found himself looking forward instead of back.

Chapter Twenty-One

Under the circumstances, Sister Benvenuto released Molly from her verbal agreement to return to the Mother House and help with the postulants.

"I still wish you'd change your mind, Molly," she said as she signed the required papers to release Molly from her vows. "But after much prayer, I've come to the reluctant conclusion that God has a different plan for your life."

"I only wish I knew what it was," Molly murmured. Although she wasn't second-guessing her decision to leave the order, the realization that she was leaving made her more than a little sad.

"It will undoubtedly be revealed in its own time." Sister Benvenuto signed the last form with a determined flourish, then rose from behind the desk and gathered the former Sister of Mercy into her arms. "Guard your heart well, dear," she said. "And have a happy life, whatever you choose."

Afraid she was going to embarrass them both by

breaking into tears, Molly managed a wobbly smile, assured the nun that she certainly would stay in touch, then walked out the door of the Mother House, feeling strangely let down and excited all at the same time.

The idea that for the first time in her life, she was completely free to choose whatever path she wanted was more than a little daunting. Fortunately, there were several immediate matters that needed taking care of. Such as finding a job. And flying to Flagstaff to have a long-overdue talk with Joe.

He was waiting at the arrival gate when her flight landed. Molly felt the familiar warmth of genuine friendship and wished it could be something deeper. Falling in love with Joe Salvatore would be so uncomplicated. She almost envied the woman who would be granted that pleasure.

His arms, as they wrapped around her, were strong and sure and comforting. But despite her unbidden response to that illicit kiss they'd shared, his embrace did not touch a single sensual chord inside her.

He took hold of her shoulders and put her a little away from him in order to look down into her face. "So. You've done it. You've left the order."

"Does it show?"

She was only joking, but to her surprise, he seemed to be considering that. After another longer, more probing look, he nodded his dark head. "I think it does. There's a spark of freedom in your eyes that wasn't there before. You have the look, Molly, me love," he said on an awful brogue that made her laugh, "of a woman who's looking life full in the face."

"And discovering that it's a little frightening," she

admitted with a light, musical laugh that drew the appreciative attention of a male passenger checking in at the counter.

Joe laughed, as well, then hugged her again. "You'll do fine. Better than fine. You're going to soar, sweetheart. I only wish I was going to be around to watch."

"Joe—"

"Later." He took her carry-on bag from her hand. "I've booked you into the hotel. We'll have dinner and you can fill me in on the latest chapter in the saga of Molly McBride."

The hotel was situated in a stand of Ponderosa pine forest on the outskirts of town at the foot of the San Francisco mountains. Although the setting was wonderfully serene and scenic, Molly's nerves were tied up in knots.

"Was it difficult?" he asked, studying her over the rim of the champagne flute. Although she was nervous about drinking wine with this man again after what had happened the last time, she couldn't refuse his insistence on toasting what he kept calling her freedom.

"Not as difficult as I thought it would be," she admitted. "I've spent so many years agonizing over the validity of my vocation, when I finally decided to leave, it seemed absolutely, positively right."

"Funny how things work out, isn't it?" he mused. "If the good Dr. Longworth hadn't gone into a tailspin after his wife's death, forcing you to return and take care of your daughter, you might have continued vacillating about your true feelings for years."

There was something in his tone. A tinge of acid

sarcasm that reminded her uncomfortably of the day Reece had accused her of having an affair with Joe.

"Of course I care about Grace's well-being. But I also understand she's Reece's daughter," Molly insisted quietly.

"So you're never going to tell her the truth?"

"No. Of course not. Lena was her mother in every way that counted. And I'd never—ever—want any child to bear the burden of knowing she was the product of a brutal act like rape."

"Good point." He refilled his glass for the second time. When he went to pour more of the sparkling gold wine into Molly's glass, she covered it with her palm.

As he drank the wine, Joe looked out the tall windows at the darkening forest beyond. Dusk was settling over the mountains, casting everything in an ethereal, silvery pale light. Molly drew in a quick breath as she watched a herd of deer approach the man-made pond behind the hotel. Their ears were up like radar detectors, every lithe muscle in the slender brown bodies tensed, prepared to run from potential danger. As the silence between Molly and Joe lingered, stretching her already-taut nerves to near the breaking point, Molly decided she knew exactly how those skittish deer felt.

"You love him, don't you?" Joe's deep voice shattered the oppressive silence.

She knew better than to ask who he was talking about. "Of course I do. Reece was my best friend even before he and Lena met. I valued his friendship then, and I still do. Especially after all he's done for me. And Lena. And, especially Grace."

"It's more than that. You love him more than a former nun loves a mere friend. Or her brother-in-law. Or even the adoptive father of her child."

"That's not true."

"Of course it is." His dark eyes held both regret and pity. "You may not realize it yet, Molly. But you will."

Much, much later, after they'd said their goodbyes and promised to keep in touch—something they both knew would probably not happen, given the impossibility of their relationship—Molly lay alone in the too-wide hotel bed, listening to the wail of a freight train echoing in the midnight hour. Even that lonely whistle couldn't drown out Joe's ominous prediction that continued to toll deep in her fretful mind.

Part Three

Chapter Twenty-Two

1994

"You aren't going to wear that, are you?"

Reece turned to look at his six-year-old daughter, who was sitting cross-legged on his bed, her frown registering her disapproval at the shirt he'd selected.

"I'd better," he said, buttoning the black pleated-front shirt, "if I know what's good for me."

"Because Meredith bought it for you." A deeper scowl suggested Grace disapproved of his choice in women even more than she did his shirt.

"When someone goes to the trouble of shopping for you, the least you can do is show appreciation for the gift," he said mildly. "The same way you wore that sweater with the purple dinosaur on the front that Uncle Alex bought you last Christmas."

Grace's sigh sounded far older than her years. "I didn't want to tell him that I was too old for Barney."

"Exactly. The same way I didn't want to tell Mere-

dith that our taste in clothing differs." Which would
be putting it mildly, Reece thought. He felt like some
sort of rap music star in the black, collarless tuxedo
shirt.

"I suppose she thinks it makes you look like a
Hollywood stud," Grace decided.

A stud? "Where did you hear that expression?"

"I don't know." She shrugged and traced the out-
line of the dark brown diamonds on the black bedspread. "I guess I just heard it somewhere."

"Obviously not on 'Sesame Street' or 'Mr. Rog-
ers.'"

"Oh, Dad." Curls bounced as his frighteningly
precocious daughter shook her head. "You're as bad
as Uncle Alex. I haven't watched them for years."

As he suddenly wondered what his daughter *was*
watching these days, Reece made a note to look into
kidproofing his cable channels.

There were days, and this was one of them, that
Reece still couldn't believe how his life had changed
in the past three years. Although he still missed Lena,
he found himself talking out loud to her less and less.
And despite Molly's coaxing, he hadn't returned to
medicine. But thanks to Theo, he had a new career.

At first he'd been furious when he'd discovered
that his aunt had taken all those short stories he'd
written, depicting the various ways he could kill the
man who'd destroyed his life, to the producer of her
soap opera who'd been in the market for a prime-time
program to pitch to the networks.

Before Reece knew what was happening, he'd been
offered an obscene amount of money for the short
dramas that had been therapy for his pain. And if that

wasn't weird enough, he was offered a job as head writer for the producer's new pet project, an anthology series reminiscent of the old "Twilight Zone."

"It's in the genes," Theo had proudly crowed at the time. "It only stands to reason that a nephew of mine would be one helluva talented writer."

Eighteen months after the series had debuted, Reece still didn't consider himself "one helluva writer."

Apparently his peers did, however, since he'd been nominated for an Emmy for the episode in which a vengeful doctor killed the carjacker who'd murdered his wife. When the thug showed up in the ER suffering a bullet wound in the chest, the lidocaine cream the doctor rubbed into the man's chest caused a fatal heart attack.

"I wish I could go with you tonight," Grace coaxed.

"It's a school night."

"Lots of kids get to stay up late on school nights," she complained.

"Not my kid."

Her frustrated sigh ruffled her jet bangs. "If you win, you're not going to tell me to go to bed on national television, like Johnny Newman's mom and dad did last year, are you?"

"I'll try to refrain from behaving like a parent." He passed up the silver and turquoise studs, opting for plain black ones instead. There was a limit to what he was willing to do to keep Meredith Rivers happy. "Am I allowed to thank you for all the help you've given to my career?"

"Like staying out of your way when you're writing?"

He laughed. "Exactly. It's true, you know." His expression sobered, his gaze softened. "I don't know what I'd have done without you these past years, kiddo."

"I don't know what you would have done without me, either." In contrast to his sudden seriousness, Grace's grin was quick, quirky and all too familiar. Molly must have looked like this at six, Reece mused. On those rare occasions she might have had something to smile about. Before her brutal father turned a little girl's already-rocky world upside down.

"I wish Aunt Molly was able to sit with me," Grace said.

"I do, too. But she had to work."

"No, she didn't."

He stopped in the act of putting on his dress shoes. "She told me she was working the night shift."

Understandably unwilling to return to Mercy Samaritan after her sister's death in the hospital, she'd taken a position as head of trauma nursing at Cedars-Sinai.

"I heard her tell Aunt Theo that she had a date. With some doctor she used to work with in Arizona. Dr. Sal something."

"Salvatore?" Reece frowned, remembering the BIA doctor who'd shown up uninvited at the house after Lena's accident. The one who'd obviously been in love with Molly. He hadn't liked the guy then. And he doubted he'd feel any different today.

"That's his name." Grace nodded. "Joe Salvatore."

"You must have misunderstood her."

"No, I didn't. They're going out to dinner, then he's taking her flying."

"Flying?"

"In a plane. Dr. Salvatore has his own plane. He flew it all the way here from Arizona. Isn't that neat?"

It wasn't exactly on a par with piloting the space shuttle to Mars, Reece thought. "Sounds pretty neat to me," he said instead.

Although he'd been disappointed to learn that Molly wouldn't be watching the awards tonight with Theo, Alex and Grace, he'd realized she couldn't take a night off to watch television. To discover she was going out on a damn date with some slick Italian doctor from her past irked. Whatever happened to loyalty?

"It's funny thinking of Aunt Molly going out with boyfriends," Grace said.

"She's allowed." When his tone sounded a bit too harsh, Reece softened it. "After all, she's not a nun anymore."

"I know. But I wish she'd marry you, instead."

"What?"

"If you and Aunt Molly got married, she could live here with us. And she wouldn't be going flying with Dr. Salvatore. And you wouldn't have to wear Meredith's ugly black shirt."

There was, Reece allowed, some sort of skewed logic in that statement. "Your aunt Molly and I are just friends."

"She loves you."

"Where did you hear *that*?"

This was definitely turning out to be a night of revelations. At least, Reece thought, this conversation was succeeding in getting rid of the giant condors that had been flapping their wings inside his gut whenever he thought about the anxiety-filled evening ahead.

He didn't care if he won an Emmy. It was an honor just to be nominated. He'd been telling himself—and everyone else who'd brought up the subject—that for weeks. Reece wondered when he'd become such a damn liar.

"Aunt Molly tells me all the time that she loves you. And me, too."

Reece relaxed. "She meant she loves us because we're her family. Like she loves Uncle Alex and Aunt Theo and Dan."

Grace appeared to consider that. "I still think it would be neat if you got married," she said stubbornly. Another Molly trait, Reece thought.

"Well, don't hold your breath waiting for me to walk down the aisle, punkin." He ruffled the glossy curls that surrounded his daughter's head like an ebony halo. "Because I've already been married."

"Eddie Bank's father has been married five times," she informed him. "And he's engaged again. To that new lifeguard on 'Baywatch.'"

Reece refrained from saying that in his opinion it was high time the forty-five-year-old director grew up and quit marrying women young enough to be his daughter.

"Well, Eddie's father and I obviously have different ideas about marriage."

Grace folded her arms across a scarlet T-shirt emblazoned with whales. After a school outing to San

Diego's Sea World, she'd turned into a committed environmentalist. "I don't know which is worse," she muttered. "Having five stepmothers like Eddie. Or no mom at all."

"You *do* have it rough," he commiserated. "I'd better call Theo and tell her to stop and pick up some cake and ice cream on the way to the house."

"For your celebration party?"

"No. For *your* pity party."

His chiding words had the desired effect. Grace giggled in good-natured surrender, and as he lifted her off the bed and into his arms for a hug, Reece thought for the umpteenth time, that his beautiful, intensely inquisitive and frustratingly stubborn daughter was, without a single doubt, the light of his life.

A shining light he'd almost extinguished with his selfish behavior after Lena's death, when he'd left Grace to emotionally fend for herself. Hardly a day went by that Reece didn't thank God, or the Fates, for Molly's interference.

She'd slipped into their lives as easily as if she'd always been there, being protective of Grace without being smothering, and tender in a maternal way that didn't intrude on his own right of parenthood. She radiated wholeness and an uncomplicated, all-embracing, warmhearted love.

She also spoke of her sister often, always with warmth and affection, and encouraged Grace to recall all those joyful times of shared pleasure that so easily get forgotten as children grow into adulthood.

When she'd first returned from Arizona, she'd had all the family members gather up things of Lena's that had held special significance for them. Theo had brought the matron of honor bouquet Lena had carried at her wedding, Alex had contributed a plaster hand-print she'd made for him for Father's Day when she'd been in the fourth grade. Dan had surprised everyone by unearthing a letter she'd written from a camp the parish had sent foster children to, begging him to break her out before she perished from the inedible food.

Reece had contributed their wedding album and a snapshot of their honeymoon, while Molly had opted for the college diploma her sister had worked so hard to earn. The eyes of all the adults gathered in the room had grown moist when Grace handed over the tattered teddy bear clad in the frilly pink net tutu her mother had sewn for her beloved stuffed animal.

"Okay," Molly had explained when the family had gathered together. "Here's the deal. Everyone's encouraged to look through these things as often as you want. The only rule is that we all have to be together whenever the memory box is opened."

Which was exactly what they'd done. In the beginning it was mostly Alex and Theo who had called the family together, in an attempt to encourage Grace to do likewise. Which, eventually, she began to do. Often. Molly had called her own counsels, and finally, one rainy Sunday afternoon, Reece had admitted his need to look through the album.

For a long time the box had stayed on a counter in the kitchen, close at hand. Then, as time went on, it was moved into the library. Finally, the last time Reece had seen it, it had been in the attic. And Grace seemed to have come to grips with her loss. As had he.

"What do I need an Emmy for?" Reece asked now as he twirled Grace around in much the same way he'd done when she was a toddler. Although she always complained she was too grown-up for such behavior, he noticed her giggles increased when he remembered to take the time to do it. "When I have you?"

"You can't put *me* on the mantel," she pointed out pragmatically. "I'm too big."

"True." And growing bigger by the day. Reece wondered, as he so often did, whether Lena was able to watch their daughter's seemingly quicksilver metamorphosis into a young lady.

If you are watching, he thought, *I hope you think I'm doing an okay job with our little girl.*

It wasn't easy raising a daughter without a mother, even with Molly's assistance. But Reece had no intention of ever marrying again. Losing someone you loved was just too painful. It was much, much easier—especially in this town with his newly acquired fame—to play the field.

He heard the door open and Theo call out their names. After having to defend his shirt yet again, Reece was finally on his way.

"Don't forget," Grace called after him, "don't say anything about my bedtime when you win your Emmy."

"My lips are sealed," he promised back over his shoulder.

As he walked out to his car, parked in the driveway, Reece looked up into the clear blue sky that would undoubtedly be filled with stars in a few hours.

He thought of Molly flying through the dark of

night with that undoubtedly oversexed BIA doctor. It caused something that felt ridiculously like jealousy to stir inside him.

"This is the biggest night of my life," he muttered as he twisted the key in the ignition of the new Jaguar he'd bought with the bonus the Emmy nomination had earned him. The engine sprang to life, humming impatiently. "The least she could do would be to stay home and offer me a little moral support."

He was nearly to Meredith's home in Brentwood when Reece wondered what Molly would have said if he'd asked her out tonight. Would she have gone to the awards ceremony with him instead of spending the evening with the Italian flyboy?

He tried to picture sweet, innocent Molly shopping for a dress at some Rodeo Drive boutique, hobnobbing with the likes of George Clooney or Candice Bergen at the party at Spagos after the awards show. He attempted to envision her indulging in a little juicy girl talk in the ladies' room with Meredith, or Sydney, or Starla, or any of the other interchangeable women he dated.

No. It was unimaginable. Molly might just as well still be a nun. Hell, he figured, although he knew she had turned thirty-one her last birthday, he'd bet she'd never been to bed with any of those bland, safe men she occasionally dated.

Not that Salvatore wasn't undoubtedly going to do his best to change that. The guy had had no qualms about hitting on her when she was a nun. Now that she was fair game, so to speak, he was undoubtedly planning to pull out all the stops tonight.

Although he knew his irritation was irrational,

Reece glared up at the cloudless sky once again and wished for rain. An old-fashioned duck strangler that would flood all the streets and runways and ground hotshot Joe Salvatore's goddamn plane.

"I still can't believe you did this!" Molly exclaimed as Joe pulled out a chair for her.

"I invited you out to dinner," he reminded her.

"You didn't tell me we were eating in San Diego."

She'd been floored when he'd driven her to the John Wayne Airport and announced they'd be dining at the famed Hotel del Coronado. The table was on a deck overlooking the sunset-gilded ocean. When he'd stopped at the hotel deli—located in an old stone wine cellar—to pick up the dinner he'd already ordered, she'd understood why he'd instructed her to dress casually.

"You didn't ask." His quick grin seemed designed to make her feel comfortable with him. "And I did mention taking you flying."

When Joe had first called her, telling her he was coming to town and would like to see her, Molly had been afraid that things would be tense between them. But, missing his friendship, she'd agreed and had discovered that they'd fallen back into the easygoing relationship they'd shared before he'd kissed her. Before he'd proclaimed his love.

"You're right." She returned his smile with one of her own. "Next time I'm asked out, I'll be sure to ask if the dinner part of the date includes a flight plan."

He bit into a French fry. "Go on many dates do you?"

"A few." Not nearly as many as Reece, she thought, comparing her occasional movie-and-pizza date with his hedonistic life-style. At least, she had to admit, most of the time he managed to keep his Hollywood life separate from his home life. And from what she'd been able to tell, Grace had not suffered any from the fact that her father was one of the most sought-after bachelors in town.

"I'm glad." He leaned back and took a long pull on his beer bottle. "I've been worried about you," he admitted. "Worried the good Dr. Longworth might break your heart."

She laughed at that. "Reece could never break my heart. He's my best friend."

"So you keep saying. Which makes me wonder—" he leaned forward and touched the tips of his fingers to her cheek "—why your face still gets warm and flushed whenever you talk about the guy."

"I have a wonderful relationship with Reece and Grace," she insisted quietly. "I'd never do anything to jeopardize that."

He gave her another long look that made Molly feel he could see all the way into her soul. "Like admitting you're in love with the guy?"

"Joe..." She backed away. "Please. I don't feel comfortable discussing my feelings for Reece with you."

"Fine." He shrugged, but the concern didn't leave his sleepy dark eyes. "Actually, I didn't ask you out to heckle you about your love life, Molly."

"Why did you ask me out?"

"For old times' sake. Because I miss you like hell. And because I wanted to invite you to my wedding."

"Your wedding?" Her lips curved. Feelings of relief and joy flowed through her like warm summer sunshine. "You're getting married?"

"Next month." He eyed her carefully. "You don't mind?"

"Mind? Oh, I think it's wonderful. I was so afraid—" As soon as she realized what she was about to say, Molly clamped her mouth shut.

"That I'd go through the rest of my life carrying a torch for you?" he asked mildly.

Once again Molly felt the hated heat flood into her face. She took a long drink of iced tea in an attempt to quench the fire.

"I really did love you, Molly. Still do, for that matter, but in a much safer way. The trouble with torch carrying," he murmured, the good-natured humor she'd always loved lightening his tone, "is that after a while you tend to burn your fingers."

She reached out and covered his hand with hers. "I love you, too." It was the absolute truth. "And I'm so happy for you.... So, who's the lucky woman?"

"Naomi."

"Naomi?" At first the idea surprised her. Then Molly realized they were a perfect match. Joe was impulsive, reckless and laughed easily and often. Naomi was serious, thoughtful and as calm as a warm tropical lagoon. She'd offer Joe an anchor, while he'd give her wings. "How wonderful for both of you!"

"We think so."

"Does this mean you're staying on with the BIA?"

"Actually, we've decided to open a traveling

clinic. Kind of pick up where you left off. Then later, after we have kids, perhaps…"

His voice drifted off as a shutter went down over eyes that only a moment earlier had danced with enthusiasm. "Hell. I'm sorry, Molly. I get talking about Naomi and our plans, which we're pretty psyched about, and my mouth just runs away with me."

"Don't worry about it. You're right to be excited about your plans. They sound wonderful. Including the children."

"You really ought to have a passel of kids of your own."

"I know." She thought it was a sign of personal growth that she could finally admit her secret desire out loud. "And I will, one of these days."

"Good." His renewed smile bathed her in a warm and approving light. "So, back to my invitation. The wedding's going to be on the rez. Think you can make it?"

"I wouldn't miss it for the world." Molly laughed with heartfelt pleasure, feeling as if the brisk ocean breeze had just blown away one of the last shadows hovering over her past.

After bestowing a dazzlingly seductive smile and a twenty-dollar tip on the parking valet who took her Porsche, Tessa made her way down the garden path to the bungalow at the Château Marmont Hotel. The hotel, secreted away behind the giant billboards and sun-bleached glitz of the Sunset Strip offered its guests an old-world charm and the ultimate in privacy.

"And tonight, we're offering a one-of-a-kind entertainment package to our Gold Star guests," she said as she brushed by a leafy green elephant-ear plant. "A private performance, so to speak, from Tessa Starr, the girl most likely to become a hooker."

She laughed at her bad joke. Thanks to the combination of pot and Valium she'd had today, she was floating. Tonight's party was with a big-money oil guy from Alaska who was looking to invest some of his black gold in the movie business.

Although her reputation for bounced checks and drugs had made her pretty much casting poison in town, causing her to finally cave in and accept Elaine Mathison's offer to come to work for her, Tessa had not given up on her dream of becoming a star. After all, this *was* acting in a way. Before each date, Elaine would give her a rundown on the client, allowing her to become whatever fantasy woman he desired.

When she'd learned that one of Elaine's other girls, Janis, had gotten this gig, Tessa had paid her two hundred bucks to call in with menstrual cramps.

"This could be your big chance," she told herself. "This could be the night you hit the big time."

Since she hadn't been given any specific instructions, she'd dressed carefully for what could be the most important audition of her life. The sea green silk dress was so thin, it was almost transparent, inviting a man to look closer to see whether or not he was imagining the naked breasts beneath it. She'd considered dispensing with underwear altogether, but since the dress was only long enough to cover the essentials, she decided that might be overkill and opted for a matching lace G-string. That, a pair of pearl studs and some spindly high-heeled sandals and she was set. As if she were hovering somewhere above her body, Tessa watched herself knock on the door. Although she'd become an expert at feigning pleasure, there was nothing fake about the quick, sharp breath she drew in when the man opened the door.

He was, in a word, *gorgeous*. His hair was thick and long enough for a girl to run her fingers through. His eyes were a goldish brown that reminded her of a lion, his nose was as straight as an arrow, his jaw could have been carved on Mount Rushmore, and his mouth... Dear God, when he smiled, she experienced a sudden need to feel that mouth between her thighs where dewy moisture was already gathering.

"Mr. Evans?" This had to be a mistake, she decided. Obviously she'd written the bungalow number down wrong. Guys who looked like this did not pay for dates. Well, some of the famous ones did, she allowed. As one well-known actor had told her, it made sex simpler. But one look told her that with this man sex would never be simple.

"That's me." His grin could have melted every ice cap left in his home state. He was wearing black jeans, a black cashmere turtleneck, and his feet were bare. He had, Tessa thought irrelevantly, the most beautiful feet she'd ever seen. She wondered if he was the kind of kinky guy who'd want his toes sucked, and hoped he was. "And you must be Janis."

His deep baritone voice wrapped around her like a black-velvet cloak. "Tessa." Her answering smile was not the slightest bit feigned. Tessa decided this had to be the best two hundred dollars she'd ever spent. "I'm afraid Janis had to cancel at the last minute. Her mother was ill."

"Too bad." His expression, as it swept over her, suggested he didn't mean that for a minute. "Would you like to come in?"

Their eyes met and in his gaze Tessa viewed myriad sensual promises. And something else. Something she would think about later when her head was clearer and her body wasn't feeling as if someone had put a torch to her skin.

"I thought you'd never ask." As she brushed by him in the doorway, she let her hip glance against the front of his jeans and felt the hardness beneath the black denim. Oh, yes. This was going to be a night to remember.

She accepted his offer of champagne and sat down in a satin upholstered wing chair, crossing her legs in a way that offered him an enticing view of her feminine attributes.

"Aren't you going to have any?" she asked as she watched him pop the top on a can of ginger ale.

"I'd better not. I'm a recovering alcoholic," he said easily. "The stuff's poison to guys like me."

"Oh." Alcoholism was not Tessa's favorite subject. Last month, when she'd been hospitalized for an accidental overdose, the doctor had suggested a Twelve Step program. Tessa had left the hospital that same day. "Well, I guess that just leaves more for me."

"You're welcome to as much as you want."

She laughed at that. "Do you know," she said in a breathy voice, "I was just about to say the very same thing to you."

It was his turn to laugh. They spent the next few minutes chatting, and although Tessa tried her best to draw him out, to learn what type of movie he was looking to invest in, and how much capital he was willing to put behind a film, his answers remained frustratingly vague.

"Well," she said finally, polishing off her third glass of champagne, "I guess you're just one of those strong silent types."

His beautiful lips quirked. "I guess I am."

"Lucky for you that's my favorite type." She rose from the chair, crossed the room on a long-legged feline glide and settled herself on his lap. With an expertise born of too much practice, she bent her head and touched her mouth to his.

The shock was hot and instantaneous, shuddering through them both like rocket fire. He pulled back far enough for her to see the smoldering embers in those tawny lion eyes.

"Tell me that was an earthquake." His ebony velvet voice had roughened. Deepened.

"I think it was us." Her own uncharacteristically shaky voice was little more than a whisper.

He paused, still holding her gaze as his fingers tangled in her hair. "More," he said finally.

"More," she echoed, weak with relief. There had been just a fleeting, terrifying second there when she'd sensed he was considering sending her away.

But he didn't send her away. Instead, his mouth met hers, harsher this time, in a breath-stealing, teeth-grinding kiss that engulfed them both in heat and sent flames licking through her blood. She opened her lips to the hot probing of his tongue, shuddered as she felt his hands on her breasts, breasts that were straining for his touch, and reveled in the immediate swell of his erection against her bottom.

He shouldn't be doing this, Dan tried to tell himself over the pounding of his blood in his ears. It was suicide. But when he felt her breasts swell beneath his palms, felt her nipples tighten to small stones, he was struck with an illicit, overwhelming urge to rip that ridiculous excuse for a dress away and take them in his mouth while he buried his throbbing penis deep inside her hot wet flesh to quench the fire raging through his loins.

The rasp of his thumbs made her nipples burn, and the hard male flesh pressing against the cleft of her buttocks made her desperate with the need to have him inside her. *Now.*

Murmuring something inarticulate that was half moan, half cry, Tessa broke away from the kiss, stood up, caught hold of the hem of the dress and began to pull it over her head.

"Don't," he said suddenly. Sharply.

"What?" She stared at him disbelievingly. Her entire body was desperate for satisfaction, and from the huge bulge in his jeans she knew that he'd been every bit as affected by the heated kiss as she was. So what the hell was his problem?

"Not yet." When his voice came out on a croak, Dan cursed himself. *What a fucking screwup. Kovaleski,* he berated himself without mercy as he remembered the video camera hidden in the arrangement of hothouse roses on the mantel. "Aren't we supposed to…I mean, shouldn't we take care of business arrangements first?"

His formerly deep voice cracked like an adolescent's at puberty. The fact that he was obviously nervous about this entire thing endeared him to Tessa. It did not, however, cool her ardor.

"Elaine should have already discussed this and charged your credit card," she said.

"Well, she did, but I thought, perhaps, if I wanted something extra…"

"There aren't any extras. Unlike so many of the other escort services in town, Elaine runs a top-class, all-services-provided establishment. Tonight is listed on the charge slip as artwork—so you won't have to explain anything to your accountant or your wife. And I'll do anything you want."

His eyes flicked over her, from her tumble of mussed, red-gold hair, down her body to her feet, still clad in those spindly sandals, then back up to her face again. "Anything?"

Her eyes met his with sensual promise. "Anything."

"And the price is still the same?"

She wondered momentarily if Elaine had gotten her mixed up with some crazed serial killer. Then dismissed that idea. Jason ran a computer check on all new johns, which kept his mother's clientele the safest in the business.

Obviously, this was just his first time paying for a fuck. "It's five thousand for the night. Whatever we do." She didn't mention that her take was sixty percent.

He sighed and dragged his long dark fingers through his hair. "Well, then." He stood up, reached into his back pocket and pulled out a small black leather folder.

Oh, hell, Tessa thought miserably as she guessed what was coming.

"You're under arrest," Dan said flatly, flashing his badge. "For prostitution."

As he read Tessa her rights, it crossed her mind that the gorgeous vice cop didn't sound any more enthusiastic about this bust than she felt.

Chapter Twenty-Three

Dan kicked himself all the way back to the cop shop for his unprofessional behavior. What the hell had gotten into him? How could he have let himself get caught up in the role-playing that was second nature in vice?

He'd busted countless hookers, but never before had he experienced the force and heat of sexual desire that had hit like an earthquake, shaking his usual iron self-control to its foundations. Another moment and it would have crumbled completely, and he would have been in deep shit.

Not that he would have been the first cop to have sex with one of the prostitutes he was supposed to bust. But most cops who started sleeping with hookers more often than not managed to get themselves washed right out of the cop business once Internal Affairs started sniffing around. And although not all the girls on the street looked like death warmed over, and offering sex in return for forgetting an arrest was commonplace, Dan had never been tempted. Until now.

Frustrated, and still horny, as he stopped at a red light on Sunset, he glanced up into the rearview mirror to check out his prisoner. She hadn't said a word since he'd cuffed her. Even now, she seemed to be in a state of shock. Or whatever dope she was on had kicked in. Not wanting her to go catatonic on him at the station, he decided to drop by the ER for a drug test to see what, exactly, the lady was on.

"We're stopping by the hospital." He felt a need to reassure her. "Just for a drug test."

She didn't respond. But her cat green eyes, already too wide in her pale face, turned panicky. If he hadn't known better, he would have thought she wasn't all that experienced at this. There was a strange aura of innocence about her that belied her seductive performance back at the hotel. He drummed his fingers on the steering wheel as he waited for the light to change.

"You're not new at this."

"No." Her shoulders slumped and he watched a defeated bleakness displace the panic in those remarkable eyes.

He wasn't surprised. But for some reason he was pissed. "Then you should know the drill." The light turned green and he returned his attention to his driving. "Getting busted comes with the territory."

She didn't answer. But the next time he glanced up into the rearview mirror, Dan viewed the silent tears streaming down her face.

After Mercy Sam's ER resident had declared that she was in no danger of dying on him, Dan took her into the station, where she was booked, fingerprinted and photographed. Through the entire process, she seemed numb, only answering the basics—name, address, date of birth. He was not surprised when, for occupation, she put actress. Every hooker he'd ever met was either an actress or a model. However, the desk sergeant confirmed her allegation.

"She was a regular in 'Roommates,'" the cop said. "Not one of the stars, but the camera loved her. Whenever she was in a scene, she was all you looked at."

That only pissed Dan off more. Having grown up in L.A., he was familiar enough with the hometown business to understand that she'd beaten incredible odds to win a spot on a network series. To throw it all away to make her living on her back was beyond his comprehension.

"So you really are an actress," he said, glaring at her across his desk.

"I told you I was." Other than the tears, the spark in her slanted catlike eyes was the first real emotion he'd witnessed.

"I know." He linked his fingers together behind his head and rocked back on the hind legs of the chair, eyeing her with renewed interest. "And I'll admit that I didn't really believe that. Because it's difficult to imagine why, when you obviously had so much going for you, you'd prefer giving blow jobs to guys with more bucks than brains."

"It's a long story."

"I've got all the time in the world. And so do you, unless there's someone you can call to post bail."

She thought about Jason and realized he'd probably kill her if she called him down to his own police station to bail her out of jail. Miles wouldn't hit her, but he had his own little ways of retaliation that she feared would be even worse than Jason's. As for their mother, Elaine had made it all too clear that her name was never to be mentioned in the unlikely event of an arrest.

At the time, Tessa hadn't considered that a possibility. Jason had assured her that the cops had known all about his mother's little enterprise for years and had always looked the other way. There was, of course, the lawyer all the girls were instructed to call in the event they might have any trouble with the authorities. But Tessa couldn't remember his name.

"No," she said quietly. "There's nobody."

Although Dan was surprised by that, he wasn't one to look a gift horse in the mouth. They'd been trying to bust the ring for months, ever since the body of a young woman had washed up in Malibu. At first it looked as if the body had been battered by the pounding it had taken against the rocks; however the autopsy had revealed that most of the damage had been done premortem. The coroner also hadn't found any water in the lungs, contributing to the theory that the girl had been dead when she'd entered the water.

When her friends in Westwood had told the investigating sheriff's deputies that the model and sometimes extra had recently begun working for a prostitution ring catering to the Hollywood elite, the sheriff's department had contacted the LAPD, which was when Dan had been brought into the case.

There had been rumors about the ring's existence for years, but the police hadn't actively pursued an investigation. Dan felt the reason for the lack of interest was that none of the brass—from the division commander all the way up to the commissioner—wanted to know whose names were on the alleged client list.

He sat there, looking at Tessa for a long time. Then decided that this was not a case for kid gloves. She'd already demonstrated an eerie ability to retreat deep inside herself. If he wanted to shake loose any information, he'd have to go for the gut.

"You know," he said, his easy, conversational tone designed to put her at ease and set her up, "you're not the first girl working this ring we've picked up."

As he'd expected, she displayed not an iota of interest.

"You wouldn't happen to know Brittany Thomas, would you?"

Although she shook her head, the faint flicker of recognition that flashed in her eyes, told him otherwise.

"Maybe if you saw a picture of her, it might refresh your memory," he suggested. He reached into a drawer for the file. Then laid the gruesome police photographs of what had once been a vibrant, beautiful young woman in front of her.

The blood drained from her already pale face as if someone had pulled a plug. She put a trembling hand over her mouth. "Bathroom," she managed.

Not wanting her to hurl all over his desk, not to mention the outrageously expensive cashmere sweater he'd bought to live up to the image of a Hollywood high roller, he took hold of her shoulders, lifted her from the chair and dragged her across the room, enlisting a female cop along the way to accompany her into the ladies' room. He'd already risked an unprofessional conduct investigation; there was no way he was going to put himself in another possibly compromising situation.

When she came out again, she'd obviously washed her face. Without makeup she looked a great deal younger than she had back at the hotel. And far more vulnerable.

"Why don't we go somewhere more private," he suggested gently. "And we can talk about Brittany."

She bit her bottom lip, but nodded her acquiescence. Not that it would have made a difference if she'd refused, but Dan had always found investigations went a lot easier if the suspects were cooperative.

He took her into the box, a small room that was one of the few things about police work television programs tended to get right. "Have a chair," he said, pulling the one that faced the mirror out for her. "Can I get you something? Some coffee? Soda? Tea?"

"A cup of tea would be wonderful," she said in a soft, sad little voice. Reminding himself that this woman had been prepared to screw his brains out all night for five thousand bucks, Dan reined in his sympathy and reminded himself that she was, after all, an actress.

"No problem. Would you like sugar in that?"

Her look of gratitude reminded him uncomfortably of Trudy, the cocker spaniel he'd had when he was a kid. "Two lumps, please."

"You got it." Before he left, he casually tossed the photos onto the table. Facedown this time.

Outside the room, he watched as she stared at the photographs. She reminded him of a woman watching a snake charmer; her expression revealed distaste, fear and an unwilling attraction, all at the same time.

"Come on, sweetheart," he murmured. "You know you want to look. You're dying of curiosity.... Just turn one of them over...and see what the future holds in store for you."

As if she'd heard him, she glanced up at the one-way mirror. And although he knew she couldn't see him, Dan looked back at her. "Do it."

He watched as she reached out, then drew her hand back. "Dammit, this could be you, baby. You ought to at least take a long hard look at what you've gotten into."

She closed her eyes briefly. When she opened them again, she took a deep breath and quickly turned over the top photograph. Dan watched her gasp, saw her hand go to her stomach, and wondered if she was going to be sick again.

She looked away. Then seemed to force her gaze back to the unpalatable scene, and stared at it for a long, silent time. She surprised him by turning over every one of the twenty photographs, each more gruesome than the previous one. Her expression had taken on that eerie disconnected look, making Dan think she'd mentally removed herself again. But when she finished looking at the last photo, the one of the autopsy, then buried her face in her hands, he knew the ploy had worked.

"Gotcha," he murmured. But as he stood there on the other side of the glass, watching her slender shoulders shake from her silent weeping, he realized that the rush of satisfaction he was accustomed to feeling under such circumstances was strangely missing.

Two days after the Emmy Award broadcast, Molly was having dinner out on the terrace of the Pacific Palisades home with Reece and Grace.

"I'm impressed," she said, watching him cook the meal on the oversize gas grill. "I didn't realize Emmy-winning writers still cooked their own dinners."

"It's only hamburgers." He spritzed some water on the flames that shot up when he turned the beef patties. "Not nearly as fancy as whatever you must have had at the Del."

Molly wasn't surprised he knew about her excursion to San Diego. After all, she had told Theo and Grace. But she was puzzled by the edge to his tone. "Actually, I had a roast beef sandwich from the hotel deli," she responded mildly. "But the view was spectacular. Almost as nice as this."

"I'm glad we come up to your high standards."

Again, his words were tinged with an unmistakable sarcasm. Molly wanted to ask what his problem was, but didn't want to get into an argument with Grace present.

"Are you going to marry Dr. Salvatore, Aunt Molly?" Grace asked.

The question caught Molly totally by surprise. She glanced over at Reece, even more surprised to discover that he was suddenly looking at her with an uncharacteristic intensity.

"Why on earth would you ask that?"

"Because Aunt Theo told Uncle Alex that you

should be married so you could have some kids of
your own. And since Dr. Salvatore took you flying in
his airplane, they thought maybe you might marry
him.''

Molly smiled at the simplistic reasoning. She also
realized that Alex and Theo had obviously picked up
on Joe's feelings for her. ''Gracious, I get the feeling
that I'm living with a junior spy,'' she hedged with a
laugh.

''Molly's not going to marry Dr. Salvatore,'' Reece
ground out as he spritzed the fire again and turned
down the flame on the barbecue.

Annoyed by his tone, Molly was tempted to ask
him why he was so sure of that, but once again managed, just barely, to hold her tongue.

''I already have you,'' she told Grace. ''Who I love
every bit as much as if you were my own little girl.''

''I love you, too. But it's not the same,'' Grace
said. ''Since you don't live here with Daddy and me
like a real mommy.''

''Well, you've got a point there.'' Molly forced a
smile and reminded herself how lucky she was to
have as much access to Grace as she did. ''And, although Dr. Salvatore and I are very good friends, I
don't think getting taken for an airplane ride is any
reason to marry a man. Besides, he's getting married
to someone else.''

''He is?'' Reece could have kicked himself for allowing his interest to show.

He tried telling himself that the only reason he gave
a damn was that if Molly married the guy and moved
back to Arizona, Grace would lose the closest thing
she'd had these past years to a mother. And, although

that was a valid excuse, Reece also admitted that the truth was that if she left Los Angeles, he'd miss Molly. A lot. More than he would have expected. More than he should.

Hell, he realized, he was jealous of Salvatore. And worse yet, any other guy Molly might be tempted to get seriously involved with.

Molly's direct gaze narrowed as she looked straight at him. "He's marrying a BIA nurse. She's a wonderful woman. I think they'll have a wonderful life."

"Lucky them," he muttered as he took the burgers off the grill.

A tenseness that had been building between them the past few months lingered as they ate their supper in relative silence, listening to Grace's convoluted story about something that had happened between Mary Beth Williams and some little boy at school. Mary Beth, Grace informed them, was the most boy-crazy girl in school.

"And she kissed him right on the lips." Grace wiped the back of her hand across her mouth, as if imagining a boy's lips touching hers.

"Gracious," Molly said, her shock not entirely feigned. As she wiped away a smear of catsup from Grace's lips, she hoped Mary Beth's predatory tendencies did not rub off on her daughter who, at this stage in her young life, seemed to prefer playing wedding with her Barbie dolls than practicing for the real thing.

"Mary Beth is definitely too young to be kissing boys," Reece agreed. "But when you get older, Grace, you'll discover that kissing isn't yucky at all."

"You should know," Molly muttered beneath her breath.

Reece seemed determined to date every bimbo in Hollywood. She'd been meaning to speak with him about the example he'd been setting for his daughter. When reporting his Emmy, *Variety* had mentioned his well-known tendency to go out with all the women who appeared on "Night Thrills."

"Excuse me?" Reece arched a chestnut brow. "Did you say something?"

"Molly said, 'You should know,'" Grace said helpfully.

"Yes." Reece's expression, as he met Molly's un-flinching gaze was a challenge. "I suppose I should."

"*Variety* did a nice piece on your Emmy win," she said, meeting the challenge. "It really is quite wonderful, Reece."

Although her tone was mild and her expression smooth, Reece knew she was referring to that crap about, as *Variety* had put it, "Longworth's girl of the week."

"You should have heard them announce Daddy's name, Molly," Grace said, oblivious of the silent battle taking place over the hamburgers, corn on the cob and tossed green salad. "Aunt Theo and I just screamed and screamed. And even Uncle Alex shouted."

"I did hear it."

Frown lines furrowed the smooth young forehead. "Did you watch the show at the hotel in San Diego?"

"Now there's a thought," Reece murmured. From his expression, Molly realized the idea of Joe and her being in a hotel together wasn't exactly a pleasant one.

"Actually, I was already back at home when they called your daddy's name."

"That was an early evening."

Molly thought she heard questions in Reece's tone and wondered if he could possibly be jealous. She decided that her imagination was definitely running away with her. Even before winning the Emmy, he could have had just about any woman in town. With competition like that, she wasn't even in the running for his attention.

"We had an early dinner so we could watch the sun set. Afterward, Joe flew back to Arizona." Molly smiled. "He said he was worried about the clinic, but I think he really just missed Naomi."

Reece knew a lot about missing the woman you loved. Although the pain had eased, he doubted there was a day that went by that he didn't think of Lena.

Before he could respond to that, the portable phone on the table rang. Reece picked it up.

"Hello. Oh, hi. Yeah, she's here. Just a sec." He handed the phone across the table to Molly. "It's Dan. For you."

Afraid something might have happened to Alex, Molly grabbed the phone. Out-of-the-blue calls usually meant some tragedy. "Dan? Is your dad all right?"

"Last I talked to him, which was this morning, he was great," Dan assured her. "I was calling to ask a personal favor."

"Anything," Molly said.

"I'm in Beverly Hills with this woman. Actually,

an informant. She's been beaten and is in pretty bad shape.''

''Shouldn't she be in the hospital?''

''Probably. But she doesn't want the cops called in, which the ER doc would probably have to do.''

Molly didn't understand. ''But you're a cop.''

''I know. But the situation's a little sticky, Molly. Anyway, I was wondering if you could come by and check her out. If she's in real danger, I'm going to have to take her to the hospital, but if it's just cuts and bruises, I'd rather handle it myself.''

Molly was more confused than ever. She also didn't want to be the one to make what could end up being a life-and-death decision. ''Give me twenty minutes to take care of a few things,'' she said. ''And I'll be there. What's the address?''

She took the pen Reece handed her and wrote the Beverly Hills address on a paper napkin, then hung up and immediately dialed Theo, and without going into details, asked if she could come stay with Grace for a little while.

''Reece and I have to go out,'' she explained.

''No problem, sweetie,'' Theo assured her. ''I was just fine-tuning a script, and Alex can watch the basketball game on Reece's television just as easily as our own. Give me a couple minutes to put a pair of shoes on and we'll be right over.''

''So, where are we going?'' Reece asked, irked by Molly's not even bothering to ask him if he had other plans for the evening. ''And why?''

Molly stood up and began carrying the empty plates into the kitchen. ''It's a bit complicated,'' she hedged. ''I'll tell you on the way.''

Twenty minutes later, Reece was about as angry as he'd ever been. "You had no goddamn right to do this, Molly."

"I'm sorry, Reece." Glancing down at the instructions Dan had given her, she turned right on Beverly Drive. "But I didn't have any choice."

He folded his arms. "Well, I do."

She found the house. It was Spanish-style with a red-tile roof, smaller than its neighbors, but still quite lovely. Or it would be with a coat of new paint and a lawn service to tend to the overgrown bushes and weed-filled lawn.

"No, you don't," she said mildly as she pulled into the driveway behind Dan's fire engine red Mustang GT. She cut the engine, pulled the key from the ignition and looked over at him. "You took an oath—"

"You'd have a better chance at bringing Elvis back from the dead than getting me to ever treat another patient. I'm not a doctor, dammit."

"I told you over two years ago, you'll always be a doctor. Besides, you've renewed your license." When he gave her a surprised look, she shrugged. "I checked. I wanted to make certain the option to do something useful with your life would still be open when you got tired of life in the fast lane with all your twenty-two-year-old playmates."

That said, she retrieved her medical bag from the back seat, got out of the car and headed for the house.

He should just stay here, Reece thought, enjoying the icy fury running through his veins. Who the hell did she think she was, talking to him that way? Didn't she realize that in his world—a lofty world far more

influential than the one he'd left behind in the ER—
he was an important man? Nobody, not even the pres-
ident of the network, would dare talk to Reece Longworth with the disregard she'd just shown him!

What he ought to do, Reece considered blackly,
was to just stay the hell in the car. What was she
going to do? Send Dan out with his gun and handcuffs
to drag him into that house?

Remembering the determination on Molly's face,
and knowing her as well as he did, Reece reluctantly
decided she might, when pushed, do exactly that.

Cursing viciously, he climbed out of the car and
slammed the door behind him. As he marched up the
flagstone sidewalk, Reece vowed that as soon as this
so-called emergency was over, he and Molly were
going to have a very long, no-holds-barred talk.

Molly thought it looked as though an earthquake
had hit in the middle of the living room. Furniture
was overturned, glass shards from a shattered gilt-
frame mirror glittered like diamonds all over the mahogany floor, a fist-size hole had been punched into
the ivory silk wallpaper.

In the middle of the destruction, Dan sat on a white
linen sofa. Next to him was a woman dressed in an
emerald green satin robe. Her face was horribly battered and she was holding a washcloth filled with ice
against her forehead.

"Christ," Reece, who'd entered the house after
Molly, muttered as he surveyed the scene.

"Hi, Molly, Reece." Dan stood up. "Thanks for
coming."

Reece nodded. The fact that Dan didn't show an
iota of surprise at seeing him made him angrier than

he'd been when he'd learned of Molly's subterfuge. Despite the fact that some perverse impulse had made him renew his license to practice medicine, he hadn't thought of himself as a physician for more than two years. He'd earned the right not to care. So, why couldn't people just leave him alone to live his life as he wanted?

But, no. Those two do-gooders, Dan Kovaleski and Molly McBride, had to drag him back into the fray.

He shook his head with frustration. "What happened?"

"The lady agreed to help me with an investigation." Reece easily recognized the self-recrimination in Dan's voice, having lived with it himself these past years. "Obviously, I miscalculated the risk."

"It wasn't your fault," she murmured, her words barely understandable due to her swollen jaw. "If I'd been more honest with you up-front—"

"Why don't you two discuss this later?" Reece suggested. "I'm Reece Longworth." He introduced himself to the battered young woman. "Looks as if I'm going to be your doctor tonight."

Tessa's good eye narrowed as she looked up at him. "Do I know you?"

"I don't believe so."

"You look familiar." She chewed on a peach-lacquered fingernail, then shrugged. "Then again, I've never been very good at remembering faces."

"In a lot of ways, L.A.'s a small town," he said. "It's possible our paths have crossed, but I'm sure I'd remember you." His smile managed to somehow reveal masculine admiration without appearing unprofessionally seductive. "Let's see what we've got here...."

His touch, while gentle, made her flinch as he ran his fingers over the swollen flesh that was rapidly turning a vivid purple and blue. As she heard the familiar caring tone, Molly felt a rush of hope.

He looked at the cut the woman had been holding the ice bag against. "You've got a pretty good gash." The bleeding above her right eye had almost stopped, but the swelling was so intense, her eye was almost closed. "I could try a butterfly bandage, but I think you'd be better off with stitches."

"Won't stitches scar?"

"Not that badly." He smiled, the slow, reassuring smile that had once calmed countless patients. The smile Molly hadn't seen for too long. "It'll be faint enough for makeup to cover. And without makeup, if it shows at all, you'll just look a little dashing." He pressed his fingers against the swollen flesh. "Like a lady pirate."

She managed a weak smile at that, flinching as it pulled her split lip.

Since the ice had slowed the bleeding, Reece decided to take the time to do a thorough exam. "Why don't we go in the bedroom?" he suggested. "Where we can have more privacy?"

Instead of being relieved by that suggestion, her eyes widened in apparent panic and she looked over at Dan.

"It's okay," he assured her. "I'm not going anywhere."

Molly heard the uncharacteristic gentleness in his voice, then watched the relief and trust flood into the woman's good eye and realized that whatever was happening here was more than just a typical cop/informant relationship.

Reece turned to Molly. "I could use some help."

"Yes, Doctor." Her tone was professionally deferential, but she knew that Reece wouldn't have been able to miss the satisfaction underlying the words. "Give Elvis my regards," she murmured as she followed him into the bedroom.

The examination revealed a great deal of bruising, but the patient didn't seem to have suffered any internal damage. She was also fortunate that no bones had been broken, although Reece did locate two ribs he suspected could be cracked.

"We'll want an X ray," he said.

"No." Tessa shook her head. "I can't go near a hospital. He told me if I talked to anyone about this, he'd kill me."

"No one's going to kill you," Molly said soothingly, stroking the blood-matted hair back from the woman's forehead. Without the ice pack, the wound had begun bleeding again. "Dan will see to that."

"Yeah, he's been a real big help so far."

Molly felt her temper rise, but managed not to point out that if the woman had been living a blameless life, she wouldn't be in whatever mess she appeared to be in in the first place.

"Here." She picked up the woman's limp hand and pressed it against the washcloth. "Make yourself useful and hold this in place."

Reece shot Molly a quick, warning look, but didn't reprimand her for her sharp tone. He frowned when he viewed the marks on the woman's stomach, then stopped when he got to her thighs. Along with the vermilion impression of ten fingers, there were crescent-shaped marks that could only have come from a man's teeth. The same marks marred the smooth flesh around her navel.

"Did he rape you?"

Tessa didn't answer. But the way she shuddered and closed her eyes when he touched the marks with a tender fingertip, told them everything. "Let me go get some disinfectant to clean those wounds," he said. Since Molly had brought her bag into the room with her, she realized he wanted an excuse to talk to Dan.

He left the bedroom and went back to where Dan was pacing the floor. "She needs to go to the hospital."

"She insists she won't go. Says he'll find out about it and kill her."

"Do you think that's possible?"

Dan's look became hard. "Unfortunately, since I know the guy—I used to work with him, believe it or not—I do. But I'm not going to let it happen, so we'll have to come up with some other plan."

"You could always just take her into custody."

"I already have. Then I convinced her to help me try to solve a murder tied to the prostitution ring she's working for. That's what got her into this in the first place." He shook his head. "No, she's right. We've got to be more careful."

"I think I've got an idea," Reece said. "But meanwhile, there's something else. She was raped."

"Shit." Dan dragged his hand through his hair. "I

figured as much. But she assured me he hadn't touched her that way.''

''People find it harder to lie to doctors than cops. Do you want me to collect evidence?''

Dan glanced over at the bedroom door, as if imagining how difficult this would be for her. ''Yeah. I want to nail the bastard for everything he's done. Since I'd lose my shield if I did what I'd like to do and simply kill the son of a bitch, at least I want to make certain he's put away for a very long time.'' Reece couldn't remember ever seeing Dan more coldly furious. Although he felt no sympathy for any man who could hurt a woman so badly, he worried the cop might decide to take things into his own hands.

''You're not going to do anything foolish, are you?''

Dan looked at him with surprise. ''Of course not. I'm a cop. I'm just going to do my job.''

''Sounds like more than that.''

''Well, it isn't.''

Reece shrugged, knowing a lie when he heard it. ''Whatever you say.''

While Reece and Dan were planning what to do with Tessa, Molly found herself growing more and more uncomfortable with the thick silence that had settled over the gloomy bedroom. As soon as Reece had left the room, the woman seemed to shrink back into some private, secret place inside her. There was a weariness about her that went far beyond the physical.

Molly felt she should at least try to offer some re-

assurance that the shame she was feeling would eventually pass.

"I know it's hard." The mattress sighed as she sat
down on the edge of the bed. She began stroking the
woman's tangled, bright hair. "And it's going to get
even harder. But you *will* get over this."

Tessa hated the pity in the woman's tone. She hated
the entire fucking situation. She should have known
better than to let that handsome vice cop talk her into
cooperating in his stupid investigation. She should
have known better than to get herself mixed up with
Elaine's sex-for-hire business in the first place. She
should have run like the devil was after her when
Jason had offered her that first pill.

Hell, she thought miserably, she never should have
come to this goddamn town in the first place. She
should have done what the general wanted and married Tom, had a bunch of little fighter pilots and been
satisfied with volunteering to act in amateur musicals
put on by the community theater.

"You don't know anything," she snapped. If she'd
ever seen a woman less likely to understand anything
about the life she'd been living, it was this one. Although she appeared to be around thirty, there was an
aura of innocence about her that Tessa hadn't felt herself since she'd let Lanny Osborne feel her up after
the high school Freshman Fling.

Molly thought it said something about the woman's
spirit that she could manage to look defiant with her
face so bruised and swollen. "I know about being
raped."

The one good eye widened in surprise. "By someone you thought you loved?"

"No." Molly's heart went out her. "Mine was a stranger. Yours was obviously much, much worse." She couldn't imagine how it would feel being so horribly betrayed by someone you loved and trusted.

Tessa turned her head toward the wall, unable to bear the compassion in this woman's gaze. "I just want to die."

"No." Molly took hold of the bruised jaw and turned the battered face back toward her. "You do not want to die. As bad as all this is, it's better than the alternative. If you don't care about yourself, think about all those people who love you. Who'd miss you."

"I don't have anyone who cares."

That wasn't quite true. She knew that were she to return home, her father would take her in. She'd have to listen to one helluva lecture about him having been right all along, and about having known what was good for her, but the general wouldn't turn her away. The problem was, she was too ashamed.

"Of course you do. You have Dan—"

"Oh, yeah. Sure. He's just wild about me. That's why he busted me in the first place."

Molly was a bit surprised at that, but decided this was no time for questions. "I've known Dan Kovaleski all my life—"

"Have you screwed him?"

"What?"

"I asked, since you seem to know the guy so well, if you've gone to bed with him. Done the dark deed. Fucked."

"He's always been like a brother—"

"That doesn't mean anything. Didn't anyone tell you? In some circles, incest is a national sport."

"We obviously run in different circles," Molly snapped, her pique steamrolling over her pity.

"Obviously."

The sarcasm scored a hit, just as the woman had intended. Molly took a deep breath and reminded herself that although she might not be a nun anymore, that didn't get her off the hook when it came to Christ's message of charity.

"Look," she said, trying again. "I'm on your side. Whatever it is. So, let's not waste time and energy you don't have fighting about things that don't make any immediate difference to your situation....

"I'd suggest we start over." She held out her hand. "Hi. My name is Molly. And yours is...?"

Her face ached, her chest hurt when she breathed deeply, and that battered place between her legs felt as if it were on fire. Tessa didn't have the strength to keep up the tough act.

"Tessa," she muttered. "Tessa Starr." *No.* Tessa Starr was the girl who thought she could become a hotshot movie actress. Tessa Starr was the whore who'd gotten her into this murderously dangerous mess in the first place. "I mean, Tessa Davis."

"Tessa?" The name was not all that unusual, Molly reminded herself. But still... She leaned closer, looking for clues on that poor injured face and found none. "You wouldn't happen to be Catholic?"

"I grew up Catholic. But obviously I haven't been to church in a long time."

Molly's heart was hammering a wild tattoo in her heart. "Were you, by any chance, adopted?"

"When I was three. My parents were killed. My adoptive parents told me that they'd died in a car accident, but I overheard them talking one time about a murder..." Her voice drifted off as she looked at Molly with surprise. "How did you know?"

"Oh, my God!"

Tessa was uncomfortable with the way the woman named Molly was suddenly staring at her. "What?"

There was no response. Tessa watched, stunned, as tears started pouring from Molly's eyes.

"Reece," she called out, "you'll never believe what's happened!"

Both men were at the door in a flash.

"I've found Tessa," Molly said, beaming through her tears. She pulled Tessa to her and held her tight, as she might Grace. "I've found my sister!"

Chapter Twenty-Four

Tessa was examined at a little-known barrio clinic in East Los Angeles operated by the Sisters of Mercy, stitched up and three hours later was ensconced in Molly's condominium where Dan had determined she'd be safe since there was no way anyone could ever connect the two women.

"I still can't believe this!" She was sitting up in Molly's bed, drinking a cup of herbal tea her older sister had made to help her sleep.

"It's a miracle," Molly decided. She also decided that both of them were due a miracle after all they'd been through.

"Do you know, I vaguely remember you and Lena. But whenever I'd talk about having sisters, my father would insist I'd imagined you both."

"What about your mother?" Molly asked, immensely curious about the home her sister had grown up in.

Tessa shrugged. "She left the day I started school.

I went off in the morning with my new book bag and when I came home that afternoon, she was gone. The general—that's my dad—said she just couldn't hack it.''

A frown moved across her battered face like a storm cloud as she thought back on that day. "Later, I decided what she couldn't hack was living under the general's thumb. I was the only kid I knew—and I grew up on military bases—who had to undergo weekly room inspection.''

"Is that why you ran away to Hollywood?" Molly could understand rebellion.

"Nah." Tessa was not about to blame anyone else for her own mistakes. "I always wanted to be an actress. And, despite what I ended up doing, I'm really good, which makes sense because I had to pretend to be something I wasn't every time I landed in a new town.''

"That must have made it difficult to figure out who you really were.''

"You got that right." Tessa sighed, wondering if there even *was* a real Tessa Davis somewhere deep down inside her.

"I guess, since your life was already so unstable, the reason your father didn't want you to remember Lena and me was because he wanted the two of you to be like a real family," Molly suggested, thinking of all the years such subterfuge had cost them. If only they'd been allowed to keep in touch, how different all their lives might have turned out!

"That's a nice thought. But personally, I think it was just one more thing he wanted to control.''

Never one to dwell on the past, Molly smiled and said, "Well, at least we're together now."

"Yes." Tessa ran her broken fingernail around the rim of the teacup. "I'm so sorry about Lena. She sounds like a wonderful person."

"She was." Molly could finally smile when she thought of her sister. "She helped me through a terrible time. I'll always be grateful."

"And she and Reece had a little girl?"

"Yes." Molly decided there had been enough revelations for one day. She'd fill her sister in on that all-important detail later. "Her name is Grace. She's six, beautiful, sweet and as smart as a whip."

Tessa smiled for the first time since Molly had met her hours earlier. "Not that you're prejudiced, or anything."

"Wait until you meet your niece," Molly answered. "You'll see she's special."

"My niece." Tessa grew silent as she thought about that. "I'm an aunt. Aunt Tessa."

"It has a nice ring."

"Yes." Tessa nodded. "It does, doesn't it?" This time her smile lit up her eyes, and although they were surrounded by swollen, bruised flesh, Molly could tell that her sister was the most stunning of the three McBride girls. "And you were a nun. Amazing."

Molly laughed at that. "Sometimes it amazes me, too."

"So why did you quit?"

"It's complicated. But mostly I realized that what I thought was a vocation was merely expedience. The religious life was a haven. It also allowed me to avoid facing reality."

"But you worked in the ER at an inner-city hospital. Surely that gave you a real taste of reality." Tessa suspected it was also why Molly could prove so nonjudgmental about her life. Undoubtedly she'd met a great many prostitutes in her line of work.

"True. But I always knew that at the end of the day I could return home. And that there would always be people—nuns who were like sisters—who cared for me and would take care *of* me. Real life doesn't come with such a secure safety net."

"Tell me about it," Tessa muttered. She took another sip of the tea. As she felt her nerves tangle again, she wished that Reece would have allowed her at least one pain pill, then realized it was probably better he'd advised her to stick to aspirin. "You probably think I'm a horrible person."

"Of course not. I think what's happened to you is horrible," Molly allowed. "But any sister of mine could never be anything but wonderful."

A warmth like nothing she'd ever known flooded through Tessa. She'd never before experienced anything that made her feel so good—not sex, or drugs, or even the fleeting feeling of power that she'd discovered prostitution could occasionally instill.

"Aw, hell." Tears started spilling out of Tessa's swollen eyes. "You would have to make me cry."

"I'm sorry."

"It's just that I feel so stupid. I wanted so badly to fit in when I first came here and Jason was so nice, and a cop, and all, and Miles knew everybody in town, so I thought I had it made. Then things started falling apart and the next thing I knew I was sleeping with some creep bookie to keep him from killing Jason, and then, well…''

She shrugged her shoulders. ''It didn't seem that much of a jump to working for their mother.''

Molly wanted to hear everything about Tessa's life. But she'd had such a horrendous day, she had to be exhausted. And they had a lifetime to get to know one another.

''You need to get some sleep,'' she suggested, taking the empty cup. ''We can start catching up in the morning. I'll take the day off.''

Tessa didn't argue. She snuggled down, holding the pillow tight in a way that reminded Molly of Grace, and fell instantly to sleep. Still filled with wonder at the gift God, or fate, had bestowed upon her, Molly bent down and brushed a kiss against the row of black stitches Reece had sewn just above her sister's right eye.

Later, as she sat on the sofa bed, looking out the window at the sparkling lights of the city, Molly thought of Lena, wondering if she knew about the reunion.

''Remember when we always thought Tessa was the lucky one?'' she murmured to her sister. Molly found nothing unusual about talking to Lena. She did it often, usually telling her about Grace or Reece, or sometimes, just life in general, and it never failed to give her comfort. ''I think we were very, very wrong about that.''

Sighing, Molly turned her thoughts to a more pleasant topic. ''Reece was wonderful tonight. I was watching him caring for Tessa at the clinic—it was his idea to take her there because he could get her in and out without any danger of any of Jason's cop friends seeing her. Anyway, he was so much like the old Reece that I didn't know whether to laugh or cry.

"I can't believe he won't go back to medicine, Lena. After all, next to you and Grace, it was what he loved most."

Love. Molly dragged her hand through her hair as she thought about the feelings that had flowed through her like warm honey as she'd watched Reece tend to her sister.

Although she'd been trying to deny it for years, Joe was so, so right about her feelings for Reece. Heaven help her, she did love him. She pressed a hand against the front of her nightgown as her heart trebled its beat at the mere thought of him.

Drawing her knees up to her chest, Molly wrapped her arms tight around them. Hours later, as the shimmering, pearlescent predawn light slipped into the room, she was still awake, her cheek on her bent knees, wondering what on earth she was going to do now.

Molly was not all that surprised when Dan called later that morning, informing her that he was going to be stopping by for lunch.

"Don't worry about fixing anything," he said. "I'll pick some sandwiches up on the way."

"Probably grilled hemlock," Tessa muttered when Molly told her the news. They'd been trading autobiographies for two hours and were only up to Tessa's fifth-grade Girl Scout troop and Molly's high school graduation.

"Don't be melodramatic," Molly responded mildly. "Dan likes you a lot. I could tell."

"He likes what I can do for him. Like closing down that prostitution ring. And busting a bad cop."

"I think it goes deeper than that," Molly said. "I've known him most of my life, and from the first time he figured out the differences between little boys and little girls, he hasn't shown any serious interest in anyone. But the way he looks at you, Tessa..." Molly shook her head. "It's different."

"He's only interested in sex. Just like all guys."

"I can't imagine Dan mixing his job with his personal life."

Tessa figured Molly might be able to picture it a little better if she'd witnessed that blazing kiss they'd shared right before he'd arrested her. But since she still hadn't figured out how she felt about what had happened between them, she wasn't prepared to share that story so soon. Not even with someone who was beginning to feel more and more like a sister.

"Oh, he didn't actually do anything," she said grudgingly. "But he sure as hell wanted to."

"Wanting isn't the same as doing," Molly pointed out, guiltily remembering the sensual dream she'd had when she'd drifted off around dawn. A dream starring Reece.

"True." Already comfortable in Molly's apartment, Tessa got up from the table and went over to the coffeepot to refill her mug. "And, I have to admit, he's kinda cute when he's being official, in a Dudley Doright sort of way."

Molly laughed. "I wouldn't advise calling him that to his face."

"Hell, I may be stupid," Tessa said with a quick grin, "but despite recent evidence to the contrary, I'm not suicidal." She sat back down across from Molly and eyed her newly found sister over the top of her mug. "So, speaking of men and women, why hasn't our brother-in-law realized you're in love with him?"

"What?" Molly stared at her, aghast.

"Reece seems like a bright guy. I can't believe he hasn't caught on. Then again," Tessa said as an afterthought, "men can be pretty clueless."

"Don't tell me it's that obvious?" Molly felt the color flooding into her face.

"I was watching you while he was collecting the rape evidence." For some reason the vaginal examination had embarrassed her more than anything she'd done working for Elaine. Needing somewhere to focus her attention, she'd instinctively turned to Molly. "You reminded me of a little girl with her face pressed against the candy store window."

"Oh, no." Molly buried her face in her hands.

"Hey, sis." Tessa leaned over and stroked her thick black hair. "It's no big deal. I only noticed because I didn't know either one of you, so I was sort of an objective observer. Anyone else would probably just think you were very close friends."

"I'm not sure about that."

Joe had sensed her feelings for Reece. And now that she thought about it, Alex and Theo had said things lately that made Molly wonder if they'd seen something, as well. And heaven knows, Grace had been pushing for her aunt Molly to marry her daddy, but Molly had simply considered that to be a little girl's normal wish for a mother.

"If it's any consolation, the guy's nuts about you, too," Tessa surprised Molly even further by saying.

"I'm sure you're wrong." Molly had watched all the beautiful actresses going in and out of the revolving door of her brother-in-law's love life and knew that he'd been far too busy to take any notice of her.

"I've made some stupid mistakes in my life, but believe me, Molly, if there's one thing I can tell, it's when there's something going on between a man and a woman. The problem is, Reece doesn't realize how he feels."

"I still can't believe you're right." Molly couldn't keep the skepticism—or the reluctant hope—from her voice.

"I am." Tessa gave her a long, judicious look. "In a few days, when I can go out again without terrifying little children with this face, you and I are going shopping."

"If you need clothes—"

"Not for me, sweetie. For you. We're going to give Sister Molly a makeover that'll knock Dr. Reece Longworth right off his feet and into your bed."

Molly's face was as hot as a Fourth of July firecracker. "That isn't what I had in mind."

"Of course it is. You're just too good to admit to mad, passionate desires. Fortunately for you, your baby sister is not so well-bred. She also knows exactly what men like." Tessa's slow, secretive smile reminded Molly of the Cheshire cat. "Trust me, kiddo, the guy's a goner."

Dan arrived later, with a suitcase of clothes and toiletries he'd recovered from Tessa's house, a bag of sandwiches and salads in foam cartons, and a woman dressed in a suit. Although the woman's skirt ended high on the thigh, the somber gray pinstripes definitely meant business.

He introduced her as Kelly Britton, from the D.A.'s office. "I brought her along to interview Tessa before her testimony before the grand jury."

"The grand jury?"

"We're talking some pretty big names here, Molly. And a longtime cop. I want everything done by the book on this one."

Molly had been so excited about finding her sister after all these years, she hadn't really thought about how, exactly, Dan was going to use Tessa. She'd naively believed he'd just use the information she gave him to arrest the bad guys, then that would be that.

Tessa blanched visibly, but before she could respond, Molly instinctively took over the role of older sister. "Shouldn't she have an attorney?"

Dan looked as if he was grinding his teeth. "Of course, if she wants one..."

"That's all right—" Tessa began.

"It's not all right." Molly cut her off. She put her hands on her hips and looked up at the attorney. "I'm sorry, Ms. Britton," she said, "but I'm very uncomfortable with this. I feel my sister should be represented by counsel."

"No." Tessa's voice was steady. Her eyes, as she met Dan's, were calm. "I trust Dan."

Her frustration building, Molly was about to point out that Tessa had once trusted another Los Angeles policeman, too, and look where that had gotten her. But she knew, deep in her heart, that Dan Kovaleski was different. She also realized, from the way he was looking at Tessa, that although he might be willing to use her to break this case, he wouldn't do anything to hurt her.

"The garden needs weeding," she said. "I'll be outside."

"We'll call you when we're done," Dan said.

Molly turned to her sister. "If you have any problems, I'll be right out back."

Tessa smiled at that. "Yes, Mother."

It did Molly so much good to witness that teasing smile that, despite her lingering concerns, she smiled back, then turned to Dan. "You take care of her. Or I'll tell your father."

His lips quirked and she watched the reluctant humor light up his golden brown eyes. "Yes, ma'am."

Two hours later, Molly had pulled every weed in the tiny plot behind the condo that only an extremely generous person would refer to as a garden. She'd applied mulch and fertilizer, staked up the tomatoes, watered everything and was now pacing the small wooden deck, wondering what on earth they were doing in there.

Last night, Tessa had already shared the highlights—or lowlights, Molly thought grimly—of her life with Jason Mathison. Surely that was enough for a conviction? She couldn't imagine that Dan was forcing Tessa to go into every sordid little detail of the past seven years.

She kept glancing up at the window, wondering if she should make up an excuse to go back inside just to check on Tessa. She'd finally decided to do just that, when the door slid open and Dan came out.

"Sorry we took so long."

"That's okay. Unless you and your sidekick brought out the bright lights and rubber hoses."

"Nah. I'm saving those for Mathison." The cold fury in his eyes frightened her. The last time Molly remembered witnessing it was when he'd been on the trail of a serial killer who had a penchant for blond little girls.

"You care about her, don't you?"

His answering laugh held not a note of humor. "Hell, Molly, she's a hooker, for Pete's sake."

"She's my sister," Molly warned softly.

"True." He exhaled a long breath and dragged his hand through his hair. "Doesn't it bother you? What she's been doing for a living?"

"It's not my place to judge."

He shot her a frustrated look. "Reece is right. Sometimes you really can be a pain in the butt, Sister Molly."

"Reece said that?" The half-teasing words stung.

Dan grimaced at her hurt tone. "Hell, he didn't really mean it.... Well, maybe just a little," he allowed. "When you were giving him a bad time about his choice of women, he got a little hot under the collar."

"I merely pointed out that I didn't think having sleepovers with his daughter in the house was a very good idea."

"You're probably right," he said, surprising Molly who suspected he'd slept with more than his share of women. "But at the time Reece felt that it was difficult living up to your high standards."

"I see." She did. Only too well. Molly sighed as

she realized that whenever he looked at her, Reece undoubtedly still saw Sister Molly. It was not an encouraging thought. Maybe Tessa was right. Maybe a makeover was in order.

Unfortunately, in order to compete with those actresses he dated, she'd need more than a makeover. How about a complete overhaul?

"It wasn't really meant as an insult, Molly. We'd had a few beers and he was just frustrated because he'd been trying so hard to be a good father to Grace."

And he'd succeeded. Despite a schedule that would exhaust most people, he managed to somehow juggle his work, his social life and Grace. Molly couldn't count the number of dance recitals and school plays she and Reece had attended. And while that might be expected, she also discovered that he—not the nanny—was the one driving his daughter to all those rehearsals.

"What happens next?" Molly asked. "With Tessa?" She didn't want to talk about her relationship— or lack of it—with Reece any longer.

"She goes in front of the grand jury on Monday."

"Will the press be there?"

"No. It's secret. We should be able to get her in and out without anyone knowing. Then, I have no doubt we'll get an indictment. For pandering, money laundering, trafficking in a controlled substance, and murder, for starters."

"Murder?"

Dan looked surprised. "She didn't tell you?"

"Obviously not."

The anger was back in his eyes. His lips were set

in a grim line that left deep ridges on either side of his mouth. "One of the other girls wasn't as fortunate as Tessa. She was killed. After she made the mistake of trying to blackmail Mathison."

Molly felt her knees threaten to buckle. "You weren't kidding, were you?" she said, looking up at the bedroom window where Tessa had spent the night. "About Jason Mathison being a dangerous man."

"That," Dan assured her, "is putting it mildly."

Molly was not surprised when Tessa brushed the subject of murder off. Frustrated, but not surprised.

"Dan says I'll be perfectly safe here," she said. "And I believe him."

As much as Molly was pleased about the faith her sister had in her new benefactor, she wasn't certain transferring her allegiance from one man to another was the best thing for Tessa. "Perhaps you should think about believing in yourself." The moment she heard herself say the words, Molly cringed, remembering Reece's complaint about living up to her impossibly strict standards.

"I used to." Tessa's laugh was bitter. "That's how I got into this mess in the first place. I was so damn cocky, I believed I could do anything. Including coming to Lotusland and not lose my soul."

"You didn't lose it. It may be a little battered and bruised. But it's still there."

Tessa shrugged. "Far be it from me to argue with a nun."

"A former nun."

Another shrug. "Whatever." She seemed distracted. "What did you think of that D.A.?"

"Kelly Britton? I really didn't get to—"

"Do you think Dan is fucking her?"

"I think you'd have to ask Dan that."

"There was something there," Tessa mused. "They were too comfortable in each other's space. If they're not sleeping together now, they have in the past."

It wouldn't have surprised Molly, but it was also none of her business. "Dan's a good-looking single man. I'd imagine any woman would be attracted to him."

"They slept together," Tessa muttered. "I just know it." She turned around and pinned Molly with an angry look. "You think I'm jumping from the frying pan into the fire."

"Not exactly." Molly chose her words with care, not wanting to endanger this fledgling relationship she was establishing with her sister. And, although she had sensed something different about Dan, something that made her think he cared for Tessa more than he was willing to admit, she wanted to protect Tessa from getting hurt. "But I can't help worrying that the way Dan came to your rescue, like some white knight, you might be confusing gratitude—"

"That's not it." Tessa dragged her hands through her hair. "It started before then. When he kissed me in the hotel room. I've never felt that way in my life before. It was like an epiphany."

Molly didn't know what to say to that, so, deciding that discretion was the better part of valor, she didn't say anything.

"You want to know the funny thing?" Tessa asked with a sad little smile.

"What?"

"Even when I was handcuffed in the back of the squad car, when he looked at me in the rearview mirror, I knew I was lost." She laughed at herself. At the ridiculous situation. "Imagine falling in love with a guy who busts you. God, I've got to be the biggest idiot in the world."

"Actually, I think I've got dibs on that crown," Molly murmured. "And besides, I've always thought loving Dan Kovaleski would be easy."

Tessa was standing at the window, staring down at Molly's garden. "He deserves better." When she turned around again, resolve shone in eyes surrounded by saffron and purple flesh. "Tessa Starr might have been a high-priced whore. But Tessa Davis was a lot better. I'm going to get her back. And then I'm going to give that snotty ice queen D.A. a run for her money."

Molly laughed. "I think that's a wonderful plan." She decided it was high time she made one of her own. "So, since Dan instructed us not to leave here until you testify, why don't you show me what to do with all that stuff he brought over in those flowered cosmetic bags?"

"You really want that makeover?"

"Unless you think I'm hopeless."

"Oh, no!" Tessa looked like a little girl who'd just been invited to her best friend's slumber party. "This is going to be fun," she promised. "And when we're done with you, Molly girl, Reece Longworth won't stand a chance."

* * *

"Are you certain they're going to be okay there?" Reece asked, worried about Molly having taken Tessa into her home.

"There's no way Mathison can connect Tessa with Molly," Dan assured him.

"He could have followed you."

"He didn't. Besides, if he does any checking, he'll discover that Tessa Starr has jumped bail and bought a plane ticket to Denver." He glanced down at his watch. "In fact, her plane should be landing right about now."

"That's pretty good." Reece lifted his glass in a salute.

"Thank you. We may not be hotshot Emmy-winning writers, but sometimes we real cops actually do come up with a few halfway decent ideas."

"Speaking of ideas, Aaron West signed a deal for a new sci-fi outer-space series," Reece divulged, naming the producer who'd hired him. "He suggested I replace him as producer on 'Night Thrills.'"

"Head writer *and* producer," Dan said admiringly. "It's obviously true. That little statue *is* pure gold. Congratulations."

"I don't think I'm going to do it."

"Why the hell not?"

"I don't know." Reece shrugged. "I guess partly because I've never thought of myself as being part of the Hollywood crowd."

"There's an Emmy in your library with your name on it that says otherwise."

"I know. But I never planned to be a television writer. Hell, I kind of fell into the business when Theo took those damn stories to the guy. Then bang, the next thing I knew I had a new career."

"She was just trying to help, Reece."

"You don't have to soft-soap it. What she was trying to do was to save my life. And she succeeded. Beyond either of our wildest dreams."

"But?"

"But something's been missing."

"Like commitment?"

Reece shot him a look. "You're a fine one to be talking about commitment. When was the last time you took a woman out twice?"

"Actually, I was referring to the kind of commitment you give your work. Not the fairer sex," Dan said equably. "You might have done a good job fighting it, but anyone who's ever watched you work knows that you were born a doctor, Reece. The same way I was born a cop, just like my dad. It stands to reason you'd feel incomplete out of the ER."

"I don't know if *incomplete*'s the word," Reece mused. "I managed to convince myself that I was happy. After all, I have a gorgeous, bright daughter, friends, I live in one of the most beautiful spots on earth, I have a job half the people in this town would throw their dear old grandmothers under a bus for—"

"Make that two-thirds," Dan broke in.

"At least," Reece agreed. "But when Molly dragged me over to that house to take care of your informant—"

"Who coincidentally just turned out to be your long-lost sister-in-law."

"Yeah." Reece shook his head. "Talk about your small worlds. Anyway, it felt damn good to be practicing medicine again."

"I don't suppose you told Molly that?"

"Are you kidding? And let her say, 'I told you so'?"

As Dan laughed, Reece laughed with him. What he didn't say was that when he'd realized how he'd felt, Molly had been the first person he'd wanted to tell. But for some reason that he couldn't figure out, Reece had suddenly felt strangely uncomfortable with her.

But later that night, as he'd sat alone in the dark, nursing a single Scotch, he realized that somehow, when he hadn't been looking, the bond he and Molly had shared from the beginning, even before that fateful day when Lena had burst into Mercy Sam's cafeteria, ablaze with pride and pleasure, had deepened. He was forced to admit that somehow, when he hadn't been paying close attention, his feelings for Molly McBride had become a great deal more than fraternal.

Chapter Twenty-Five

"**W**ell, what do you think?" Tessa put down the slender lipstick tube, leaned back and studied her creation with a critical eye.

"I don't know." Molly stared in bemused wonder at the vision in the mirror. "I don't look like myself."

"Of course you do." Tessa grinned. "You clean up real good, girl. Which only makes sense since all the McBride girls are natural beauties."

The incautious words hovered in the air between them like a miasma.

"Aw, hell," Tessa muttered. "Talk about throwing cold water on a great afternoon."

"No, we *should* talk about Lena," Molly insisted. "Otherwise it would be as if she had never existed. And you're right, she was gorgeous. She looked just like Mother." Molly got up, walked over to the nightstand and took out a photo of Karla McBride. And another of Lena.

"Oh, my God!" Tessa stared down at the dual pho-

tographs. "I saw her. A few years ago, on New
Year's Eve. I remember thinking how stunning she
looked that night." She shook her head. "No wonder
Reece looked familiar when he first showed up at the
house. He was with her. I could tell they were head
over heels in love, but they seemed to be having a
serious discussion. And she looked nervous."

"I remember that night." Molly realized she'd definitely made progress when she could look back on
those days immediately following the rape without
emotional pain. "She was going to tell Reece all
about how our parents had died. About Daddy shooting Mama. She was worried he wouldn't love her
when he learned the truth about her background."

Tessa laughed at that. "I saw the way he was looking at her. She could have told him she was the re-
incarnation of Ma Barker and it wouldn't have made
a bit of difference."

Molly laughed, too. What a gift her sister was!
"That's pretty much what I told her."

"It must be tough." Tessa gave her a shrewd look.
"Being in love with your sister's husband."

"Oh, I wasn't in love with Reece then. Not that
way," Molly said quickly. Too quickly, she realized.
Had she always been in love with him? she wondered.
Just a little?

"He'd be an easy man to be in love with," Tessa
said sagely, repeating what Molly had said about Dan.
"In any way. You'd better snatch the guy up, before
some predatory actress gets her grubby hands on
him."

Molly truly wanted to. Oh, dear heaven how she
wanted to. But...

"What would people say?"

"Why do you give a flying fuck?"

Despite her nervousness, or perhaps because of it, Molly laughed. "Well, no one can accuse you of beating around the bush."

Tessa's expression turned serious. "A lot of women would do murder to have that man look at them the way Reece looks at you when you're not looking. He's mad for you, Molly. Even if he hasn't figured it out for himself. All he needs is a little nudge, and he'll fall into your lap like a ripe plum."

"I can't." Too unnerved to sit still, Molly stood up and began to pace.

Tessa's curse was brief and ripe. "If I'd known my big sister was a coward, I'd just have soon stayed an only child."

Molly spun around and speared her sister with a lethal glare. The temper the nuns had tried to whip out of her flared as hot as the Santa Ana winds. "I'm not a coward!"

Tessa glared back. "Then prove it."

Was it really so wrong? Molly asked herself as she met her sister's challenging stare. She wasn't bucking for sainthood. Why shouldn't she go after what she wanted?

"I wouldn't have the faintest idea how to seduce a man."

A spark of satisfaction lit Tessa's green eyes. "Hell, it's not that hard, especially since men all want to be seduced in the first place. All you have to do is think sexy thoughts and follow your instincts."

"I don't have those kinds of instincts."

"All women do. It's in the genes. Believe me, you

just have to loosen up and forget you were ever a nun. "There's nothing wrong with going after the man you love."

Molly sighed. "I still think I'd end up feeling just like Mary Magdalene tempting Jesus."

"For your information, Magdalene wasn't a whore, just possessed, and she never tempted the guy. You're not the only McBride sister with a Catholic education," Tessa said with a toss of her head as Molly's expression revealed surprise.

"You don't have to drag Reece to bed, Molly. But what's stopping you from calling the guy and asking him out to dinner? Fortunately, we're the same size, since I doubt if you have any decent bait in your closet."

With that single remark, she somehow managed to make Molly feel like a failure as a woman. Reminding herself that an attractive, intelligent man had once wanted to marry her, she tried not to be too hurt by Tessa's appraisal.

"I don't want to leave you alone."

"I won't be alone. Dan'll be here."

"Did he tell you that?"

"No. But I guarantee he'll come running when I tell him about my little black book."

Molly's eyes widened. "You don't mean—"

"Honey, some of the biggest names in town are in that book. Including the police commissioner and mayor. Oh, and a local television anchorman known for his political ambitions." Tessa's smile lacked humor. "I told you, our business was the cream of the Los Angeles elite."

"This case will blow the city sky-high," Molly predicted.

"That's the idea," Tessa agreed cheerfully.

Molly was more than a little relieved when Reece agreed to meet her at a neighborhood pizza place.

"Is that the best you can do?" Tessa groaned. "How romantic can you expect a guy to get over pepperoni?"

"I don't expect romance. I'm just testing the waters."

"That's probably what Jonah said before he was swallowed by that whale," Tessa muttered as she went to take her turn on the phone.

Neither sister was at all surprised when Dan arrived within minutes of Tessa's phone call. Although he looked momentarily surprised by Molly's transformation, it was apparent that his mind was on his work.

"So, where is this alleged book?" he demanded, forgoing preliminary polite conversation.

"You are such a typical male," Tessa complained dryly. "Always in a hurry. Keep your pants on, Officer, and I'll tell you everything. In good time."

"I thought you already told me everything you knew."

"Now that would have been foolish, wouldn't it? I had to be sure I could trust you before I brought in the heavy hitters. I also didn't trust that bimbo from the D.A.'s office."

"She's not a bimbo."

"Of course she is. Or were you too busy admiring her agile legal mind to notice the hickeys on her neck?'' Before he could respond to that, she turned to Molly. ''Didn't you say you had somewhere to go?''

''Well—'' Molly twisted her hands nervously in front of her ''—I did have plans. But they can be changed.''

''Don't worry,'' Dan said brusquely, ''I'll stay here with Tessa until you get back.''

''Scoot,'' Tessa broke in before Molly could warn him she could be late. ''I'm in good hands here with Officer Law and Order.'' Having taken two of the Valium she'd managed to liberate from her bathroom medicine cabinet before they'd taken her to that clinic, she was feeling much more at ease with the grim-faced cop.

Enough so, that she couldn't help wondering if she ought to take a bit of her own advice. After that kiss they'd shared, Tessa had not a single doubt that sex with Officer Daniel Kovaleski would register at least a ten on her personal Richter scale.

And although he couldn't have behaved more professionally when he and that blond prosecutor were interviewing her, every so often, she had caught him looking at her mouth, a distant look in his magnificent gold eyes, as if he were still remembering her taste.

Oh, yes, she considered, as she kissed Molly goodbye at the door, pressing a condom into her hand, insisting that she take it—''just in case''—seducing the sexy vice cop would be a breeze.

Molly's heart was pounding so fast, she was certain she must be having a heart attack. Or at the very least a major league anxiety attack. What in heaven's name did she think she was doing, trying to seduce her sister's husband? Why had she allowed herself to take Tessa's advice?

"After all," she said into the darkness as she drove to her meeting with Reece, "if Tessa were any expert on love, she wouldn't have messed up her life so badly."

Her younger sister might know a great deal about how to please a man. At least in bed. But love was something entirely different. Love was deep and abiding and ran as unceasingly as a river flowed to the sea. Love was constant. And in her case, inescapable.

Every nerve in her body was tingling. As Molly passed Our Lady of Perpetual Help Church, she considered stopping, then changed her mind. She'd always been able to find peace in her religion, but not tonight.

The unadulterated truth was that she wanted Reece. Truly, madly, deeply. She wanted him with every fiber of her being, and to pretend otherwise, particularly in the sanctity of the Church she'd served with all her heart, would be the epitome of hypocrisy.

Needing a private moment, she pulled into a nearly deserted parking lot, found a secluded spot far from the supermarket and cut the engine. Then leaned back and closed her eyes, willing her heart and her mind to calm.

Molly had always been able to pray anywhere, at any time; even in the chaos of the emergency room, private conversations with her God had always come easily. But it wasn't God she needed to talk with tonight.

"Oh, Lena," she whispered, "I tried so hard to

keep this from happening. I shut my mind to thoughts of him for so many years, because I knew how deeply you loved him. And how much he loved you. You were the sun his entire life revolved around, which was why his world shattered to pieces when you left it.''

Uncaring of the shadow and mascara Tessa had applied, Molly pressed the heels of her hands against her closed lids. ''But although I know it was not your choice, you did leave. And during these past years, as I've tried to fill the gap left in your daughter's— our daughter's—life, I fell in love with your husband.''

It was the first time she'd actually said the words out loud, and just hearing them made them so real. So inescapable.

''I never...ever...would have acted on those feelings if you hadn't...'' She could not say the fatal word aloud. ''If you were still alive,'' she said instead. ''But you're not, Lena, and although Reece professes to be happy dating a different woman every night, I know he's only fooling himself. He deserves more. A real home, with a wife who'll love him. A woman patient enough to wait until he realizes that he loves her back.''

Molly dropped her hands to her lap and blinked hard against the threatening tears. It was not a simple thing she was asking of Lena. Nor, she knew, would it be an easy matter to convince Reece that they belonged together. But, although patience had never been Molly's long suit, her love for him had become so much a part of her, that she had no choice but to try.

"Heaven help me, Lena, I want to be that woman," she said softly, vaguely ashamed of her feelings, although she knew her sister undoubtedly already knew the secrets of her heart. "And I want you to know that I don't want to replace you...in either Reece's or Grace's heart. I just want the opportunity to build a life with them." She hitched in a deep, painful breath then let it out with a shuddering sigh. "Because I love them both so very much...with all my heart and soul."

Oblivious to the shoppers coming and going in the parking lot, Molly kept her eyes closed and her heart open. Open enough that she could sense her sister's presence. The tension that had cropped up between them in the final years of Lena's life had vanished, and as a comforting warmth surrounded her, Molly knew she was in the presence of the woman who'd so lovingly cared for her during that anxiety-filled time after the rape, when she'd been carrying Grace.

Sitting there, alone in the dark, Molly felt Lena's love. And her permission.

"You aren't the only one who's been praying for Reece to be happy," Lena's calm clear voice echoed in her head. "And I know you can make him happy, Molly. Which makes me so very happy."

Although all the windows were closed, a faint breeze touched her cheek, like the caress of a hand, or petal-soft lips. "Take care of my darlings. The way you always took care of me." The voice grew softer, a whisper now as it faded away, back into the ether. "Love them, Molly. The way you always loved me."

Despite her best intentions not to cry and ruin Tessa's handiwork, the tears were in danger of winning when a sudden rapping on the driver's window pulled Molly from her reverie.

The elderly man standing outside the car was bathed in the spreading yellow glow of the shopping-center lights. His face, wrinkled from age and years of California sunshine, was etched with concern.

"Are you all right, miss?"

Molly lowered the window. "Yes, thank you." She wiped away the single tear that had managed to escape and was trailing down her cheek.

"I thought you might be ill."

"No." She smiled reassuringly and felt the warmth left behind by her sister flow through her. "I was feeling a little unsettled, but I'm fine now."

"Are you sure? I can go back in the store and have the manager call someone."

"No," Molly repeated. She had already spoken with the one person who could ease her mind. "Really, I'm fine. But thank you so much for caring."

He seemed a bit embarrassed by her gratitude. "Well, since you're all right," he mumbled, "I guess I'll be on my way. But a word of warning. Don't be so quick to open your door or window. It's not that safe for a young woman—especially one as lovely as you—on the streets at night."

Molly knew that only too well. Thanking him again for his concern, and enjoying having a male—even one well into his seventies—call her "lovely," she restarted her car and continued on her way to her meeting with the man she loved.

Reece arrived at La Bella Pizza Palace before Molly and decided that the brightly lit pocket-size restaurant with the four wooden tables and long counter for take-out was about the furthest thing from a palace he'd ever seen. It was just as well, he decided considering the thoughts he'd been having about Molly lately—not to mention his dreams! There was no way he could contemplate having sex with his sister-in-law with all these bright lights glaring down on them. Not to mention the twelve-year-old mall rats playing the Space Invaders video game less than six feet away.

He ordered a beer and was wondering what was so important that she needed to talk with him privately, away from the house and Grace, when she walked in the door and every coherent thought in his head scattered.

Her dark hair had been pulled back from her face with a pair of silver combs, allowing it to cascade down her back like an ebony waterfall. She was wearing a silky pink top the color of strawberry sherbet that, while not exactly formfitting, hugged curves he'd never suspected she possessed. And her legs, clad in white jeans seemed a mile long.

She'd done something to her face, as well. The flesh above her startling blue eyes was smudged with a soft pearly-hued wash that echoed her pale pink lips. She looked soft and sweet and innocent. And sexy as hell.

The high heels on her sandals—higher than any he'd ever seen her wear—caused a soft feminine sway of her hips that stirred emotions he'd been trying to ignore for months.

"Hi." As she sat down in the white wooden chair across from Reece, the subtle scent of white flowers slipped beneath his skin. "I'm sorry I'm late. I hope you haven't been waiting too long."

"Just long enough for two galaxies to be blown to smithereens," he managed, feeling uncharacteristically tongue-tied.

She glanced over at the video game that was bursting forth with a triumphant victory march. "Actually, that's a fun game. Have you ever played?"

Even with every ounce of his attention focused on those glossy pink lips, Reece didn't hear what she said.

"What did you say?"

"Space Invaders. Have you ever played it?"

The floral fragrance fogged his mind and his thoughts. "I don't think so. Grace is more into Barbie dolls and stuffed animals."

The way he was looking at her—as if really seeing her for the first time—made Molly feel excited and terrified. She tried to remember all the flirting instructions Tessa had given her while they'd been waiting for Dan to arrive.

Number one was look the guy in the eye. Which hadn't sounded that difficult. But Tessa hadn't explained what to do if the target wouldn't stop looking at her mouth.

Deciding it might break the ice between them, Molly stood up again. "How about I challenge you to a game?" she asked. "Loser buys the pizza?"

The words coming out of those luscious pink lips sounded like the familiar Molly of old. But Lord, how the rest of her had changed! Knowing that if he even allowed his gaze to drift down to those soft breasts, he wouldn't be able to stand up without flashing one hellacious boner at the old lady behind the counter, Reece dragged his gaze back up to her eyes and realized that although they were like crystal at the center, the outer rings were a rich dark morning-glory color exactly like Grace's.

"You're on." His acceptance of her impulsive bet was little more than a croak. As he followed her the few steps across the room, Reece wondered why the hell he'd never noticed that Molly had a terrific ass.

He watched her ask the boys if they could have a turn and was unsurprised when they agreed. As they backed away from the machine, they continued to stare at her like the males on a deserted island might stare at a mermaid that had suddenly washed up onto their beach.

He watched with admiration as she blasted away at the alien invaders through several levels before finally having her spaceship blown up. His own turn at the controls lasted less than a minute.

"It takes a while to get the hang of it," she consoled him. "How about two out of three?" She looked back over her shoulders at her adolescent audience. "Would you boys mind if we tried again?"

As the boys shook their heads, Reece decided that she could probably ask them to throw themselves off the Santa Monica pier and they wouldn't hesitate.

This time he managed to make it to the third level before being blasted into nano fragments. When Molly was finished she was not only elevated to starship captain, the display of fireworks that lit up the screen announced that she'd saved the world and her score was being added to the official record.

"I'm sorry." Caught up in the competition, Molly

remembered, too late, Tessa's instructions to always let the man win.

"You should be. When I took you up on that bet, I never expected you to cheat."

"Cheat?"

Reece heard the murmur of angry voices and realized he was about to talk himself into a pizza-parlor brawl with her young admirers. "It's damn near impossible to think with your perfume distracting me."

"Oh." She smiled at that, a slow, sultry siren's smile so different from the bright, friendly one she usually bestowed on him.

They stood there, only a few feet apart, too close for comfort. And not nearly as close as he'd like to be. "How hungry are you?" Reece asked suddenly.

Molly read the unmistakable invitation in his eyes and realized that contrary to what she'd told Tessa, there would be no testing of the waters tonight. Feeling more reckless than she ever had in her life, she decided to dive right in, even if she did end up over her head.

"Not very." Her voice was soft and a little shaky. "How about you?"

"I had a late lunch." That was a lie. Actually, he'd spent the entire day on the phone calling various hospital board members, but he didn't want to destroy whatever was happening here with discussions about his work. "What would you say to a rain check on the pizza? And going for a drive, instead."

Forgetting the rest of Tessa's flirting tips, and refusing to play coy, Molly put her hand in his outstretched one. "I'd say yes."

* * *

"This is amazing!" Dan was turning the pages in the black journal, stunned by what the entries revealed. Tessa had alleged the journal to be a copy of a source book Elaine used to brief the girls on their various customers. The names of many of the city's heaviest hitters were represented, along with their sexual preferences and a detailed record of the times and places of their dates. There were also enough out-of-town names to fill several pages of Who's Who listings in finance, politics and academia.

"You've gotta be exaggerating about this one."

She glanced down at the hand-written entry. The Southern senator was renown for his fiery speeches upholding family values.

"Dog collars are very popular. Not to mention leashes."

"And rolled-up newspapers?"

"The *Washington Post*," she said with a quick grin. The Valium had her feeling wonderfully relaxed. Almost as if she were wrapped in fluffy pink cotton candy. She had to restrain herself from crawling onto his lap.

"Amazing." He shook his head. The deviant behavior didn't surprise him, but he was astounded by the list of customers.

"Every man has his secret fantasies." She looked at his ruggedly cut lips, remembered their taste and longed to feel them on every inch of her warming flesh. "I'll bet a few of yours are just as kinky, in their own way."

"You'd lose." He damn well wasn't going to discuss his sexual fantasies with this woman. Not when all it took was the memory of that shared kiss to make him hot.

"I can't believe you're a boring old missionary-position man." She pressed a palm against the erection that had begun to stir beneath his jeans. "And you can't be gay." She leaned forward and traced a line around his lips with the tip of her tongue. "I can tell by a man's kiss when he wants me."

"You're right. I'm not gay." He took hold of her wrist and returned her hand to her own lap. "Just discriminatory."

His cool tone cut its way like a chilled scalpel through the soft drug-induced fog surrounding her mind. Tessa was engulfed by an icy flood of embarrassment that was quickly followed by anger.

A sound like the retort of a pistol rang out. Tessa was surprised to see her hand resting on his cheek. Surprised, but not at all regretful. The bastard deserved it, she told herself.

His expression revealed not a flicker of response. Only that same cool disdain that had made her strike out at him in the first place.

"Now that you've gotten that out of your system, perhaps we can get back to work." His tone was mild but she felt a muscle jerk beneath her fingertips. "I want to know which of these guys you think your boyfriend might have been shaking down."

"*Blackmail*'s such an ugly word." She took her hand away; the white fingerprints contrasted vividly with his tanned face.

"Not nearly as ugly as murder."

The warning, softly spoken, hit home. As she reluctantly turned her attention back to the damn journal, it crossed Tessa's mind that were they to ever meet, Detective Daniel Kovaleski and the general would probably get along like gangbusters.

Molly was surprised when Reece pulled into the driveway of a condominium in Brentwood.

"I leased it a few months ago," he said in answer to her unspoken question when she glanced over at him. "After you complained about women staying over at the house with Grace there."

"Oh." Some of the excitement she'd been feeling drained out of her. Knowing that he'd brought all his other women to this secret trysting place made their long-awaited experience less special. And made her feel more than a little cheap.

"It's not the same," he assured her, as if he possessed the ability to read her mind. "Would it make you feel any better to know that I've been arguing with myself about this for months? And that while I'm still not sure it's the right thing for us to be doing, I also know that you mean far more to me than any other woman I've brought here?"

His words, instead of making her feel better, only succeeded in embarrassing Molly more. What kind of woman would he think she was? It was the nineties, for heaven's sake, nearly the millennium and she was behaving like some throwback to the past century.

"You don't have to say that, Reece, really." She forced a smile that wobbled only slightly. "I'm a big girl. I know what I'm doing."

Looking at her earnest face, illuminated by the slanting silver moonlight streaming in the car window, Reece felt a rush of tenderness.

"We could go to a hotel."

"No." That would even be worse. She couldn't imagine sitting in the lobby waiting for him to register, neither of them with any luggage. She might as well be wearing a scarlet A on her chest. Molly groaned inwardly. She was truly hopeless. Now she was thinking like some helpless heroine from an eighteenth-century novel. "This is fine, Reece. Really."

He gave her a long look. *This is quicksand, pal,* he warned himself. *One more step and you could end up stuck for good.* Even knowing that, he found himself unable to resist. Sighing his surrender, he leaned across the center console and brushed his mouth against hers. Once. Twice. A third time.

Her lips reminded him of rose petals, soft and velvety and oh-so-sweet. He deepened the kiss, and as her lips parted, then opened, like blossoms opening to the lure of a sultry summer sun, Reece knew he was lost.

Somehow—Molly had no memory of it happening—they made their way from the car into the condo. The furnishings, all chrome and glass and black leather, seemed unsuited to the Reece she'd always known.

"I leased it furnished," he said as he viewed the puzzled frown lines on her forehead as her glance swept the room.

"It's very nice," she lied.

Reece shrugged. "It's okay, I guess," he lied back. When he'd first seen the condo, he'd thought it possessed all the personality of an operating room. Since he was only interested in the bed, it could have been draped in silk and satin like a pasha's seraglio for all he cared. "Would you like a drink?"

Molly almost smiled at that, thinking back on the night she'd drunk wine with Joe and ended up kissing him. The night she'd dreamed that it had been Reece whose mouth had created such burning need.

"I don't think so." The few kisses they'd shared in the car already had her head buzzing. If she was going to go through with this, Molly fully intended to remember every detail in the morning.

"Well." Christ, he couldn't ever remember being so damn nervous with a woman. Reece felt like some anxious, horny teenager about to experience sex for the first time.

They stood only a few feet apart, looking at each other. Molly was unreasonably uncomfortable, wondering if he was comparing her to all the other glamorous, sexy women he'd brought to this place and was finding her lacking.

She need not have worried. Reece was fascinated by this woman who was both foreign and familiar all at the same time, and absolutely enthralled by the open desire shining in her wide blue eyes.

"I'm scared," she admitted breathlessly.

Reece understood that she was not referring to the physical act. She wasn't the only one concerned about what the impact of what they were about to do would have on their relationship.

"Me, too." He managed a smile. "Scared to death." He touched his hand to her face. "It'll be all right."

"Yes." She covered his hand with hers. "And I promise to respect you in the morning."

He laughed at that, a rich, bold laugh that banished the lingering discomfort. Molly's ability to diffuse awkward situations was one of the things he'd always loved about her.

Loved? The word reverberated through his mind like the civil defense siren that used to sound every noon in downtown L.A. This wasn't about love, Reece reminded himself. Oh, it was a lot more than the lust he'd felt for all the other women—the ones *Variety* had called "Longworth's playmates."

But love? No way. Love was too dangerous. Too sneaky. It lulled you into complacency, got you to trust, to relax in its warm golden comfort, then in one fell swoop, pulled everything away, leaving you alone. And empty.

Closing his mind to that perilous thought, Reece laced their fingers together and began walking toward the bedroom.

Chapter Twenty-Six

The bedroom was decorated in the same sparse, sterile style. The huge bed dominated the room.

Molly looked up at Reece, her anxious heart in her eyes. "I don't know what to do."

If any other woman had said that to him, Reece would have taken it as a sign to run. But the woman standing in front of him, looking up at him with a blend of desire and uncertainty was Molly—his Molly—and that made all the difference.

"Don't worry." He rocked forward on the balls of his feet and touched his mouth to hers. "I do."

It was not a hard kiss. It did not plunder, not even when he slipped his tongue between her lips and swept the dark moist interior of her mouth in an enervating way that made her go weak at the knees and forced her to hold on to his shoulders. Part of her felt on the verge of crumbling to the floor. Another part felt as if she were floating, high above them, in some misty, glorious place.

The dazzling kiss went on and on, creating warm ribbons of golden light that flowed through her veins like liquid sunshine.

"Ah, Molly," he murmured against her mouth, "if you had any idea how many times I've dreamed of this."

Her eyes, which had fluttered shut, flew open. "Me, too," she admitted hesitantly.

She felt his smile curve beneath her lips. "I'm glad I wasn't the only one suffering." He wrapped his arms around her and drew her into the cradle of his thighs. "But this is even better than my dreams."

She sighed her pleasure. "Mine, too."

He continued to kiss her lovingly, lingeringly, until Molly's entire world became focused on his mouth. She'd never known it was possible to feel so much from just kissing. She'd never realized a kiss could make you fly.

After a time, he took her hands from around his neck and placed them against the front of his shirt. "I think we're wearing too many clothes."

She felt his heart pounding beneath her fingertips in a hard, pulsating rhythm that echoed her own. "You want me to undress you?"

"Only if you want to. In fact, if you'd rather stop—"

"No." Even as her nerves rose to torment her yet again, Molly knew she'd die if they stopped now. "No," she repeated more firmly as her fingers went to work on his shirt.

How could one man's shirt have so many buttons? Her fingers seemed to have turned to stone. For every button she managed to unfasten, it seemed as if three more popped up to take their place. Nearly weeping with frustration, she glanced up at him and received an encouraging smile in return.

"We have all the time in the world." He smiled and ran a fingertip along the tender flesh of her bottom lip, reddened from the way she'd been worrying it with her teeth. Grace did the same thing whenever she was concentrating, Reece realized.

Reassured and a bit emboldened, she returned to the task. Success! Finally she was able to push the crisp cotton aside and gaze in wonder at his muscled dark chest.

After another frustrating moment struggling with the buttons at the cuffs, she managed to push the shirt off his shoulders and down his arms. It landed on the floor at their feet and went ignored. Following her instincts, she leaned forward, touched her mouth to his gleaming chest and felt his deep guttural groan vibrating against her lips.

"My turn." Displaying far more dexterity than she'd managed, he dispatched the buttons running down the front of her silk blouse. Within seconds, it was fluttering downward like a tropical pink bird, and landed atop his shirt.

Her breasts, clad in a skimpy bit of pink lace she'd borrowed from Tessa, felt unnaturally heavy. And although she never would have believed it possible, they'd begun to throb in anticipation of his touch.

"Lovely," he murmured as he traced the scalloped lace with his finger, leaving a trail of sparks on her already heated flesh.

When he followed the burning path with the tip of his tongue, Molly imagined water sizzling on a hot skillet. Her nipples, pressing against the lace, desperate for his touch, began tingling painfully.

Touch me, they seemed to be crying out. *Taste me.*

Displaying the patience that had once made him the best ER doctor she'd ever worked with, Reece touched his mouth to the startlingly sensitive spot where her shoulder and neck met, then continued to kiss his way along her collarbone.

"Reece…"

"Mmm?" After skimming his lips hotly up her throat, then back down again, he seemed intrigued with tasting the crook of her elbow.

"Please." If anyone had ever suggested she'd ever plead for a man's touch, Molly would have scoffed at the possibility. But at this moment, she was willing to beg, if that's what it took to get that treacherous mouth back up to her breasts. "Touch me."

"I am." He trailed his fingers down the inside of her other arm.

"Not there." Unable to bear the tension another moment, she combed her hands through his thick hair and literally dragged his head up to her breasts. "Here."

"Ahh." He nuzzled the soft yielding flesh, then once again proving himself an expert when it came to women's clothing, unfastened the front clasp of her bra so quickly, it seemed to dissolve in his hands before he sent it flying. "You are so beautiful."

Her breasts were round and ripe and tipped with pale pink nipples. Reece cupped them in his palms while running his fingers over those rosy crests. When she began to tremble, he bent his head and took one between his lips, laving lightly at first, then sucking in a way that made her gasp in stunned pleasure. When her hips began to move instinctively against his thighs, Reece realized that although Molly might not think she knew how to make love, her body definitely knew what to do.

The way she was moving against him, the heat of her body, the soft little sighs she was making, conspired to make him forget that he'd vowed to take his time, to be careful with this precious gift she was bestowing upon him. Fires burning in his loins, Reece scraped his teeth against one of the taut nipples and felt her immediately stiffen.

Damn! Cursing himself for his impatience, he looked down into her face and witnessed the sheen of tears glazing the wide, midnight blue pools of her eyes.

"I'm sorry, I—"

"No." She pressed her fingertips against his mouth. "Please. Don't apologize. I was loving it. You can't be blamed for old, knee-jerk responses."

"I should be more careful. I got carried away."

"Please, Reece, don't treat me like something that might break." She held her arms out from her sides, as if offering herself, body and soul to him. Which, of course, she was. "I want you to treat me like a woman."

The tension in the room disintegrated as he realized she was telling the absolute truth. "Well, then," he drawled around his own answering smile, "if you insist."

Drawing her back against him, he kissed her again, harder this time. His hands moved over her with a practiced touch that had her own palms roaming over his chest, up his arms, across his shoulders, down the muscled smoothness of his bare back.

He sat her down on the bed and unfastened her sandals. When he touched his mouth to the arch of first her right foot, then her left, Molly bit her lip to hold back her cry.

"Don't do that." He kissed her again, soothing the wounded pink flesh with his tongue. "I don't want you to hold anything back, Molly, love. I want to know everything you're feeling. I want to be sure I'm bringing you pleasure."

"Oh, you are," Molly assured him as she kissed him back in an openmouthed wanton way that she'd never imagined she'd want to do with any man. Tongues tangled, lips ground against one another, teeth clashed.

"Oh, God, I knew it," he said as he managed to unfasten her jeans and pull them down her legs. He released her mouth to kiss his way up each leg.

The hot touch of his mouth was making her legs quake. Her body bowed as Molly lifted her hips off the mattress, seeking...needing...something.

"Knew what?" she managed as the erotic heat took her breath away.

"That you'd be sweet." He dispensed with the final silky barrier with ease.

The heat flowing through her veins had coalesced into a tight ball that pulsed like a newly born star. A roaring filled her head. When he touched his tongue to her ultrasensitive clitoris, the star exploded within her, around her, flinging her somewhere far above herself.

She couldn't breathe. She was dying. Surely it

wasn't possible for anyone to live through such heat. But Reece was merciless. As she felt herself crashing helplessly back to earth, he sent her up again. And again, each crest higher, each climax more shattering than the last.

"Please." She wanted to reach for him, to pull him deep inside her, but her arms lay limp and useless at her sides. "Reece, I need you."

He'd planned to be gentle. Worried that she'd link the rape with their lovemaking, he'd vowed to be tender. But the animal within had burst free when she'd responded with such surprising passion to his lovemaking, bringing with it a possessive need to plunder. Reece had wanted her hot and hungry, writhing and screaming. And by God, that's just the way he'd had her. And it still wasn't enough.

He left her only long enough to strip off the rest of his clothes and sheathe himself in the condom he was never without. Then he drew her back into his arms and resumed kissing her, slow, deep, devastating kisses that went on and on. When he slipped his hand between her thighs and pushed aside the soft slick folds to slip a long finger inside her, he found her hot and wet and tight.

Molly had worried that her old terror would kick in when he sought to penetrate her, but now, as a second finger joined the first, stroking her in an intimate way no man had ever done before, pleasure overruled fear.

"You're so wet," he murmured, feeling himself on the verge of explosion as her body softened, opening for him.

"I know." Molly was amazed to discover that she

wasn't the slightest bit embarrassed by the sucking sound of his fingers moving in and out of her body. On the contrary, it was the most erotic sound she'd ever heard. "I can't seem to help myself."

"Don't try to help it." He leaned down and kissed her, his tongue thrusting into her mouth, its rhythm echoing the wild pulsating one between her legs. "Wet is good." When she bucked against his hand, he thought he was going to explode. "Wet and hot is very, very good."

His own desire was nearly out of control now, causing his caresses to become less controlled. He suckled on her breasts as his hand probed deeper, he groaned as she reached between them and wrapped her fingers around his throbbing erection.

"You're so big." Her eyes, which had drifted shut to better concentrate on these new sensual sensations, flew open. "We'll never fit."

"Believe me, love—" he kissed her again, a soft featherlike promise "—we'll be a perfect fit."

He knelt between her silky thighs. "I'll try not to hurt you."

"You could never, ever, hurt me." She twined her arms around his neck and drew his head down to hers for a long, passionate kiss. When she began sucking on his tongue, the last of Reece's control slipped away.

"Put your legs around me, Molly, love."

She wrapped her legs around his hips, crying out with surprise and ecstasy as he surged forward, fully embedding himself inside her.

"Oh!" She never could have imagined that anything could have felt so wonderful. She never could have imagined that having Reece inside her could make her feel so complete.

When she began to move against him, Reece feared he wouldn't last long enough to show her just how good sex could be.

"Honey." He put his hands on her hips, stilling her restless movements. "Please, just lie still and let me…" He lifted her hips and went even deeper, until he could feel himself pressing against the back of her womb. "Oh, yes." It came out on a guttural groan of masculine pleasure against her throat. "God, you feel so good. So tight. So warm."

He was shaking from need for her. He was burning up from the inside out. He'd wanted to watch her, to witness her expression as he took her up over that final peak. But smoke clouded his mind, and a red haze shimmered in front of his eyes, blinding him as he plunged harder, deeper, faster.

All the time she arched against him, keeping up with the merciless pace, her hands moving up and down his back, clenching his buttocks, pulling him even deeper inside her velvet wet warmth.

It was mad. It was ferocious. And it was glorious.

Her vaginal orgasm racked her body; she shuddered convulsively beneath him. Engulfed in a rush of heat, her body clutching at him like velvet fingers, Reece lost all control, shouting out her name as he gave in to his own explosive release before collapsing on top of her.

Not wanting to crush Molly, he shifted them onto their sides, deftly managing the maneuver without slipping out of her. They lay there for a long, silent time, breathless. Spent.

"I don't think I'll ever be able to move from this spot," he groaned when he was finally able to speak again.

The idea sounded fine to Molly. Better than fine. It was wonderful. "I never knew," she murmured, pressing her lips against his damp neck, tasting on her tongue the salt born of his exertion. "Never in my wildest imagination did I believe it possible for people to feel so much and not burn up from the feeling."

Neither had Reece. Sex with Lena had been hot and wonderful, a manifestation of their love. Sex since her death had been hot, but his heart had never been involved in the action.

But sex with Molly had been like throwing himself on a fiery funeral pyre, only to rise again, reborn. He remembered thinking, just before his own orgasm, that if he were to die at that moment, his only regret would be that he wouldn't be able to do this again.

Christ, for a woman with absolutely no sexual experience, she'd been perfect. They'd been perfect together, which didn't make any sense since the first time with any woman was at best a getting-acquainted session, at worst a devastating mismatch. But when he'd first kissed Molly, it had been as if she'd been created specifically with him in mind. And every step along the way had only upheld that quixotic feeling.

Reece had never felt exactly like this after making love and that scared the hell out of him. *Quicksand,* he reminded himself grimly. He'd known it was there, had waded in anyway and was now buried in the damn stuff up to his neck.

Molly had never felt so good. So complete. As she lay in Reece's arms, basking in the warm afterglow of their lovemaking, she refused to believe that what they'd just done was a sin. She loved Reece, with all her heart, and that, she decided, made all the difference.

It was only when she felt him suddenly flinch that she realized she'd spoken out loud.

"Molly..." He pushed himself up on one elbow and brushed the tousled hair away from her face. "What we did was wonderful. Hell, it was better than wonderful. It was world-class. But it had nothing to do with love."

She wished she hadn't opened her big mouth. But now that she had, Molly refused to lie about her feelings just to make him more comfortable with their situation.

"Maybe not for you," she said, trying to ignore the little stabbing pain in her heart caused by the unwelcome realization that she'd taken their lovemaking far more seriously than he had. "But you're certainly not the first man to want to make love to me, Reece—"

"I suppose you're referring to that flyboy BIA doctor?"

If he hadn't already assured her that he didn't love her, Molly would have thought, from his tone and dark expression, that Reece was jealous.

"I'm not going to discuss particulars," she said mildly. "But I've had a few offers since leaving the order. And the reason I turned those men down was because I didn't love them. Like I love you."

"Look, honey—"

"I have a name," she reminded him, afraid she was

about to hear a speech he gave often in such circumstances.

"Don't you think I know that?"

"Truthfully, I don't know what to think about you anymore. I used to think I knew you. Now I'm beginning to wonder."

He sat up and raked his hands through his hair. "I'm the same guy I've always been."

"No. You're not. You never played around with other women when you were married to Lena."

"Of course I didn't. I loved Lena. More than life itself. But she died, remember? And now if I want to have sex with a different woman every night—hell, ten women every night, there's nothing to stop me."

"Doesn't it get stale?" she asked, genuinely curious.

"You seemed to enjoy it well enough."

"I was in love." On this, Molly would not give in.

He swore. "You can't be in love with me."

She met his frustrated look with a calm one of her own. "I agree that you're not being very lovable right now. However, I can't help my feelings. I do love you, Reece. I have for years. But there's no reason for you to get so upset about it."

"It's not that I don't want to—"

"Isn't it?"

"Lord, no wonder you had to leave the order. You'd probably argue with Saint Peter."

That stung, just a little, but it was certainly not the first time Molly had been accused of being stubborn. "Do you always insult women right after you make love with them?"

"I told you—"

"I know. It wasn't love."

Her wide, patient morning glory eyes tore at something elemental in him. Reece cursed. "You don't understand."

"I'm trying to."

"It's like love is some kind of cosmic joke. Or jinx. Every time I love someone, I end up losing them. First my parents, then Lena…" He dragged his hands down his face. "It's just too damn hard, Molly."

"Surely you don't believe Lena's death had anything to do with your loving her? Or her loving you?"

"She was on the way to the store to buy stuff for my birthday cake."

Momentarily sidetracked from her own needs, Molly stared at him. "Reece, what happened to Lena was a tragic accident. She was in the wrong place at a horribly wrong time. It had nothing to do with you."

"Perhaps not. But it still hurt, Molly. A lot. I don't think I could ever survive that much pain again."

"You love Grace."

"Of course. But I didn't have a choice, dammit. She's my daughter."

"Love is a gift, Reece," she said quietly. "It's given freely. You don't have to feel guilty if you can't feel the same way."

His expression told her this was not exactly what he'd been hoping to hear. "I don't know what you want from me."

"Nothing." She smiled up at him when she wanted to cry.

Wanting to put the discomfort behind them, she brushed her mouth against his unsmiling one. "I take that back.'' She plucked at his lips. ''There is just one little thing....''

It was happening all over again. Just one kiss and she was pulling him back into the flames. ''Molly...''

''It's just sex, Reece.'' Her hands moved down his chest, branding him with her delicate touch. ''What's to stop you from doing it again?''

''How about the fact that I can't perform on command?''

Her fingers brushed against his erection. ''Want to bet?''

At her touch Reece surrendered to the inevitable—to Molly. He rolled her over, slipped into her without a ripple and once again let his body and, he feared, his heart, take over his mind.

''I can't believe it!''

Molly had never seen Dan more furious. He was pacing her living room floor like a caged tiger who hadn't eaten raw meat in a month. ''I don't understand. You said Tessa was scheduled to appear before the grand jury today—''

''That was the plan. Until the damn judge called in sick. Along with three of the jurors.''

''Perhaps they all came down with the flu?''

The look he shot her suggested otherwise. ''It's no coincidence. Someone got to them.''

''Surely that's impossible,'' Molly protested.

''Not for Jason,'' Tessa muttered. She was sitting on Molly's couch, and although the day was warm, she was wearing a sweatshirt and fleece leggings. She was so, so cold. ''He's got informants all over the city. It wouldn't be that hard for him to find out who was on the jury, then threaten them.''

Having witnessed the results of Jason Mathison's violent streak, Molly suspected he could prove horribly intimidating. But surely a judge would be beyond such tactics?

"The guy's probably one of Elaine's clients," Tessa said when Molly professed such doubts. "There's no way he's going to help make that list public."

"Which is why the damn ring has been able to exist with impunity for so many years," Dan ground out. "A large percentage of the movers and shakers in L.A. are on that list."

"That's why you cops spend your time busting the poor working girls on Sunset," Tessa said. She began rubbing her arms to warm them. "Because they're the only ones you can get a prostitution conviction on. Even if they are back out on the street in ninety days."

Dan cursed again. Then looked at Tessa as if finally seeing her. "Are you all right?"

"I'm fine." Or would be if only she could figure out a way to get some pills. Her secret stash was running low; she'd had to cut way back to save enough to get her through the grand jury appearance. After her testimony she'd hoped Dan would quit standing guard over her like a police dog, long enough for her to make a buy.

God, you're a mess, she told herself. *It's not like you're hooked on crack or heroin. Why the hell can't you grow up? How hard could withdrawal from a few prescription pills be?*

Molly gave Tessa a long look, as well. "Dan's

right. You're not at all well." She'd been so wrapped up in her own problems with Reece—who hadn't spoken to her since he'd brought her home Friday night—that she hadn't even noticed her sister was suffering.

Tessa hated the way they were looking at her. "It's just the air-conditioning. The room's too cold." How could she be so cold when it felt as if coals were burning inside her head?

"You seem nervous."

"Wouldn't you be?" Tessa could feel the anxiety creeping up on her. "I was all psyched up to testify, and now Dirty Harry here informs me that the court date's been postponed. Of course I'm nervous." That was putting it mildly. Little bursts of electricity were sparking beneath her icy skin. "I don't suppose anyone around here has a cigarette?"

"I didn't realize you smoked." Molly's eyes narrowed.

"She didn't during the interrogation," Dan said.

She couldn't stand it any longer. "Would you both just shut the hell up? What's the matter with wanting a fucking cigarette? Who are you, the Surgeon General's smoking patrol?"

Molly sat down beside her, and when Tessa tried to look away, Molly took hold of her chin and turned her face toward her. "You've been taking pills."

"Of course I haven't." Tessa forced a laugh. "Jesus, how could I get drugs with the two of you hovering over me all the time?"

"Good question," Molly said. "And one we can talk about later. After we get you to a clinic."

"What?" Tessa leapt to her feet. "What the hell

are you talking about?'' She began to pace, as Dan had done earlier, but with much more hectic energy.

''How about the fact that you're in deep withdrawal?'' Dan asked.

Tessa turned on him, her hands fisted on her hips. ''Spoken just like a former drunk. This is where I get the Twelve Step lecture, right?''

''I wouldn't think of it.'' His tone and his expression remained mild. ''Unless you want me to.''

''I don't.''

He shrugged. ''Fine. However, since you're obviously in withdrawal, not to mention being on the verge of a psychotic episode, your sister's right. You need help.''

He turned toward Molly. ''I'm going to call Reece and ask him to try to get Tessa into a clinic.''

Ignoring Tessa's heated protests, he placed the call while Molly retrieved a blanket from the cedar chest at the end of the bed. ''It'll be okay,'' she assured her sister, as she wrapped it around Tessa's trembling shoulders. ''You'll be okay.''

Her teeth chattering from the godawful chill, Tessa only wished she could believe that.

Molly realized just how important Reece had become in the Hollywood community when, with a single phone call, he managed to circumvent the waiting list and get Tessa into Phoenix House, a popular rehabilitation clinic catering to the movie community.

''Two weeks isn't that long,'' she assured Tessa as she hugged her goodbye.

''That's easy for you to say. You're not the one

who's going to have to deal with Nurse Ratchett for fourteen days.''

''She didn't look that bad.'' A bit humorless, Molly thought, but not cruel. And, although she wanted to protect her sister, she realized that Tessa needed someone with a no-nonsense attitude toward her addiction.

''She won't be able to get anything past that dragon.'' Dan echoed Molly's thoughts as they walked out of the clinic. Hopefully by the time Tessa was released, the grand jury would have convened with a new judge.

''Like she did me?'' Molly still couldn't understand how Tessa could have been using drugs without her noticing. .

''You're a classic caretaker, Molly. A rescuer. But the problem is, while you're a dynamite ER nurse, you don't have any real experience with drunks and addicts.

''You're like a guy without any lifeguard training who's walking along the beach and sees a person drowning. Feeling a gut-level need to help, he rushes into the surf, swims out to the victim, who thrashes around so much, they both end up drowning.''

''That wouldn't have happened to me.''

''Yes. It would have.'' He turned to her and took both her hands in his. ''Believe me, I've seen it happen too many times to count. Trying to fix your sister up all by yourself would eventually end up draining all your confidence and energy. And Tessa still would be an addict.''

His grim expression softened and he leaned forward and brushed his lips against hers. ''You're a bright, wonderful woman, Molly. But you have an unfortunate tendency toward denial.''

"I know.'' He wasn't telling her anything she hadn't told herself a thousand times. "I'm working on that.''

He laughed. And winked. "Me, too.''

Linking their fingers together, he continued walking with her back to the car.

Watching them out the window, Tessa felt a sharp jolt of something that even as messed up as she was, she could easily recognize as jealousy.

"I don't care,'' she muttered, turning away from the window to begin pacing again. Where the hell was that doctor, anyway? They'd promised her something to take the edge off. "Only an idiot would fall in love with some ex-alcoholic cop.''

Only an idiot. The description, Tessa admitted with chagrin, fit her perfectly.

Chapter Twenty-Seven

A week after Tessa was admitted to the rehab clinic, Molly was sitting in her kitchen with Dan, sharing a pizza, two bottles of nonalcoholic beer and some eye-opening conversation about addiction. Although Molly had known he'd had a drinking problem, she was amazed to discover exactly how bad it had gotten before he'd sought help.

"I never knew," she admitted, nonplussed that this man she'd believed she knew so well had been so out of control.

"Most drunks are great liars. And, in the cop business, it's pretty easy to cover up. Because you get a lot of help from the troops."

"The old us-against-them mentality." Molly had witnessed it hundreds of times with cops in the ER, whether they were shooter or victim.

"Hey, we're the good guys. The rest of the world are assholes," he agreed easily. When he realized what he'd said, he flushed. "Sorry about that."

"You don't have to apologize. I've heard worse." She grinned and stood up as the doorbell rang. "In fact, I've been called worse."

Dan was still laughing about the thought of anyone calling Saint Molly an asshole when she opened the door to Reece.

"Oh, hi." Her unruly heart, which had leapt at the sight of him, made her voice breathless.

"Hi." He glanced past her, as if trying to locate the source of the male laughter. "If I've come at a bad time…"

"Of course not." Molly moved aside, inviting him in.

She was wearing a tangerine-colored dress that looked like an oversize T-shirt, and ended a good four inches above her knees, showing her long legs to advantage.

"Dan's here. We were having pizza."

"Sounds like fun." Reece frowned as he walked into the cheery yellow room and found the cop looking all too comfortable sitting at the antique farm table he knew Molly had refinished herself.

"I thought I'd drop by to make sure you got Tessa checked in," he said after exchanging a curt greeting with the cop.

"We did. And thanks again for pulling all those strings. I don't know what I would have done without you."

"You would have thought of something. And I have no doubt Dan would have been more than happy to help."

Hearing the edge in his friend's voice, Dan glanced from Reece to Molly, then back to Reece again. Sensing the sexual tension shimmering between them, he decided it was time to leave.

"Gotta go." He stood up and hugged Molly. Suddenly nervous to be alone with Reece, she hugged him back, holding on tight. "Are you sure you can't stay?"

"Nah." He grinned down at her. "You'll do fine," he murmured for her ears only. "See ya," he said with a nod to Reece, who nodded back.

Waiting in the kitchen, listening to their murmured conversation at the door, Reece reminded himself that he had no right to be irritated by Dan's presence.

If Molly wanted to invite the entire goddamn police department over for pizza, it wasn't any of his business. Just because they'd made love didn't give him any right to dictate her friends. She had her life, just as he had his. It was what he wanted, what he'd demanded.

So why the hell was he so pissed?

"Would you like some pizza?" she asked as she returned to the brightly lit kitchen.

"No." He shook his head. "I think you know what I want, Molly." He hadn't been able to get her out of his mind for days. "I haven't been able to sleep."

"I'm sorry." It was the only lie she'd ever told him. And Molly didn't feel at all guilty about it.

"I can't work, either. I've got a script due tomorrow and I haven't written a single decent line."

She tossed back her hair. "Are you blaming me for destroying your concentration?"

His eyes locked on hers. "Who else?"

He moved quickly, before she had time to answer. Or breathe. Her gasp was swallowed by his mouth as he scooped her up into his arms.

"Shouldn't we talk about this?" she asked as he carried her out of the kitchen.

"Later."

The male hunger in his heated kiss thrilled Molly. The need made her want to weep with relief. After days of ignoring her, Reece had come back. Just as she'd hoped. Just as she'd prayed.

"Later," she agreed breathlessly, wrapping her bare legs around his waist as she rained kisses on his face.

They tumbled together onto the bed in a tangle of arms and legs. Molly's dress was whipped over her head before she could draw a breath; a moan ripped from her throat as he covered her breast with his mouth, dampening the flowered bra, creating an enervating heat.

"No." Although it took every ounce of self-control she possessed, she pulled away.

"No?" Reece looked at her disbelievingly.

"It's my turn." Kneeling over him, she began ripping at the buttons on his shirt. As impatient as she, he helped her, and when the rest of their clothes were gone, he pulled her back down to him, his kiss hot and greedy and filled with sharp, edgy need.

She sprawled atop him, hot flesh molded to hot flesh, hearts pounding in a wild, shared rhythm.

"Oh, God, I want you." He filled his hands with her breasts.

When his teeth tugged on a rigid peak, Molly felt a jolt of electricity shoot from his mouth to that tingling, hot wet place between her legs.

"I want you, too," she managed on a ragged gasp as he reached between them and cupped that throbbing heat. "But first it's my turn to drive you mad."

Reece wanted to assure her that their days apart had already done that, that he'd been going crazy with need for her. But before he could tell her all that, she began touching him, stroking him, caressing him with her hands and her mouth, sparking smoldering embers.

This time it was she who rolled the condom down his tumescent flesh, and although she fumbled a little, Reece found her insistence both sexy and endearing.

Still surprising him with her uncharacteristic assertiveness, she straddled his hips, lowered herself onto his straining shaft, surrounding him with her slick tight heat, then began rocking her hips back and forth in a way that caused an almost painful friction between them.

When Reece felt Molly's body begin to spasm around him, he grabbed her hips, forcing her down even as he slammed upward. A tidal wave flooded over him, dragging him down into a churning, red-black sea. When he finally surfaced, he was laughing.

"Did I do something wrong?" Worry marred her forehead.

"Aw, baby, I'm sorry. Of course you didn't. You were wonderful. And I laughed because I feel so damn good." He rolled her over and gave her a long wet kiss. "*You* feel good."

She smiled and cuddled up against him. And as they lay there, arms and legs entwined, Reece realized that the quicksand was rapidly closing in over his head and he couldn't even get up the strength to care.

"Well, that sure should have done it," he murmured.

She lifted her head. Her eyes were still dark with

passion, as deeply blue as a storm-tossed midnight sea. "Done what?"

"Gotten you out of my system."

"I certainly hope not." Since she'd decided not to push Reece into admitting emotions he wasn't prepared to face, Molly forced a bright and breezy tone. "Because I surely haven't gotten you out of mine." She nuzzled his neck. When she nipped at his earlobe, he felt a renewed stir of hunger.

"You should have told me you were insatiable," he said as he rolled them over, urging her legs apart.

She gave him a sassy, very unnunlike grin. "You should have asked."

Her long limber legs wrapped around him; her body bowed; her dancing dark eyes fluttered shut on a sigh of pleasure as he filled her.

"I love you," she said, unable to censor her words when her heart was so overbrimming with emotion.

He bent his head and kissed her. A soft heartfelt kiss suggesting a promise his head was not yet prepared to make. "I know."

It was all either of them was to say for a very long time.

She just couldn't do it. Tessa paced her room, smoking one of the ten cigarettes a day she was permitted, still fuming over the earlier group-therapy session. How dare all those losers get on her case! Just because she hadn't grown up in some rat-infested tenement, like Marcus. Or been raped by her father when she was twelve like that screwed-up loser Roseanne.

"Did they think it was easy, having to go to a different school every year?" she muttered as she glared out the window at the rose garden. Her chore for today had been to cut off all the dead blooms. Her fingers were still bleeding from that work session. "I need a manicure." She dragged her hand through her hair. "And a shampoo."

Hell. What she needed was a pill. Just one lovely little yellow Valium. Or a pretty purple Xanax. Anything to stop her nerve endings from jumping inside her skin.

It wasn't fair they were keeping her prisoner! Hell, for all the freedom she had, she might as well have been in jail.

"Which is where Dudley Doright would probably put me, if he could." She took a last long drag on the cigarette, burning it all the way to the filter, then ground it out in a clear glass ashtray on which a phoenix bird had been painted. Nice bit of advertising, Tessa decided, wondering if she was expected to take the ashtray home with her at the end of her stay and leave it out on the coffee table for her friends to see.

Everyone knew addicts had junkie friends. Putting decals on ashtrays was certainly a cheaper way to get the word out than those television ads Phoenix House ran, which showed a beautiful blonde in a flowing dress sitting in the rose garden.

"No one ever mentions she's going to be expected to prune those fucking roses herself," Tessa muttered as she lit another cigarette and drew the smoke deep into her lungs. The nicotine calmed. But not enough.

As she continued to pace and smoke, Tessa plotted her escape.

Molly was gone when Tessa let herself into the apartment with the spare key she'd stolen from Molly's kitchen junk drawer. She was relieved that her sister wasn't home. Relieved and a little disappointed.

She dialed the number she knew by heart.

"Hello?"

At the sound of that all-too-familiar deep voice, Tessa began to shake. *No,* some little voice deep in the far reaches of her mind counseled. *You don't really want this man back in your life.*

"Hello?" the deep voice repeated.

She closed her eyes and pressed the receiver against her chest, thinking how easy it would be. He could be here in ten minutes. With just what she needed.

And then what? the little voice piped up. *Next time he beats you up—and you know there will be a next time—you could die. Is that really what you want?*

Two weeks ago, she might have said yes. But that was before Molly. And before she'd managed to stay straight for the longest period of time in years.

With an unsteady hand she hung up the phone.

Jason looked down at the caller ID unit attached to his phone. He'd known she wouldn't be able to hold out. The cunt needed her pills like a baby needed milk.

"And I'm going to make certain you get them, sweetheart," he assured her as he retrieved the throwaway pistol he kept in the box beneath a loose floorboard in his bedroom. "All the pills you need."

A quick call gave him the address she'd called from. When it turned out to be less than ten minutes away, Jason decided this was definitely his lucky day.

* * *

"I'm sorry," the ER clerk who answered the phone said, "but Molly's off today. Can I take a message?"

"No." Tessa took a deep breath and assured herself she could hold on. Just a little longer. "Thank you, anyway." She pressed the Lucite button down and dialed Information again, this time getting the central number for the LAPD.

It took a while to track him down. When he answered, Dan's voice revealed impatience. "Yeah, this is Detective Kovaleski."

His voice was so curt, Tessa almost hung up. Reminding herself that this man might be her last chance, she said, "Dan?"

"Tessa?"

"It's me," she answered in a frail fractured voice nothing like the smartass one she'd used with him the last time they'd been together. "You know that Twelve Step lecture I said I didn't want?"

There was a brief silence. Then, "Yeah…I remember."

"Well—" she drew in a ragged breath "—I think I'm ready."

There was another pause. "You're not at the clinic, are you?"

She shook her head, then realized that there was no way he could hear the gesture over the phone lines. "No," she said finally. "I'm at Molly's."

She was vastly relieved when he didn't yell at her for running away from Phoenix House or lecture her about breaking the rules.

"I'll be right there."

She felt as if fires were sparking beneath her skin. "Please hurry."

"I'm on my way."

She replaced the receiver on the cradle. Then prayed Dan would get here in time to save her from herself.

"Are you certain you don't want to come in?" Molly stood on the sidewalk, her back against Reece's parked car. They'd spent a leisurely morning making love, then had passed the afternoon at the beach with Grace, who'd proven a natural surfer on her new Boogie board.

"Of course I do." He leaned against her, playing idly with her hair. "But if I don't get that script written…"

"I know." Her smile held not an iota of regret. "I shouldn't have kept you from your work all day."

He smiled back and, mindless of the fact they were on a public street, brushed his lips against hers. "I'm just going to have to learn some self-restraint where you're concerned."

She wrapped her arms around his waist. "Not too much, I hope."

"No. Not too much." The kiss lingered, warmed. "I have to go."

"I know."

Neither of them moved.

"I need an incentive."

"How about a paycheck?"

"Won't work. I'm already obscenely rich, remember?"

"That's right. I keep forgetting." His warmth was turning her to wax. Molly wondered why, after all those years working ER, she'd never known it was possible for a human body to melt. "How about I promise to show you the new things I bought from Victoria's Secret...when you're finished?''

He leaned back far enough to look at her. "You went shopping at Victoria's Secret?"

"The day after we first made love." She'd known that once he'd had time to get used to the idea of them together, he'd be back. And she'd intended to be ready.

"What did you buy?"

"Oh, a little bit of this and that. The underwear you said you liked today. A nightgown." Her eyes danced with a blend of newly tapped sensuality. "And a teddy."

The mental vision of Molly scantily clad in a satin-and-lace teddy was enough to make him hard. "Ah, sweetheart," he groaned, covering her smiling mouth with his, "if you're trying to convince me to go back to work, you're going about it the wrong way. How about we go inside, you can give me a fashion show, *then* I'll get back to work?"

"And have me be responsible for another week of reruns?" She put her hands on his shoulders and pushed. "The sooner you get the script finished, the sooner I can show you my new garter belt."

"Oh, Lord. I never realized you were such a cruel woman, Margaret Mary McBride."

"I never realized it, either." Her grin was that of a woman who'd discovered a secret weapon with which she could rule the world. She went up on her toes and kissed him again. Hard. "Call me when you're finished."

"You've got a deal." He kissed her again, longer, ignoring the wolf whistle of a kid riding by on a mountain bike. Then he reluctantly got into the car and drove away, vowing to finish the damn script in record time. It was the last one of the upcoming season. Once he'd completed it, he could take a long hard look at his life and make some important decisions.

Molly was still floating on air when she walked into her condo. At the sight of her sister sitting on her couch, white-faced and trembling, she came crashing down to earth.

"Tessa?"

"Oh, Molly." It came out on a wail. "I'm so, so sorry."

Having learned a great deal about addiction from Dan, Molly was not overly surprised by her sister's lapse. "It's okay, honey," she assured her. "You made it ten days. That's a good start."

"I wasn't talking about that," Tessa said on a sob.

"Then what—"

"I believe she was referring to me," a calm male voice offered.

Molly turned toward the voice. As she saw the man pointing the gun toward her, she had a vision, like an acid flashback, of another armed man.

And in that fleeting moment, although she had no idea how she would get out of this dangerous situation, Molly vowed that this time things would be different. This time she was not going to end up a victim.

Instead of returning to work as he'd told Molly he intended to do, Reece drove to the cemetery. Unlike the first time he'd come and failed to find comfort, subsequent visits had brought, if not peace, at least acceptance.

As he walked across the emerald green grass he passed a group of mourners gathered for a funeral. A distant pain stirred, but Reece tapped it down. Today was not about endings, he reminded himself. But beginnings.

In the distance he heard the drone of a mower's engine. The scent of freshly cut grass mingled with the tinge of salt on the slight breeze from the sea. When he reached Lena's grave, he knelt down, took the bright tulips from their green tissue paper wrapping and placed them in the sunken cup beside the marker, then filled the cup with water from the plastic bottle of Evian water he'd picked up at 7-Eleven.

He ran his fingers over the name etched into the pink-hued marble, just as he'd done that first day he'd garnered the courage to come here. And although he knew it was only his imagination, Reece thought his wife's name warmed beneath his touch.

"I suppose you know why I've come," he said finally. In the beginning, when he had first talked to her, his words had been born of anger and a feeling of betrayal. These days the conversations centered around more mundane issues—a story he was working on, Grace's ballet recital, Molly's work at the ER, and most recently, the surprise discovery that Tessa was living right here in Los Angeles.

"I also suppose, being a woman and more in tune with things like this, you figured out long ago how I feel about Molly. I didn't mean for it to happen," he said, unknowingly echoing Molly's earlier sentiments. He dragged his hand through his hair. "Hell, I don't even know *when* it happened. But it has. And I just need to know that you're okay with it."

More nervous than that long-ago day when he'd

first proposed, he absently plucked at the crimson flower petals. Pollen from the stamen stained his fingers bright yellow.

"I thought I would die when you left me," he said gruffly. "I *wanted* to die. But I didn't. And Alex and Theo and most of all, Molly eventually managed to convince me that I had an obligation to Grace…to our daughter…to keep on living.

"So I did. And eventually I could go hours, then days, without thinking up suicide scenarios."

He sighed heavily, finding those dark days painful to think about. Putting aside the hurt, Reece concentrated on the hope.

"You'll always have a very special place in my heart," he assured the woman he'd fallen in love with at first sight. "And it's not that I love you less, Lena, because that could never happen…. It's just that I love Molly now."

There. He'd said the words out loud without being struck by lightning. And the sky hadn't fallen in.

While he sat there in quiet contemplation, thinking of Lena and Molly and Grace, and how their lives were so inextricably interwoven, Reece felt something brush against his cheek, then ruffle his hair.

It's only the breeze, he assured himself. Coming in from the coast. Even though he willed himself to believe that logical explanation, as he walked back to his car, Reece imagined he detected Lena's scent wafting on the sun-warmed air.

A phalanx of police cars was parked out in front of Molly's condo. Klieg lights lit up the area, making it as bright as day. Behind the police barricade, spectators stood in groups, talking about the action as if they were watching a taping of "NYPD Blue," while video crews from every television station in the city were jockeying over the best vantage positions.

"That's a rogue cop holding those women hostage," Dan Kovaleski reminded the members of the SWAT team who'd arrived to try to take out one of their own. "He knows the drill."

If only he'd been a few minutes faster. He'd sensed something was wrong the minute Molly had answered the door and told him that Tessa wasn't there. Then she'd politely thanked him for his interest and assured him that her sister was bound to show up. Eventually. But he'd seen the fright in her eyes and when he'd found Jason Mathison's motorcycle parked on the next street, Dan's fears had been confirmed.

"We'll need a clear shot," the SWAT commander said. "I sent my best man up on the roof across the street. Two others are behind the van. And a third's at the back of the place, just in case he tries to make a break for it."

The team had been instructed to stand by when Dan had first called in the hostage situation. Since Mathison was still refusing to surrender, they appeared to be the last chance. Dan could only hope that they were as good as they claimed to be.

"What the hell are you going to do?" Reece demanded. He'd driven like a bat out of hell to get here when Dan had called him at home to break the news. "If they shoot Molly—"

"They won't," Dan said, wishing he could sound more confident. The unpalatable truth was, whenever a hostage situation ended in a shooting, it was more than likely that one of the hostages, or one of the cops was going to end up bleeding. "They're good, Reece. Really good."

Reece wasn't taking comfort from that. All he could think about was Molly's face when he'd tried to explain why he couldn't love her.

"Christ, if anything happens to her—"

"She'll be okay." Dan could not allow himself to think otherwise. He also couldn't forget that he'd been the one to bring Tessa into Molly's life in the first place. It had seemed like a happy coincidence. But if Molly ended up getting killed because of his need to play the hotshot cop, he knew he'd never forgive himself.

"How the hell did Mathison find her anyway?"

"I'm guessing that after she left Phoenix House, Tessa called him, trying to score some drugs. Then changed her mind."

"But Mathison traced the call."

"Even civilians can do it these days if they've got caller ID and a reverse directory," Dan pointed out. "You've written the scenario yourself."

"Shit." If the cops managed to get that scumbag out of the house alive, Reece would personally strangle the guy with his bare hands. "Goddammit!"

"It'll be okay," Dan said again.

The men exchanged a grim look. It had to be.

"This isn't going to work," Molly said, schooling her voice to a calm she was a very long way from feeling. Only years of ER experience kept her from revealing that she was on the verge of screaming. Or fainting.

"Why don't you shut the hell up?" Jason said.

Molly managed, just barely, not to flinch as he spun

away from the window, and pointed the 9 mm pistol at her head. "I'm sorry," she said carefully. "It's just that I'd hate to see anyone die."

"Too bad. Because you and your cunt sister are at the top of a very short list to do exactly that."

Her heart was pounding in her ears, making it difficult to hear. Molly wished she was braver. She wished she wasn't afraid to die. She wished she could go back in time to this morning, when she was lying in bed with the man she loved.

If wishes were horses, she remembered her mother saying. *Beggars would ride.* Karla McBride had, unfortunately, been an authority on unfulfilled wishes. And terrified though she was, Molly had no intention of ending up like her mother.

Although she was sitting down, Molly's knees were shaking. At the other end of the couch, Tessa was curled into a tight, miserable ball, looking like a pound puppy terrified of being kicked again.

"You might have gotten away with it, if only Dan hadn't come over here when he did," she said, trying to make some sort of contact with him.

She remembered one of Reece's television programs, when a woman being held hostage managed to befriend the man who'd kidnapped her. If she could only keep him talking long enough to figure a way out of this. Or to buy time for Dan to do something....

"Yeah. And who do we have to thank for letting the fucking cat out of the bag?" Jason's handsome face turned ugly. "You tipped him off somehow, didn't you?"

"You were standing behind the door," Molly reminded him. "You know I didn't say anything."

"The hell you didn't!" He bent down and

screamed into her face. "You bitch, this is all your fault!" He swung, hitting her on the cheek with the pistol. The same bone that had been shattered all those years ago by the rapist.

"Don't you dare hit my sister!" Amazingly, Tessa sprang to her feet like a wildcat, threw herself onto his back and buried her teeth into his neck.

"Goddammit!" Roaring in pain and fury, Jason tried to shake her off, but her legs were wrapped around him in a vise grip, her hands were pounding on his head and her teeth had drawn blood. "You fucking cunt whore! I'm going to kill you!"

Although shocked, Molly was not too stunned by the unexpected attack to take advantage of any opportunity. She picked up a flowered vase from an end table and brought it down hard on his head.

"You're going to die, too!" he shouted as the shards of pottery fell over his shoulders and the gash at the back of his head began to bleed.

While he was staggering from that blow and still trying to shake a determined Tessa off his back, Molly raced into the kitchen, rushed back with a heavy cast-iron skillet, lifted it up with both hands and hit him again with all her strength.

The cursing was replaced by a muffled *oof.* Jason stared at her, his eyes glazed.

The gun fell out of his hand and went skittering across the floor.

Then finally, like a grizzly who'd finally realized it had been shot, he went tumbling down on top of the coffee table, which shattered beneath his weight, taking Tessa with him.

"Are you all right?" Molly asked frantically as she

tried to extricate her sister from the broken wood and unconscious man.

"I've never felt better." Tessa's unnaturally high voice was tinged with a hysteria Molly recognized all too well since she was feeling it herself. "You'd better get that gun. In case Sleeping Beauty wakes up."

"Good idea." Molly gingerly picked up the deadly weapon with shaking hands.

She and her sister stared at each other, looked down at the man sprawled at their feet, then wrapped their arms around each other and began to laugh.

Time seemed to take on a slow-motion quality as the front door of Molly's condo slowly opened.

Every rifle rose to firing position.

Nerves stretched to the breaking point, Reece heard the squeak of the door, then Dan's sharp, indrawn breath.

"Hold your fire," Dan shouted as he viewed the two women standing in the doorway.

"What the hell is Mathison up to now?" Reece asked, fearing for the worst.

"I don't know." From what he knew of his former partner, Dan didn't believe he'd let his hostages go without a fight.

"Is Molly holding a gun?" Reece asked in disbelief.

Dan zeroed in on the pistol she was holding between visibly shaking hands. Several possible scenarios flashed through his mind, none of them pretty.

"Aw, shit...Molly," he called out, "put the gun down, honey. Everything's going to be all right."

"Of course it is," Tessa yelled back. "Because my big sister knocked the son of a bitch out."

"Only after Tessa jumped on his back," Molly tacked on.

Dan and Reece exchanged a brief, disbelieving look, then as Molly bent down and carefully placed the pistol on the lawn, they took off running toward the house. Behind them, the commander instructed the SWAT team to continue to hold fire.

"She decked him with a vase," Tessa crowed, her face flushed and wet with tears. "And a frying pan."

"I couldn't have done it if Tessa hadn't attacked him first," Molly said. Her blue eyes were bright with moisture and, Reece considered, instinctively thinking like a doctor, some hysteria.

"We make a helluva team, sis," Tessa said.

Molly's answering grin could have lit up Los Angeles for a month of smoggy Sundays. "Yes. We do."

After a very groggy Jason Mathison had been handcuffed and put in the back of a patrol car, Molly and Reece stood in the middle of her lawn in each other's arms.

"Do you have any idea how frantic I was?" he murmured against the top of her head. "Thinking I might lose you?"

"Yes. Because I was worried about the same thing. That you'd lose me."

He pulled his head back and smiled down into her face. Her lovely, lovely face. "I'll admit it sounds irrational, but when I began to realize how much you meant to me, I was afraid that if I allowed myself to care for you too much, fate would make something horrible happen to you. Like my parents' plane crash. And Lena's dying."

"I know you felt that way, but—"

"But it didn't make any difference," he interrupted, needing to get the long overdue declaration said. "Because even after I refused to admit how I felt, I still ended up almost losing you." He took a deep breath. "I love you, Molly McBride."

She linked her fingers around his neck. "I know."

Of course she did, Reece thought. Molly had always known everything about him. It was one of the reasons she frustrated him so often. It was also one of the many reasons he'd fallen head over heels in love with her.

"Are you going to marry me?"

Feminine instincts she'd once told Tessa she didn't possess told Molly this was no time to be coy.

"You bet I am." Dual feelings of relief and happiness flowed through her like a golden sunlit stream, washing away her earlier fear. Molly laughed as she went up on her toes and pressed her lips against his.

Tessa watched her sister kissing the man she so obviously loved and felt a tinge of envy. But mostly she felt pleasure at the idea of Reece and Molly beginning a new life together.

Speaking of new lives...

"About that Twelve Step lecture," she said, looking up at Dan.

He folded his arms and lifted a chestnut brow. "What about it?"

"How about you give it to me while you drive me back to Phoenix House?"

A ghost of a smile twitched at the corner of those gorgeous male lips Tessa vowed to someday taste again. When they were both ready.

"Lady, you've got yourself a deal." He took her hand and tucked it through his arm. "Let's go."

Epilogue

December 24, 1996

It was Christmas in Los Angeles. The season of joy. As she returned home from the chapel with her husband and daughter, Molly couldn't remember ever being happier.

"I've got to call Mary Beth," Grace announced the moment they entered the house that smelled of pine and balsam.

"It's late," Molly said. "And it *is* Christmas Eve. I'm not certain Mary Beth's parents will be wild about—"

"Puleeze, Mom," she wheedled prettily. "I promised to tell her all about the wedding."

Molly knew better than to ask if such news couldn't wait until morning. The wedding was all the girls had been talking about for weeks. "Try to keep it short."

"I will, promise!" She gave Molly a hug, then dashed up the stairs.

"That's a relief," Reece said as he threw himself down on the living room couch.

Molly was smiling as she turned toward her husband. She knew it was silly of her, but having Grace call her Mom never failed to warm her heart. As for Reece... Nearly eighteen months ago, she'd stood in this very room in front of friends and family and promised to love and cherish this man. No promise had ever come easier.

"What's a relief?"

She sat down beside him, snuggling into his embrace as he put his arm around her shoulder. In the corner, the fairy lights adorning the towering twelve-foot fir tree sparkled like stars in a midnight sky.

It had taken an entire weekend for the three of them to put up the tree, another weekend to bake the gingerbread shapes hanging side by side with the hand-blown crystal ornaments she and Reece had brought back from their honeymoon in Ireland, but Molly decided the effort had definitely been worth it.

"I'm relieved that it was an eight-year-old running up those stairs. And not the almost grown-up stranger who came down them a few hours ago.

Molly knew all too well what he meant. When she'd first viewed their daughter, dressed in the wine red bridesmaid dress and wearing a slender string of pearls, she'd caught a disconcerting glimpse of the woman Grace would too soon become.

"Children grow up faster these days."

"Try telling me something I don't know." Reece sighed as he thought of all the teenage mothers he and Molly were forced to deal with on a daily basis. Babies having babies, forgoing prenatal care, showing up in Mercy Sam's emergency room—where they'd both returned to work—when it came time to deliver. "I don't suppose you'd agree to locking her in a closet until she's thirty."

Molly laughed. "She's a good kid. She'll be all right."

Reece was more pragmatic. "And if she isn't?"

Molly refused to think unpleasant thoughts tonight. Watching Tessa and Dan exchange vows had wiped away the lingering sense of pain she'd always experienced on this day. Although her sister had never said anything, Molly suspected she'd chosen Christmas Eve specifically for that reason, and she loved her all the more for such sensitivity.

Thinking of how Tessa had turned her life around—getting off drugs, winning the role as the vixen on Theo's soap opera, signing that new contract for a made-for-television-movie, even making time to volunteer in a battered women's shelter—made Molly believe anything was possible.

She patted Reece's cheek with wifely reassurance. "Then we'll deal with it."

He laughed and shrugged off the momentary parental fear. "Just what I should have expected Molly Sunshine to say." He kissed her, a deep, slow kiss that she knew would always possess the power to curl her toes.

"Did I happen to mention that you were the most beautiful woman at that chapel today?" he asked when the blissful kiss finally ended.

"The bride is always the most beautiful woman at

her wedding,'' Molly corrected breathlessly as his lips continued to pluck at hers. It was ten o'clock and she'd been fantasizing about tonight for hours. Molly hoped Grace did, indeed, manage to keep her conversation with her best friend short.

"Tessa was lovely. But you, my love—" he kissed his way down her throat "—were stunning. I swear, the way you were glowing, you could have been the bride."

She'd been planning to tell him later. After they'd made love. She'd wanted to save her news for a Christmas present. But now, since he'd brought it up...

"Actually," she said, with far more aplomb than she was feeling, "if I was glowing, there's a very good reason."

Reece drew back and looked down into her face. He could see tiny Christmas trees reflected in her eyes, but realized that the lights shining in those blue depths were from something else altogether.

"Are you saying...?"

Molly gently framed his face with her hands. "This time next year, Santa will have to add another Longworth child to his list."

Her warm, serene, satisfied smile reminded Reece of every painting of every Madonna he'd ever seen. He felt a surge of wonder. He'd been so grateful for Molly and Grace that he'd never dared consider asking for more.

He pulled her into his arms again, holding her tight. "I do love you, Molly McBride Longworth."

As joy sang its sweet song in her veins like a chorus of silver bells, Molly laughed and lifted her face for her husband's kiss. "I know."

New York Times Bestselling Authors

JENNIFER BLAKE
JANET DAILEY
ELIZABETH GAGE

Three *New York Times* bestselling authors bring you three very sensuous, contemporary love stories—all centered around one magical night!

It is a warm, spring night and masquerading as legendary lovers, the elite of New Orleans society have come to celebrate the twenty-fifth anniversary of the Duchaise masquerade ball. But amidst the beauty, music and revelry, some of the world's most legendary lovers are in trouble....

Come midnight at this year's Duchaise ball, passion and scandal will be...

Unmasked

Revealed at your favorite retail outlet in July 1997.

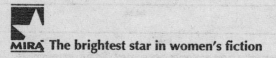

MIRA The brightest star in women's fiction